J

The Prophet of Fire

SALZWASSER
VERLAG

John Ross MacDuff

The Prophet of Fire

Reprint of the original, first published in 1864.

1st Edition 2022 | ISBN: 978-3-75259-328-0

Verlag (Publisher): Salzwasser Verlag GmbH, Zeilweg 44, 60439 Frankfurt, Deutschland
Vertretungsberechtigt (Authorized to represent): E. Roepke, Zeilweg 44, 60439 Frankfurt, Deutschland
Druck (Print): Books on Demand GmbH, In de Tarpen 42, 22848 Norderstedt, Deutschland

THE

PROPHET OF FIRE.

THE
PROPHET OF FIRE;
OR,
THE LIFE AND TIMES OF ELIJAH,
WITH THEIR LESSONS.

BY

J. R. MACDUFF, D.D

"Thus saith the Lord of Hosts, Behold, I will make my words in thy mouth FIRE." JER. v. 14.

"Elijah stood up as a FIRE and his word burned as a lamp." ECCLUS. xlviii. 1.

Third Thousand.

LONDON

M.DCCC.LXIV.

PREFACE.

The author hesitated in committing these pages to the press, for the same reason which he believes has deterred others, viz., that the life of the greatest of the Prophets of the kingdom of Israel has been already so graphically portrayed, and its sacred lessons enforced, in the admirable volume of Dr Krummacher.

It is not certainly with the presumptuous expectation of either rivalling or excelling that well-known work, that he has ventured to occupy the same ground. The gifted and now venerable pastor of Elberfeld, whose writings have enjoyed a long and deserved popularity, will always retain his own peculiar pedestal in the Christian Church as the biographer of the Tishbite. But what is true in all departments of literature, is surely specially so in the case of sacred literature and Bible biography, that no human works—not the very best—can possibly be exhaustive :—there are always harvest-gleanings, if not sheaves, for the diligent reaper. A character like that of Elijah, at once so unique and so complex, and a life so varied in incident, must ever be suggestive of new lines and phases of thought. More than this, much interesting light and information since Krummacher wrote, has been thrown upon the times of the Great Prophet and upon the scenes of his labour, tending further to illustrate and vivify the events in his heroic career. While the writer, therefore, has endeavoured to give as faithful a photograph as he can, of "the grandest and most romantic character Israel ever produced,"* he has made it his special aim, to draw manifold practical and gospel lessons from a history so replete with evangelic truth, as well as so suggestive of noble life-thoughts for this earnest and busy age.†

* Dr Stanley's "Sinai and Palestine," p. 325.

† I have taken care to make reference in foot-notes to any sources of information to which I have been indebted. I have to acknowledge my obligations, among other modern writers, especially to Dr Stanley's works, Kiel on Kings, and an excellent and learned article on "Elijah" in Dr Smith's Bible Dictionary. Also, as throwing further light on the localities connected with the Prophet's life, to the travels particularly of Van de Velde, Dr Robinson, and Dr Bonar. Although deeming it unnecessary to make in all cases specific reference, I have gratefully to acknowledge the help derived throughout from Dr Krummacher.

The name given to this volume, "PROPHET OF FIRE," will afford its own explanation. It seems the most befitting of epithets as applied to him who was truly one of the SERAPHIM (the "flaming ones") of earth;—"a burning and shining light;" —a beacon-blaze of warning set on the hill-tops of Israel. Pagan mythology has put a gleaming thunderbolt in the hands of Olympian Jupiter. Such was our Prophet in the hands of the living and true God;—Jehovah's messenger of wrath to a guilty age. In the words of the Son of Sirach, quoted in the title-page, "He stood up as a *Fire*, and his word burned as a lamp." The most graphic and memorable incidents, moreover, in Elijah's life, seem, so to speak, to be illumined with the element and symbol of FIRE. It was the empire of Baal—the *Fire*-god—he came to shake and overthrow. *Fire* fell at his intercession on the sacrifice at Carmel. God shewed him, as we shall see, in the sublime manifestation at Horeb, the reflection of his own character in the *Fire* which preceded the "still small voice." He called down *Fire* on the captains of fifties; and in a chariot of *Fire* he went up to Heaven. To him, with a better acceptation, the name of the old Canaanite king specially belonged—*Adoni-bezek*, ("the lord of lightning.") Like a fiery meteor, he appears all at once in the sacred firmament, and as a fiery meteor he vanishes. A remarkable Jewish legend regarding the birth of Elijah is quoted by Krummacher:—"His father on that occasion is said to have seen a vision, in which a number of men, dressed in white and shining garments, appeared to stand round the child, and then wrapped him up, with every token of reverence, *in swaddling bands of Fire, and fed him with blazing flames.* The priests are said to have interpreted the vision thus: —that the family of Elijah should come to great distinction, and that he himself should judge Israel with the Fire of his mouth. And what prediction was ever more exactly fulfilled."* "Recalling his life and his terrible vengeance," remarks a very different writer, "it seems as if this man had the thunder of the Lord for a soul, and that the element in which he was borne to heaven was the one in which he was brought forth."†

It is in another sense as the PROPHET OF FIRE, that he reads the great lesson to the Church of the future. As such, he has a living voice for the

* Page 17. † Lamartine's "Holy Land," vol. i., p. 189.

times. It is *Fire* we need; not the fire of fitful impulse;—not the flame of intemperate bigotry;—not the kindlings of unregulated enthusiasm;—not the ignis-fatuus gleam of bewildering human reason;—not the strange fire of deified intellect—sparks of their own kindling, with which the sons of Aaron are prone as ever to dishonour and desecrate God's altar. But the living fire of burning words and burning deeds, lighted from the inner sanctuary;—men instinct with divine, God-derived energy,—who feel that they have got their high consecration from Him, who alone "takes the censer and fills it with the fire of the altar."* All other spurious fires will sooner or later go out in darkness. This alone is the true vestal flame of heaven, which burns pure and bright, and shall thus burn for ever.

PROPHET OF FIRE! resume thy sacred mission! And in days when the mournful question is too often prompted—"Where is the Lord God of Elijah?" may the God "who answereth by Fire" raise up many "in the spirit and power of Elias," who shall rekindle the smouldering ashes on the Church's altar, to consume the dross, and refine the gold.

* Rev. viii. 5.

PREFACE.

"And since we see, and not afar,
The twilight of the great and dreadful day;
Why linger till Elijah's car
Stoop from the clouds? Why sleep ye? Rise and pray,
Ye heralds seal'd,
In camp or field
Your Saviour's banner to display.

"Thou Spirit, who the Church didst lead
Her eagle wings to shelter in the wild,
We pray Thee, ere the Judge descend,
With flames like these, all bright and undefiled,
Her watch-fires light,
To guide aright
Our weary souls by earth beguiled!"

KEBLE.

CONTENTS.

I.

Birthplace, Appearance, and Character.

"And Elijah the Tishbite, who was of the inhabitants of Gilead."—
1 Kings xvii. 1.

"Who maketh his angels spirits; his ministers a flaming fire."—
Psalm civ. 4.

BIRTHPLACE, APPEARANCE, AND CHARACTER.

THE life of ELIJAH is, in the truest sense of the word, a poem, —an inspired epic. It is surrounded throughout with a blended halo of heroism and saintliness. Though neither angel nor demi-god, but "a man of like passions," intensely human in all the varied incidents and episodes of his picturesque history,—he yet seems as if he held converse more with heaven than earth. His name, which literally means "My God the Lord," or "Jehovah is my God," introduces us to one who had delegated to him superhuman powers; not only an ambassador from above, but the very viceroy and representative of Omnipotence. He announces himself as standing before the Lord of hosts,* as if he were a retainer in the heavenly palace, rather than a citizen of the lower world; coming forth from time to time from his mysterious seclusion to deliver his message, and then retiring again into solitude to wait fresh communications from on high.

No one in Scripture story possesses a more thorough individuality; and this is all the more remarkable, as we have only a few broad touches descriptive of his personal appearance, and of his mental and moral character. But these are

* 1 Kings xvii. 1.

so bold and impressive, that there is no mistaking him. He stands out in massive relief from the sacred canvas. Others of illustrious name, who occupy a far larger share of the inspired page, appear shadowy and undefined in comparison with this illustrious product of nature and grace.

He is presented to our view without a note of premonition, — ushered at once on the stage of stirring action full panoplied,—in the colossal manhood and maturity of his being. This is all our introduction to him, as he confronts the guilty monarch of northern Palestine: "And Elijah the Tishbite, who was of the inhabitants of Gilead, said unto Ahab, As the Lord God of Israel liveth, before whom I stand."* We have no antecedents in his history. No reference to ancestry, home, education, father, mother, companion, or friend; and this, too, throughout all the rest of his career, till nigh its close. He appears before us—the Melchizedek of his age—nursed in the wilds of nature for his great and momentous calling. There is a marked contrast in this respect between him and other well-known names in the roll of Hebrew writers. Pilgrim and wayfarer as he was, with his moveable dwellings and altar, we are familiar with Abraham as "the Father," — the patriarchal chief or sheik, surrounded with the hum of living voices and desert tents,—with wife and sister's son and children, slaves and herdsmen—ever ready, when occasion requires, to dispense the rites of Eastern hospitality. In the life of Moses, we come in contact at every turn with the same human relationships and sym-

* "He comes in with a tempest," says Bishop Hall, "who went out with a whirlwind."

pathies. We can think of his own mother singing Hebrew lullabies by his cradle. We are allowed to picture him in his boyhood, disciplined under the strange influence of the court of Pharaoh, instructed in the sacred schools of Heliopolis "in all the wisdom of the Egyptians." Even in his wilderness exile, the loneliest period of his life, we find him associated, as a family man, with the household and flocks of Jethro. Samuel, kindred in many respects as he was with the Tishbite in his prophetic calling, was surrounded with the sanctities of a double home and parentage. We see, on the one hand, the mother who, from his lisping infancy, "lent him to the Lord," year by year bringing him his "little coat" to the sanctuary at Shiloh. On the other, the venerated foster-father on whom he duteously waited in that curtained tabernacle where "the lamp of God was burning," instilling into his susceptible soul his earliest lessons of heavenly wisdom. David's whole life is domestic, full of tender delineations of strong human sympathies and clinging friendships, manifested alike in the family homestead, the martial camp, and the palace of Zion. Even Elisha, as a writer has remarked, "had his yoke of oxen, parents to bid adieu to, a servant, Gehazi, in attendance on him, the sons of prophets in converse with him. But the mention of Elijah is at intervals, as one appearing in peopled neighbourhoods —no one knew from whence—in the desert, on the hill-tops —seen and recognised as by surprise, in the hairy garment of the prophet;—the solitary of God—as one without scrip or purse,—even, it may be, as He who had not 'where to lay His head'—having food to eat which man wot not of." *

* Dr Williams on the Characters of the Old Testament, p. 225.

Among the many influences which are known to mould and develop individual character, external nature must not be overlooked. The grand and sublime has always proved a "meet nurse" for heroic spirits; and, were this the place, we might illustrate the statement by examples. Gilead,—Elijah's birthplace, the cradle of his youth, and where he remained until the time of his shewing unto Israel,—was that wild, rugged, in many parts picturesque country, lying east of the Jordan—the "rocky" region, as the word implies, with its deep ravines and water-courses, its sheepfolds and herds of wild cattle, in contradistinction to Bashan, "the level or fertile land." It was a region uncultured in more than its physical aspect. "Galilee of the Gentiles," on the western side of the border river, was proverbially a rude province compared with the civilised tribes of the south of Palestine. But this was, in a still greater measure, the character of those secluded uplands of Gilead. Contiguous as they were to the roving tribes of Arabia, subject to continual invasions or forays of Bedouin freebooters, the walled towns and villages, common on the western side of Jordan, were here unknown. With the exception of a few mountain strongholds, the inhabitants were obliged, in their nomad existence, to be satisfied with the tent of canvas or goats' hair. And this primitive patriarchal life survived the advancing civilisation of other parts of the country. "To an Israelite of the tribes west of Jordan," says a recent writer,* "the title 'Gileadite' must have conveyed a similar impression, though in a far stronger degree, to that which the title 'Celt' does to us. What the Highlands were, a century ago, to the

* See Smith's Dictionary of the Bible, *in loco*.

towns in the lowlands of Scotland, that, and more than that, must Gilead have been to Samaria or Jerusalem." In this very country had been reared some of the warriors of a former age. "Because Machir was a man of war, therefore he had Gilead and Bashan." * Jephthah the Gileadite, the wild, lawless hero of his time, issued from these "mountains of prey," and his hapless daughter, with her group of maidens, awoke the echoes of their savage gorges with pathetic wailings. And now, He who had, in a still remoter age, nursed Moses His servant for his great exploits amid the solitudes of the Sinai desert, trains up a worthy successor in the same great Temple. The soul of Elijah was tutored for his prophetic mission amid the rushing streams, "the pipings of flocks," the awful solitudes, and the rough freebooter-life of the most distant territory of the sacred tribes. Jehovah, in the selection of the human instrument for a great revival in Israel, would magnify the sovereignty of His own grace;—He brings balm from half-heathen Gilead to heal the hurt of the daughter of His people;—He chooses no Rabbi nor learned doctor of the schools—no Hierarch with the prestige of hereditary office or outward form of consecration,—but a lay preacher from the Highlands of Palestine,—a man who had graduated in no school but nature—who had been taught, but taught only of Heaven. Forth he comes, A PROPHET OF FIRE, a burning and a shining light, in one of the darkest periods of Hebrew history—and "many were to rejoice in his light."

Some, indeed, have supposed that Elijah was not Hebrew in his origin at all,—that the blood of roving Ishmael was

* Joshua xvii. 1.

in his veins,—that he sprang from a tribe of Gentiles who inherited from the patriarch Abraham the knowledge of the one true God, and retained it longer than the heathen around, owing to their proximity to the land of Canaan;—that such a selection, moreover, was purposely made by God to rebuke the wayward apostasy of His chosen Israel, and shew them that even from strangers and foreigners He could raise up honoured men for the vindication of His truth and the accomplishment of His purposes.* Be this as it may, if we draw a portraiture of Elijah even from the materials afforded us in Scripture, we recognise in his outward mien more of the Bedouin than the son of the chosen race. There stands before us a muscular figure, tawny with the burning suns of Palestine, with long, shaggy raven hair hanging loose over his shoulders. A modern writer, in speaking of Samson's unshorn locks, compares him to the Merovingian kings, "whose long tresses were the sign of their royal race, which to lose was to lose royalty itself."† We cannot pronounce in the case of the prophet of Gilead of what these flowing tresses were the symbol,—whether they were the badge of his Divine mission, or as, with the son of Manoah, the token of his strength,—or that, like him, he had taken the vow of the Nazarite. In any case, they form a marked feature in his outward appearance. He is specially spoken of, in a subsequent period, by Ahaziah's messengers‡ as "a hairy man," (lit., "a lord of hair.") The children of Bethel, when they came forth and mocked Elisha as "the bald head," did so because struck with the contrast between him

* See Kiel, vol. i., p. 267. † Stanley's Jewish Church, p. 364.
‡ 2 Kings i. 8.

and the familiar appearance of his shaggy predecessor. Around his shoulders he had flung a loose cape or striped blanket, made either of rough sheep or camel hide, fastened at his breast with a leathern girdle. Whatever may have been the case with his untonsured head, this mantle appears to have had some singular significance attached to it. It was to him what the rod was to Moses. It seemed at once the outward badge of his prophetic office, and the instrument by which his miracles were performed. It screened him at one time when he held intercourse with God in the entrance of the desert cave,—he wrapped it round his face: at another, he would roll it up like a staff, as we shall find him doing at the close of his history, when at its magic touch Jordan was driven back. It was the legacy which dropped on the shoulders of his successor from the fiery chariot when the whirlwind bore him to heaven.* Nor must his physical strength and powers of physical endurance be forgotten in this rapid portraiture. That must have been no ordinary man, surely, who, before the coming night-storm, and after the toils of an exhausting day, could accomplish such a feat of pedestrianism as to run sixteen miles, and withal outstrip the fleet coursers in Ahab's chariot in reaching the gate of Jezreel. That must have been no average strength that could sustain the hardships and privations of Cherith, and the long forty days' fast of Horeb.

Such, then, in personal aspect seems to have been THE GREAT ELIJAH:—with no priestly vestment but that hairy

* It has been noted that the rough cloak or mantle, perhaps in imitation of the Tishbite, was worn by the prophets at a much later period of Hebrew history. See Zech. xiii. 4.

tunic of the desert—wanting in courtly attire and perhaps courtly manners and etiquette, but with regal mien and bearing too;—a glorious champion of truth and righteousness. His name must have been a household word in every home of Israel and beyond it. Something awful must have been the terror inspired by the man who had the elements of nature delegated to his control; who could seal up the heavens at one time—lock up from a whole nation for years the treasures of the clouds: at another, draw fire from these clouds like a sword from its scabbard, and strew the earth with a hundred dead! Even the suddenness of his appearances and disappearances are startling and dramatic. He towers—like one of the sons of Anak—morally as well as physically high above those around him. He reminds us of the brave heroes—though with nobler elements of grandeur in *his* case—who came across Jordan in high flood to join a former exiled king of Israel—"whose faces were like the faces of lions, and were as swift as the gazelles upon the mountains." In one word, he was an incarnation of Power. If early Greece or Rome (not Palestine) had been the theatre of his deeds, he would have had his place amid the gods of Olympus. As it was, there was no name (that of Abraham and perhaps Moses excepted) more venerated in subsequent ages among his countrymen. But yet, with all his moral and physical superiority, with all his mortifications, his strange ascetic life, Elijah is spoken of, for our encouragement, as "a man of like passions."* And it is this which makes his biography so interesting and instructive. With all his greatness, he had his weaknesses and failings—and failings,

* James v. 17.

too, just in the points of character we should least have expected. The reprover of Ahab,—the bold, bearded son of the desert who feared God, and knew apparently no other fear,—so elevated above the foibles, weaknesses, caprices of his fellows—so indifferent to human opinion, whether in the shape of commendation or censure,—can become a craven and coward on hearing the threats of an intriguing woman. Champion as he was,—a shaggy lion from the coverts of Gilead, who can challenge single-handed a multitude of idolatrous priests,—he cowers away in moping despondency from work and duty. We shall see in all this—when we come to dwell minutely on these varied incidents—a reflex of our fluctuating selves, which we may take, not to foster or encourage similar collapses, but to prevent us being needlessly disconcerted by the experience of kindred changeful moods in the spiritual life. "There was but a step," it has been remarked, in the case of Paul, "between the third heavens and the thorn in the flesh;" there was but a step in the case of Elijah between the heights of Carmel and the cave of Horeb. This Peter of the Old Testament was, like all characters of strong, fervid, vehement temperament, easily elated, easily depressed. He reminds us of the engine careering along our own highways—a very Hercules in strength—the type and impersonation of grandeur and power: but laid on its side, amid the mangled wrecks it has dragged along with it, nought is more helpless.

Elijah's life, however, as that of "a man of like passions," is instructive in more than this. Not only was there in his character a union of weakness with greatness, but, despite of all his apparent solitariness, unworldliness, asceticism, isolation from his fellows, there were not wanting elements of tenderness. The earthquake, the whirlwind, the fire, which he saw in the Sinai desert, and after all these "*the still small voice,*" formed the reflection of his own inner nature—a union of the terrible with the gentle. The denouncer of Ahab, the rebuker of kingly iniquity, the slayer at the Kishon, the homicide who, in one day, with his own hands, purpled its waters with the blood of four hundred and fifty priests,—we shall yet see with what considerate tenderness he ministers to the distress of the lonely widow of Zarephath, and with what loving affection he clings at the last to the friendship of the faithful Elisha. Stern characters are often misunderstood. There is frequently a union of opposites in the same nature,—the stern may appear to predominate, when gentleness and goodness are there, if the world would but believe it. The official severity of the homeless Prophet was tempered and softened with these latter qualities; while his every action, with the one solitary exception, was governed and pervaded by sterling principle, uncompromising rectitude, unflinching adherence to the will of God. Much as Ahab hated his truthful denunciations, he could not disguise his respect for his candour, boldness, and devotion to Him he so faithfully served. These lofty attributes doubtless Elijah owed not to himself. It was God's training and grace, the power of His Spirit working within him, that made him the man and the hero that he was. The classic fable regarding Hesiod, the unlettered herdsman, but who became the Father of poetry, was a reality in the case of THE PROPHET OF FIRE;—a heavenly flame coming suddenly down and resting on his head, he became the greatest of his age. The Lord had said to him, as to the prophet of Chebar, "Behold, I have made thy face strong against their faces, and thy forehead strong against their foreheads. As an adamant, harder than flint, have I made thy forehead: fear them not, neither be dismayed at their looks, though they be a rebellious house." * Indeed we often think of the Tishbite as an example of a character surcharged with elements of great power, which, if misdirected, must have been terrible for evil. Left to his own wayward, impetuous, fiery nature, his strong impulses and iron will, the bold Bedouin of Gilead might have grown up to be the scourge and destroyer, the tempter and corrupter of Israel,—not its Restorer, Reformer, and Saviour,—a vessel of wrath instead of a vessel of mercy. An angel in might, he might have turned a demon in depravity;—a "Prophet of Fire," not to illumine, but to scathe. His was a temperament in which evil impulses, had they once obtained sway, would have swept him down rapidly to ruin, and hurried thousands along with him, spreading his evil and baneful influence through a whole generation. But he had been enabled to consecrate all this latent power to the cause of righteousness. Perhaps, after many a silent soul-struggle, of which the world knows nothing, in the solitudes of his Fatherland, the devil in his nature had been expelled and exorcised; and he had adopted as his life-motto—"THE GOD OF ISRAEL WHOM I SERVE, AND BEFORE WHOM I STAND."

As a closing practical thought, let us remember how little it often takes to divert elements of character towards good or towards evil. How many, with downward, depraved pro-

* Ezek. iii. 8, 9.

pensities, have, by godly training, or by dint of moral courage and determination, combined with the grace of God, struggled manfully against the stream, and are now firm on the side of religious principle. How many, on the other hand, with, it may be, nobler natural elements of character,—full of hope and promise,—have, in an evil hour, by *one false step*, initiated the backward and the downward course to ruin! By one false turn of the helm, they have made shipwreck of faith and of a good conscience.

And, though we must not anticipate, we shall find that God did not leave His servant—this "light of Israel," whom He had kindled "for a FIRE"*—without high recompense. He made a stormy life close with a glorious setting: when the cloudy, fitful, changeful moods of his own spirit had, by varied discipline, subsided into calm faith, and obedience, and trust,—he was borne upwards to that rest for the storm-tossed, where "earthquake, and whirlwind, and fire" are known no more, to listen through eternal ages to the "still small voice." Enoch-like, "he was translated that he should not see death; and was not found, because God had translated him: for, before his translation, he had this testimony, that he pleased God."†

* Isa. x. 17.

† We need hardly wonder that the great German composer should have selected the history of Elijah, with its rapid alternations, its shifting dramatic effects, to give the loftiest and most varied expression to the art of which he was so consummate a master. Mendelssohn's translation into music of this great life poem,—in which there is such abundant scope for the rendering of the plaintive and pathetic, as well as for the grand and sublime,—is, in the highest sense, a triumph of genius. Even the words to which the music is set, shew that he has thoroughly appreciated alike the character of the Prophet and the scenes through which he moved.

II.

National Apostasy.

"And Elijah the Tishbite, who was of the inhabitants of Gilead, said unto Ahab, As the Lord God of Israel liveth, before whom I stand, there shall not be dew nor rain these years, but according to my word."—1 Kings xvii. 1.

"THROUGH THE WRATH OF THE LORD OF HOSTS IS THE LAND DARKENED, AND THE PEOPLE SHALL BE AS THE FUEL OF THE FIRE."—ISAIAH IX. 19.

"AND THE THIRD ANGEL SOUNDED, AND THERE FELL A GREAT STAR FROM HEAVEN, BURNING AS IT WERE A LAMP, AND IT FELL UPON THE THIRD PART OF THE RIVERS, AND UPON THE FOUNTAINS OF WATERS."—REVELATION VIII. 10.

NATIONAL APOSTASY.

AHAB was at this time on the throne of Israel;—his residence was at Jezreel, and the windows of his ivory palace looked along the vast plain of Esdraelon, one of the most fertile and exuberant portions of Palestine. His was a gloomy reign. His predecessor, Jeroboam, by setting up golden calves at Dan and Bethel, had paved the way for the shameless idolatry which now disgraced the land and provoked the Divine judgments. Compared with Ahab's apostasy, however, that of Jeroboam was a trivial and modified departure from the true worship. The latter may be regarded rather as a desperate, and, in the circumstances, a world-wise stroke of state policy. On the revolt of the ten tribes and their formation into a northern kingdom, the first sovereign was naturally jealous of the effect which attendance at the old festal gatherings in Jerusalem might have on his new subjects. These might revive, in the separated tribes, the ancient love of unity, and attachment to the time-honoured capital. "Jerusalem is builded as a city that is compact together: whither the tribes go up, the tribes of the Lord, unto the testimony of Israel, to give thanks unto the name of the Lord."* If he is to perpetuate his dynasty and save the dismemberment of his infant kingdom, he too must meet the religious wants

* Ps. cxxii. 3-4.

and aspirations of his people, by having a "city" or "cities of solemnities;"—he must have sacred shrines and sacred rites to vie in splendour with the ceremonies of Mount Zion. For this purpose he made selection of the two extreme border towns —Dan in the north, and Bethel in the south. Both were already invested with sacred recollections in connexion with the earlier history of the chosen race, and in them he erected two temples, with rites of corresponding magnificence. "His long stay in Egypt had familiarised him with the outward forms under which the Divinity was there represented; and now, for the first time since the Exodus, was an Egyptian element introduced into the national worship of Palestine. A golden figure of Mnevis, the sacred calf of Heliopolis, was set up at each sanctuary, with the address, 'Behold thy God, which brought thee out of the land of Egypt.'"*

Guilty as Jeroboam was in introducing so flagrant a violation of the Divine command,—erecting "a similitude like to a calf which eateth hay," he seems to have had no intention of superseding the national religion by pagan worship. It was different, however, with his weak and servile successor. Ahab's "abominable idolatries" owed, if not their origin, at all events their chief instigation, to a guilty matrimonial alliance he had formed with Jezebel, daughter of Athbaal, King of Tyre. Little could be expected from the antecedents of this Tyrian princess; her own father having himself originally been a heathen priest, and having afterwards mounted the throne of his brother as a usurper. Greatly Ahab's intellectual superior—crafty, bold, designing, unscrupulous, cruel,—she wielded from the first a fatal influ-

* Neh. ix. 18. Smith's Dictionary, *in loco.*

ence over her weak and pliant partner. He soon forgot the solemn inheritance that had been transmitted to him in that sacred land. Shrines and temples sacred to Baal and Astarte, the tutelary deities of Phœnicia, covered the hill-tops and valleys, "marked by the grove of olive or ilex round the sacred rock or stone on which the altar was erected."

This false worship, indeed, was no novelty in Hebrew history. We find it had struck its roots deep—even so early as the time of the Judges. Gideon's thrashing-floor at Ophrah, was close by a rock, surmounted by a spreading Terebinth, and under its branches the altar and image of Baal. One part of his mission, as his new name of Jerubbaal imported, was to overthrow the worship of the Phœnician idol, and reassert the supremacy of the God of Israel. The Angel of the Lord appeared to him, at his wine-press, with a message of "*peace*." That same night of the Divine appearance, he cut down the consecrated grove on the rock, and converted the long-defiled altar into a place of sacrifice for Jehovah, using the felled trees as fuel for his burnt-offering. The citizens of the little town, enraged at the sacrilege, demanded of Joash to give up his son to instant death. Joash, however, the Gamaliel of his age, stood on his defence by appealing to the reason of his hearers, and boldly asserting, that if Baal were indeed a god, he needed no puny human arm to vindicate his sovereignty, or inflict his vengeance. "Will ye plead for Baal? Will ye save him? If he be a God, let him plead for himself."* Who knows but the remembrance of this advice of the old Abiezrite may have suggested and shaped

* Judges vi. 31.

Elijah's subsequent appeal on the heights of Carmel.* Be this as it may, the land, during the reign of Ahab, with which we are now concerned, swarmed with priests of the heathen deity imported from pagan Tyre. Four hundred of them sat at the royal table, and stimulated their royal patrons to deeds of vengeance. The worship of Jehovah of Israel came to be denounced as disaffection to the government—a slight on the court religion. The torch of persecution was lighted. The prophets of the Lord were hunted down,—driven into caves, and saved from utter extermination only by the merciful interposition of Obadiah, a saint in the household of the Nero of his day.

What a guilty and presumptuous attempt to thwart the Divine purpose in portioning off the chosen people from the rest of the world! The Hebrew nation had been appointed as a perpetual protest against the polytheism of the surrounding kingdoms. By one dastardly act of the new monarch of Israel, the wall of separation was thrown down. The modified calf-worship of Jeroboam now lapsed into unblushing idolatry. God was dethroned; and Baal, (or Baalim,) a plurality of Lords, was set up in His place. The one living, self-existent, all-pervading JEHOVAH was superseded by a divinity of good or evil, (as might be,) presiding over the

* "Everywhere throughout the land lingered the traces of the old idolatrous sanctuaries—Baal-gad, Baal-Hermon, Baal-Tamar, Baal-Hazor, Baal-Judah, Baal-Meon, Baal-Perazim, Baal-Shalisha—like the memorials of Saxon heathenism, or of medieval superstition, which furnish the nomenclature of so many spots in our own country; and even in families, as in that of Saul's, we find that the title of the Phœnician god appears; as in the name so common in Tyre and Carthage—Maherbal, Hannibal; Asdrubal."—*Stanley's Jewish Church*, p. 291.

several elements of nature. One mountain summit would have its altar to the sun - another to the moon—another to the stars. One grove would have its temple, or shrine, or image dedicated to the brooks and rivulets—another to the rain of heaven—another to the falling dew—another to the seasons. The summer would have *its* shrine to a *propitious* Baal; the winter with its storms would have *its* altar and libations of blood to the malevolent Being whose wrath needed to be appeased. The worshipper's main conception of this hundred-headed god was connected with the attribute of *power*. The Phœnician Baal was called by the Greeks the Hercules of Tyre—the embodiment of might, if not of cruelty. They lost sight of the God of holiness, and rectitude, and love. They were awed by the wrath and judgment which was the habitation of Baal's throne:—they knew nothing of the mercy and righteousness and truth which went before the face of the true God of their fathers.

The time had arrived for judgment. The cup of the iniquity of Ahab and Israel was full. The cloud was charged. It is about to burst on the devoted land. Is there no gleam of light to relieve this thick darkness? Is there no trumpet-tongued messenger, no "minister of FLAMING FIRE," to vindicate the rights and prerogatives of Israel and Israel's Jehovah—to witness for the great essential truth—the *unity of God;*—taking up the old watchword,—"Hear, O Israel, the Lord our God is ONE Lord?" Yes! God has "come to send *fire* on the earth;" and, in the person of Elijah, "it is already kindled." He has in him a champion ready harnessed for the battle, who will be bold to speak His word before kings, and not be moved. The fan is in his hand, and he will thoroughly purge his floor—hurl "Baalzebub, the prince of devils," from his seat, and quench the fire on his defiled and defiling altars. "It is time thou work, Lord, for they have made void thy law." "Let not the heathen say, Where is now their God?"

It was, then, in the midst of this scene of darkness, apostasy, and blood, that forth came the great Tishbite. The Jewish prophets were compared to vigilant watch-dogs.* But Elijah was no "dumb dog that cannot bark;" "sleeping, lying down, loving to slumber." His was not the trumpet to give forth a wavering or uncertain sound. Standing face to face with guilty Ahab, he startles him with the avowal—"My God—the God of Israel—the God of thy Fathers—and he who ought to be *thy* God—JEHOVAH *liveth!*" "As the Lord God of Israel *liveth,* before whom I stand, there shall not be dew nor rain these years, but according to my word." To understand aright the force of this asseveration, we must view it in the same light as the subsequent scene on Mount Carmel, viz., as a challenge made by the Prophet to settle the question by a solemn appeal to the great power or powers (be who they may) who rule the universe, and who have the elements of nature under their control. It was as if he had said to his royal master—'I shall prove that thy base idolatries cannot aid thee in the hour of need. I shall undertake to demonstrate that a plurality of gods is but a plurality of nonentities. Here is the test. In the name of my God I utter it. *You* have invested the Baalim you worship with lordship over the processes of outer nature—you have *your* pretended Baal or lord who has the

* Isa. lvi. 10.

clouds of heaven in his hand—who can unseal or close their watery treasures at his will. You have your pretended deity —who spangles morning by morning the pastures on the hills of Israel with *dew*-drops, or leaves them dry like the fleece of Gideon. I shall disprove your polytheism;—I shall unmask the lie of these Phœnician priests whom you feed at the royal table;—I shall solve the momentous problem, not by word, but by awful *deed*. I shall prove that this dew and these rain-clouds are *not* Baal's giving;—that his priests might rend the sky from morn to even with importunate supplication, and there would be no response. But I shall demonstrate that they are in the hands of that "*living* God," whose servant I am, and "before whom," though unseen, "I stand." And here will be the proof. I assert, in the name and by the authority of Him whom I worship, and whose unworthy servant I am, that neither Dew nor Rain shall fall on the parched plains and valleys of Israel except at my bidding. From this day henceforth these skies shall be as brass, and this earth as iron. Let thy Baalim throng disprove it if they can. Let them, if they can, thwart this act of delegated omnipotence. Let them, if they can, force open the bolted doors of heaven, and exude dew-drops from the gasping earth. Let them, if they can, bribe the miser fountains to unlock their hoarded treasures. *Then*, but not till then, will I listen to the tale of thy dumb idols, and renounce my belief in that Great Being who maketh the clouds His chariot;—who giveth rain from heaven, and fruitful seasons, filling our hearts with food and with gladness. I know my God liveth. From this day forth, trees and grass scorched and blighted—the arrested growth of the vegetable world—waterless channels and cattle lowing on hungry pastures, during "these years," shall prove the truth of my solemn declaration.' We are told of no reply on the part of Ahab. He may have been struck dumb—quailing under the withering words;—or perhaps the sequel may rather intimate that his brow darkened with vengeance, and that he turned to his palace to take summary means of avenging and rebuking "the madness of the prophet." Be this as it may, it is enough for us to know that as months rolled on, it became terribly evident that nature all around—the heavens above and the earth beneath—confirmed the utterances of the man of God. The blossoms of the fig-tree drooped—the shoutings of the vintage in the fruitful valleys of Ephraim and Zebulon ceased;—no oil was distilled from the olive-tree,—the flocks pined and languished in field and stall—a fearful famine overspread the land;—whilst the feeble remnant of the faithful, in their cave-retreats, sang together that song of Zion—"By terrible things in righteousness wilt thou answer us, O God of our salvation."*

We shall close the chapter with a few practical lessons from this opening portion of the Prophet's history.

Let us learn the insidious power of error, and guard against it.

With regard to nothing had God fenced around His law more solemnly than the introduction of idolatry. The protest, sounded amid the blazing accompaniments of terror on Sinai, was repeated and reiterated in the written Oracles. The most rigid injunctions were given for the extirpation of

* Ps. lv. 5.

the Canaanites, lest an intermixture with a pagan race might corrupt the primitive worship; and not only were the idolatrous nations themselves to be expelled and exterminated, but all vestiges of the idols and idol-altars and groves were to be swept away. "Ye shall utterly destroy all the places wherein the nations which ye shall possess served their gods, upon the high mountains, and upon the hills, and under every green tree. And ye shall overthrow their altars, and break their pillars, and burn their groves with fire; and ye shall hew down the graven images of their gods, and destroy the names of them out of that place." After such a stringent admonition as this, who can estimate the daring presumption and impiety of a whole covenanted nation, from king to peasant and vine-dresser, trampling in the dust the most sacred article in the charter of their religious liberties;—forgetting the strong hand and stretched-out arm of Him who led them through the depths of the sea;—selling themselves as votaries to bloodthirsty idols,—worshipping Remphan and the host of heaven!

There is not much danger, in this our land and day, of a relapse into idolatry;—of a cultured intellectual age making all at once a rebound of a thousand years into the darkness of heathen and pagan delusion; although the histories of Greece and Rome tell us too plainly, how the most exquisite intellectual refinement may be in lamentable conjunction with degrading superstition. Neither do we share in the dread entertained by some, in this era of broad common sense, of a relapse into the puerilities and mummeries of Popish superstition. Protestantism—love of intellectual, moral, and spiritual freedom—is too deeply-rooted for that. But we are *not* proof against other more insidious and specious forms of religious error. The next phase which infidelity will assume, and indeed *has* assumed, is that of "a philosophy falsely so called," whose principle and lurking element of danger is the exalting proud reason in the place of childlike faith; sitting in arbitrary and high-handed judgment on the declarations of God's Word; undermining the foundation-truth of the atonement; stripping the cross of Christ of its chiefest glory; and regarding the Bible—the precious casket in which these truths are contained—not as of fine gold, more precious than Ophir, but rather like the image of Nebuchadnezzar, partly of gold and partly of iron and clay. Unbelief, varying in its phases and developments, is the same in every age. The monitory word can never be out of place or season, even when we think a rampart of impregnable strength and defence is girdling Church and nation and religious privileges—"Beware, lest ye also, being led away by the error of the wicked, fall from your own steadfastness." "Take heed, brethren, lest there be in any of you an evil heart of unbelief in departing from the living God."

Let us learn, as a second lesson, that *Divine judgment follows national apostasy.*

It has been often remarked that individuals may, in this world, escape punishment for personal crime,—but nations never. Retribution, in the case of *individuals,* may be reserved for a future condition of reward and punishment, where the present unequal distribution of good and evil will be corrected and adjusted. But the case of nations is different. With them, in their aggregate capacity, there is no such after state of dealing; and therefore their reward or their doom is meted out and accomplished here. What is history? what is prophecy? but a comment on this. Look at these "burdens," pronounced one after another by the ancient seers;—the burden of Egypt, the burden of Tyre, the burden of Nineveh, the burden of Babylon, and, most affecting and significant of all, the burden of *Jerusalem*;—what are these, but God's own solemn indictments, as apostate nation after apostate nation is cited at His bar? In the case of each nation or city, the awarded vengeance is in proportion to their crimes. As they have sowed the wind, so do they reap the whirlwind. When the body politic becomes morally diseased, like the putrid corpse or carcase cast out on the street, the winged messengers of retribution are at hand to prey upon it, in accordance with the Jewish proverbial saying, which was so literally fulfilled in their own signal doom,—"Wheresoever the carcase is, there shall the eagles be gathered together." Ahab and his whole people, save a feeble remnant, had been guilty of glaring national delinquency. They had dishonoured the God of their fathers;—they had adopted and nationalised the mythological creed of the heathen nations;—they had deified nature, and given to a separate Baal lordship over the elements;—they had made fire and hail, snow and vapour, stormy wind, each to fulfil the word of a presiding divinity;—disowning the *one God* who sat enthroned behind the elements He had formed; and who had declared that "while the earth remaineth, seed time and harvest, and cold and heat, and day and night, and summer and winter, should not cease." Jehovah resolves to mete out judgment in accordance with their guilt. He makes those very gifts of nature the instruments of their punishment which had been the means of their sin. They had *undeified* Him in nature; He will make nature wield the lash of retribution. They had given to others a sovereignty over the "rain" and the "dew;" He makes these arrows in His own quiver to be the weapons of vengeance,—with what measure they mete, it was to be measured to them again. "I have spread out my hands all the day unto a rebellious people, which walketh in a way that was not good, after their own thoughts; a people that provoketh me to anger continually to my face; that sacrificeth in gardens, and burneth incense upon altars of brick. . . . These are a smoke in my nose, a fire that burneth all the day. Behold, it is written before me; I will not keep silence, but will recompense, even recompense into their bosom, your iniquities, and the iniquities of your fathers together, saith the Lord, which have burnt incense upon the mountains, and blasphemed me upon the hills: therefore will I measure their former work into their bosom." *

Let us remember that the Great Lord and Governor of nations acts upon fixed and unchanging principles still. We may not undeify Him by the worship of graven images—by bowing the knee to stocks and stones. But there are other national idols which may provoke righteous retribution. The eager thirst for gold—the hasting to be rich—and, worse than this, when riches, given as a great trust, are either selfishly hoarded or guiltily squandered. Ah! as the jealous eye of that God who will not give His glory to another, sees this modern Baal—hundred-headed *Mammon*—claiming the

* Isa. lxv. 2, 3, 6, 7.

homage of his million votaries, let us not wonder if ever and anon He should speak in accents of rebuke and judgment through the great national sin,—put a sudden arrest on our perishable, material, unsanctified prosperity; and, in the midst of shut markets and excluded supplies abroad,—closed factory doors, quenched furnaces, and silent shuttles at home,—utter the great truth which, whether individually or nationally, we are so slow to hear—that "Life," true greatness and true glory, consists not in the abundance of the things which we possess. If the silver and the gold of modern times be taken as symbols of the dew and rain of Israel,—that which is most valued, clung to, depended on,—can we wonder should some Prophet of Fire,—some burning messenger of wrath and retribution,—stand in the midst of our mighty marts, and, with a voice of thunder, proclaim—"As the Lord God of Israel liveth, before whom I stand, there shall not be dew nor rain these years, but according to my word!"

A third lesson we may here learn is—that *God invariably raises up suitable instruments in every great crisis of His Church's history.*

The Church life—the spiritual life of Israel—could not have been at a lower ebb than at this period under the reign of Ahab. His own faithful people were counted by units. Thousands were bowing the knee to Baal, and kissing his impious shrine. But Jehovah has His hero prepared for the times. It was one, moreover, as we have already noted, very specially gifted that was needed. It was no Jeremiah—plaintive, tender-hearted, crushed himself with the national woes, the tear standing on his cheek. It was no John of Apostolic times, or Melancthon of Reformation times—gentle, devout, contemplative, sensitive—a heart overflowing with benignity and love. It was no Thomas of Apostolic times, or Erasmus of Reformation times—calm, speculative, philosophical; and, in the case of the latter, the man of learning, yet the timid, cautious time-server. It was not even a man of the stamp of Paul of Tarsus—bold, brave, unflinching; with the culture and refinement needed to grapple with the sages of Athens, the courtiers of imperial Rome, and the sharp-witted merchants of Corinth; but deficient in powers of physical endurance—weak, and uncommanding in bodily presence. It was one in type and mould like John the Baptist, or like Luther—a Goliath in mind and body—one who could fearlessly confront Pharisee and Sadducee—Herod and Herodias—king, priest, and soldier—who could stand unmoved, as the great German Reformer did, amid the crowned heads and priestly potentates in the Diet at Worms, and fearlessly declare that though it were crowded with devils, he would face them all.

Such was emphatically the Tishbite,—bold, brave, trained to habits of endurance. The gigantic evils of the times needed a giant to grapple with them;—one who could confront wickedness in high places—be the scourger of court vices, and dare anything and everything for the sake of truth. God has ever His star ready to come forth in the midnight of gloom and despair; when the sword drops from the hand of Moses, He has His Joshua ready to take it up; when the Philistian champion defies the armies of Israel, He has ready the stripling youth with the sling and the pebble-stones to smite him to the dust; when His people are led captive, He has Daniel and Cyrus, Joshua and Zerubbabel, ready at His word to turn again the captivity of Zion "as streams in the south." He has only to "give the word," and "great is the company of them that publish it." Should seasons of gloom, and darkness, and apostasy, again overtake the Church; should rampant infidelity threaten to rise to a perilous ascendancy, and to trample out the fires on God's holy altar; trust Him!—a thunder-voice will be ready. A man of might will be sent to break the impious spell. The Church historian of the future, as he closes one chapter of terror and dismay, will open the next with the words—"And ELIJAH said ——."

Learn, once more, *the power of individual influence.*

We shall not at present speak of Elijah's influence. To this we shall have occasion, in a future chapter, more particularly to advert; how, under God, this one man rallied an apostate nation—saved his country by saving its religion, and made thousands and tens of thousands in after ages, when he himself was gone, rise up and call him blessed: "He stood in the breach, and the plague was stayed!" Let us rather, at this point, mark what a corrupt, debased, sensual, and selfish life can do. Let us see what may be the awful consequences of one *guilty* act,—of what a progeny of vice and ruin it may be the prolific parent. Ahab, in himself, appeared to have some naturally good and amiable qualities. But he is one of those of whom it is said he "*sold himself* to work iniquity." The stream which might have been flowing through his land dispensing endless blessings in its course, became a stagnant pool, breeding and diffusing corruption. The defect of his natural character seems to have been indolence, sloth, selfishness, love of ease. Wavering and fickle, he was an easy tool for the intrigues and artifices of others. And then came the fatal crisis—the act of which we have a little ago spoken, which consummated his own ruin and his people's apostasy—his marriage with an unprincipled and bigoted idolatress. He paid the penalty which multitudes have done who have in an evil hour scorned the Divine monition—"Be ye not unequally yoked together with unbelievers: for what communion hath light with darkness? and what concord hath Christ with Belial? or what part hath he that believeth with an infidel?" Doubtless, Ahab's was spoken of and chronicled in its day as a splendid union. Tyre was at this time in its glory—the sovereign of that queenly city could enrich the palace and park of Jezreel with a golden dower. The fretted ceilings of the ivory palace may have been his royal gift—the cunning work of renowned Phœnician craftsmen. Israel's king may have been lauded and congratulated by the neighbouring princes as a favoured man. Alas! dearly bought was that gilded pageantry—the pomp and pride of having these retainers liveried in purple wrought on Tyrian looms! "Ichabod, the glory has departed"—the ark is taken—the god of Ekron is hailed as the god of Israel: and all through the instrumentality of this unhappy, —this ungodly alliance of Jehovah's covenanted king with an uncovenanted heathen. Ahab's whole life is a mournful illustration of resisted and scorned warnings—slighted messages of remonstrance and mercy. The God he rejected strove with him to the last. But the guilty partner of his throne and of his crimes, made him spurn at once the messenger and the message; and over that bloody grave into which their mangled bones were at last consigned, is inscribed the epitaph—"*Who made Israel to sin.*"

Would that in this age of "trust in uncertain riches" it were borne more sacredly in mind, that it is not gold, but moral worth that is the amplest marriage-dowry. Rank, position, wealth, accomplishments, may be but the tawdry gilding underneath which lurk moral debasement and ruin. Think not of Ahab alone, for his was a miserable, characterless, soulless life. But look at *Lot*. See that man of God—that "righteous man." He made the guilty venture of contracting an irreligious marriage. Mark the result! See it in his "vexed soul," his weeping eyes, his laughed-at pleadings; his wife a monument of vengeance, his blackened home, his blackened name, his unknown and unhonoured grave. "A brand plucked from the burning." "SAVED; YET SO AS BY FIRE!"

III.

The Retreat.

"And the word of the Lord came unto him, saying, Get thee hence, and turn thee eastward, and hide thyself by the brook Cherith, that is before Jordan. And it shall be, that thou shalt drink of the brook; and I have commanded the ravens to feed thee there. So he went, and did according unto the word of the Lord: for he went and dwelt by the brook Cherith, that is before Jordan. And the ravens brought him bread and flesh in the morning, and bread and flesh in the evening; and he drank of the brook."—1 KINGS xvii. 2–6.

"SO THE SPIRIT LIFTED ME UP, AND TOOK ME AWAY; . . . BUT THE HAND OF THE LORD WAS STRONG UPON ME."—EZEK. III. 14.

THE RETREAT.

ONE of the striking dramatic incidents here occurs, which we shall often have occasion to note in the course of the Prophet's life.

Where he met the king of Israel, and delivered the abrupt communication considered in last chapter, we know not. It may have been at some unexpected moment; as when Isaiah met King Ahaz "in the highway of the fuller's field;" or when the monarch was seated on some state-day in regal magnificence, with Jezebel at his side, amid a blaze of courtiers, in the palace of Jezreel; or on some religious festal occasion, when the six hundred priests of Baal, clad in their official vestments, were doing homage to the Phœnician idol, and rending the air with the cry—"O Baal, hear us!" All this, however, is left to conjecture. But the message having been delivered, the God, whose behest it was, proceeds to secure the safety of His faithful servant—alike from court vengeance and from being involved in the national calamity. He directs him to flee to a lonely spot—probably amid the wilds of his own native Gilead—and there to wait farther intimation of the Divine will. In prompt obedience to the monition, "he went and did according to the word of the Lord; for he went and dwelt by the brook Cherith, which is before Jordan."*

* It would only perplex the reader to give the various conjectures on the topography of Cherith, from Eusebius, Jerome, and Josephus, to those

We can picture to ourselves his strange solitude. Some narrow gorge, uninvaded by human footstep, fenced in by nature to form a prophet's chamber—the awning of this "pilgrim-tent" constructed of the interlacing boughs of fig, oak, and oleander; the blue vault of heaven overhead, leading him by day to consoling thoughts on the Great Universal Presence; the sun shining with tempered lustre, answering to the deeper sunshine of a quiet conscience within; the stars by night, like the wakeful eyes of ministering angels, keeping watch over his lonely couch as he pillowed his head on the dewless leaves:—with that better pillow still for the weary—the sublime consciousness of having done his duty, and subordinated his own will to that of the Highest. What a contrast—his evening meal and chamber of repose, with those of the monarch in whose guilty ear he had recently proclaimed the judgment of God! —the ivory palace, filled with imported luxury—the retainers, gorgeous with Tyrian purple and dust of gold—the royal couch, curtained with Phœnician draperies and redolent of Phœnician perfumes. A stranger was the rough Bedouin

of modern travellers. Dr Robertson, Stanley, and Van de Velde mention with probability, among other claimants, the *Wady Kelt*, near Jericho. On a careful examination of authorities, however, we are disposed strongly to adhere to the view stated—giving it a position much farther north, on the other side of Jordan. As Elijah, at the time, must have been either at Samaria or Jezreel, the *Wady Kelt* was not in the direction indicated by the Divine command, "*eastward* before Jordan." In Hebrew, the word "before," has invariably the geographical meaning of "east." So that the expression, "before Jordan," pointed to its eastern bank. Both Jerome and Eusebius place it thus—on the other side of the border river. Keil adds the remark, with reference to the Wady Kelt, that "its close proximity to Jericho, then rebuilt by Hiel, would at this time make this exact spot scarcely fit for a secure place of concealment."

Prophet to all such dainties. His table, the green sward, —his retainers, the winged fowls of heaven,—his bed, the hollow of the rock—its coverlet, his rough hairy mantle,—his lullaby, the music of the rippling stream, which, as it babbled by—the one tuneful brook of a silent land—sang morning and evening a hymn of God's faithfulness. But, as we picture him, with thankful, contented heart, strengthening in summer's drought the stakes of his hut; or in winter's cold, gathering, like the apostle of Melita, the scattered leaves and dry wood to kindle and feed his lonely fire;—as we imagine him thus, night by night composing himself to rest, have we not a living commentary on words with which he may have filled his waking and sleeping thoughts—"A little that a just man hath is better than the riches of many wicked." "When thou liest down thou shalt not be afraid; yea, thou shalt lie down, and thy sleep shall be sweet." "The curse of the Lord is in the house of the wicked; but he blesseth the habitation of the just."

Let us pause here, and ponder, as a first lesson, *the power of prayer.*

The whole land was pining under the most fearful of judgments. Every brook, save that lonely rill of Cherith, had failed. No dewdrops spangled the forests with their crystal jewels,—no rain-torrents answered the silent inarticulate cry of the gasping earth. The ground upturned by the ploughshare had become rigid furrows of iron—the dust lay thick on the highways—the heavens above were a blazing furnace. All day long, from the chariot of the sun, there seemed to be discharged bolts of scorching fire. Nature lay prostrate and helpless under the withering curse. And how was this? St James tells us, "Elias *prayed earnestly* that it might not rain, and it rained not on the earth by the space of three years and six months." Oh, wondrous power!—a mortal pleading with God!—Omnipotence being moved by weakness! The seasons arrested in their course;—nature's processes curbed;—the windows of heaven closed, and the fields and granaries of earth emptied and spoiled—all—all owing to the voice of one man!

And does not the example of the Tishbite refute the oft-repeated objection to prayer—'What need is there to try to move God? He has all things "foreordained, whatsoever comes to pass." It can only be a bold, presumptuous dreamer who can think of altering or modifying the Divine decrees. If He has resolved to send judgment, He needs not the pleadings of a mortal to remind him of His purposes.' Not so did our Prophet reason;—his was a truer and nobler philosophy. Well did he know that Ahab's wickedness had provoked the Divine displeasure; and if God himself had not announced to His faithful servant the specific form of retribution, He had, at all events, doubtless, given him to understand that judgment was prepared and ready to descend. But this does not release or exonerate Elijah from what he felt to be alike his duty and his privilege. We find him on his knees—praying—and "praying earnestly;"—just as if the awful lesson about to be read to Israel depended on these feeble petitions. God, had He seen meet, without any human intervention, might have "thundered in the heavens," and the Highest given His voice, "hailstones and coals of fire;" He might have "sent out His arrows and scattered them—shot out lightnings and discomfited them." But "the Prophet of Fire," knowing the appointed medium through which the Being he served fulfils His behests, employs the conducting-rod of *prayer* to fetch down the lightning from His treasuries. It reminds us of the Apostles—the "Prophets of Fire" of a later age. The promise of a fiery baptism of a different kind had been given them. But, nevertheless, they continued, we read, "with one accord, in prayer and supplication;" and it was while thus engaged—assembled "with one accord in one place"—that there came the descent "as of a rushing mighty wind," and "cloven tongues like as of fire sat upon each of them."

How constantly are similar illustrations of this prevailing "*power*," brought before us in the case of believers of old. It was by *prayer* Jacob wrestled and prevailed. It was by *prayer* Joshua arrested the fiery wheels of the sun's chariot. It was by *prayer* Daniel shut the lions' mouths, and cheated death of its prey. It was *prayer*—the prayer of good King Hezekiah and the pious remnant among those who owned his sceptre—that saved Jerusalem from utter destruction, and the people from captivity. He carried his desperate case and cause,—he spread the railing letter of the Assyrian invader before God in an agony of *prayer*. Next morning, the hushed tents of Sennacherib—the ground strewn with his dead—was the divinely-renewed testimony that "the effectual fervent prayer of a righteous man availeth much."

And *we* have the same blessed refuge—the same strong consolation—in our hours, whether of impending national or individual sorrow. Whatever be the cloud that may be gathering, this is our sheet-anchor—our polar-star in the day of trouble—"The Lord's hand is not shortened that it cannot save, neither his ear heavy that it cannot hear!"

Let us learn, further, from this incident in Elijah's life, *the triumph and sure recompense of faith.*

It was a bold and brave thing, surely, to utter such a prayer, and confront Ahab with such an announcement. Indeed, independently of the wrath of the Israelitish monarch, the *malison* Elijah had pronounced could not fail to rouse the indignation of the whole kingdom. That savage-looking seer of Gilead would be hated and denounced by the starving thousands on whom his imprecation had fallen, as a "troubler in Israel." But, bold as a lion, he fulfils his mission as the ambassador and vicegerent of Heaven. He knows that he has been divinely called to vindicate the cause of truth and righteousness. Ahab may load him with irons—he may seize and torture him in hopes of coercing a revocation of the hateful utterance. Famishing with hunger, the people may also be hounded on to vengeful extremities against this prophet of evil tidings. But in tranquil composure he waits the result. He is like the daring soldier who has fired the train, and who, with the consciousness of having bravely done his duty, is prepared for the worst, even should he be involved in the awful havoc—buried under the blood-stained ruins.

We cannot, indeed, claim for Elijah, as "a man of like passions," exemption from all doubt or misgiving in the present emergency. Unquestionably he had, as all have, a weaker side, even in what we suppose the least assailable part of his nature. It was no common heroism which was needed to outbrave the vengeance of an infamous court, a debased and infuriated priesthood, a people stung to madness by want. The very blight and prostration of the external world, too, must have been a touching spectacle to a feeling heart. The trees draped in ashen leaves—the cattle lowing on arid pastures—innocent children making a vain appeal for food to parents miserable and helpless as themselves! But a higher impulse than his own had prompted the prophetic woe. He knows that it was no selfish, wayward caprice on his part, but the will—the righteous decree—of the God and King whose servant he was. He will not retract the retributive utterance; he will allow no debate or parlance between duty and expediency. Others may have sought to deter him; his own heart at times may have prompted more timorous counsels. Under the same feeling of oppressive solitariness which impelled him subsequently with pusillanimous spirit to take flight to Horeb, he might now have purchased immunity from danger by refusing to deliver his message, and fleeing, like another Jonah, for shelter amid the mountains of his native Gilead. But he will obey God rather than be deterred by the frowns, and fears, and even sufferings of men. With the calm confidence and resolve of a kindred spirit, he can say—"*In the Lord put I my trust; how say ye to my soul, Flee as a bird to your mountain?*"

Nor is he left without the sure reward and recompense which follow simple trust and bold action. As the angel was sent to Peter in his dungeon, or to Paul in the storm, just at the crisis-hour when help was most needed;—so does the same God provide now a refuge for His Prophet. When he had no earthly home or friend,—when king and people were confederate against him;—One who was better than home, and friend, and king—the "*El-Shaddai*," the "*All-Sufficient*," comes with the cheering word—"Get thee hence, and turn thee eastward, and hide thyself by the brook Cherith that is before Jordan." Moreover, not only does He furnish him with a refuge, but He makes provision for the supply of his daily wants; and in order to manifest His power and boundless resources, employs for this purpose the unlikeliest means and agencies. He makes the ravenous birds of the forest have their instincts in abeyance, in order that they may minister to His servant. "And it shall be that thou shalt drink of the brook; and I have commanded the ravens to feed thee there!"

The Lord God of Elijah is still to this hour faithful to His promise—"Them that honour me, I will honour." "The young lions may lack and suffer hunger; but they that seek the Lord shall not lack any good thing." Manly work done in His service—sacrifices made in His cause—will sooner or later be repaid with usury. It is because the presence and power of a personal God are so little felt and realised that our faith is so weak, and our ventures in His cause and service are so small. When the soldiers of Gustavus Adolphus, the greatest king of Sweden, wished to dissuade him from risking his life by exposure in battle, it is said his grand reply was—"*God Almighty liveth.*" The motto of the Gilead Prophet was the same—"The Lord God of Israel *liveth*, before whom I stand!" With his faith anchored on that simple but sublime assurance, he hastened to his rocky, sterile abode, knowing that his "bread would be given him, and his water would be sure." And all that his "God had spoken came to pass."

On reaching his secluded retreat, lo! the joyous, unwonted sound of the brook broke upon his ear. The ravens, too, were there waiting their strange mission. When the gates of the morning opened, they flocked with the miraculous bread;—when the gates of evening closed, down they flew, bearing the promised sustenance.* Night by night, as the curtain of darkness fell around, wrapping himself in his mantle, and composing his head on his leafy pillow, he could exultingly say—"The Lord is my light and my salvation; whom shall I fear? the Lord is the strength of my life; of whom shall I be afraid?"

It may have seemed at first sight indeed strange, this long period of suspension from busy life, this seclusion from the scene of action where his voice and presence were so needed. It was enough for him, however, that his God

* "I cannot see that bird, but I must needs think of Elijah, and wonder no less at the miracle of his faith than of his provision. It was a strong belief that carried him into a desolate retiredness to expect food from ravens. This fowl we know is ravenous; all is too little that he can forage for himself, and the Prophet's reason must needs suggest to him that in a dry barren desert bread and flesh must be great dainties, yet he goes aside to expect victuals from that purveyance. He knew this fowl to be no less greedy than unclean; unclean as in law, so the nature of his food. What is his ordinary prey but loathsome carrion? Yet since God had appointed him His caterer, he stands not upon the nice points of a fastidious squeamishness; but confidently depends upon that uncouth provision, and, accordingly, those unlikely purveyors bring him bread and flesh in the morning, and bread and flesh in the evening. . . . . Upon the sight of them, he magnified with a thankful heart the wonderful goodness and truth of his God, and was nourished more with his faith than with his food.

" O God, how infinite is Thy providence, wisdom, and power! We creatures are not what we are, but what Thou wilt have us; when Thy turn is to be served, we have none of our own. Give me but faith, and do what Thou wilt."—*Bishop Hall's Meditations.*

willed it to be so, and patiently to wait the disclosure and development of the Divine purposes. Moreover, can we doubt that this season and place of deep solitude proved to Elijah a meet and needed training-school to prepare and qualify him for the grander achievements that were before him? It was so in the history of the most illustrious saints, both in Old and New Testament times. Moses had forty years' separation from the world in the Sinai desert, before entering on his unparalleled mission as the liberator and leader of the many thousands of Israel. John had his loving spirit fed and refreshed and disciplined in the solitudes of Patmos. John's loving Master had His days and nights of sacred seclusion on the mountains of Judea and Galilee, where His holy human soul was strengthened for arduous conflict. Paul, in training for the great work of the apostolate, had three years of retirement amid the deserts of Arabia. Luther,—the Elijah of his age,—had his spirit braced for hero-deeds during an uninterrupted season of prayer and the study of the sacred oracles, in the lone castle of Wartburg in the forest of Thuringia. In the same way would the "Prophet of Fire" carry with him his torch to this vestibule of nature's temple—not to quench it, but rather, by holding more intimate fellowship with the great Source of Light, to get it kindled with a purer flame from the inner sanctuary. We are told nothing regarding his occupations during these months of loneliness. But may we not think of him truthfully as "alone, yet not alone;" seated under the rock-clefts, with the music of the brook in his ear,—his heroic soul, filled with mighty thoughts, musing devoutly on his great work, and earnestly seeking to be braced for his momentous life-struggle? May not nobler winged attendants than the birds of heaven have brought down messages of comfort to refresh and invigorate his spirit? Ay, by mystic and hallowed communings with the Lord of angels, may he not have been enabled to perfect the self-surrender and self-consecration of his whole nature, getting his will more and more merged and absorbed in the will of the great Being he delighted to serve? He would ever after, in all probability, cherish the remembrance of Cherith as a place and occasion of calm and elevated joy; and can we doubt that, when he emerges from his obscurity, he will come forth more fully harnessed for the battle,—the fire of his earnest soul burning with a purer, intenser, and more tempered lustre?

And is it not so with God's people still? When He has for a time secluded them from a busy world,—sent them away from life's thoroughfares to hold pensive communings with their own hearts in the lonely wilderness of trial, have they not been led to feel and to recognise, not only a gracious needs-be in the Divine dealings, but, following in Elijah's spirit the teachings and directions of the great Disposer, have they not found that they come forth from their season of affliction better fitted for their work and disciplined for their warfare,—moreover, that in their very hours of sadness, He opens up for them unimagined sources of solace and consolation? In taking them to Cherith, He does not permit them to go unbefriended or alone. What Patmos was to John, or Cherith to his great prototype, so can He make the gloomiest of seasons bright with the manifestations of His own grace and love

He will not suffer the Cherith of sorrow to be without its brook of comfort and its winged messengers of peace. He provides streams of consolation specially suited for His people in all their seasons of trial. *Sickness* is such a Cherith; when secluded from life's active duties—health withdrawn—strength prostrated—body and mind enfeebled; —pain extracting the cry, "in the morning, Would God it were evening; and in the evening, Would God it were morning." Yet how many can look back on such seasons and tell of their brooks of solace? Bible promises welling up with new beauty like streams in the desert;—a nobler and truer estimate of life imparted;—nearer and more realising views of God and heaven. *Bereavement* is such a Cherith. When the scorching sun of sorrow has withered up life's choicest flowers, and dried its sweetest sources of pleasure, "the wilderness and the solitary place are made glad." He who has taken away, comes in the place of "the loved and lost." Our very sorrows, like the sable-plumaged ravens, are transformed into messengers of comfort. God fulfils His own promise by the bestowment of "the hidden manna:" we may come forth from the severe soul-conflict, like Jacob, wrestling, but it is like him also, with "a *new name.*" And even in the prospect of *Death* itself;—though called like Elijah to "*Cherith which is* BEFORE JORDAN;"—the *All-Sufficient*—the living God—is there, amid the turgid waters of "the border river," to cheer and support us, saying, "Fear not, I am with thee; be not dismayed, for I am thy God." Whatever be our circumstances; our discouragements, disappointments, sorrows—"fightings without, and fears within"—worldly calamities, temporal losses; let us not utter the misgiving word, "Where is the Lord God of Elijah?" Let us rather take as our motto, under all the varying conditions of life, "JEHOVAH-JIREH"—*The Lord will provide.* Let us do our duty, and God will fulfil His word. Let us go to our Cheriths, and God will have ready His promised brook and ravens and manna. Let us prepare the fire and the wood, and God will provide His own lamb for the burnt-offering.

IV.

Cherith and Zarephath.

"And it came to pass after a while, that the brook dried up, because there had been no rain in the land. And the word of the Lord came unto him, saying, Arise, get thee to Zarephath, which belongeth to Zidon, and dwell there: behold, I have commanded a widow woman there to sustain thee. So he arose and went to Zarephath. And when he came to the gate of the city, behold, the widow woman was there gathering of sticks: and he called to her, and said, Fetch me, I pray thee, a little water in a vessel, that I may drink. And as she was going to fetch it, he called to her, and said, Bring me, I pray thee, a morsel of bread in thine hand. And she said, As the Lord thy God liveth, I have not a cake, but an handful of meal in a barrel, and a little oil in a cruse: and, behold, I am gathering two sticks, that I may go in and dress it for me and my son, that we may eat it, and die. And Elijah said unto her, Fear not; go and do as thou hast said: but make me thereof a little cake first, and bring it unto me, and after make for thee and for thy son. For thus saith the Lord God of Israel, The barrel of meal shall not waste, neither shall the cruse of oil fail, until the day that the Lord sendeth rain upon the earth. And she went and did according to the saying of Elijah: and she, and he, and her house, did eat many days. And the barrel of meal wasted not, neither did the cruse of oil fail, according to the word of the Lord, which he spake by Elijah."—1 KINGS xvii. 1-17.

"AND I WILL BRING THE BLIND BY A WAY THAT THEY KNEW NOT; I WILL LEAD THEM IN PATHS THAT THEY HAVE NOT KNOWN: I WILL MAKE DARKNESS LIGHT BEFORE THEM, AND CROOKED THINGS STRAIGHT. THESE THINGS WILL I DO UNTO THEM, AND NOT FORSAKE THEM."—ISAIAH XLII. 16.

CHERITH AND ZAREPHATH.

THE Prophet of Israel had now been nearly a year in his desert retreat. There he remained passive regarding his future disposal, leaving the evolution of events in the hands of Him who had given His angels charge over him to keep him in all his ways. He knew that he was under good and gracious guidance. So long as the brook murmured by his side, and the winged retainers supplied his table, he took no unnecessary thought for the morrow, assured that the needed strength would be apportioned for each day.

But as this period was expiring, the brook began to sing less cheerily; once a full rill or cascade, which, night by night, was wont to lull him asleep, it becomes gradually attenuated into a silver thread. In a few days it is seen only to trickle drop by drop from the barren rock—until, where pools of refreshing water were before, there is nothing now left but sand and stones. So long as the rivulet flowed, it was a pledge and guarantee of God's watchful providence and continued care. True to His word, the Lord had hitherto, in this "Valley of Baca" made for His servant "a well." But now, as each new morning recalls a diminished supply, till at last song of bird and song of stream are alike silenced, it seems as if the Divine promise had failed, and He who "sendeth the springs into the valleys which run among the hills," had "altered the word which had gone forth out of His mouth!"

To one, indeed, like Elijah, with his naturally impetuous, and, it may be, impatient temperament, no trial could have more thoroughly tested the strength and reality of his faith than this. Though he could brace himself for great exigencies,—though he could face Ahab undaunted, and hurl his malediction in the face of angry courtiers and idolatrous priests,—he was not so well fitted to bear with equanimity this slow wearing-out ordeal,—watching the sacramental sign and token of Jehovah's faithfulness gradually decreasing and filtering away;—marking day by day the subsidence of the water in the little pools around, till his cherished shelter turned out no better than all other earthly refuges—a refuge of lies. May we not imagine injured pride and unbelief doing their best to whisper in his ear, 'Prophet of Fire! the pledge of the Divine presence has failed thee; the altar-flame has forsaken thy rocky shrine; thou hast lost thy Protector now. Go, God-deserted one!—take thy staff and mantle;—find out for thyself some safe retreat from this burning drought;—the Lord has forgotten to be gracious, and in anger He has shut up His tender mercies!' But "he staggered not through unbelief." "The man of like passions" successfully combated his own weakest point—his natural failing of hastiness and irritability. During these last solitary musings at Cherith, he clings only the more ardently to his life-motto and watchword—"Jehovah liveth;" and waits in calmness and submission an answer to the silent prayer—"What wilt Thou have me to do?" Nor does he wait in vain. The old well-known voice, in due season, breaks upon his solitude with a new communication of grace and mercy.

And has not this been often God's way and method of dealing? It was when the disciples were in their hour of extremity, during the storm on Gennesaret, giving themselves up to the hopelessness of despair, that, "in the fourth watch of the night," when darkness was deepest and danger greatest, the great Deliverer appeared on the crested wave—"Jesus went unto them walking on the sea." It was when the bereft of Bethany had, as they imagined, consigned the fond treasure of their affections to everlasting silence; and as they were sitting in their pillaged home, wondering at the mysterious delay on the part of the one Being who could alone have arrested that winged arrow which had laid low the pride of their hearts;—at that crisis-hour, the great Conqueror of death appears, to revive the smouldering ashes of their faith, and reanimate the joy and prop of their existence! Yes, how often, in the experience of His people still, does God thus delay His succouring mercy to the very last, that they may see His hand, and His hand alone, in the gracious intervention or deliverance, and be brought to say, with grateful, adoring thankfulness—"Unless *the Lord* had been my help, my soul had almost dwelt in silence." And even when He does *not* appear visibly to succour;—when some fond brook of earthly comfort is left to dry in its channel—or when deliverance from some threatened earthly trial or threatened evil is not vouchsafed, it is in order that we may, the more significantly and submissively, listen to His own voice saying to us, as He did to Elijah,—"*Arise.*" For, observe the difference between the failing of the world's consolations and refuges and joys and those of the true Christian:—when the worldly man mourns his dried-up brooks, he has lost his all—he has nowhere else to turn: there is nothing left him but the tear of despair—the broken heart—the grave. But in the case of the Believer, when one comfort is withdrawn, his God has other spiritual comforts for him in reversion. Miserable indeed are those who have nothing but the poor earthly rill to look to! For, sooner or later, this must be its history, (as multitudes, in their Cheriths of sorrow, can bear testimony,) "And it came to pass, *after a while*, that the brook dried up!"

But even with the new provision God has made for His Prophet, there comes a fresh trial of faith. The new arrangement made for his safety and sustenance is the last which, in his meditative moments, Elijah would have imagined. He is commanded to go to Zarephath, a distant city in the territory of Phœnicia. Had he been told to take temporary refuge in some of the Trans-Jordanic kingdoms, amid the tribes of the Amorite mountains, or amid the freebooters of Arabia—the roving hordes of the desert—it would not have been so startling nor so strange to him. But in order to reach this distant Sarepta, he must, in the first instance, traverse nearly a hundred miles of the blighted famine-stricken land of Israel; subjecting himself to want and peril among a people to whom his name was hateful and terrible, as identified with their sufferings. And, it might seem more unaccountable still—that the selected place of his refuge should be in the very kingdom which was responsible for the evils which had overtaken his unhappy country:—Phœnicia, the land of Baal—the old home of Jezebel—itself at that moment suffering under the judgment of God; for over it also the dark wings of the Angel of Famine were brooding, as well as over the adjoining territory of the Hebrews. The very directions regarding his sustenance might have been humiliating to a proud heart. There was something romantic and prophet-like about the appointments of Cherith,—the rocky chamber with its crystal brook and sable-plumaged attendants. Elijah was there a privileged unit of the nation, getting, as his forefathers in the Sinai wilderness of old, day by day the divinely-appointed manna and the running stream. He would perhaps have learned to love his brook as much as Jonah did his gourd and his bower, and be "exceeding glad" for it. But now he has to go as a mendicant, an expatriated pilgrim, to seek his food and home at the hands of a Gentile stranger—a heathen of a strange country—an impoverished widow. But there is no hesitancy on his part—"The word of the Lord," (the living Jehovah,) had come unto him, saying—"Arise! get thee to Zarephath, which belongeth to Sidon, and dwell there: behold, I have commanded a widow woman to sustain thee." The voice is no sooner heard than obeyed. Casting his mantle around him, forth he goes on the long and perilous journey,—travelling probably by night to elude observation and avoid danger. Depressed, indeed, he could not fail at times to be, during that long and trying route, were it from nothing else than seeing the visible traces of God's judgment on every side, among the people to whom he was linked by imperishable ties. For himself, he knew that the Lord was his keeper. His long and faithful guardianship of him at Cherith, with all the encouraging memories of that secluded home, would brace his faith and inspire confidence for the future. He had there learned that all things are possible to him that believeth. We may imagine the girded traveller—lonely, yet confident, —"sorrowful, yet alway rejoicing"—"cast down, but not destroyed,"—cheering his spirit as he pursues his way with the words of the great minstrel of his nation—"O my God, my soul is cast down within me: therefore will I remember thee from the land of Jordan, and of the Hermonites, from the hill Mizar."

Let us, like Elijah, be prepared for the Divine will, whatever it be. It may be mysterious. The summons in our case, as in his, may be to get us from some cool shady retreat,—some brook of refreshing,—to a Zarephath, (*lit.*, "a place of crucibles" or "furnaces" for melting metal).* But there is some wise and gracious necessity in all God's dealings. We shall come to understand and adore their yet undiscovered, undeveloped meaning. Let us, meanwhile, hear the voice addressed to us, which was addressed to a loving disciple of a future age—"Said I not unto thee, if thou wouldst believe, thou shouldst see the glory of God?"

There is surely no small comfort in the thought, suggested alike by Cherith and Zarephath, that the bounds of our habitation are divinely appointed. Our lots in life—our occupations, our positions, our dwellings—what the fatalist calls our destinies—what heathen mythology attributed to the Fates,—all this is marked out by Him who "seeth

* "It was probably a station of glass-houses; so that the name may be taken as analogous to what we call 'smelting-houses,' or furnaces. Some suppose it was a place famous for refining metallic ores—a blast furnace." —*See Calmet.*

the end from the beginning." "The lot is cast into the lap, but the whole disposing thereof is of the Lord." It is He who takes us to Cherith — a place of solitude — a distant dwelling—it may be a distant land. It is He who takes us *from* solitude — from grove and woodland and murmuring brook,—from the green fields of childhood and youth, and brings us to some busy Zarephath—some thronged city with its "stunning tide of human care and crime." It is He who takes us to our sweet shelters of prosperity with their sparkling brooks of joy. It is He who, when He sees meet, hurries us into the "house of crucibles"—"the melting furnaces." He gives the *gourd*—He sends the *worm*. Oh, it is our comfort to know, in this mysterious, ravelled, manifold life of ours, that the Great Artificer has the threads of existence in His own hands—weaving the complex pattern, evolving good out of evil and order out of confusion. He who sent Elijah alike to Cherith and Sarepta for his own good, as well as the good of others,—sent Onesimus, the runaway slave, to Rome,—and Lydia, the seller of purple, to Philippi,—and Zaccheus, the tax-gatherer, to Jericho. But one and all of these, and other notable examples, were brought thither for their souls' everlasting welfare; and the new song was put into their lips—"Blessed be the Lord, for he hath shewed us his marvellous kindness in a strong city!" How many still can tell the same. Their choice of abode seemed to them something purely arbitrary and capricious. A mere trifle seemed, as they thought, to have determined or altered their whole future. But the finger of God had, unknown, been pointing. The inarticulate voice of God had been saying, as to Elijah, "*Arise.*" "He led them forth by the right way, that they might go to a city of habitation. Oh that men would praise the Lord for his goodness, and for his wonderful works unto the children of men."

At last the Prophet has crossed the border territory, descending the mountain slope towards the southern entrance of the town. SAREPTA or ZAREPHATH, the modern *Surafend,* occupied a long ridge, overlooking the blue waters of the Mediterranean on one side, while its view northwards was bounded by the snow-capped summit of Hermon.* Its streets were hallowed by the footsteps of the seer of Israel; and, in after times, by the Presence of a Greater than he. For the probability is that in this same city, the Syrophœnician who pleaded so earnestly for her daughter, had her faith commended, and her child restored.

Close by the city gate, Elijah beheld a woman, with sunken cheek and pallid eye, busied in gathering a few broken branches dried and withered by the long-continued drought. The wearied traveller accosts her. He solicits what in the circumstances was no ordinary boon, "Fetch me," said he, "a little water in a vessel that I may drink." Probably no drop of the refreshing element had crossed his lips since he drained the last mouthful from the cleft at Cherith. From the peculiarity of his raiment, this Gentile stranger seems at once to recognise him as a prophet,—not of Baal, but of

* "The identity of Surafend with Sarepta is unquestioned. It is a village seated aloft on the top and side of one of the hills, the long line of which skirts the plain of Phœnicia, conspicuous from far by the white domes of its many tombs of Mussulman saints. It throws no light on the story of Elijah, beyond the emphasis imparted to his visit by the complete separation of the situation from the Israelite territory on the other side of the hills."—*Stanley's Sinai and Palestine,* p. 273.

the God of Israel, and the adjoining kingdom. She speaks of Jehovah as *his* God;—probably cognisant, too, of the fact that it was the God of the Hebrews who had sent the famine.* She at once assents to the request he had made. When on her way, however, for the draught of water, he recalls her by preferring a more startling petition, that she bring along with it "a morsel of bread." The demand unlocks and unseals the hidden story of her woe. With the tear in her eye, she avows her inability. She is preparing for a sad and solemn future. That sunset in the western wave, is among the last her eye is to see! And had it been her own fate alone that was then engrossing her thoughts, these hot tears would not flow so fast. But there was another fond life in her home. One child had been left to cheer her widowhood. Why is he not here with her now, to help that last gathering for the evening meal? We can dimly surmise the reason. The parent had been able to buffet hitherto these long months of wasting famine; but the youthful sufferer, we may imagine, had sunk prostrate on the couch, from which, the heart that fondly doted upon him, feared he was never to rise. The few remaining crumbs in the empty barrel are barely sufficient to make one last meal. In the cruse of olive oil, there are but a few drops

* There are some who would make this woman an Israelite, or, at all events, a worshipper of the true God. This we cannot think. Dr Kitto well remarks—"That she was a worshipper of Him, as some have thought, is not likely, and betrays some ignorance of the extent to which the heathen were disposed to recognise the gods of other nations as gods—and powerful gods—but not as *their* gods. Besides, she says '*thy* God'—an addition which she would not be likely to have made, had the Lord been her God also."—*Daily Readings*, p. 223.

left to spread on the cakes. She is preparing to dole out the last pitiful morsel. Her emaciated hands are now engaged in gathering a little fuel to bake the scanty remains of her exhausted cupboard; then, casting herself by the side of her boy, she will calmly wait the slow lingering departure. The Prophet turns to her, and says—"Fear not; go and do as thou hast said." He tells her, however, to bake first a cake for him with the remnant of the flour,—"Make me thereof a little cake first, and bring it unto me, and after make for thee and thy son: for thus saith the Lord God of Israel, The barrel of meal shall not waste, neither shall the cruse of oil fail, until the day that the Lord sendeth rain on the earth." With alacrity she obeys the voice of the Hebrew stranger. She hies her to her lowly abode, little dreaming of the blessing in store for her from that dust-covered seer of Israel; and that she was yet to experience the truth of the gospel saying, "Whosoever shall give to drink unto one of these little ones a cup of cold water only in the name of a disciple, verily I say unto you, he shall in no wise lose his reward."

Let us now proceed to gather a few special lessons from this new chapter in the Prophet's history, both in connexion with the conduct of the *widow;* and also in connexion with the dealings of the *widow's God.*

Mark, in the case of the widow, *her disinterested kindness.* Place ourselves for a moment in her position. A starving, dying woman, reduced to earth's last morsel, with her own and only child sinking fast in her desolate cot under the grip of biting famine. What rare unselfishness! when this stranger prophet (an alien in blood and in religion) comes and reveals himself a fellow-sufferer,—the tear of commiseration steals to her wan cheek and sunken eye. No miserable exclusive feelings of difference in creed and country are suffered to interfere with the outflowings of tender compassion. Great was the sacrifice, in that season of burning drought, to part with a cup of water; and far more to surrender some of the crumbs of that rapidly-exhausting barrel. But with a combination of faith and unselfishness which have few parallels in Scripture, she hastens, in obedience to Elijah's request, to relieve his distress, and permit him to share the last pittance of her cupboard.

How lovely, in this selfish world, are such pictures of unselfish consideration for the wants, and sufferings and woes of others! How many are there who, if it be well with themselves, have no care for the necessities of their neighbours:—who, if their own families are prospering, and their own cup filling, and their own circle uninvaded by want and sickness, listen with apathetic ear to the appeal of the helpless,—turn with averted look from the pleading claim of tattered rags and bleak homes! This woman's generosity was a freewill-offering, in the midst of her own intense sufferings; when pinching poverty was blanching her lips and ploughing deep furrows in her cheek. Alas! is it not to be feared—is it not to be confessed with shame (I speak regarding cases of virtuous poverty, of well authenticated want and suffering)—that a similar generosity and kindness is often withheld, even where the giving involves no sacrifice —no diminution of daily comforts? How frequent is the miserable spectacle, of men becoming more hardened and incased in selfishness with the very increase of their worldly substance;—God storing their granaries with plenty, speeding their wheels of industry, wafting their ships with propitious gales, whilst they only pile up more greedily the gilded heap. And even if, in some such cases, there be entertained an undefined purpose of posthumous liberality; they miss the *present* blessedness of being almoners of the Divine bounty, and of lighting up the bosoms of the wretched and outcast with a sunshine of joy. Selfishness is the irreconcilable antagonist of Christianity. He cannot be a Christian who lives for self. "Whoso hath this world's goods, and seeth his brother have need, and shutteth up his bowels of compassion from him, how dwelleth the love of God in him?"

Let us learn, from the case of the widow of Zarephath, *the power of feeble influences.* She was a poor, lowly, depressed, hunger-stricken woman,—unknown, perhaps, beyond the doors of her neighbours in the Phœnician town. Yet see exemplified that great power in moral dynamics—"the power of *littles.*" It was but a little incident this, in a little-known life—the giving a little morsel of bread—and a small cup of water,—a single word, and no more, of strengthening and comfort. But how manifold and important the results of that one *little* act! To *herself*—the prolongation of her own natural life, and that of her son;—the commencement, as we believe, in both, of a nobler spiritual existence—God blessing her household, like that of Obed-edom of old. To the *Prophet*—introducing him in that time of drought and famine to a congenial home:

perhaps his wavering faith revived and confirmed, not only by witnessing the unselfish love and kindness of this heathen woman,—but by hearing, in that heathen land, and from heathen lips, what he had not listened to for a whole year until now,—his own life-motto falling like heavenly music on his ear—"The Lord thy God, JEHOVAH, liveth!" To *the Church of God*—in having on record this beautiful example of simple faith and unselfish deed. How many, in the extremity of want, have learned a lesson of trust and hope from reading of the widow of Sarepta! How many a bereft child of poverty, in the depth of her agony, with a blank future before her and her little ones, has risen from this page blotted with her tears, thanking God, and taking courage! Wheresoever this Bible is read, or this gospel is preached, there what this woman has done shall be told as a memorial of her.

Never despise the power of feeble influences. Often when the giant's spear, the greaves of brass, and the panoply of iron could do nothing, God has made use of the sling and brook-pebbles, the "broken pitchers," and "trumpets of rams' horns." It is worthy of note that this 'power of littles' is specially illustrated in Holy Writ, in connexion with two *widows*;—the one in the Old Testament and the other in the New. The widow of Sarepta, giving the last handful of her drained barrel:—the widow at the temple-treasury, casting in her two mites. Never let any one say, 'I am of no use in the world—I can do no good—I can exercise no influence;—God has clipped my wings—I am like a chained bird—I would soar, but I cannot!—this cage of poverty or of sickness keeps me shut up from the elements of activity and usefulness.' Imprisoned one, "if you cannot soar, you can sing." If yours is the cage and not the wide blue sky, you can warble your song of cheerfulness and submission to the will of God. Remember, the song of the caged and captive bird has put, before now, music and high resolves into the patriot's heart. Nay, nay,—the widow who, it may be in the midst of poverty and wretchedness, exercises faith in God;—the stricken sick one, laid for years on years on a couch of languishing, yet making that couch a radiating centre of holy influences,—can preach a silent sermon which will arrest and convince, when all the eloquence of press and pulpit may be but as sounding brass and a tinkling cymbal. The domestic servant preserving intact her own honesty in the midst of purloining associates,—the schoolboy defending purity and virtue, and frowning on vice in the midst of his playmates;—the shopkeeper foregoing the tempting bribe or gain, in which sterling honour might be tainted or compromised;—the Sabbath-school teacher gathering the waifs of poverty, and vice, and neglect, week after week, under his kindly eye;—the district-visitor leaving the kindly word and kindly advice in the homes of the poor, or giving the kindly smile or kindly grasp when the timid word cannot come;—the lowly working man gathering his children on his knee, and imbuing their young hearts with the never-to-be-forgotten lessons of early piety:—these are but illustrations and exemplifications of those countless *little* efforts—feeble influences—which have made the world greater and wiser and happier. Mechanical science has to make the confession that she has lost the secret of those great powers which of old poised in mid-air the blocks of huge stone we still gaze upon with wonder in the pyramids of Cairo, and in the gigantic temples of Memphis and Thebes. But in *moral* dynamics the power of *littles* still remains. That lever is in every one's possession. If relics are disowned and repudiated in our Protestant Church, there are relics, better than material ones, to which we love to cling. That Barrel of meal and that Cruse of oil have been handed down for 3000 years as *moral* relics—heirlooms to the Church—lowly but significant trophies of faith, and love, and humble trust, which she delights to suspend on the walls of her temple! Go back in thought to that widow of Sarepta, and take courage from her example in doing *little* things for God and for His people. Hear her song of praise and thankfulness—"Trust in the Lord and do good; so shalt thou dwell in the land, and verily thou shalt be fed. Commit thy way unto the Lord. Trust also in him, and he shall bring it to pass. And he shall bring forth thy righteousness as the light, and thy judgment as the noonday."

But to pass from the widow to *the widow's God* The first and most prominent reflection suggested is, *the sovereignty of grace.* This was the great lesson the Saviour himself drew from the incident, on the occasion of His preaching in the synagogue of Nazareth. "In the days of Elias," He says, "when the heavens were shut up, and when great famine was throughout all the land, there were many widows in Israel." God could have hidden His prophet in the home of one of these. It might have been the cupboard of a Hebrew widow he replenished:—*her* home he rescued from famine,—*her* heart he made to sing for joy,—the story of *her* faith and kindness He selected to go down in enduring memorial to the Church of the future. But He who acts how and when and as He pleases, directs His servant across the boundaries of the chosen kingdom, to the unlikeliest spot and home on the shores of the Great sea. He sends him amid one of the heathen races,—to Baal's land, and to an idolatrous worshipper of Baal's shrines. He takes the children's bread and casts it to Gentile dogs!

Let us adore the freeness of His mercy. God's thoughts are not our thoughts, neither are His ways our ways. Man has generally some reason for conferring his favours—some claim arising from person or pedigree, from character or attainments. But *His* sole motive in conferring favours is His own free and gracious purpose. "It is not of him that willeth, nor of him that runneth, but of God that sheweth mercy." He takes a Manasseh filling Jerusalem with blood, and makes him a monument of forgiveness. He takes a Saul breathing out his blasphemies, and converts him into the great Apostle. He takes a Samaritan leper and fills his tongue with gospel praise, while the nine of Jewish birth and privilege go thankless and ungrateful to their homes. He takes a rude heathen jailer, or an unprincipled tax-gatherer of Jericho, or a profligate woman of Capernaum, or a felon in his last agonies, while many encircled with the halo of natural virtues or with the prestige of religious education and training, are left to perish in their ungodliness and unbelief and pride! He took as the founders of His Church and the ambassadors of His cause—not philosophers of Rome, nor polished Greeks, nor learned Rabbis,—but a handful of unlettered fishermen from the villages of half-heathen Galilee. And it is the same principle we recognise still in His dealings. He often passes by the great, the powerful, the rich, the learned, the educated—ay, even the virtuous and the amiable; and He crowds the marriage-supper of the King,—from the highways and hedges,—with the poor and the illiterate, the outcast and prodigal. He often leaves palace and castle and stately mansion and lettered hall, and enters the humble cottage and the poor man's garret. He leaves the nominal British Christian,—the polished European, and He takes the poor Bechuana of Africa, or the cannibal of the South Seas, and converts these children of darkness into children of light. He leaves noble vessels to lie on the sands on which they have been stranded, and He takes the mean unsightly craft around them and sets them floating on the waters. May not this be the solemn reflection of some whose eyes fall on these pages? My old companions—those at one time better and more promising than I—have been long ago scattered as wrecks on life's ocean, entangled in the swirling vortex, and hurried down into nameless depths of infamy. And how is it that I am made to differ?—that that tale of misery and ruin—that which, in the case of others, has broken a parent's heart, whitened his hairs with the snows of premature age, and sent him sobbing and halting to the grave,—how is it that I have escaped these dread temptations; and that, while others have broken loose with a worse than maniac's madness, I am this day sitting at the feet of Jesus, clothed and in my right mind? Not unto me, O God! not unto me, but unto Thy name be all the glory! I read the reason, written in gleaming characters, in the heights and depths of Thine own Infinite love. By Thy grace (Thy free, sovereign, unmerited grace alone) I am what I am!

Let us farther learn *God's recompense of unselfish kindness.* So far as we can infer, this poor woman assented to the appeal of the famished, fainting Prophet, without any hope of recompense or reward. Those who are themselves suffering calamity are generally most ready in their straitened circumstances to lend a kindly ear to the woes of others. Just as we may have seen that the mother, with naked feet and hungry children, singing her mournful song on the streets, is most willingly and generously relieved by those who have known, by sad personal experience, what similar exigencies are. The widow of Zarephath went back for the vessel of water to assuage the Prophet's thirst with the heavy thought and certainty burdening her heart, that the hours of her own life and that of her boy were numbered. But God is not unmindful of her work of faith and her labour of love in that she ministered to one of His saints. Hers was the "scattering and yet increasing." She had paid her little mite into the bank of Heaven: in lending to His servant, she had lent to the Lord; and back comes the hundredfold interest,—the payment with a divine munificent usury. She experienced, temporally and spiritually, the reality of a gospel promise, afterwards uttered by the lips of Truth itself,—"Do good and lend, hoping for nothing again, and your reward shall be great, and ye shall be the children of the Highest." The barrel and cruse are replenished;—the shadows of death are warded off from her home;—and Heaven's blessing descends, better than all. In giving of her earthly pittance, this idolatress learned, that the God of Israel was not like Baal, but a living Being in whom the lowly, the poor, and helpless might trust. In exchange for the "daily bread which perisheth," she received the nobler recompense of the heavenly. Her lone heart was taught a truth which no Baal could utter—"Thy Maker is thy husband, the Lord of hosts is his name, and thy Redeemer the Holy One of Israel." "She and he and her house did eat many days: and the barrel of meal wasted not, neither did the cruse of oil fail, according to the word of the Lord which he spake by Elijah."

The old economy dealt largely in temporal blessings. Good deeds then, were generally acknowledged by temporal recompense. It is different under the new economy. Its recompenses and rewards point rather to the future. But this does not lessen or impair the truth and certainty of the Divine promises,—"Them that honour me, I will honour"—"Give, and it shall be given unto you, good measure pressed down and shaken together and running over"—"If thou draw out thy soul to the hungry, and satisfy the afflicted soul, then shall thy light rise in obscurity, and thy darkness be as the noonday. . . . And the Lord shall guide thee continually, and satisfy thy soul in drought." If not now, there *is* a time of recompense at hand for all pure, lofty, beneficent, unselfish, disinterested kindness done in Christ's name, and out of love for Him and His people. On the Great Day of God, what is to be the test and evidence of a saving personal interest in Jesus? What is the touchstone which the great Saviour-Judge Himself is to apply in the case of the myriad crowd sisted at His bar?—"I was hungry, and ye gave me meat; I was thirsty, and ye gave me drink; I was a stranger, and ye took me in. . . . Inasmuch as ye did it" to the greatest, such as that Prophet, or to the least, such as that famishing Lazarus at the gate, *"ye did it unto* ME!"

And if there be one other thought yet suggested to us, it is this—*God's tender care of the Widow.* How specially was the Widow's case provided for under the Old Testament economy:—"Ye shall not afflict any *widow,* or fatherless child. If thou afflict them in any wise, and they cry at all to me, I will surely hear their cry." "When thou cuttest down thine harvest in thy field, and hast forgot a sheaf in the field, thou shalt not go again to fetch it: it shall be for the stranger, and for the fatherless, and for *the widow.* . . . When thou beatest thine olive-tree, thou shalt not go over the boughs again: it shall be for the stranger, for the fatherless, and for the *widow.* When thou gatherest the grapes of thy vineyard, thou shalt not glean it afterward: it shall be for the stranger, for the fatherless, and for the *widow.*" Who can fail to remember, in New Testament story, the scene outside the gate of Nain? How kindly and beneficently the great Sympathiser approaches the chief mourner, and utters first the gentle "*Weep not;*" and then the word of power which brings back her loved one to her side! There were, we may well believe, other homes and other parents in Galilee similarly bereft at that moment and needing succour. What took the Saviour's steps to the city of Nain? Why select that funeral crowd amid the many wending their way at that doleful sunset hour to the long home? Are we wrong in surmising that, had any disciple asked the question,—had they ventured to probe His heart of love,—He would have given, in all probability, the touching reason assigned by the Evangelist, when his enumeration of the elements and ingredients in that bereft one's sorrow rises to this climax,—"*And she was a widow!*" That Divine love and sympathy remain unchanged. God is to this hour, as He ever was, "a judge of the widow in His holy habitation." The name of that Saviour who stood at the gates of Nain, and mingled His own tears with the widow's there, is "Jesus Christ, the same yesterday, and to-day, and for ever." God's promises are the same to all,—irrespective of rank, or age, or country. Around this Treasury of comfort for the lone sufferer and sorrower, rich and poor may meet together. The cottager's widow in her lone hut, and the widowed monarch in her sackclothed halls, are heirs to one and the same promise of the widow's God,—"Leave thy fatherless children, I will preserve them alive; and let thy widows trust in me."

V.

Lights and Shadows.

"And it came to pass after these things, that the son of the woman, the mistress of the house, fell sick; and his sickness was so sore, that there was no breath left in him. And she said unto Elijah, What have I to do with thee, O thou man of God? art thou come unto me to call my sin to remembrance, and to slay my son? And he said unto her, Give me thy son. And he took him out of her bosom, and carried him up into a loft where he abode, and laid him upon his own bed. And he cried unto the Lord, and said, O Lord my God, hast thou also brought evil upon the widow with whom I sojourn, by slaying her son? And he stretched himself upon the child three times, and cried unto the Lord, and said, O Lord my God, I pray thee, let this child's soul come into him again. And the Lord heard the voice of Elijah; and the soul of the child came into him again, and he revived. And Elijah took the child, and brought him down out of the chamber into the house, and delivered him unto his mother: and Elijah said, See, thy son liveth. And the woman said to Elijah, Now by this I know that thou art a man of God, and that the word of the Lord in thy mouth is truth."—1 KINGS xvii. 17-24.

"BEHOLD, I HAVE REFINED THEE, BUT NOT WITH SILVER; I HAVE CHOSEN THEE IN THE FURNACE OF AFFLICTION."—ISAIAH XLVIII. 10.

LIGHTS AND SHADOWS.

In our last chapter we left Elijah under the roof of the widow of Zarephath. The famine was still raging amid the thousands around. But as each morning's sun rose on the inmates of this tranquil home, lo, the barrel and the cruse which the evening meal seemed to have exhausted were again replenished. God's mercies were "new to them every morning, and His faithfulness every night."

We can only venture to surmise how the Prophet's hours, in this secluded dwelling, would be spent. We can follow him in thought, as betimes, perchance, he wandered up the rocky ridges which flanked the town, gazing now on the everlasting snows of Hermon, now on the wood-crowned top of Tabor;—thus beholding both "Tabor and Hermon" "rejoicing in God's name." Or, as at other times, he would wander along the shores of "the great and wide sea," in adoring contemplation of Him who taketh up the waters in the hollow of His hand, and who "giveth the sea His decree." Yet again, when the barrel had yielded its evening supply, and the lamp had been lighted from the unfailing oil-cruse, we can picture him unfolding to these two children of Pagan Phœnicia, the name and works and divine character of the God of Israel;—dwelling on the glorious promise spoken to the fathers, but in the blessings of which all the families of the earth were to participate. We can picture him narrating to them the eventful scenes in his national annals—Egypt—the exodus—the wilderness—the conquest of Canaan—the wonders of the old prophetic age—the splendour of the reigns of David and Solomon. We can think, perhaps, of Prophet and widow and child joining their voices together in the psalms of the great Hebrew minstrel,—many of them so applicable to their own circumstances and experience:—"Happy is he that hath the God of Jacob for his help, whose hope is in the Lord his God; which made heaven and earth, the sea, and all that therein is; which keepeth truth for ever; which executeth judgment for the oppressed; which giveth food to the hungry. . . . The Lord preserveth the strangers; he relieveth the fatherless and widow." Or, more appropriate still in that heathen Tyrian home:—"And the daughter of Tyre shall be there with a gift; even the rich among the people shall entreat thy favour. Instead of thy fathers shall be thy children, whom thou mayest make princes in all the earth. I will make thy name to be remembered in all generations: therefore shall the people praise thee for ever and ever!"

We have every reason to believe that these two heathen-born Phœnicians—mother and child—would, under the training of the Hebrew stranger, be brought to a saving knowledge of divine truth. Whilst led to see that Baal was a dumb, insensate idol, they would be taught also to love and reverence that God who had vouchsafed deliverance in the hour of their extremity, and for soul as well as body, learn to offer the prayer—"Give us this day our daily bread." Moreover, "that church in the house" forms a significant incident in sacred story, prefigurative of gospel times. Suggestive surely was the fact of a messenger of Heaven, a seer of Israel, being sent to a home in distant Phœnicia to unfold to heathen hearts the way of salvation. In this sense Elijah occupies the illustrious position of a first missionary to the Gentiles ;—bequeathing by his example to the Church of the future—the Church of our own age—a lesson of the duty which we owe to our benighted brethren in pagan lands,—when, in obedience to the commission of its Great Head, the heralds of the cross go forth into all the world and preach the gospel to every creature.

But a dark season is at hand for that lowly home at Zarephath. Perhaps it was with this widow, as with many among us still :—in her state of comparative prosperity,—of exemption, at all events, from the pressure of famine so severely felt all around,—she may have been beginning to forget the hand which was filling her empty cupboard, and warding off want from her dwelling. Miraculously fed from day to day—seeing the barrel and the cruse each morning recruited with the needed supply,—she may have begun to feel too confidently secure ;—that her "mountain was standing strong ;"—and that she might safely calculate on a permanent immunity from the inroads of trial.

How apt are we, after a season of long-continued blessing —unbroken prosperity,—to indulge in this spirit of boastful independence : taking our daily comforts—food—health—friends—children, as matters of course. We may see in the case of others,—these strong pillars—these "beautiful rods," —bowed and broken ;—but our inmost thought and feeling is, "I am all secure—I need not fear !" So may have meditated the Sarepta widow. And the last trial she would ever have anticipated, would probably be the very one that was in store for her. With appalling suddenness, the little life,—the light of her dwelling,—is extinguished! "There is no breath left in him." Since this loved and only child had been given back to her from the gates of famine and death, we may imagine her heart-strings had twined more tenderly then ever around him; he was every day growing up more of a companion and solace to her,—a pledge of unspeakable blessing in her latter years—when his arms would toil for her, and his prayers would comfort her, and his hands at last would close her eyes in death. Sad, indeed, that that one lone star which twinkled in her firmament should be quenched. Better it had been if, two years ago, his sun had gone down in opening day, than have so mournful a setting now. His being spared only to be taken, seemed a cruel mocking of her grief and tears. All her hopes and joys perished in that hour of woe. She could bear to see the barrel of meal yielding a diminished supply,—she could endure to look on an empty, unreplenished cruse—but to gaze on that withered flower, lying cold and lifeless in her bosom,—to lose HIM, this was death indeed!

We cannot, perhaps, wonder that for a time, faith, and patience, and submission, were tempted to give way. In the bitterness of her bereft soul, she thus upbraids the Prophet, "What have I to do with thee, O thou man of God? Art thou come unto me to call my sin to remembrance, and to slay my son?" The words were a cutting reflection on Elijah, as well as an insinuation against Elijah's God. It was as if she had said, "What have I done to provoke at thy hands so terrible a calamity? Is this thy recompense and requital for sheltering thy defenceless head? In pity, I gave thee welcome to my humble roof. Have these been thine answered prayers for thy benefactress? Has thy God come, in this fearful retributive sense, to be the 'Judge of the widow?' Hast thou come, a wolf in sheep's clothing, to slay my son?" How striking is the contrast between this agony of her impassioned grief and the calm composure manifested when she first met Elijah. Then, her child's death was equally imminent, and threatened, too, under a more terrible form. Her words on that occasion, in speaking of partaking with him of her last morsel, were these, "That we may eat it and die." She had familiarised herself with the approach of the last enemy: it was the passive, silent, submission of blank despair. Now, however, it was "*sudden death*,"—death unexpected—death when she was handling the full cup. It was her gourd withering, not by a process of slow, gradual decay—drooping leaf by leaf; but it was, as with Jonah, the luxuriant plant—coiled fresh and beauteous round her evening bower—becoming, in a night, a mass of blighted, withered leaves. In the words of the patriarch of Ur, "The morning was even as the shadow of death."

Nor can we fail to admire Elijah's conduct in the trying circumstances. We know to what course his natural character would have impelled him. Hurt at the unkind and unjust reflection—his fiery nature might have prompted him to retaliate. He might, with an angry word, have answered the ungenerous suspicion breathed by that broken heart. But there is no syllable of recrimination or resentment. He says nothing (as he might have done) about the blessing he had been, and brought, to her household. He makes no reference to the barrel and the cruse beside them, the silent witnesses of God's mercy and goodness. Deeply touched at the impressive sight of death—and, perhaps, with a tender love for the youthful victim—he makes kind allowance for the anguish of the childless widow. Saying, "Give me thy son," he takes the cold marble, the dead body, in his arms, and carries it to his own couch. In Eastern dwellings in these times,—as at the present day,—there was generally a room higher than the rest of the building, called "'allîyeh," or, as it is here translated, "loft," where strangers and guests were accommodated. In the better class of houses, it was regarded as the place of honour. To this upper room, Elijah bears the lifeless child. That quiet chamber echoes to the voice of impassioned prayer. The Prophet, though he had dissembled and controlled his feelings before the sorrowing mother, evidently felt keenly the severity of the blow. He dreaded lest the dealings of his God might be misjudged by that crushed mourner, and "he cried unto the Lord, and said, O Lord my God, hast thou also brought evil upon the widow with whom I sojourn, by slaying her son?" Laying the corpse upon the bed, he stretched himself upon it,—not for the purpose of imparting, as some have thought, natural warmth to revive and quicken the dormant physical energies —but rather, it would seem, to communicate the quickening power of God.* He knew that He who had "brought the evil" could alone remove it. Three times, as he overlaid the dead body, did the importunate cry ascend, "O Lord, my God, I pray thee let this child's soul come into him again!" The prayer is heard:—the limbs begin to move;—the eye

* See Keil, *in loco.*

dilates;—the pulse beats. Back comes the departed spirit. "The Prophet of Fire" has rekindled the cold ashes on this desolated hearth; and carrying in his arms the living trophy of God's goodness, he hushes the sobs of the mother with the joyful announcement—"*See, thy son liveth!*" Her tears are dried. Her murmurings cease. Her faith in Israel's Jehovah is confirmed. "Now"—is the utterance of her bounding heart—"by this I know that thou art a man of God, and that the word of the Lord in thy mouth is truth."

From this touching and suggestive episode in the Prophet's history, we may gather, as one out of many practical lessons, that *bereavement is not necessarily a Divine judgment on account of any special sin.* The widow, in the first moments of her grief, as she sat with her dead son upon her lap—the hot tears coursing down her cheek—was led to form the hasty conclusion, that God had sent her this heavy chastisement as a rebuke and retribution for some previous transgression. "Art thou come unto me to call my sin to remembrance?" Many, we know, in the season of bereavement are apt to draw a similar unwarranted deduction;—saying to themselves what Job's unfeeling friends reproachfully addressed to him, as they pointed to the miserable bed of dust and ashes on which he lay—"Such, surely, are the dwellings of the wicked; and this is the place of him that knoweth not God." But we may thus often misinterpret the reason and motive of the Divine procedure. Our Lord, in one of His great miracles—curing the blind man at the temple gate—declared emphatically, in opposition to the false and gratuitous assumption of the Pharisees, that it was in consequence of no sin either of the sufferer or his parents that he had been doomed to grope his way in darkness at noontide, but "that the works of God might be made manifest in him." Let us not, therefore, hastily surmise when God at times sees meet to empty the chairs and hush the loved voices of our households, that some specific sin must have evoked that special judgment and drawn forth the arrow from the Almighty's quiver. At the very moment when the darkness of death was shadowing the home of Bethany, "Jesus," we read, "loved Martha, Mary, and Lazarus."

We may farther learn from the incident we have been considering, that *no amount of good works, or of active service in the cause of God, will exempt us from trial.* This widow had rendered the greatest benefit which the Church of Christ at that age could receive, by affording shelter to its most valued servant and defender, the great Prophet of Heaven. Yet she was smitten. Her generous pity and kindness to God's vicegerent could not shield her from the assaults of trial! It becomes us, whatever be the Divine dealings, never to ask with the voice of complaint and querulous upbraiding, "If the Lord be with us, why hath all this befallen us?" No good deeds or lofty virtues, or self-denying services, will purchase for us immunity from His righteous ordination, that through much tribulation we must enter into the kingdom. Whatever be our lot or portion, be it ours to "rejoice with trembling." The vessel best manned and equipped may strike on the sunken rock, as well as the meanest and most unseaworthy craft. Nay, God's most favoured saints are often put in the foremost ranks of chastisement. Upon the most fruit-bearing trees of His garden He often uses His pruning-knife. Trial, in its varied forms, has ever been employed by Him as a powerful means of leading to deeper convictions of sin, as well as a salutary quickener of spiritual graces. He knows what discipline is best fitted to draw the soul to Himself; and often does He shew that none is *so* effectual as that which was employed in this home at Zarephath—snapping the ties which bind us to the creature—disuniting us from earthly to bind us to heavenly things. How many can tell—"I date my first deep sense of sin,—my first lively apprehension of Christ and of Divine realities,—to the hour when my dwelling was rifled of its cherished treasures. I should have been to this moment sunk in the sleep of death, had He not roused me from my perilous dream, and taken husband or wife, brother or sister or child!"

This, however, reminds us of *the deep mystery there is in many of God's providential dispensations.* Amid all the homes of that region, who would have expected that the one to be so terribly smitten, was that which had, for two years, kindly screened the head of the expatriated Prophet of Israel. Surely, we might think, if there be one dwelling more than another secure from the assaults of the dread invader, it will be that of the widow of Sarepta, and of the hope and solace of her declining years, who, if spared, might be spared to be an honoured instrument in the defence and maintenance of the true religion.* And yet, behold, the desire of her eyes and the delight of her heart taken away by a stroke!

* According to a Jewish tradition, as quoted by Jerome, this boy became the servant who afterwards accompanied Elijah, and finally became the Prophet Jonah.—*See Smith's Dictionary of the Bible.*

How often are we baffled and confounded by similar dealings; — useless lives spared, and useful lives taken. Decayed scaffoldings, crumbling props remaining,—and the strong and vigorous, the virtuous and useful, swept down in a moment! There is no key now to these dark dispensations. Many a weeping eye cannot read them through blinding tears. But the day is coming when we *shall* read them;—when they shall be luminous with love. Earth may not, as in the case of the widow of Phœnicia, give us back our dead;—no prophet's voice can reanimate the silent ashes,—no anguish of prayer recall the winged spirit. But we joyfully believe the day is coming when we shall write under every mystic providence, "He hath done all things well." Yes, bereaved ones, ye shall no more weep over early graves, when ye yourselves pass upwards to the realms of glory, and hear from your loved ones as they are waiting to greet you at the door of heaven, that by an early death they were "taken away from the evil to come." Meanwhile let us rejoice, like Elijah, in the assurance, that "*the Lord reigneth;*"—that all bereavements and chastisements are His appointments;—"*Thou*" (the Prophet says, addressing his God in prayer)—"THOU" (the living Jehovah) "*hast brought this evil.*" Oh comforting thought! enough to dry all tears and silence all murmurings—"Is there evil in the city," in the cottage, in the palace,—is there evil which blights some unknown poor man's dwelling,—is there evil which clothes a nation in mourning, "*and the Lord hath not done it?*"

The narrative farther exhibits, what we have already had occasion to note in the Prophet's life, and to which we shall have frequent cause to revert,—*the energy and power of prayer*. Not when he supplicates that Heaven should seal up its rains and dews from a whole nation,—not when on Carmel, as we shall find him ere long, invoking discomfiture on Baal and his priests,—is his prayer more earnest than now, in this lowly dwelling, when not the lives of thousands, but the life of one little child, is the subject of his intercession. He seems, indeed, to have felt personally deeply moved under this sudden bereavement. The strong, heroic, brave man could bear with equanimity any ills affecting himself, but he was stung to the quick under the imputation of his benefactress. He could not brook the allegation of bringing evil on the home of one who had opened her door to a friendless stranger. His prayer is an urgent appeal to God—(we had almost said a bold remonstrance)—as a just and merciful and righteous Being. "It cannot be, Lord," he seems to say; "Thou canst not suffer this reproach to descend on me and on Thy great Name! Thou, who hast made the widow's cause Thine own, oh, recompense not thus her kindness to me! Let not this heathen woman say, as she points to her childless home and buried treasure, 'Where is now thy God?'" We can imagine the Tishbite pacing up and down his little chamber in importunate, impassioned prayer,—but yet with no doubt as to the result of his intercession. It was a mighty demand, indeed, for a mortal to make,—a request that had no previous parallel in praying lips. It was nothing short of this,—that unassailable Death be stormed in his own strongholds;—that the iron crown be plucked from the head of the King of terrors. When Elijah *does* manifest faith, it is always of the noblest type. He would doubtless now revert to his life-motto,—the first utterance of his prophetic mission,—"Jehovah liveth." Confiding in the "*El Shaddai*," he feels confident that He who gave him his brook at Cherith, will restore this more sacred living brook which had been so suddenly dried in its earthly channel. Strong in faith, giving glory to God, he proceeds to the couch where the lifeless child lay, and to the act of awakening. Once more he stands before us as delineated by St James, "the righteous man," bearing the glorious testimony as to the "availing,"—the "*much* availing power"—of "*effectual fervent prayer!*"

Finally, we have here a glimpse given us of *the doctrine of the Resurrection*. This was a truth dimly unfolded in Old Testament times. Its full revelation was reserved for Him who, under a more glorious economy, "abolished death, and brought life and immortality to light." As the gladdening words sounded in the mother's ears, "See, thy son liveth!" not only was that widow herself taught that the God of Elijah had a power which no Baal ever had, in imparting life to the still ashes,—reanimating the cold clay, and putting light into the rayless eyes; but it was a parable to the Jewish Church of that great gospel disclosure, that there is a day coming "when all that are in their graves shall hear the voice of the Son of God, and they that hear shall live." Nay, more; from the fact which is expressly recorded in the inspired narrative, that Elijah brought down the living child from the upper chamber into the house, "and delivered him to his mother," we have the precious thought suggested, under a significant figure, that in that glorious resurrection-morning friends will be reunited to friends;—there will be undying reunions of the departed in the

Church of the glorified;—mothers restored to the embrace of children, and lost little ones given back to their parents! How will the happiness of that day of complete triumph be augmented and enhanced, as death-divided relatives, re-linked in bonds of purified earthly affection and love, will be able to exclaim to one another, See, my son! my parent! my brother! my long-lost one!—see, HE LIVETH!

VI.

Obadiah and the Search for Provender.

"And it came to pass after many days, that the word of the Lord came to Elijah in the third year, saying, Go, shew thyself unto Ahab; and I will send rain upon the earth. And Elijah went to shew himself unto Ahab: and there was a sore famine in Samaria. And Ahab called Obadiah, which was the governor of his house: (now Obadiah feared the Lord greatly; for it was so, when Jezebel cut off the prophets of the Lord, that Obadiah took an hundred prophets, and hid them by fifty in a cave, and fed them with bread and water.) And Ahab said unto Obadiah, Go into the land, unto all fountains of water, and unto all brooks; peradventure we may find grass to save the horses and mules alive, that we lose not all the beasts. So they divided the land between them to pass throughout it: Ahab went one way by himself, and Obadiah went another way by himself."—1 KINGS xviii. 1–6.

"NEITHER THEIR SILVER NOR THEIR GOLD SHALL BE ABLE TO DELIVER THEM IN THE DAY OF THE LORD'S WRATH: BUT THE WHOLE LAND SHALL BE DEVOURED BY THE FIRE OF HIS JEALOUSY. . . . SEEK YE THE LORD, ALL YE MEEK OF THE EARTH, WHICH HAVE WROUGHT HIS JUDGMENT; SEEK RIGHTEOUSNESS, SEEK MEEKNESS: IT MAY BE YE SHALL BE HID IN THE DAY OF THE LORD'S ANGER."—ZEPHANIAH I. 18; II. 3.

OBADIAH AND THE SEARCH FOR PROVENDER.

ELIJAH had come to the lowly dwelling where still he tarries—a homeless Jewish prophet—an unbefriended stranger. Now, we have good reason to suppose, he was regarded, alike by mother and son, as an angel of God—a Heaven-sent messenger of mercy,—who had "delivered their souls from death, their eyes from tears, and their feet from falling."

We know not how long he continued at his adopted home after the miraculous raising of the child. But be the time long or short, he quietly waits the Divine will regarding his departure. As we have already noted, in speaking of the place of his former seclusion at Cherith, so still more on the present occasion might he have been disposed, with his ardent impulsive spirit, to fret under this long withdrawal from active public work. Three of the best years of his life spent in inaction! He who could exercise (as we shall find afterwards) an almost magic power over multitudes, why should he be pent up for this protracted period in a cottage of Gentile Phœnicia, when he might have been doing mighty deeds amid the many thousands of Israel? Why should so noble a vessel be left lazily sleeping on its shadows in the harbour, when, with all sail set, it might have been out wrestling with the storm, conveying priceless stores to needy hearts? But it was enough for Elijah, now as formerly, to feel assured that it was part of the Divine plan. He felt that he was glorifying his God,—just because he was occupying his assigned and appointed place for the time,—as much in that humble habitation as he did on the heights of Carmel. The Christian poet represents those angels in heaven who "only stand and wait," as "serving,"—doing their Lord's will,—as truly as the swift-winged messengers who carry to and fro the behests of His pleasure: and of the Church militant on earth, "Thus saith Jehovah," by the mouth of His prophet, "In returning and *rest* shall ye be saved: in *quietness* and in confidence shall be your strength." We can serve God in rest and in quietness,—in the noiseless tenor of an uneventful existence,—as well as in the feverish bustle or prominent position of an active one. Let this be the comfort of those whose lot may be lowly, obscure, uninfluential. They are accepted according to what they have, not according to what they have not. The domestic servant in her kitchen; the mechanic with his begrimed hands at his daily toil; the weaver at his shuttle, the cobbler at his stall; the ploughman at his team, the lone sick one on his or her couch of languishing;—these being each in the way of duty, or necessity, may, in their peculiar sphere and work, as truly glorify their Maker and Redeemer, as the philanthropist at his desk solving great social problems, or the minister of the gospel in his pulpit, swaying thousands by his words! Elijah, however, did not love for its own sake inglorious ease. So long as it was his Lord's will, he remained seated under this pleasant vine and fig-tree. But, like a true soldier, he was prepared at the bugle note to start from his pillow, assume his armour, and rush into the fight. That summons in due time was heard. "After many days the word of the Lord came to Elijah in the third year, saying, Go, shew thyself unto Ahab, and I will send rain upon the earth." He did not hesitate. With cheerful alacrity he grasps his pilgrim staff, flings the hermit mantle once more around his shoulders, and crosses into the valleys of Samaria.

How his spirit must have been bowed with sadness as he traversed the famine-stricken land! Wherever he looked, the scourge of God—the scourge of sin met his eye. The green pastures and the still waters, of which the great Hebrew poet sang, gleamed no longer under the joyous sunshine. Hushed were the notes of the shepherd's pipe, and the bleatings of the flocks. The sickles hang rusting on the closed granary doors. A hundred skeleton forms flitted with glazed eyes across his path;—the vintage shoutings had ceased;—the fig-tree no longer blossomed;—there was no fruit in the vine;—the labour of the olive had failed;—the fields yielded no meat. Oh, what a comfort, amid these scenes of misery, to repose on the word of the living Jehovah, "I *will* send rain upon the earth;" knowing that what the Lord had spoken he would faithfully perform; that perhaps but a few brief days would elapse, ere the funeral pall should be rolled aside, and the shadow of death turned into the morning.

But a new character here reveals himself in the sacred narrative in the person of *Obadiah*, the prime minister or steward of Ahab's palace. We are called to witness in him another wondrous instance of God's sovereign grace. We have had occasion, in a recent chapter, to refer to a signal example of that sovereignty in the case of a heathen widow —a votary of Phœnician Baal. We have now a miracle and monument of divine mercy in the court of a wicked and licentious king of Israel—for "Obadiah feared the Lord greatly."

How, we may ask, could a worshipper of Jehovah reside in the midst of so much degeneracy, idolatry, and crime? How could the lily rear its head amid these thorns—this sheep of the fold survive in the midst of ravening wolves? We answer—just in the same way as divine grace, in the earlier part of this century, moulded and quickened and sustained such men as Wilberforce, Fowell Buxton, and others, in the midst of the lax, irreligious society, and the dissolute, licentious court-life of England. Ay, and just as, in the midst of much obloquy and derision in the present day, there are those in the high places of the land, who are able boldly to take up their cross, and who count this the brightest gem in their coronets—"We serve the Lord Jesus." The natural influence of the corrupt moral atmosphere of Ahab's court, would be to rear, in the person of the chief officer, a cruel, unscrupulous tyrant—the creature and myrmidon of Ahab and Jezebel—who would climb to power and favour by his severity against the prophets of the God of Israel. If Obadiah had been a base time-server, his life aim would have been to second and stimulate the diabolical designs of the royal persecutors. But the grace of God and the fear of God were in his heart, and he knew no other fear. Under the insolence of oriental rule, he might well have dreaded the combined influence of the queen and the idolatrous priests on the despot's will, in compassing his degradation and ruin; but, sustained by the power of religious principle, this righteous man was bold as a lion. He gave one specially unmistakable proof of his heroism and true moral chivalry:

for when Jezebel was involving the prophets of Jehovah* in an indiscriminate massacre, Obadiah hid and sheltered them by fifties in a cave, and fed them on bread and water. It is easy for *us*, in an age of fashionable profession, to espouse the Christian name, and subscribe the Christian creed, and call ourselves worshippers of the Lord God of Elijah. But it was no ordinary test of spiritual courage to stand alone, a witness for Jehovah in the midst of a godless palace;—to rear a solitary altar—a solitary protest on the side of insulted Goodness—when polluted incense was rising from Baal's shrines all around, and the very people of the land were in guilty accord with their monarch, ignoring their great heritage—the truth bequeathed to them in sacred trust—"Jehovah liveth!" Obadiah, moreover, is a remarkable testimony to that singular respect which sterling character and worth command, even from irreligious men. Uprightness, purity, consistency, honesty of purpose, have always an irresistible influence and charm even to base natures. Bloated vice stands rebuked and abashed in the presence of virtue. The wretched slave of sin and pollution respects the purity which degrading habit forbids himself to practise. Herod—the parallel of Ahab in the gospel history—hated John's religion and that of his Master; but he could not help admiring and respecting his honesty, self-sacrifice, self-denial, and boldness. "When a man's ways please the Lord, he maketh his very enemies to be at peace with him." As it was with Joseph in the court of heathen Pharaoh, or Daniel in the palace of heathen Babylon, Obadiah's piety, worth, and goodness exalted

* These were probably "the sons of the prophets"—or those taught in the prophetic schools or colleges; of whom more hereafter.

him to the highest honours which his sovereign had in his power to bestow. Ahab may have hated from his heart the Jehovah-worshipper;—but he revered and reverenced the faithful counsellor, with his stainless honour and unblemished life.

But Obadiah is brought before us in connexion with a mission in which he was engaged in conjunction with his royal master;—a mission which, oriental writers tell us, is frequently still undertaken in seasons of temporary drought by chiefs and petty kings in Syria, Persia, and Hindostan. Fountains of water—so precious in pastoral districts, and specially in the desert—are spoken of in the figurative language of the East as "eyes;" and when these eyes—these fountains—in a season of great scarcity are closed, it seems to be considered a sort of royal prerogative to visit them in person; as if some charm or talismanic power were possessed by the chiefs of the land to reach or bribe their locked-up treasures. It was in accordance with this immemorial usage that Ahab said unto Obadiah, "Go into the land, unto all fountains of water, and unto all brooks: peradventure we may find grass to save the horses and mules alive, that we lose not all the beasts. So they divided the land between them, to pass throughout it. Ahab went one way by himself, and Obadiah went another way by himself."

We shall conclude this chapter by drawing two lessons from the conduct of Ahab as here presented to us.

Let us note *the meanness and cruelty of a selfish nature.* How terrible—how appalling must have been the scenes which presented themselves to the eye of the king in this strange journey! But what are we told was his object in thus traversing his dominions, either all alone or probably with his staff of followers? Noble would it have been to minister consolation to the dead and dying, even by his presence and sympathy, or to devise means in the desperate circumstances to ameliorate the condition of his famishing subjects. But he has no higher, no other object than to save his stud—his mules and horses! Let the horses and mules—let the royal herds browsing in the park of Jezreel, —let *them* be saved. Let the coursers be fed and kept alive which grace his cavalcade or draw his chariot,—let fountains and brooks and patches of verdure be diligently sought for *them;* but let the people be left to their miserable fate!

Has this intense selfishness, this guilty squandering on personal pleasure, to the exclusion of the claims of human misery and woe, been confined to Ahab or his age? Alas! may not the conduct of Ahab be seen in many still, who lavish a fortune on the beasts which perish, while they withhold the humblest mite from the starving orphan or the perishing brother or sister? Do we then condemn these or kindred luxuries? By no means. In this mighty country, wealth was given to be enjoyed, as well as employed. Whatever a man's tastes may be, if innocent and ennobling, let these, within due limitation, be cultivated and gratified. Only, (and here is the qualification,) the pampering of self must not be at the expense of the prior and pre-eminent claims of the destitute and needy. A man is entitled to turn, like Ahab, to his stables; to his horses and mules,—his carriages and equipages; only after he has resolved this question in the sight of God, and of his own conscience, "Have I done my duty to the poor? Have I answered, according to my means, the calls of distress? Have I given my proportion to that languishing mission cause? Have I helped as I ought that starving charity?" Yes! Then, *have* your luxuries as you like, and enjoy them with satisfaction. When one goes,—shall we say, to see some country seat, with its lordly demesne;—some modern park of Jezreel with its antlered children of the forest feeding in picturesque groups, or bounding through the glades;—or when, leaving the park, you enter the ancestral halls which wealth has been permitted to enrich with rare works of art,—walls glowing with lavish decoration, hung with the priceless creations of genius,—how is the pleasure of gazing on all enhanced, when you are told that the owner scatters with princely liberality the gifts of fortune; that he is known for miles around as the benefactor of the poor; and that missions abroad and charities at home would feel terribly the blank of his name and generosity! Or, how a new sunshine seems to light up hall and corridor within, and landscape without;—as, from some oriel window, you gaze on school and church amid the village trees, which Christian munificence has reared, or on smiling cottages, which the open hand and the large heart have built for the aged and infirm to spend the evening of life! But take another case. How the dream of delight and satisfaction vanishes, when you enter the drawing-room which wealth has furnished with lavish costliness;—enter it with the roll or subscription-paper in your hand—headed with the urgent claim of a starving neighbourhood, or, it may be, a starving empire;—and from the jewelled hand to which you consigned it, you have it returned with the answer, "*I cannot afford it!"* Cannot afford it!! The grotesque figures on wall and tapestry, on slab and pedestal, silently refute the lie. The dumb creations of genius smile blushingly and incredulously from their gilded heights. The pampered dog on his velvet couch glances up with reproachful look. The horses standing at the door, fling the foam from their polished bits in sympathetic sarcasm and scorn! This is not an overdrawn picture. Such extreme instances may be rare; but such *could* be photographed from real life. There *are* such houses with this splendid, selfish misery;—gilded dungeons with cold icicles for their tenants; frigid themselves, and freezing all around; who have abundance to lavish on self, but nothing to spare for their brother man—or the cause of the Divine Brother-man who died for them! Wealth is an awful trust! How solemnly will the thought of mis-spent wealth confront many on a death-bed. What would Ahab, if time for reflection had been allowed him at the hour of his death,—what would *he then* have thought of this saying of his manhood—manhood in its prime and glory?—"Go into the land, unto all fountains of waters, and unto all brooks: peradventure we may find grass to save the horses and mules alive, that we lose not all the beasts."

We may learn yet farther, *the terribleness of unimproved warnings.* What a mournful picture have we here. For three years God had tried this monarch with sore judgments. He had shut up heaven, closed the fountains of the land, decimated his people with famine. The voice seemed too loud, too solemn and awful to be disregarded. We might have expected to see Ahab, like the heathen king of Nineveh, put sackcloth on his loins and dust on his head, calling his people to humiliation and repentance. But, alas! the Divine monition seems utterly disregarded. God has emptied His quiver upon him: but arrow after arrow has bounded back from that heart of adamant. He has neither tear for his own guilt, nor tear for his suffering subjects. So far as we are told, the one miserable, petty thought which fills that narrow soul is, to get provender for his stable, and save his mules and horses. Ah, terrible, indeed, it is, when judgments thus lead to an open defiance and resistance of the Divine will; a mocking of His hand, a laughing to scorn of His righteous reproofs: no penitence, no remorse; but rather a more intense selfishness. This miserable king fought against his trial—fought against God,—rushing against the bosses of the Almighty's buckler!

Let those on whom chastisement has been laid remember that affliction itself is no blessing unless it be improved. It is the reverse. An unsanctified trial becomes a curse. It indurates if it does not soften. It is like the heat of the sun, which melts the wax, but hardens the clay. Affliction never leaves us as it finds us. If it does not bring the soul nearer to God, it sends it farther from Him. If the result is not *amelioration*, it is *deterioration*. And what then? When the Divine patience has been wearied and exhausted, the irrevocable doom must go forth—"Ephraim is joined to his idols, let him alone!"

For the space of *three years* God had spoken to Ahab by severe judgment; for *three years* He had blighted his land, and arrested the fall of rain and dew. It was for the same period, the husbandman, in the Gospel parable, waited for fruit on his cumbering fig-tree,—"Behold, these *three years* I come seeking fruit on this fig-tree and find none; cut it down, why cumbereth it the ground?" Three years! Far, far longer than this, may He have been dealing with many of us! dealing by mercies—dealing by chastisements. What has been the result? Has it been, as in the case of Ahab, only a stouter-hearted rebellion—an intenser selfishness—a deeper love of the world—a life of pleasure, which is a life of death? the guilty cumberer—a cumberer still; robbing the ground of space which others would more worthily occupy;—drinking in dews and sunshine for its own useless existence, which might load other boughs with plenteous fruit, and make the world better and happier. Can such expect always to be borne with? Can such dream of continuing to presume on the Divine forbearance? The voice of the Intercessor, in the case of such, may even now be heard, *for the last time,* pleading with despised and injured Mercy: "Lord, let it alone *this year also:* and if it bear fruit, well, —and *if not,* then, *after that,* thou shalt cut it down!"

VII.

The Convocation on Mount Carmel.

"And as Obadiah was in the way, behold, Elijah met him; and he knew him, and fell on his face, and said, Art thou that my lord Elijah? And he answered him, I am: go, tell thy lord, Behold, Elijah is here. And he said, What have I sinned, that thou wouldest deliver thy servant into the hand of Ahab, to slay me? As the Lord thy God liveth, there is no nation or kingdom whither my lord hath not sent to seek thee: and when they said, He is not there; he took an oath of the kingdom and nation, that they found thee not. And now thou sayest, Go, tell thy lord, Behold, Elijah is here. And it shall come to pass, as soon as I am gone from thee, that the Spirit of the Lord shall carry thee whither I know not; and so when I come and tell Ahab, and he cannot find thee, he shall slay me: but I thy servant fear the Lord from my youth. Was it not told my Lord what I did when Jezebel slew the prophets of the Lord, how I hid an hundred men of the Lord's prophets by fifty in a cave, and fed them with bread and water? And now thou sayest, Go, tell thy lord, Behold, Elijah is here: and he shall slay me. And Elijah said, As the Lord of hosts liveth, before whom I stand, I will surely shew myself unto him to-day. So Obadiah went to meet Ahab, and told him: and Ahab went to meet Elijah. And it came to pass, when Ahab saw Elijah, that Ahab said unto him, Art thou he that troubleth Israel? And he answered, I have not troubled Israel; but thou, and thy father's house, in that ye have forsaken the commandments of the Lord, and thou hast followed Baalim. Now therefore send, and gather to me all Israel unto mount Carmel, and the prophets of Baal four hundred and fifty, and the prophets of the groves four hundred, which eat at Jezebel's table. So Ahab sent unto all the children of Israel, and gathered the prophets together to mount Carmel. And Elijah came unto all the people, and said, How long halt ye between two opinions? If the Lord be God, follow him: but if Baal, then follow him. And the people answered him not a word."—1 KINGS xviii. 7-22.

"AND AFTER THREE DAYS AND AN HALF THE SPIRIT OF LIFE FROM GOD ENTERED INTO THEM, AND THEY STOOD UPON THEIR FEET; AND GREAT FEAR FELL UPON THEM WHICH SAW THEM."—REV. xi. 11.

THE CONVOCATION ON MOUNT CARMEL.

For three and a half years, a price had been set on the head of Elijah. The bloodhounds of Ahab had been on his track, but had failed to discover his lurking-place. Obadiah, in search of provender for the cattle belonging to his royal master, had taken the westerly direction from Jezreel, along the great plain of Esdraelon. At some turn of the highway, on this great battle-ground of Hebrew history, all at once he confronts the strange figure of the missing prophet, with his mantle and staff. The royal Chamberlain, startled at the unexpected apparition, prostrates himself to the earth, and exclaims, in half-doubting bewilderment, "Art thou my lord Elijah?" He had perhaps supposed, like many, that with the announcement of the drought, Elijah's prophetic work and mission had been finished; and that he had either retired to his native Gilead, or had possibly been taken to heaven to receive a prophet's reward. High in rank and position as Obadiah was, it shews the blended reverence and awe with which he regarded the seer, when he falls down "on his face before him," addressing him as "*my lord*," and speaking of himself as "*thy servant*"—the obsequious language of a slave to his master. Elijah's command is to go forthwith to Ahab—"Go, tell thy lord, Behold, Elijah is here." Obadiah, at first, with what in the circumstances, perhaps, was not altogether, as has been supposed, a blameworthy or pusillanimous hesitation, remonstrates. He knows the dark purposes of hate and revenge in his master's bosom towards the Prophet; that the people, too, maddened with the horrors of famine, would be eager to second the vengeance of their king. If Elijah fell into their hands, his head would to a certainty be hung that night on the gate of Jezreel. If, therefore, in obedience to the prophet's wish, he proceeded to inform the king that the troubler is found; he concludes either that Elijah will forfeit his life, or else that the God of Elijah, to defeat the king's purpose, will transport his servant miraculously to some other Cherith or Sarepta, and shelter him there. On the latter supposition, Obadiah dreads the consequences to his own person. The monarch would wreak upon *him* his disappointed revenge. He would charge him as being in secret league with his enemy, and deal with him as a traitor to the throne. The Tishbite relieves his apprehension. He gives him the promise, that that very day, ere the sun set over the brow of Carmel, he would shew himself to his royal master. Obadiah is reassured, and assents to Elijah's directions.

The message is delivered. The king in hot haste sets out from his palace, and soon the seer and he stand face to face. How strangely diverse the two characters! The prophet of Jehovah, and the champion of Baal; the upholder of the true religion, and the abettor of lies; Light confronting darkness —Truth confronting error. They meet like two charged thunder-clouds, and we watch, with bated breath, the bursting of the storm.

When the impetuous monarch finds that the prey he has been seeking for years, is at last within his grasp;—could we wonder should the instigations of the queen and his own uncontrollable passion drive him to cruel extremities, and the dust of the highway be stained with the Tishbite's blood? When Ahab reins up his horse, he is the first to speak. But the very sight of that commanding figure—the brave heroic seer—seems at once to unman him. His narrow soul shrivels in his presence. Instead of summary vengeance;—instead of the order we expected to hear given to his armed retainers, "Let the traitor die!" and their swords at the summons leaping from their sheathes;—his rage expends itself in the feeble challenge—"Art thou he that troubleth Israel?" The God of Elijah has the heart of that king in his hand, and turns it "even as He turns the rivers of water;" He has said to the proud waves, "Thus far shalt thou go, and no farther." "Art thou he that troubleth Israel?" How does Elijah meet the charge? He imagines himself alone loyal to the God of his fathers, amid the thousands of an apostate kingdom; with the full consciousness that monarch, queen, princes, courtiers, priests, people, were leagued against him. Do we find him cowering in abject terror at Ahab's feet, imploring on any terms for life; or else, endeavouring to disarm the king's wrath, by telling him that the occasion of it is now at an end,—that he has Divine authority for commanding that the windows of heaven be opened, and for unbarring the long-closed gates of famine; so that, if the accusation has been hitherto correct as to his being a 'troubler in Israel,' he will prove to be so no more? Nay! his are no such coward lips. The eye of 'the Prophet of Fire' flashes;—and he rejoins in a voice of thunder—"*I* have not troubled Israel; but *thou* and thy father's house, in that ye have forsaken the commandments of the Lord, and followed the Baalim."

Brave, undaunted man!—noble type of every faithful minister of God—boldly speaking out the truth; uninfluenced either by fear or by flattery;—scorning all compromise, all unworthy servility, and taking as a guiding principle the words of the great Apostle—"If I please men, I am not the servant of Christ." Many there are who will listen long enough, and patiently enough, to *general* descants on the truth;—to *general* denunciations of sin, or eloquent expositions of virtue and holiness;—but who resent closer personal remonstrance—the faithful charging home of the darling sin. Herod bore with the stern Preacher of the desert, so long as he kept to his *general* theme—Repentance. But when he came to speak plainly of Herodias, "It is not lawful for thee to have her;"—then the frown gathered on his countenance, and the outspoken reprover was sent in chains from his presence. Would that we had more Elijahs amongst us,—fearless rebukers of all vice and wrongdoing;—who, unmoved and undeterred by the world's fashion and opinion, would unsparingly lash the conventional follies and sins of the times, whatever these may be.

But to return—What is to be done? Elijah, as master of the occasion, dictates to his sovereign what the urgent nature of the crisis imperiously demands. In the name of his God, he proposes to gather together "all Israel" to Mount Carmel. A mighty throng it is to be, and the place selected is befitting convocation-ground.* "Carmel," remarks a distinguished

* "Carmel has derived its modern name from the great prophet. *Mar Elyas* is the common designation, Kürmel being occasionally, but only

traveller, "is not so much a mountain, as a ridge, an upland park extending for many miles into the interior of the country." Changed, as in many respects it is at this day, in its outward aspect, and in minor details, the prospect from its plateau,—the same grand outlines of unvarying nature,—still remain. If the town of Acre, dimly visible in the far north, and Cesarea, now in ruins, in the extreme southern view, were both yet future cities in the days of Elijah; the Prophet's eye, from these familiar heights, would at all events fall, equally with that of the modern traveller, on the distant bay of the one, and the bold promontory of the other; —on the near plains of Sharon and Esdraelon;—on the river Kishon, rolling its sluggish waters through the windings of the intervening hills, on "the rocky dells, with their deep jungle of copse;" above all, on the giant northern boundary of the Lebanon range and the blue expanse of the Mediterranean. Enough of fertility still is left in the present wild and uncultured state of this great headland of western Palestine, to attest the beauty and fruitfulness of the past, when herds of cattle browsed on rich pastures; graceful forests of oak and olive, fig, sycamore, and pine clothing its undulating slopes; and to vindicate the truth of Isaiah's figurative language, when, describing the future glory of the Church of Christ, he compares it to "the excellency of Carmel."*

seldom, heard. It is also the usual name of the convent, though dedicated "In honorem B. B. Virginis Mariae."—*Smith's Dictionary, Art. Carmel.*

* Carmel was famous also for its vineyards. King Uzziah had three hundred husbandmen and vine-dressers (2 Chron. xxvi. 10.) Some of these are still kept in repair by the Druses. Modern travellers describe its "impenetrable brushwood of oaks, and other evergreens, tenanted in the wilder parts by a profusion of game and wild animals;"—"but in other

"At the eastern extremity," says the same authority just quoted, "which is also the highest point of the ridge, is a spot marked out, alike by tradition and by natural features, as one of the most authentic localities of the Old Testament history. . . . Here is no town, only a shapeless ruin; yet the spot has a name, 'El-Maharrakah,' 'The Burning,' or 'The Sacrifice.' . . . But, be the tradition good or bad, the localities adapt themselves to the event in almost every particular. The summit thus marked out is the extreme eastern point of the range, commanding the last view of the sea behind, and the first view of the great plain in front, just where the glades of forest sink into the usual barrenness of the hills and vales of Palestine. There, on the highest ridge of the mountain, may well have stood, on its sacred 'high place,' the altar of the Lord which Jezebel had cast down. Close behind, on a wide upland sweep, under the shade of

places bright with hollyhocks, jasmine, and various flowering creepers." "The whole mountain side was dressed with blossoms, and flowering shrubs and fragrant herbs."—*Porter, Martineau*, &c., as quoted in Bible Dictionary, Art. "Carmel."—"At every step the ancient glory of Carmel became more and more evident to me. What a memorable morning in this wild flower-garden! The hawthorn, the jasmine, and many another tree and shrub, whose sweetly odorous and elegant bunches of blossom are unknown to me by name, are now in flower. The oak, the myrtle, and the laurel have tempered their deep winter green with glittering leaflets of a lighter hue. And what a variety of flowers are trodden by the traveller on his way! There is not one I have seen in Galilee or on the plains along the coast, that I do not find here again on Carmel,—from the crocuses on the rocky grounds to the fennel plants and narcissuses of the Leontes; from the intense red, white, and purple anemones of the plains to the ferns that hide themselves in the dark sepulchral caves. Yes! Carmel indeed is still Carmel: the fruitful—the graceful—the fragrant—the lovely mountain that he was in the days of old."—*Van de Velde*, vol. i., p. 318.

ancient olives, and round a well of water, said to be perennial, and which may therefore have escaped the general drought and have been able to furnish water for the trenches round the altar, must have been ranged the multitudes. Full before them the whole plain of Esdraelon, with Tabor and its kindred ranges in the distance. On the rising ground at the opening of its valley the city of Jezreel, with Ahab's palace and Jezebel's temple distinctly visible."* Such was the theatre for "a conflict more momentous than any which their ancestors had fought in the plain below." It was a momentous question which was to be decided—"*Who is the Lord?* JEHOVAH OR BAAL?" Is the God of the Patriarchs to be re-enthroned on His altars and in the hearts of the children of Abraham? Are the silver trumpets to gather a willing people in the day of His power? Or are these heirs of the old covenant to barter their birthright for a base superstition? By a worse than Philistine invasion, is the bitter cry of "Ichabod!" to ascend from the broken heart of the solitary Prophet, the last ray and relic of the departing glory?

Imagine the vast concourse gathering. The flanks of the mountain teem with the living mass. As they are assembling, perhaps at sunset, and pitching their tents on the varied slopes of the elongated hill, so as to be ready for the great scenes of the morrow,—let us note the *three parties* of which the multitude is composed;—for that crowd on Carmel is a typical picture of the Church and the world to this hour.

Our eye first falls on the royal tent, with the spear in the ground and the rich Tyrian banners floating overhead.

* Sinai and Palestine, pp. 350–1.

An hour ago, deafening plaudits rose from the throng, as the prancing coursers swept past, bearing thither the monarch with his courtiers. Close by them are those most deeply concerned in the issues of the day;—rank on rank of Phœnician priests, flaming in gorgeous vestments of purple bespangled with gold. There are eight hundred and fifty of them altogether; four hundred and fifty of these are *Baal's* ministers; you may know them by the sun-symbol on their embroidered dress; and these four hundred with the symbol of the crescent moon, are the priests of the goddess Astarte, who have been housed in the royal palaces of Israel, and have places assigned them at Jezebel's table; these again, supported by thousands around, who, in blindfold ignorance, had followed the creed of their atheist king. Such constitute one of the companies in that heterogeneous crowd. They have that adjunct which impiety and irreligion often have upon their side—human power and influence. They have sold themselves to work iniquity. They have publicly dethroned Jehovah, and espoused idols, saying, Who is the Lord Jehovah, that he should reign over us?

The second class or company was small indeed. For aught we can tell, there may have been several composing it. Obadiah's faithful hundreds may have come out from their caves,—those rocky caverns which are still shewn in the gorges of Carmel as their supposed hiding-places. But Elijah is the only representative of this second group who is mentioned in the sacred narrative. Though there be nothing imposing about him externally;—though he wears the roughest garb;—though he has been living for years in cave or lowly hamlet, dependent for his daily meals, now on the birds of the forest, now on the charity of a poor Gentile widow;—yet there is something truly royal about that solitary man as he stands like a lone rock towering amid the chafing waves! He has One on his side (and he is conscious of it) 'mightier than the mightiest.' He knows that as a prince he has power with God, and is about to prevail. He is there the delegate of true, believing, leal-hearted Israelites,—worshippers of the living Jehovah,—those who are still stanch in their allegiance to their fathers' God,—uninfluenced by court-intrigues or by the fear of man;—who had wept many a secret tear over the grievous national apostasy,—and in cave and lone forest, "faithful among the faithless," had oft breathed the ancestral prayer, "Arise, O God, and let thine enemies be scattered."

But there was still a third, and by far the most numerous class, to which adhered the bulk of the people. It was made up of those who were swayed between opposing views,—divided in opinion,—hesitating upon which side to declare; conscience, perhaps, pointing one way, and self-interest another;—a false feeling of deference to the king—blind, obsequious loyalty, leading them to adopt the idolatrous court-faith: on the other hand, all the sacred memories of their history, and the recorded kindness of the God of Israel, rebuking them for the baseness of their apostasy. It was for *them*,—this fickle, undecided rabble, but who really constituted the numerical strength of the kingdom,—it was for their sakes Elijah demanded the convocation: "Gather to me," he says, "*all Israel*." Again, it is "*the people*" whom he addresses with the startling words, "How long halt ye between two opinions?" He saw they were labouring under a ruinous delusion,—ruinous to themselves, and most insulting to the God he served. They evidently imagined they could compromise matters;—that they could amalgamate the worship of Jehovah and Baal. They were not willing to forget that they were the historical descendants of those who had seen the Divine Majesty shining gloriously on Teman and Paran,—for whose sakes the tongue of the Red Sea had been rebuked, and Jordan driven back. They were not disposed altogether to discard their ancestral traditional creed; but they desired to incorporate it with the licentious rites of the idols of Tyre. If persecution threatened to descend against those who refused thus to blend the Phœnician with the Hebrew ritual, they were not so wedded to the latter in its integrity, as to be ready to suffer or to die for it. They could not dream of undergoing the martyr-life of those who were hiding in the mountain-caves of Samaria, fed on bread and water. They would appease Ahab, and absolve their own consciences, by espousing both creeds. They would retain that of their fathers, but blend with it the impurities of the Phœnician worship.

Have we not here a vivid and truthful picture of the professing Christian world in every age? It, too, has ever had its *three* distinct classes. The Baal-worshippers,—the atheist class,—whose virtual religious creed is "no God." Speak to them of the God of Elijah, and their secret retort is, "Who is the Lord, that he should reign over us?"—"Depart from us, for we desire not a knowledge of thy ways." Such are the slaves of custom in religion as in everything else;—who have no conscience of their own;—no settled convictions of duty. They do as Ahab does. Their miserable religious theory is, that all creeds are alike; or rather, if their feelings were analysed, that all religion is a pretence and delusion;—the lie which superstition has palmed, and which credulity has perpetuated. Having overthrown the altar of God, they are sacrificing daily incense at the Baal-shrines of self, pleasure, lust, and sin!

A second class are the true worshippers of God;—(and, blessed be His name, there has never yet been an age, and never shall be, when these are not found.) The thousands, or the ten thousands; or, it may be, only the *units*, who have "not bowed the knee to Baal:"—His true Israel—the salt of the earth—pillars which prevent the fabric of society tottering to its base. Those who love His name, and do His commandments, and seek to promote His glory. Those who, like Elijah, would sooner die than be unfaithful to Him, or do homage at an unhallowed shrine. The Enochs and Noahs of patriarchal times. The Lots amid the iniquity and worldliness of Sodom. The Daniels amid the snares of Babylon. The "few names," even amid the grievous indifference of Sardis, who have "not defiled their garments." The hundreds around us, who, amid manifold temptations,—the ridicule of evil companions—the power of degrading worldliness—the enticing snares of vice,—are faithful to their God and Saviour. In one word, those who are Christians indeed,—who know holiness to be happiness, who have avouched the Lord to be their God, and would not barter the joys of true religion for all the gains and gold of earth, and all the gilded baubles of worldly ambition.

One other class still remains; and we fear, as in Elijah's time, by far the most numerous. It is the mass—the vast mass of the *undecided*. Those who are half-hearted Christians—"borderers"—hovering on the confines of light and darkness—of truth and error: who have not repudiated religion,—nay, who nominally profess to be on God's side; but who, in reality, are on the side of Satan. Waverers, like the waves of the unstable sea, "driven by the wind and tossed!" They have the wish to die happy and go to heaven at last; but they cannot make up their minds, as yet, to renounce their favourite sins. They wish to flee to Christ as their Saviour;—but *not yet*. They wish to give up the world's follies and sins;—but *not yet*. They wish to shake themselves free of their enslaving lusts;—but *not yet*. Their immortal interests are all this while trembling in the balance. They have had their convictions, their impressions, their serious thoughts, their hours of penitence; the tear of remorse has stood in their eye, and a trembling prayer has faltered on their tongue;—but they have never yet had courage or resolution to make the great decision, to cast in their lot unmistakably on the side of God. They are living for both worlds, and losing both. They have enough of religion to make them unhappy, but not enough to save their souls! A little religion is the most miserable of all states. It becomes an accuser, not a comforter. It is the thorn in the flesh—the lash of the scorpion. Better remain at Jezebel's table, than come feeble, irresolute, half-hearted, to Carmel;—to hear the thunder tones of the Prophet;—to see the fire of God descending. Yet scorning it all.

Look at the effect of Elijah's bold remonstrance. The people were awestruck. He had touched their consciences. They felt his appeal and rebuke to be only too true. They stood silent and self-condemned! And the same feeling of self-condemnation must come home to multitudes still: that they have for years, and that, too, while enjoying many religious privileges, been living on in guilty uncertainty as to their soul's everlasting salvation;—attempting to unite impossibilities; — attempting to join what Heaven has divorced:—to serve God and Mammon,—Jehovah and Baal,—holiness and sin! Nothing is so displeasing to God as this divided heart;—this attempting to blend and incorporate what can as little be blended, as oil can commingle with water, or darkness with light. "I would," he says, "thou wert either cold or hot." He demands the whole heart or nothing. There can be no middle course—no intermediate ground. The saying is solemnly explicit, "He that is not with me is against me."

Are there some among us, who, like the multitudes on Carmel, are silent under the question?—who feel that theirs has been worse than indecision;—the hollow name to live, while they are spiritually dead? God is not willing that you should perish. He is ready to meet you on Carmel with His overtures of mercy—the remonstrances of His own unwearying love! Listen to His voice and expostulation, 'O ye sons of men, how long will ye love vanity? How long barter the finite for the infinite, the temporal for the imperishable? O Israel, thou hast destroyed thyself, but in me is thy help found!' He sets before you life and death, salvation or destruction, heaven or hell. Listen to the great gospel declaration,—the alternative is for you to select,—"If thou seek Him, He will be found of thee; but if thou forsake Him, He will cast thee off for ever!"

VIII.

The Answer by Fire.

"Then said Elijah unto the people, I, even I only, remain a prophet of the Lord; but Baal's prophets are four hundred and fifty men. Let them therefore give us two bullocks; and let them choose one bullock for themselves, and cut it in pieces, and lay it on wood, and put no fire under; and I will dress the other bullock, and lay it on wood, and put no fire under: and call ye on the name of your gods, and I will call on the name of the Lord; and the God that answereth by fire, let him be God. And all the people answered and said, It is well spoken. And Elijah said unto the prophets of Baal, Choose you one bullock for yourselves, and dress it first; for ye are many; and call on the name of your gods, but put no fire under. And they took the bullock which was given them, and they dressed it, and called on the name of Baal from morning even until noon, saying, O Baal, hear us! But there was no voice, nor any that answered. And they leaped upon the altar which was made. And it came to pass at noon, that Elijah mocked them, and said, Cry aloud; for he is a god: either he is talking, or he is pursuing, or he is in a journey, or peradventure he sleepeth, and must be awaked. And they cried aloud, and cut themselves, after their manner, with knives and lancets, till the blood gushed out upon them. And it came to pass, when mid-day was past, and they prophesied until the time of the offering of the evening sacrifice, that there was neither voice, nor any to answer, nor any that regarded. And Elijah said unto all the people, Come near unto me. And all the people came near unto him: and he repaired the altar of the Lord that was broken down. And Elijah took twelve stones, according to the number of the tribes of the sons of Jacob, unto whom the word of the Lord came, saying, Israel shall be thy name; and with the stones he built an altar in the name of the Lord; and he made a trench about the altar, as great as would contain two measures of seed. And he put the wood in order, and cut the bullock in pieces, and laid him on the wood, and said, Fill four barrels with water, and pour it on the burnt sacrifice, and on the wood. And he said, Do it the second time: and they did it the second time. And he said, Do it the third time: and they did it the third time. And the water ran round about the altar; and he filled the trench also with water. And it came to pass at the time of the offering of the evening sacrifice, that Elijah the prophet came near, and said, Lord God of Abraham, Isaac, and of Israel, let it be known this day that thou art God in Israel, and that I am thy servant, and that I have done all these things at thy word. Hear me, O Lord, hear me; that this people may know that thou art the Lord God, and that thou hast turned their heart back again. Then the fire of the Lord fell, and consumed the burnt sacrifice, and the wood, and the stones, and the dust, and licked up the water that was in the trench. And when all the people saw it, they fell on their faces; and they said, The Lord, he is the God; the Lord, he is the God. And Elijah said unto them, Take the prophets of Baal; let not one of them escape. And they took them; and Elijah brought them down to the brook Kishon, and slew them there." —1 KINGS xviii. 21-40.

"THUS HATH THE LORD GOD SHEWED UNTO ME; AND, BEHOLD, THE LORD GOD CALLED TO CONTEND BY FIRE."—AMOS vii. 4.

THE ANSWER BY FIRE.

In the previous chapter, we found the appeal of Elijah to the people on Mount Carmel responded to by "mute expressive silence;" they "answered not a word." This may probably have been the result of conflicting emotions. In the case of some, who in their hearts were Jehovah-worshippers, it may have been the silence of guilty fear or cringing expediency. They may have been stifling their deep-felt convictions of truth in presence of the king and priesthood. With others, (the fawning, obsequious creatures of Ahab,) it may have arisen from dread of incurring the vengeance of the Prophet of Cherith; lest he who had manifested such power in material nature might visit them with sudden and condign retribution, should they dare openly to avow themselves the abettors of idolatry.

Let us hasten at once to the sublime sequel. There is no picture in all history, sacred or profane, more thrilling or impressive. No wonder that poetry, painting, and music have conjointly seized on this memorable day and scene as fit theme and subject for their grandest efforts. Elijah feels, and feels deeply, that ere the clouds of heaven break, and the curse of famine be rolled away from the land, the people, in the aggregate, must be brought back from their wretched apostasy, and that, too, by some great public acknowledgment of their sin. As theirs had been a national alienation from their fathers' God, so must theirs be a public renunciation of their abominable idolatries, and a renewed recognition of the one living Jehovah.

The mighty throng are still hushed, as the Prophet—God's consecrated minister between the living and the dead—prepares yet farther to speak. Ere we listen to his address, we may in a few words recall, how very peculiarly he himself was situated in the midst of that vast concourse.

Other hearts, as we have already seen, true and loyal to Jehovah, were beating responsive with his at that moment throughout the land. But they were witnessing in sackcloth; they were languishing in dungeons, or hidden in caves and fastnesses. On this consecrated mountain-height —this high altar of nature—the Tishbite stood alone;—a sheep amid wolves—an isolated beacon-light amid the floods of ungodly men,—a solitary cedar of God wrestling with the storm. It is difficult for us thoroughly to realise the strain on his faith and courage when thus deprived of human sympathy and support. The Waldenses of the Middle Ages, or the hero-martyrs of our own land, were in as imminent peril as he; but they were sustained in their endurance and privations by the words and deeds of fellow-sufferers. Cave and forest, alpine fastness, mountain, moor, and dungeon, were cheered by sympathetic hands and hearts. That assemblage on Carmel, too, be it remembered, was no despicable multitude—no vulgar rabble. The political influence and strength of the nation were there. Elijah was coming into collision and hostility with the throne and the altar;—with a debased king and priesthood;—the court religion—the fashionable creed of the hour. With what intense emotion must he have uttered the opening words, "I, even I, only, remain a prophet of the Lord." His proposal is, that the Deity, which either party professes to worship, should decide the great question which has convened them on that high arena; that each should take a bullock, cut it in pieces, and lay it on wood on a separate altar of burnt-offering. The usual way of consuming the sacrifice was by applying a lighted torch to the fuel or faggots underneath. But the Prophet suggests, on this occasion, an appeal to miraculous intervention;—that the Baal-worshippers and the Jehovah-worshippers should each invoke an "answer *by fire;*" and that whichever offering was miraculously ignited, should be regarded as conclusively determining the point at issue. The crowd at once assented to the reasonableness of the test. Their unanimous response was—"It is well spoken." An appeal which had thus commended itself to the spectators, could not well be resisted by the Baal priests. Indeed, the fairness of the proposal was unanswerable; for Baal being the reputed god of Light or Fire; it was a virtual appeal to his own element—a defiant challenge and reference to his own sacred emblem. Nor was the proposed method of arbitration strange or unfamiliar to the Jehovah-worshippers —the true Israel of God. Their sacred records and national annals furnished many examples of answers by fire, from the earliest, in the case of Abel's sacrifice, to the latest, within the memory of that generation, at the magnificent scene of the temple consecration under Solomon.

The moment has come. Elijah concedes the precedence to his 850 antagonists. "Rise, ye priests of Baal; choose one of the oxen, and lay it on your altar!" Forth they come in their gorgeous Tyrian purple and gold. The bullock was prepared, and laid on the wood. It was still early morning when they began their wild orgies. The excitement increased with advancing day. The cry, "O Baal, hear us," again and again ascended to the brazen sky. Mountain height responded to mountain height, "but there was no voice, nor any that answered." Amid their frenzied dances, they look up wistfully to the heavens for the appearance of the descending symbol. Louder and still louder rises the vehement imprecation, 'O Baal, hear us!—ye lords many, hear us!—ye forest gods!—ye mountain deities!—gods of rivers!—and, above all, thou blazing Sun—Baal's burning throne and sacred shrine,—send down a lighted torch, burning coals from thine altar fires!' Louder and louder, deeper and deeper, waxes the hoarse-voiced chorus! Till noon it continues;—the maddened priests leaping upon the altar. But there is no answer. The heavens are still;—the altar is silent;—Baal's oracle is dumb;—the appeal is in vain! And now, as the sun has reached its meridian, Elijah interposes. He has been, hitherto, like the rest, a silent spectator. But at the height of noon, as the orb the others worshipped is pouring his fierce rays on their heads, he calls out, in words of cutting irony, "Cry aloud; for he is a god: either he is talking, or he is pursuing, or he is in a journey, or peradventure he sleepeth, and must be awaked." But the fretting sarcasm only increases the mad and frantic ravings and incantations of the ministers of Baal. When noon is past, they begin to "prophesy." They have wrought themselves now into a state of desperation. Drawing their knives and lancets, they inflict gashes on their bodies, and cover themselves with blood.* Still, all is in vain. Their god will not arise. On the heights of the mountain, the unkindled wood and the untouched altar remain, during the long afternoon of that momentous day, just as they were erected at early morn. The discomfited priests retire bleeding and exhausted to their tents. Their cause is lost. Baal is not God!

Here, however, in passing, may we not well pause and gather for ourselves a lesson of humbling rebuke? How devoted were these abettors of a blinding superstition! We cannot read the passage, and pronounce their part in the gigantic conflict, a heartless formality—a dumb show—the pantomime of hypocrites. No! Self-deceived, as they were, they were, at least, men in earnest. Elijah—himself all earnestness—must have honoured their zeal, though mourning that it was so misguided and misapplied. What a reproof to our ofttimes lagging faith; our lifeless prayers; our cold, negative

* "Many ancient writers—Seneca, Lucian, Statius, Apuleius, &c.—notice this custom, from whose statements Movers (p. 682) thus describes the processions of the strolling bands wandering about with the Syrian goddess:—'A discordant howling opens the scene. Then they fly wildly through one another, with the head sunk down to the ground, but turning round in circles, so that the loose-flowing hair drags through the mire: thereupon they first bite themselves on the arms, and at last cut themselves with two-edged swords which they are wont to carry. Then begins a new scene. One of them, who surpasses all the rest in frenzy, begins to prophesy with sighs and groans, openly accuses himself of his past sins, which he now wishes to punish by the mortifying of the flesh, takes the knotted whips, which the Galli are wont to bear, and lashes his back, cuts himself with swords, until the blood trickles from his mangled body.' This description perfectly agrees in the main points with the practice of the prophets of Baal here. Here, also, the conclusion or highest degree of frenzy is the prophesying, (v. 29,) which began only when noon was past, and continued till the time of the evening sacrifice."—*Kiel on Kings*, p. 281.

zeal in God's service. These heathen devotees of Carmel, worshippers of a figment,—a dumb idol,—with their knives and lancets, and self-inflicted tortures,—how will they rise up in the judgment against many lukewarm professing Christians, and condemn them!

But now the time of the evening sacrifice — Israel's own sacred hour—has come. Elijah had allowed his opponents full time and scope for the required proof. He now comes forward and challenges personally the flagging attention of the crowd. Close by were the ruins of an altar, which had once been erected to Jehovah, but which, probably with many others in the land, had been demolished by one of the exterminating edicts of Jezebel.* Summoning the people to draw near, he repaired the ruined place of sacrifice. There is something impressive in the calm dignity of the Prophet, after these long hours of demonstrative vehemence and delirious excitement. We can picture him, with his sheepskin cloak, and shaggy hair, and stately figure;—with no noisy clamour, or extravagant gesticulations, but rather with dignified self-reliance, standing amid the fevered multitude, and beginning with reverend hands to uprear the dismantled altar. There is always a quiet majesty about

* Carmel seems to have been regarded by the Jews as "a holy place:" hence the probable reason of Elijah's selection of it on this occasion. By a subsequent reference in 2 Kings iv. 23, the people seem to have been in the habit of resorting thither on the new moon and Sabbath. The same discriminating writer who has noted this circumstance, adds:—"In later times, its reputation was not confined to Palestine. Pythagoras was led to it" (as a sacred spot.) . . . "Vespasian, too, came thither to consult the oracle of the god whose name was the same as that of the mountain itself an oracle without image or temple." See also "The Land and the Book," p. 483.

truth. How calmly stood Paul before Felix and Agrippa. With what meek, unruffled, expressive silence stood Incarnate Truth Himself before Pilate and Herod,—the Lamb "dumb before His shearers:" it was the same dignified calmness of demeanour which had previously unmanned the assassin band at the gate of Gethsemane: "As soon as He had said unto them, I am He, they went backward and fell to the ground!" It was so now, on Mount Carmel. Ahab was agitated with conflicting fears. The people were in a frenzy of excitement. The priests were filled with delirium and rage. Elijah alone was unmoved,—confident in the righteousness of his cause. He had everything perilled on the next sunset hour. Failure!—and his own body, like that of the offered sacrifice, would be cut in pieces, and the Kishon be stained with his blood. Failure!—and the power and glory of his God would be compromised;—every altar of Israel would be profaned, and Baal would sit triumphant in his impious shrines. But "Jehovah liveth,"—his first utterance—was his motto still; and he felt confident that that watchword would be caught up, ere these night-shadows fell, and be repeated from lip to lip by the congregated thousands of Israel. Of the dilapidated altar, he took twelve stones, "according to the tribes of the sons of Jacob, unto whom the word of the Lord came, saying, Israel shall be thy name!" There was much significance in the act. It was a rebuke he read, not to the Baalites; but to the true Israel of God. By this 'parable in stone,' he would tell them that the disrupted monarchy—the breaking asunder of the ten tribes from the twelve—was unrecognised by God;—that it was a sinful breach in their unity as the covenant nation;—that they were still essentially one in the sight of Jehovah;—having one common altar, though partitioned and dismembered by reason of their own guilty jealousies and strifes. Nay, he would point them on to the time when God's own purpose would be fulfilled regarding them, "And I will make them one nation in the land upon the mountains of Israel; and one king shall be king to them all: and they shall be no more two nations, neither shall they be divided into two kingdoms any more at all: neither shall they defile themselves any more with their idols, nor with their detestable things, nor with any of their transgressions: but I will save them out of all their dwelling-places, wherein they have sinned, and will cleanse them: so they shall be my people, and I will be their God," (Ezekiel xxxvii. 21, 22.) Would that we had more Elijahs in the midst of us; ever and anon to bear their protest against the unseemly schisms and divisions which mar the strength and beauty and fair proportions of the Church of Christ! Blessed will that time be, when divided churches and divided nations shall become one in heart and one in worship; one in undivided aim for the good of men and the glory of a common Lord. When the distinctions of sect and party, which are now like the separate pools on the rocky shore, shall be swept over by the ocean-tide of Divine love; all united and mingled into one; and the old heathen exclamation become the testimony of an admiring world, "See how these Christians love one another!"

And now the wood is laid in order on Elijah's altar. The bullock is cut in pieces, and a deep trench is formed all around; moreover, in order to prevent any possible suspicion of imposture,—such as would throw discredit on the reality of the miracle,—the Prophet gives orders to the people to go down, either to the adjoining well, or to the Kishon,—some have even surmised, though this is inadmissible, to the sea,*—and fill four barrels of water to be poured over bullock, wood, and altar.† This is done four times in succession, till the trench is filled. He was cognisant of the fact, that the idolatrous priests of surrounding nations stooped at times to unworthy fraud and artifice in the case of similar answers by fire; sometimes by concealing torches,—sometimes by kindling the subjacent wood, through excavations under the altar. In order that no such base arts might be attributed to him, he soaks the whole pile with the antagonistic element of water. While the altar is thus dripping and saturated,—he proceeds to take his turn in the great testing struggle.

The period of the day was known to the whole Hebrew nation as "the hour of prayer." The priests in the Temple at Jerusalem, were at that same moment offering their evening oblation as the sun was sinking behind Mount Olivet, as now it was going down over Carmel, or hanging like a golden lamp over the burnished waters within sight. Behold the Prophet of Fire, wrapped in his mantle, on his knees in supplication! A breathless stillness—like the portentous quiet which reigns in nature before the bursting of the thunder-cloud—pervades the heterogeneous throng. With bated breath, king, priests, people, look on, while thus he addresses

* The great distance from the sea would have rendered it impossible to go hither and thither in one afternoon.

† Josephus distinctly states that it was from the neighbouring well (ἀπὸ τῆς κρήνης) the water was obtained.—Ant. viii. 13, § 5.—Quoted in Dr Smith's "Bible Dictionary."

his God: "Lord God of Abraham, Isaac, and of Israel, let it be known this day that thou art God in Israel, and that I am thy servant, and that I have done all these things at thy word." The first utterance in his prayer is "JEHOVAH!" There was but a moment of solemn pause. The prayer ascends;—the FIRE falls. Bullock, wood, dust, stones, earth, all are consumed by the devouring element. The flame of Heaven has incontrovertibly, in the face of all spectators, authenticated the Prophet's word and mission, and flashed condemnation on his opponents. The people, on seeing it, fell on their faces; and a mighty shout rends the air, ringing from the mountain-summits, along the plain of Esdraelon, mingling with the rippling waves on the adjoining shores—"*Jehovah he is the God! Jehovah he is the God!*"

Sudden is the next step in the drama. Jehovah being re-enthroned; the priesthood of Baal must at once be crushed,—extirpated root and branch—from the land they had so long cursed with their shadow. The recent general reverence of the people for this false worship now turns into rage. Catching up the malison of their great national minstrel, "Confounded be all they that worship graven images,"—they drag, (at Elijah's command) the ringleaders down the side of the mountain, and the Kishon carries to the sea, in its crimsoned stream, the tidings of righteous vengeance.* Elijah, in this

* Van de Velde mentions, that a knoll is pointed out between the ridge and the plain, called *Tell Kasis*, "the hill of the priests," and that the modern name of the river is Nahr el Mukatta, "the river of slaughter."

It may be interesting here to give the vivid delineation of the localities in the words of this writer. The more so, as he was the first traveller, we believe, who identified the site of "the Burning," as confirmed by the subsequent visit and description of Dr Stanley, previously apparently harsh and cruel act, only performed what Ahab as theocratic Regent had failed to do. It was not the vindictive massacre of a barbarous conqueror; but the faithful servant and vicegerent of God fulfilling a stringent Divine command; —a command, indeed, which admitted of no evasion;—for the extermination of idolaters.* The Tishbite has now attained the fulfilment of his heart's ardent longing—the glory of

quoted. After speaking of the difficulties of approaching the place, "covered as it was with a dense wilderness of natural timber, trees, and copse," "the mules painfully struggling forward through the thick jungle," he proceeds :—"One can scarcely imagine a spot better adapted for the thousands of Israel to have stood drawn up on, than the gentle slopes around. The rock shoots up in an almost perpendicular wall of more than two hundred feet in height, on the side of the vale of Esdraelon. On this side, therefore, there was no room for the gazing multitude; but, on the other hand, this wall made it visible over the whole plain, and from all the surrounding heights; so that even those left behind, and who had not ascended Carmel, would still have been able to witness at no great distance the fire from heaven that descended on the altar. . . . Here we were certain the place *must* have been, for it is the only point of all Carmel where Elijah could have been so close to the brook Kishon as to take down thither the priests of Baal and slay them—return again to the mountain and pray for rain—all in the short space of the same afternoon. Nowhere does the Kishon run so close to Mount Carmel as just beneath El-Mohhraka. . . . Two hundred and fifty feet beneath the altar-plateau, is a vaulted and very abundant fountain, built in the form of a tank, with a few steps leading down into it, just as one finds elsewhere in the old wells or springs of the Jewish times. Possibly the water of this spring may have been consecrated to the Lord, so as not to be generally accessible to the people even in times of fearful droughts. In such springs the water remains always cool, under the shade of a vaulted roof, and with no hot atmosphere to evaporate it. While all other fountains were dried up, I can well understand that there might have been found here that superabundance of water which Elijah poured so profusely over the altar."—Pp. 325-6.

* See Krummacher's excellent remarks, p. 130; with references given to the Mosaic statute.

God and the good of Israel. All his personal privations had been nothing, to his sorrow of heart on account of the people he was commissioned to teach, and warn, and instruct, being held spell-bound by an evil power. His life-prayer, his life-adjuration, if they only had had ears to hear it, was this— "*O Israel, return unto Jehovah thy God, for thou hast fallen by thine iniquity;*" and in his earnest, fervent supplication at this hour on Carmel, he tells the reason of his urgency, (v. 37,) "Hear me, O Lord, hear me! that this people may know that Thou art the Lord God, and that thou hast turned their heart back again." His prayer was heard. As they saw the forked flames descending on the Prophet's sacrifice;—conscience-stricken at the remembrance of their apostasy, and inwardly marvelling at the Divine patience and forbearance,—the grateful thought must have passed through many hearts in that crowd, "It is of the Lord's mercies that *we* are not consumed!"

"Take heed, brethren," says the apostle "lest there be in any of *you* an evil heart of unbelief, in departing from the living God." The tendency of the corrupt heart is the same in all ages,—though modified by peculiar circumstances,—to "forsake the Fountain of living waters, and to hew out broken [leaky] cisterns, that can hold no water." Let us no longer act the part of traitor Israel, by calling to our Baal,—whatever the form of the seducer be,—"O Baal, hear us." There will be no answer. There *can* be none,—if our cry be for anything else than the infinite Jehovah, to fill the aching voids and necessities of our natures. May it be ours rather to make the confident appeal, "*Our* God is in the heavens. *Their* idols are silver and gold, the work of men's hands. They that make them are like unto them; so is every one that trusteth in them. O Israel, trust *thou in the Lord.*" We cannot now expect such miraculous answers to prayer for the confirmation of our languishing faith as were vouchsafed to the mighty pleader of Carmel. But in another spiritual sense, the God of Elijah *still* "answers by *fire.*" Fire! It is the emblem of the work and agency of His blessed Spirit. He still "baptizes with the Holy Ghost, and with fire." Moreover, that highest of boons is procured in the same way as was the fire of Carmel;—in answer to prayer. Our Father who is in heaven, gives his Holy Spirit "*unto them that ask him.*" Spirit of God! descend upon us in Thine enlightening, quickening, refining, purifying influences. In order to insure Thy coming, we have not, like Elijah, to slay any bullock; we need prepare no burnt-offering. Our great Propitiation has already been made. The Son of Man and Son of God, has already offered Himself a bleeding victim. On this priceless sacrifice the fire of Divine wrath has descended. He, our true Elijah, has upbuilt the altar of ruined humanity. His ransomed people are its living stones. Through everlasting ages it will continue, the peerless monument and memorial of the Divine faithfulness, holiness, and love. "Unto principalities and powers in heavenly places will be made known by the church, the manifold wisdom of God."

And finally, in closing the chapter, let the eye once more rest with admiration on the prime actor in this magnificent drama. Mark his firmness and self-reliance;—his meek spirit of dependence on Divine aid. Hating expediency;—resolved to stand or fall with truth;—superior to the world's censure—heedless that the majority is against him—with the consciousness of God being upon his side, He boldly confronts the floods of ungodly men, and *alone* he triumphs. Some who read these pages may possibly be placed in similar circumstances. Standing solitary in the midst of scoffers: stigmatised as "*peculiar:*" surrounded by those who ridicule Elijah's God, and who sneer at their blind, credulous reverence for some obsolete Jewish Scriptures. Fear not. "Quit you like men. Be strong." You may be in the minority;—all good men ever have been so. The "broad way" is the crowded way. The true way is the one with the narrow gate. But "them that honour me," says God, "I will honour." "Be thou faithful unto death, and I will give thee the crown of life."

To any who may be guilty of scorning Divine mercy, we cannot say, "Fear not." Nay, rather, remember ye, too, the God of Carmel answers still "*by fire.*" Yes, *by fire,* shall be His awful answer on that day when there can be for you "no more sacrifice for sin!" The Bible speaks of those who are "reserved unto *fire.*" It speaks of a time when "God shall not keep silence, when a *fire* shall go before him, and it shall be very tempestuous round about him." When "the Lord Jesus, whom you now despise, shall be revealed from heaven, with his mighty angels in *flaming fire,* taking vengeance on them that know not God." Forbid, that when the discovery is too late;—when all our refuges of lies crumble into dust, and all the gods we have worshipped are proved to have been dumb idols;—forbid that *then,* we should for the first time, be awoke up to the conviction, which, during a whole life of sin and apostasy, we have disowned and denied,

"That the Lord he is the God,—the Lord he is the God;" and that our only personal interest in this 'living Jehovah,' through an endless eternity, is this—"Our God is a consuming FIRE!"

"*Seek ye the Lord, and ye shall live; lest he break out like* FIRE *in the house of Joseph, and devour it, and there be none to quench it in Bethel.*" "Seek the Lord while he may be found; call upon him while he is near: let the wicked forsake his way, and the unrighteous man his thoughts: and let him return unto the Lord, and he will have mercy upon him; and to our God, for he will abundantly pardon."

IX.

The Sound of Rain.

"And Elijah said unto Ahab, Get thee up, eat and drink; for there is a sound of abundance of rain. So Ahab went up to eat and to drink. And Elijah went up to the top of Carmel; and he cast himself down upon the earth, and put his face between his knees, and said to his servant, Go up now, look toward the sea. And he went up, and looked, and said, There is nothing. And he said, Go again seven times. And it came to pass, at the seventh time, that he said, Behold, there ariseth a little cloud out of the sea, like a man's hand. And he said, Go up, say unto Ahab, Prepare thy chariot, and get thee down, that the rain stop thee not. And it came to pass, in the meanwhile, that the heaven was black with clouds and wind, and there was a great rain. And Ahab rode, and went to Jezreel. And the hand of the Lord was on Elijah; and he girded up his loins, and ran before Ahab to the entrance of Jezreel."—1 KINGS xviii. 41–46.

"THOU, O GOD, DIDST SEND A PLENTIFUL RAIN, WHEREBY THOU DIDST CONFIRM THINE INHERITANCE, WHEN IT WAS WEARY."—PSALMS LXVIII. 9.

THE SOUND OF RAIN.

FROM the hills of Galilee; from the plains and valleys of Zebulon and Issachar, and the mountains of Ephraim;—thousands on thousands, we found in last chapter, were gathered on the heights of Carmel, to decide the great question whether Baal or Jehovah were God. The afternoon had closed with the signal discomfiture of the Phœnician priests; and Jehovah, by the loud shouts of the awe-struck multitude, had been owned and acknowledged as the God of Israel. In consequence of this public renunciation of Baal-worship, and this equally solemn and public recognition of the God of their fathers, Elijah feels that he can now with confidence expect the removal of the drought which for three years and a half had cursed the land, and the return of blessings to the famine-stricken people.

The bodies of the false prophets are lying in ghastly heaps unburied on the margin of the Kishon. The king has gone up, amid the wooded slopes of the mountain, with his nobles and retinue, to feast themselves after these exciting hours. The multitudes are seen dispersing; some for repose and refreshment, others wending their way towards their distant homes. But the Prophet feels that his mission is not yet fulfilled;—one grand sequel is still required to complete the most memorable day of his life.

Quitting the terrible Aceldama on the river's banks, and again casting his sheepskin cloak over his shoulders, he ascends to a higher and remoter portion of Carmel, removed from the din alike of the multitudes and of the royal tents below. From his elevation, the old familiar scene of barrenness and desolation met his eye;—waterless channels at his feet;—the noted verdure of Carmel turned into ashes;—no living blade to relieve the dull monotony for miles and miles;—so far as his vision could extend, the earth gasping at every pore. Rest and refreshment he greatly requires, alike for his weary body and jaded spirit. He had tasted nothing since morning; and now the setting sun had gone down behind the western ridges of the mountain. But, like his great Antitype, "his meat is to do the will of Him that sent him, and to finish His work." In company with a young attendant, he resorts to this secluded spot in order that he may plead with Jehovah, (now that he had shewed himself unto Ahab,) to make good His faithful promise, "I will send rain upon the earth." He might well have urged the excuse of an overwrought and overtasked frame for postponement till the following morning; but if—like many earthly conquerors—he had failed to follow up his victory, it would have marred the completeness and grandeur of the day's transaction. Both king and people might have left the scene, and missed the great closing lesson. Elijah, however, never hesitates. Whether it were by some intimation made by special revelation to his inner sense; —or whether, more probably, by some outward token, such as the gentle rustling on the tops of the forest-trees premonitory of storm, we cannot pronounce. But it was on hearing "the sound of abundance of rain" that he himself ascended to his sequestered sanctuary; instructing his servant at the same time to proceed to a yet higher promontory or spur of the mountain, from which he could command a full view of the waters of the Mediterranean to the remote horizon.

The sun of that long day had already set; but, as is the case in Eastern evenings, a bright radiance lingered on mountain, plain, and ocean. The sky still preserved the same monotonous aspect it had worn during the years of drought. Its azure depths were undimmed with a cloud. The great sea beneath it, slept in quiet serenity.

Let us pause for a moment at this impressive point in the narrative. What a place of hallowed calm after the exciting scenes and turmoil of that day of days! Ye who are engaged in the busy thoroughfares of life;—fevered and fretted with its anxieties;—from morning to evening your ears and your spirits stunned with the loud, never-ebbing tide; do you know what it is, when night is gathering its shadows as at Carmel, to ascend to some quiet oratory to be alone with God, and get your spirits calmed and refreshed amid this "Sabbath of the soul?" Or ye, who, like Elijah, may have experienced, during the day, some eminent tokens of blessing in your worldly undertakings;—the fire coming down on your sacrifice;—your fears disappointed;—your fondest hopes and wishes realised;—some successful stroke in business,—some unexpected deliverance from harassing anxiety and vexation,—the occurrence of some prosperous and joyful event in your family circles;—do you deem it alike your hallowed privilege and duty, to take the first opportunity of owning the hand of the gracious Restorer of all good, and the gracious Deliverer from all evil; ascending the silent, lonely Carmel-height, that you may, like the Prophet, pour out your soul in fervent gratitude,—record your vow, and offer your oblation of thanksgiving? Beautiful, indeed, is Elijah's humility. He was undoubtedly the hero of the hour. He was more truly King in the sight of Israel than Ahab. As a prince he had power with God, and had prevailed. The keys of Providence seemed to hang at his girdle;—his voice had rent the heavens;—at his summons the flames had descended;—the fiery sword had leapt from its cloudy scabbard, flashing vengeance on his enemies. Had he sought it,—a triumphal procession might have borne him laurel-crowned and garlanded to Jezreel. The chivalrous songs and minstrelsy that welcomed the illustrious sovereign of the preceding age, might have been accorded to him also. But no vainglorious thought tarnished the splendour of the moral victory. Never is he greater, on this illustrious occasion, than when,—the shouts of the multitude over,—he retires with his servant to a lone spot on the mountain; proclaiming, that, for all the deeds of that day of renown, he arrogates no praise, no glory to himself, but gives it all to the God whose legate he felt honoured to be. He cast himself down upon the earth, and "put his face between his knees."* We scarce recognise the man; he seems for the moment to have lost his personal identity. A few hours before, he was "the Prophet of Fire;" the lightning flashing from his eye; or, standing by the Kishon, a girded

* Travellers have observed the same attitude in prayer at this day among the Dervishes.

homicide, the sword gleaming in his hands. Now he is "clothed with humility." Bold and strong as a sturdy oak of Bashan in the presence of the dense *human* crowd;—he bows his head like a bulrush in the presence of the Lord of hosts. 'Lord,' he seems to say, 'I am but sinful dust and ashes. I am but a man of like passions with that fickle multitude below. I am but a vessel, a lump of clay in the hand of the potter. Not unto me, not unto me, but unto Thee, the living Jehovah, before whom I stand, be all the glory!' If we may imagine him, in these first moments of prayer, glancing back at the long hours of conflict which had terminated in the miraculous symbol;—and seeking, moreover, in the retrospect, to give utterance to a full heart of thanksgiving;—would it not be, if not in the words, at least in the spirit of the sacred bard of his nation,—"Sing unto God, ye kingdoms of the earth: O sing praises unto the Lord; to him that rideth upon the heaven of heavens, which were of old; lo, he doth send out his voice, and that a mighty voice. Ascribe ye strength unto God: his excellency is over Israel, and his strength is in the clouds. O God, thou art terrible out of thy holy places: the God of Israel is he that giveth strength and power unto his people. Blessed be God."

But it was for purposes of prayer, rather than praise, that the Prophet had ascended the slopes of the mountain. While he himself remains in rapt supplication;* his servant seven

* Dr Stanley, in his interesting description of the celebration of the Samaritan passover on Mount Gerizim, speaks of some of the assemblage "kneeling or crouching with their faces wrapt in their clothes, and bent to the ground towards the Holy Place on the summit of the Mount."—*Lectures on Jewish Church*, p. 515.

successive times hastens to the upper height to bring intelligence of the visible answer.* "Go up now," was the command; "look toward the sea." But six times did he return with the strange and disappointing intelligence, "*There is nothing.*" Noble, however, was the Tishbite's undaunted faith; —unswerving his confidence in a prayer-hearing God. He staggered not for a moment through unbelief. He knew that Jehovah was not, like Baal, "asleep or on a journey." That what He had shortly before spoken,—not only was He "*able* also to perform," but He *would* also perform. Though, therefore, the vision tarried, he patiently waited for it. He knew that "at the end it would speak, and not lie." As his attendant comes back, time after time, with the dispiriting announcement, it only seems to quicken his faith, and to strengthen within him the resolve of the old wrestler of Jabbok, "I will not let thee go except thou bless me." Moreover, he would not allow either this promise of God or the precursive indications of the storm—"the sound of abundance of rain,"—to supersede the duty of supplication. When he heard the rustling in the tops of the trees—the low moaning sound—the harbinger of rain and tempest,—he might have reasoned with himself, as many are still inclined to do, 'What need is there to cry to Jehovah, when I already hear the mutterings of His voice? Why need I call for rain, when

* The distance to that height must not have been great, for the passage runs—"Go again seven times." Now such is the position of El Mohhraka, that these circumstances might all quite well have been united there. On its west and north-west side, the view of the sea is quite intercepted by an adjacent height. That height, however, may be ascended in a few minutes, and a full view of the sea obtained from the top.—*Van de Velde.*

every tree-top is already countersigning the faithful word given at Zarephath?' But how differently does he act! These waving trees have poetically been spoken of, as so many bells summoning this lone worshipper to prayer.* Nor was it in vain that Elijah sped him to his mountain oratory. His servant descries, hovering in the western horizon, a tiny cloud, like a man's hand;—to an Eastern, habituated to the signs of the sky, a trustworthy token of approaching storm and rain.† He speeds down to the pleading Prophet with the longed-for intelligence. It is enough. The Lord has given the word: He is about to send "a plentiful rain," to refresh His inheritance "when it was weary." An urgent message is conveyed to Ahab to prepare his chariot and haste him to his distant palace, ere the Kishon be flooded with the waterspouts, and the dusty roads have been stiffened

* Krummacher.

† "Of several instances that occur to us, one of the most graphic is that given by Mr Emerson in his letters from the Ægean. He is at sea in a Greek vessel in the Levant. One morning, which had opened clear and beautiful, it was announced that a squall might be expected. No sign recognisable by European landsmen appeared; but, on attention being properly directed, 'a little black cloud' was seen on the verge of the horizon, towards the south, which was every instant spreading rapidly over the face of the sky, and drawing nearer and nearer to the vessel. Order was immediately given to strike sail and to prepare the vessel for scudding before the hurricane. But scarcely an instant had elapsed ere the squall was upon us, and all grew black around; the wind came rushing and crisping over the water, and in a moment the ship was running almost gunwale down, while the rain was dashing in torrents on the deck. As quick as thought the foresail was torn from the yards, and as the gust rushed through the rigging, the sheets and ropes were snapping and cracking with a fearful noise. The crew, however, accustomed to such sudden visitants, were not slow in reefing the necessary sails, trimming the rigging, and bringing back the vessel to her proper course, and in about a quarter of an hour, or even less, the hurricane had all passed away; the

into moist, tenacious clay, rendering them impassable.* Meanwhile, cloud after cloud rises, till the sky becomes a frowning battlement; and ere Elijah can reach the royal pavilion, every tree on Mount Carmel is wrestling with the storm! The monarch has already started, amid pelting rain and howling wind; but, fleeter than his swift coursers, are the feet of the Bedouin Prophet. Strange close to the chivalrous proceedings of this high convocation; to witness Elijah, with pilgrim staff and girded loins;—weary in body, but with unchafed and unsubdued spirit;—running in front of the royal chariot until he gets in sight of the gate of Jezreel!† As the stern reprover of Ahab's guilt, he had been brought till now into unwilling antagonism with his sovereign. But, in consequence of the king's public renunciation of idolatry, and the overthrow of Baal-worship; he takes the earliest opportunity of displaying his deference and loyalty as a subject.‡ Perhaps

sun burst out again through the clouds that swept in its impetuous train; the wind sunk to its former gentleness, and all was once more at peace, with the exception of the agitated sea, that continued for the remainder of the day rough and billowy. To this Mr Emerson adds the interesting fact, that it is mainly the dread of such sudden bourasques as the present that compel almost every vessel in the Levant to shorten sail at the close of day, since in cloudy weather it would be next to impossible during the night to discern the cloud which announces the approach of the tempest, in time to prepare for its reception, and to a ship with all her canvas spread, the effect might be terrific."—*Dr Kitto.*

* See Van de Velde's travels, *in loco.*

† Jezreel is identified with the modern Zerain—a poor collection of twenty houses on a hill in the Esdraelon plain.—See Van de Velde and Robertson, *in loco.*

‡ "Elijah, as God's minister, had overwhelmed the king with shame and confusion in the presence of his subjects. The natural tendency of this would be to lower him in their eyes, and lessen their respect for his authority. It was not the intention, however, to weaken the government,

there were joyous thoughts—alas! never to be realised—which were then filling his soul, regarding his sovereign, which imparted fresh fleetness to his limbs, and energy to his spirit. It would have been to him the noblest of the day's triumphs, if Ahab had become, from that hour, an altered man;—consecrating the remainder of his life and reign in undoing the fatal influences of an unhappy past; and, by the overthrow of abominable idolatries, inaugurating a new era of blessings for Israel. Indeed, from the king's pliable, im-impressible nature, we may fairly surmise, that the marvels of this day in Carmel had, for the time, spoken to him with irresistible power;—that the Prophet had heard the sovereign's voice, mingling with that of the people, in forswearing the impostures by which he had been so long spell-bound, and in reasserting the supremacy of Israel's Jehovah. Notwithstanding, therefore, the buffetings of the storm,—the wind sweeping along the plain, and the torrents falling on his head, and drenching his shaggy locks—on, with elastic step

nor to encourage rebellion. The prophet was, therefore, divinely directed to give a testimony of respect and honour to the king as public and striking as from necessity had been the opposition and rebuke to his idolatry. The mode of doing honour to Ahab by running before his chariot was in accordance with the customs of the East even to this day. I was reminded of this incident, more than twenty years ago, at Jaffa, when Mohammed Ali came to that city with a large army to quell the rebellion of Palestine. The camp was on the sand-hills south of the city, while Mohammed Ali stopped inside the walls. The officers were constantly going and coming, preceded by runners, who always kept just ahead of the horses, no matter how furiously they were ridden; and in order to run with the greater ease, they not only 'girded their loins' very tightly, but also tucked up their loose garments under the girdle, lest they should be incommoded by them. Thus no doubt did Elijah."—*Thomson's "The Land and the Book,"* p. 485.

and kindling eye, sped the seer, never pausing for breath until the charioteer drew rein in front of the royal palace. True Arab, however, in extraction, though he probably was, and with all the marvellous physical endurance of his tribe, it is almost impossible to suppose that, after the unremitting toils of the livelong day, Elijah should have been equal to such an undertaking, had he not been endowed with supernatural strength. But we read that "the hand of the Lord was upon him." That same God who had braced him with moral courage from morn to even, gifted him physically for the closing duties of that great occasion. He could emphatically echo the words uttered aforetime by joyous lips, after a similar season of deliverance and triumph: "We went through FIRE and through WATER, but thou broughtest us out into a wealthy place." Never perhaps, before or since, was the unfailing Divine promise fulfilled on so vast a scale,—"As thy day is, so shall thy strength be."

If, in speaking of this day's transaction in the preceding chapter, we beheld, in the fire coming down from heaven and devouring the sacrifice, a dim but suggestive picture of the Divine acceptance of a nobler Propitiation: may we not still farther, in these water-floods which followed,—the sky sending down its refreshing showers,—see an impressive symbol of the great sequel in the gospel dispensation, the descent of the Holy Spirit; and more especially on the Church of the latter day, when "the dry land shall become springs of water;" while in Elijah himself, prostrate in supplication, we have the representative of the Church herself, "*asking* of the Lord rain in the time of the latter rain;"—the God of

Elijah, moreover, uttering the challenge—"Prove me now herewith, if I will not open you the windows of heaven and pour you out a blessing, that there shall not be room enough to receive it."

Other symbolic teaching, too, may be gathered from this scene, with reference to God's dealings with individual believers. Is it their conversion? It is first the fire of conviction; then the healing, comforting, refreshing influences of the Spirit,—bringing home the blessed sense of pardon and forgiveness through the blood of the cross. Is it His method of procedure with them in their times of trial? Comfort and solace follow affliction. First the *fire*, then the *rain*; first the wounding, then the healing; first the flames of the fiery furnace, then the refreshing comforts of the Holy Spirit. First the mown grass laid low by the scythe, then the promised fulfilled—"He shall come down like rain upon the mown grass, as showers that water the earth."

Let us, in closing, listen to the cheering word—"Get thee up, for there is the sound of abundance of rain." Glad and grateful must that moment have been to the many thousands of Israel,—when the gasping earth, that had for three long years suffered in dumb agony, drank in the refreshing full flood of God;—when the true Church, who had beheld in that sky of brass and these furrows of iron, the visible tokens of the Divine curse,—now witnessed the heavens unfolding their black, inky scroll, with the joyful tidings that the curse was removed. Can we participate in this joy in a loftier spiritual sense? Do we see the curse of sin taken away;—God propitiated? and from the "rain" with which He is "filling the pools," are we drawing all needful supplies for our parched souls? Can we say with the Prophet—"O Lord, I will praise thee: though thou wast angry with me, thine anger is turned away, and thou comfortedst me. Behold, God is my salvation; I will trust, and not be afraid: for the Lord Jehovah is my strength and my song; he also is become my salvation. Therefore with joy shall we draw water out of the wells of salvation." If we are drooping and desponding;—if our cry is, "My flesh longeth for thee in a dry and thirsty land where no water is," we again echo Elijah's words—"Get thee up, for there is the sound of abundance of rain." Our privileges are many. The Spirit of God is ever and anon moving "on the tops of the mulberry trees." The small clouds have been rising, and copious showers have fallen. Go, get thee, like Elijah,—get thee to the oratory!—pray that the cloud may spread, that it may stretch across the heavens. At present we may have only the drops before the shower. But there shall be "abundance of rain"—"showers of blessing," for the mouth of the Lord hath spoken it.

But let there be a word of solemn *warning* to us also. There is deep responsibility in that "sound of the abundance of rain." If at any time in our individual experience we should hear the "rustling on the tree-tops," let us not reject or neglect the monitory voice—"Arise, get thee up!" There is no one but can tell of such solemn seasons, when this rustling was heard,—"the voice of the Lord God walking amid the trees of the garden." Think of the past! That *sick bed* was a rustling sound of the coming rain;—when, from the long slumber of unbroken health, conscience woke up to a sense of the uncertainty of life, and the possible certainty and suddenness of death. That solemn *bereavement* was a rustling amid the tree-tops;—the moaning and wailing of earth's night-blast;—the sudden blackening and overcasting of the azure sky: oh, how solemnly did the warning voice sound amid the stillness of the death-chamber, or standing by the grave; —"Get thee up!"—leave the din of the world behind thee; —Get thee up—prepare thy chariot—the deluge of wrath may be ready to overtake *thee*;—"Escape for thy life!"—there may verily be but a step between thee and death. That *solemn sermon* was a rustling on the tree-tops: do you remember it? When the word came home with irresistible cogency;—when the message (perhaps delivered with stammering lips) was like an arrow in the hand of the mighty, and went direct to your heart of hearts? Up,—at the sound of the abundance of rain,—go, like that importunate intercessor for Israel, and rest not till the little cloud have overspread the whole horizon of your being, and showers of heavenly blessing descend on your soul. Yes, and amid your own vacillating feebleness, like that of the wavering crowd on Carmel, look above, to Him,—the true Elijah,—who is pleading your cause on the mount of God; and in the gathering rain-cloud is fulfilling His own precious promise—"And I will pray the Father, and he shall give you another Comforter, that he may abide with you for ever."

X.

The Flight to the Wilderness.

"And Ahab told Jezebel all that Elijah had done, and withal how he had slain all the prophets with the sword. Then Jezebel sent a messenger unto Elijah, saying, So let the gods do to me, and more also, if I make not thy life as the life of one of them by to-morrow about this time. And when he saw that, he arose, and went for his life, and came to Beer-sheba, which belongeth to Judah, and left his servant there. But he himself went a day's journey into the wilderness, and came and sat down under a juniper-tree: and he requested for himself that he might die; and said, It is enough: now, O Lord, take away my life; for I am not better than my fathers."—1 KINGS XIX. 1–4.

"ELIAS WAS A MAN SUBJECT TO LIKE PASSIONS AS WE ARE."—JAMES V. 17.

THE FLIGHT TO THE WILDERNESS.

We left Elijah in last chapter a hero,—accomplishing deeds of unparalleled prowess and faith. The words employed at a future time by the Redeemer regarding his great follower, seem equally applicable to him,—"Among those born of women there is none greater." As the stars in their courses, nigh this same river Kishon, had fought against Sisera,—so were the very elements of nature made subservient to the Prophet's will—"fire and hail," and "stormy wind" authenticating his divine mission. After such remarkable and encouraging tokens of the Divine presence and power, we expect to find him more the champion of truth than ever; in his undaunted career, going "from strength to strength;"—the torch kindled on the altar of Carmel, burning with increasing brightness as he bears its radiance among the homes and cities of Israel. As we see the bold, lion-hearted man, running amid the rain-torrents along the Esdraelon highway, in front of the royal chariot,—his mind filled with the day's wonders,—we almost fancy we can hear him exultingly exclaiming, "It is God that girdeth me with strength, and maketh my way perfect. He maketh my feet like hinds' feet, and setteth me upon my high places. . . . Jehovah *liveth;* and blessed be my rock; and let the God of my salvation be exalted," (Ps. xviii. 32, 33, 46.) As he halts at the gate of Jezreel, we doubt not it is with a noble resolution to follow up his triumph on the morrow. We expect to see the leader of God's armies rush, like another Jonah, through the metropolis of revolt, with the message of Divine rebuke and mercy,—" O Israel, thou hast destroyed thyself, but in me is thy help found,"—confirming the capricious monarch and the wavering people; and if there be frowns still lingering on brows, which yesterday's defeat has clouded and humbled, what of that? Will not his answer be ready, "The Lord [the living Jehovah] is on my side; I will not fear what man can do unto me!" "Now know I that the Lord saveth his anointed; he will hear him from his holy heaven with the saving strength of his right hand," (Ps. xx. 6.)

Alas! a new dramatic, we may rather call it a new tragic, turn, unexpectedly occurs. This Asahel—swift of foot, and mighty of soul—degenerates into a craven and coward. We almost fail to recognise the Elijah of yesterday in the unworthy renegade of to-day. On Carmel, he had willingly and without one misgiving or hesitation, staked his life on the answer by fire. These knives and lancets, which his bold irony had whetted, would, in the event of failure, have inflicted on his person a terrible retaliation. Yet, with all this certainty before him, he went fearless, in the strength of the Lord, against the mighty. Now, how different! Poor human nature reveals itself. "The tower of David, builded for an armoury, whereon there hang a thousand bucklers and all manner of weapons of mighty men," becomes in a moment a humiliating ruin. Come and see what the best and bravest of God's saints are when left to themselves. "O Lucifer, son of the morning. how art thou fallen!"

Let us briefly rehearse the narrative.

Ahab, on reaching Jezreel, without delay conveys to his queen the astounding intelligence of the day's conflict and victory: that Elijah, by the most irrefragable proof, has vindicated his authority and established the supremacy of JEHOVAH; that her idol-god is dethroned,—her priests massacred,—and that the solemn amen and shout of the people had ratified the proceedings. The monarch's own fickle spirit, as we have remarked in last chapter, could not fail to have been impressed by all he had witnessed; and doubtless he would cherish the hope that Jezebel, if she did not acquiesce in the popular enthusiasm, would, at all events, deem it a matter of political expediency, to waive her own prejudices and prepossessions for the public weal. He had mistaken the temper and will of his supercilious consort. The storm that had burst over Carmel gathered afresh over her brow. Her rage is irrepressible. 'What! to have the cherished dream of years dissolved thus rudely in a moment! To have her ancestral faith dishonoured and degraded; her priestly confessors stript of their sacred garments, and their blood spilt like water. To have her husband and his whole subjects duped and hoodwinked, and all this by a half Hebrew, half Arab fanatic—the upholder of a worn-out effete system of old-world belief! No! it cannot be endured!' And if Ahab venture to interpose in this fit of frenzy, and speak of the double miraculous attestation; she has her reply ready. The so-called fire-answer was only the crowning successful trick of the wily old impostor; the rain falling at his prayer was the merest accident of weather—a freak of capricious nature. No, no! the shouts and vows of Carmel—so far as her influence is concerned—shall never be ratified within the palace of Jezreel; the heavens may again be shut up; the famine may drain the life of the nation—but on no account shall Baal's altars be overthrown. By all the gods of Tyre, the insult perpetrated by this Gilead Prophet shall not pass with impunity. The blood of her priests shall not be borne unavenged to the shores of Phœnicia! That hour a messenger is sent to Elijah to confirm the threat—that ere the shades of to-morrow's evening gather over the hills of Samaria, his life should be as the life of the ghastly corpses strewing the banks of the Kishon.

And though not precisely stated, we are left too plainly to infer from the sequel, the effect which this outburst produced on the mind of wavering, pusillanimous Ahab. By the time the whirlwind of his consort's passion had expended itself—alas! his goodness, too, had become that of the morning cloud and early dew. The deep impression of the Fire and Rain answers, was already obliterated from his abject soul: his voice is now loud as that of Jezebel in denouncing the whole day of miracle and triumph as a gigantic imposture; and Elijah more than ever, "a troubler in Israel" —a fanatic homicide,—whose deed of recent blood can only be expiated by his life.

What was the result of this threatening message and sudden reverse of feeling on the conduct of the Prophet? We might well have expected, from his antecedents, that he would maintain either a dignified silence, or send to the haughty idolatress a dignified answer and reproof, worthy of the ambassador of the living Jehovah: a message, in the spirit of that sent by a later champion of the faith, to the Jezebel of her age,—"Go," said Chrysostom to the person sent by the Empress Eudoxia, with a threat of vengeance, "Go, tell her I fear nothing but sin." Or if this base appeal to natural fears and to induce an unworthy flight, were for a moment entertained by him, that he would straightway exorcise the coward thought with worthier resolves. He who had not winced or quailed, when he stood, in single-handed combat, against six hundred antagonists;—who had braved, for years, summer's drought and winter's cold—could it be supposed that for a moment, he would stagger under the impotent threat of a woman? Impossible! And yet so it is. Paralysed with terror,—overpowered and overmastered as if by some sudden temptation,—Elijah resolves on escape. "He arose and went for his life." Mournful transition! We look in vain for the proud vessel which, a few hours before, we beheld holding on its triumphant course amid buffeting storms. All we can now discern is a forlorn castaway, in the midst of a dark sea, without sails or oars or rudder,—drifting on, he knows not where,—with no star to guide him, and no voice to cheer him in the waste wilderness of waters! Accompanied by his servant, and probably under the cover of night, he hurries across the mountains of Samaria; onwards. thence, to the extreme south of Judah in the direction of the Arabian desert. We can follow him in thought, "far away from the hills of Judea—in the wide upland valley, or rather undulating plain, sprinkled with shrubs and with the wild flowers which indicate the transition from the pastures of Palestine to the desert, marked also by the ancient wells dug far into the rocky soil, and bearing on their stone or marble margins the traces of the long ages during which the water has been drawn up from their deep recesses. At last he seeks shelter in the town of Beersheba—'the well of the oath'—the last point reached by the patriarchs—the last centre of their wandering flocks and herds, where Abraham planted the grove of light feathery tamarisk, and called on 'the name of the Lord, the everlasting God.'"* How the memories of the great Father of his nation—so fragrant around that sacred spot—must have rebuked his coward flight! He must have read on every crumbling altar-stone the record of the patriarch's faith, and the reproof of his own degenerate spirit. Nor is he satisfied with the refuge which the walls of Beersheba afford him. One of the best kings of Judah (Jehoshaphat) then swayed the sceptre of David's house; and as Beersheba was situated within his territory, the fugitive Prophet—with such a guarantee for his security and safety—might well have been contented there to remain. But his whole nature seems demoralised and panic-stricken. He had lost, alike all confidence in God and trust in man. He cannot brook even the company of his servant, or suffer him to share his heavy secret. Leaving his attendant to his fate in the city, he himself plunges into the depths of the wilderness;—the wild arid waste terminated in the far south by the tremendous gorges and precipices of Sinai. On, on, on, he plods, during a long weary day, till the sun sets over the burning sands. No ravens of Cherith are there to minister to him;—no sympathising voices of Sarepta to cheer him. The journey, even for his iron bodily frame, seems too

* Stanley's Jewish Church, pp. 35, 36.

much. Footsore, travel-worn;—with aching head and fevered brain,—he casts himself at the foot of a bush of desert broom,—one of those shrubs with white blossoms, familiar to travellers in these cheerless wadys, and under which the Arabian to this day shelters himself, alike from the sun's heat and the night winds.* There, on a hard pillow lies the forlorn pilgrim;—muttering, with faint lips, a prayer, (how different from the recent one of Carmel!) "He requested for himself that he might die, and said, It is enough, now, O Lord, take away my life, for I am not better than my fathers." "*It is enough!*"—that is, 'I need go no farther; I feel I can get no comfort;—my life is embittered with cruel failure; what can I hope for, if the trumpet-tongued miracles of Carmel fail to convince? My sun has set behind these distant waves of the great sea. I had hoped to have a grave in Israel,—But 'It is enough.' Let me die, uncoffined, unsepulchred! Let the desert sand be my winding-sheet;—let the desert winds sigh and chant my requiem!' In the deep,

* See Rob., vol. i., p. 136. "The desert-broom or *rithm* ('genista') is in leaf, stalk, stem, colour, and everything but flower, like our own broom. The flower is smaller, and is white, with a slight tinge of lilac. The 'brooms' of the desert are the same flexile plant-shrubs as elsewhere."—*Dr Bonar's Desert of Sinai*, p. 389. Dr Stanley notes that "the 'retem,' with its high canopy and white blossoms, gives its name to one of the stations of the Israelites, (Rethmah.)"—*Sinai and Palestine*, p. 20. "Buckhardt found the Bedatoin of Sinai burning the roots of the juniper into coal; and says that they make the best charcoal, and throw out the most intense heat. The same thing seems to be implied in Ps. cxx. 4, when David threatens the false tongue with 'sharp arrows of the mighty, *with coals of juniper.*'"—*The Land and the Book*, p. 611. It has been suggested, with probability, that these were the coals on which, as we shall presently find, Elijah's cake was baken—the same desert shrub affording him alike shade and fuel.

awful silence of that night-season, what visions must have clustered around his pillow, as he laid down his weary head to sleep. The crowd and the shouts of Carmel—the descending fire—the blackening heavens—the refreshing rain—the impressed king—the exulting people—his own prayer! And then, these phantoms, as they troop before him, chasing one another in succession through his fevered brain, leave, in this chaos of thought, the altar and sacrifice on which the fire descended, standing by itself, lonely, desolate, forsaken—the monument of his triumph—the memorial of his guilt and shame;* and, worse than all,—would not the reflection goad him like a scorpion-sting, the thought of the joyful thousands of penitent Israel who had woke up at his bidding to hope and faith—deserted all at once by their leader; some relapsing into the old idolatrous worship; others, if true to their convictions, given over unshielded to the fiendish vengeance of Jezebel,—their blood flowing like water in the streets of Jezreel,—calling, in vain, for aid and succour from the crouching coward of the wilderness;—the creed of the palace, "Baal he is the Lord!" effacing the nobler confession of Carmel, like the writing on the sand obliterated by the rising tide! Oh, who would covet that uneasy head in the Beersheba desert? Every star in the sky used at Cherith to look down upon him like an angel of light. But now these heavens are a dark inky scroll, written in letters of lamentation, and mourning, and woe;—sorrow, anguish of spirit, wounded pride—were that night his bitter portion. The torch of "The Prophet of Fire" lay quenched and blackened at his feet. A prince and a great man in Israel had

* See this well described by Krummacher.

ignominiously fallen. "Put not your trust in princes, nor in the son of man in whom there is no help. His breath goeth forth: he returneth to his earth: in that very day his thoughts perish!"

We may well learn, from this sad crisis in Elijah's history, the lesson of *our own weakness, and our dependence on God's grace.* In the divine life, often the most dangerous and perilous time for the believer, is after a season of great enlargement; when he is saying to himself, "My mountain standeth strong." The spiritual armour is loosely worn;—he gets supine after the flush of victory: the bold, bounding river, that we have just witnessed taking leap after leap in successive cataracts, loses itself in the low, marshy swamps of self-confidence. In prosperity, moreover, whether that prosperity be outward or inward, worldly prosperity or soul prosperity, or both combined,—the Lord often puts His favoured servants at such seasons to the proof, to test the strength and reality of their faith. He did so with Abraham. After a season of signal and unexampled blessing, "God did tempt Abraham;"—the death of an only son and covenant-heir was the fiery ordeal. But the patriarch stood the trial. He came forth purified from the furnace, the possessor of a richer heritage of covenanted promises! He did so with Paul. Lest he should be exalted above measure, He brought him from the third heavens to endure the smarting of some earthly thorn. But he also came forth unscathed. His "buffeting" led him to prayer. He leaves the furnace, glorying in his infirmities; exulting in the power of Christ, and in a deeper personal interest in the blessings of His grace. Elijah had been thus "exalted." In his elation, he had too confidently calculated on success. His naturally impetuous spirit, in the hour of triumph, would be in no mood to brook courtly opposition or to receive the threat and affront of an insulting message. His strength gives way just where we would have least expected,—under an appeal to the lowest emotion of a man's nature,—*fear.* We are often exhorted to "beware of *besetting* sins;" but a different lesson is brought home to us from Elijah's experience. It is rather to beware of sins that are least besetting;—loopholes in the citadel of the heart through which we have least dread of being successfully assailed. If there was one sin, judging from the Prophet's previous history, by which he was less likely to be overtaken than another, it was the sin of weakness or a craven spirit. God often suffers His people thus to lapse, in order to shew what broken, bruised, fragile reeds in themselves they are. Ah! "when thou thinkest thou standest, take heed lest thou fall." "Be not high minded, but fear." When even an Elijah,—like Samson, when shorn of his locks,—becomes weak as other men;—what need is there for those of inferior moral and spiritual stature—the "Feeble Minds," and "Little Faiths," and "Ready to Halts" to remember, that it is by grace they stand! When a mighty denizen of the forest succumbs to the blast of temptation; what need is there for the saplings to tremble in grappling with the storm!—"Howl fir-tree, for the cedar has fallen."

Beware of taking any step without the Divine sanction. If Elijah, on hearing of Jezebel's rage, had made prayer still his resort; and asked in simple faith, "Lord, what wouldest thou have me to do?" it would have saved him many a bitter hour and tear. But he constituted himself judge of what was right, took his own resolution, and abandoned himself to flight. "He fled *for his life;*" but, in doing so, he lost sight of this golden thread of comfort and joy—that *life* is in the hand of God. He ignored, for the time, his glorious old watchword,—flung aside the glowing lamp which had hitherto guided his path—"Jehovah liveth, before whom I stand!" Hitherto, with the docility and confidence of a child, he had followed God's leadings alone. Cherith, Zarephath, Carmel, were like so many finger-posts on life's journey, bearing the inscription, "*This* is the way, walk ye in it." But now, he followed the dictate of his own cowardly fears, and wounded, fretted pride. Dearly did he pay the penalty of his folly! "There is a way which *seemeth* right unto a man, but the end thereof are the ways of death."

Let us be careful *not* to follow our own paths; not to take any solemn and important step unless it be divinely owned and recognised. "In all thy ways acknowledge Him, and He shall direct thy paths." "Blessed is the man whose strength is in Thee, in whose heart are Thy ways." Lot followed *his* own way;—it was to the well-watered plain—the luxurious capital in the vale of Siddim. He rushed blindfold into evil. Carnal reasons alone lured him thither. It was the result of no prayer,—no divine impulse. Jonah followed *his* own way; but not with impunity, did the fugitive rush, in blind madness, from God and from duty. He was tossed into a raging sea;—left an outcast on a desert shore;—carrying, moreover, the brand of a wounded conscience,—a fostered spirit of peevishness and discontent with him through life,—we fear to the grave. So long as Elijah did his God-appointed work earnestly, unflaggingly, all went well with him. When he paused, hesitated, faltered,—or rather, when, in an impetuous moment, he cast away the noblest opportunity ever prophet had;—shut himself up in a wilderness;—settled down into inaction,—shedding ignoble tears under a bush in the desert;—then the great soul and its magnanimous purposes is gone. He has become a fretful, petulant child, morbidly brooding over his disappointed hopes. He flings away the oars of duty and obedience;—his strong brawny arms have ceased to pull the bark in which his God had bid him struggle,—and now he is at the mercy of winds and waves.

Beware of murmuring under trial. Elijah's desert prayer was one of pride, presumption, irritability, impatience, peevishness,—"It is enough, take away my life." Even had his success on Carmel been marred and counteracted by the evil influences at work in Ahab's court, and a new era of persecution had in consequence been initiated in Israel;—his duty was patient submission to the Divine will, cherishing the humble confidence and assurance that light would sooner or later arise out of darkness. Instead of this, he breathes the prayer, of all others least warrantable for any creature of God to utter,—"*Let me die.*" There are circumstances, indeed, when such a prayer *is* permissible;—when it becomes a noble expression of believing faith and hope. Such was the case when the great Apostle, in subordination to the Higher will which was ever his guiding principle, made the avowal of "a desire to depart and be with Christ, which was far better;"—making, however, the reservation, that so long as his Lord had work for him in the Church on earth, he would cheerfully remain. Elijah's prayer was altogether different. It was the feverish outbreak of a moment of passion. How forbearing and gracious was God in not taking him at his word! Had he done so, the Prophet would have died under a cloud,—his name would have been associated with cowardice;—his character would have been a mournful example of greatness ending in ignominy. He would have lost the glorious closing scene of all—the chariot of fire, and the deathless victory.

Each of us has, or may yet have, his day of trial;—sickness, bereavement, crushed hopes, bitter disappointments, crossed wishes,—stings and arrows from quarters least expected. How are we to meet them? Are we to give way to peevish, fretful repining? Are we to say, 'I am wearied of life. I would I were done with all this wretchedness. What pleasure is existence to this wounded, harassed, smitten spirit? Nay, take courage. It is not "*enough*." The Lord has work for you still to do. It is not for you, but for Him, to say, at His own appointed time, as He said to Hezekiah, "Thou shalt die, and not live." If we have ever been guilty of uttering such a rash prayer as that of Elijah,—"Take away my life,"—let us be thankful God has not given us the fulfilment of our own wish,—the ratification of our own desire,—and allowed us to die, unmeet and unprepared!

But we must not close this chapter, picturing the Prophet in his desert denuded of all hope or faith,—with no relic remaining of his own former self. His spiritual life for the moment may have been reduced to a spark; but the spark was there, and his God will yet fan it into a flame. Even in his peevish, querulous utterance, as he lies under that juniper tree, he *prays.* Even in the far desert he has not forgotten (oh, how *could* he forget!) the ONE who, for years, had been his almighty Protector, Guide, Friend! "It is enough, *O Lord*"—"*O Lord!*" "My flesh," he seems to say, "longeth for *Thee* in a dry and thirsty land where no water is." "As the hart panteth after the water-brooks, so panteth my soul for Thee, O God." "It is enough!" 'Man has deceived me;—earthly hopes and expectations have proved like this desert's mirage;—"*It is enough, O Lord,* I turn to *Thee.*' Yes, let us leave Elijah on that prostrate couch of unworthy exile,—yet still, mingling accents of fretfulness with accents of *prayer.* This poor, battered-down flower seems, in the moment of its humiliation, to turn towards the Great Sun. Arise, Prophet of the desert! thy God has still for thee a noble, unfulfilled destiny. Thy future is in His hands. Say not, in thy blind, disappointed pride, "It is enough!" Let Him work out His own plan of infinite wisdom. Arise! thou hast much yet to do and dare and suffer for His sake. He will yet turn thy mourning into dancing, take off thy sackcloth, and gird thee with gladness. Arise! take thy torch with its expiring flame: The God who gave it thee, is yet to revive it, and make thousands bless both Him and thee for its undying radiance. The day is coming when thou *shalt* say, "It is enough,"—but not, until, thy work finished, the chariot and horses of fire are waiting ready to bear thee to thy eternal reward!

XI.

The Angel's Visit.

"And as he lay and slept under a juniper tree, behold, then an angel touched him, and said unto him, Arise and eat. And he looked, and, behold, there was a cake baken on the coals, and a cruse of water at his head. And he did eat and drink, and laid him down again. And the angel of the Lord came again the second time, and touched him, and said, Arise and eat; because the journey is too great for thee. And he arose, and did eat and drink, and went in the strength of that meat forty days and forty nights unto Horeb the mount of God. And he came thither unto a cave, and lodged there; and, behold, the word of the Lord came to him, and he said unto him, What doest thou here, Elijah?"—1 Kings xix. 5-9.

"And the Lord said unto Satan, The Lord rebuke thee, O Satan; even the Lord that hath chosen Jerusalem rebuke thee: is not this a brand plucked out of the fire? . . . And the angel of the lord stood by."—Zechariah iii. 2, 5.

"Man did eat angels' food."—Ps. lxxviii. 25.

THE ANGEL'S VISIT.

We return to the lonely prophet, sitting sullen and dejected under the bush of the desert. "Lo," he had said in his despondency, "I will wander far off, and remain in the wilderness. I will hasten my escape from the windy storm and tempest." Jaded in body and racked in spirit, sleep—nature's great restorer,—"the chief nourisher in life's feast"—overtakes him. He had prayed that he might *die;* and as his eyes were now closing, he might have wished it were the last long slumber that knows no waking. But God's thoughts are not man's thoughts. "He giveth his beloved *sleep.*" He rocks this petulant child to rest in his desert cradle; but he is to wake with tearless eyes, refreshed, invigorated, gladdened. "Weeping may endure for the night, but joy cometh in the morning."

Leaving the Seer wrapt in slumber, let us pause and note *God's tender interest in His people.* And this especially in seasons, when we might have imagined they had forfeited all claim on His care and compassion. "He considers their soul *in adversity.*" As this fugitive from duty is stretched under the juniper tree, with his sheepskin mantle for a covering, lo, a bright angelic being,—probably during the darkness of night—is seen approaching the sleeper's couch, bending over his sun-browned face, furrowed with fatigue and sorrow. It is one of those spirits to whom has been assigned the lofty mission of 'ministering to those who are heirs of salvation.' It may have been one of the very throng who had encamped around the hero-prophet in the day of his triumph. With what mournful sympathy and interest would he now steal to his side, in the hour of his humiliation!

The personal and visible ministry of angels was no strange occurrence in Hebrew history. In this same wilderness, a thousand years before, Ishmael's cries and Hagar's tears were answered by an angel's directing voice and presence. A century later, another houseless fugitive from Beersheba had laid him down, like the prophet, amid heaps of rough stones, to sleep. Angelic beings were sent to guard the pillow of the wanderer, and convert the rudest of couches into the gate of heaven. Generations after Elijah had been borne to heaven in his flaming car of victory, a lowlier chariot was seen moving along the neighbouring desert of Gaza. A dejected but earnest soul was seated in it reading his Bible, and longing to know "the better way." An angel from heaven comes to the city of Samaria, and instructs Philip the Evangelist to intermit his work and hasten far off to the wilderness to minister comfort to that one lone traveller. Yet again—in the sea of Adria, an Alexandrian vessel has been overtaken by storm. For days the crew seem abandoned to their fate, drifting along the trough of the maddened sea. God has one loved, treasured soul in that ship, and for his sake, lo, an angel from the upper sanctuary is commissioned to speed at midnight; to whisper a word of peace and comfort to the apostle-prisoner.

"There stood by me that night," said St Paul, "the angel of God, whose I am, and whom I serve."

Did the Church need these celestial protectors and guardians only during the period of her infancy and nonage; and did the ministry of angels lapse with the Old Testament dispensation? Nay; we believe,—though unseen to mortal eye,—though we cannot trace their footsteps nor hear the rustling of their wings,—it is a thoroughly scriptural and comforting truth, (and never more so than in our seasons of trouble,) that we are still environed by these bright sentinels from the spirit-land,—hovering, now, over a sick-bed, now, smoothing a pillow of suffering, now, gathered amid the hush of our solemn assemblies, now, mingling with the weeping mourners at a couch of death, and bearing the ransomed soul in its arrowy flight to the upper sanctuary. It is interesting to think, that no sooner are the gates of the morning opened, than these glorified "ministering ones" are abroad on earth on their errands of love and mercy to its waiting crowds. Here is a sorrowing spirit to heal; there is a body of pain to soothe; here is an aged pilgrim struggling in the Jordan, they go to help him through; there is an infant on its tiny couch of death, they hasten to pluck the bud, to gather the lily, and carry it to the garden above.

But to return to the sleeper. A gentle hand touches him, a gentle voice speaks to him, "Arise and eat." Partially roused, yet almost unconscious of the angel's presence, the Prophet raises himself from his pillow, and sees placed at his head—(all the provisions which to this day a Bedouin needs)—"a cake baked on the coals, and a cruse of water." He seems scarcely to have partaken of the provided food when sleep again overtakes him; and then a second time, —probably when morning dawned,—the gentle touch and heavenly voice are heard and felt, accompanied by the additional words—"because the journey is too great for thee." Now broad awake, the strange celestial form appears before him; and, more impressive and touching to his spirit, the celestial voice falls on his ear. It must have been like a ray of light breaking through a storm-wreathed sky, this bright messenger giving him the assurance that his God still cherished him;—took a tender, loving interest in his well-being;—and, notwithstanding his miserable coward flight, had delegated a special envoy from heaven to spread a table for him in the wilderness, and whisper to him accents of comfort! His soul, like that of aged Jacob, revives. 'God cares for me,' is the simple thought which rekindles the smouldering fires on his heart-altar. It is to him better than all the miraculous provision. He envies not the prophets of the groves, with their dainties at Jezebel's table. He has meat to eat which the world knows not of. The living Jehovah of Cherith and Sarepta is still his. He has "found him also in a desert land, and in the waste howling wilderness," keeping him "as the apple of His eye." The Prophet can make his waking song that of the sweet psalmist of Israel,—"If I take the wings of the morning and flee to the uttermost parts of the sea, even there shall thy hand lead me, and thy right hand shall hold me."

It is the *goodness* of God which still leadeth to repentance. Let every trembling backslider, whose eye may fall on these pages, know the unwearying love with which that God follows you, even when, sadder far than in the case of Elijah, you can tell of weeks and months and years of guilty alienation. He finds you in the deep slumber of spiritual indifference under your juniper-tree;—some miserable, false, delusive, worldly shelter which you have deliberately preferred to "the shadow of the Almighty." How righteously might He have left you to be a mark for the poisoned arrows of the tempter, and to have slept the sleep of death! But He sent His angel of mercy,—some solemn providence, shall we say,—that with angel-touch woke you, and with angel-whisper bade you 'arise.' The warning voice was heard; but the warning was but for a moment. The old drowsiness supervened;—you were locked, as ever, in the dream of spiritual callousness and unconcern. Has He abandoned you to your fate? Has He given His angel the commission, 'Let him alone; let him sleep on now and take the final rest of despair?' Nay, that angel of the Lord, whether wearing the bright shining wings of prosperity, or the sable wings of sorrow, has come, like the messenger sent to Elijah, the second time, and "touched you;"—assured you of the loving interest your God has in your restoration;—addressed the monitory word, reminding you of the solemn journey before you, but pointing you to the blessed gospel provision He has made, if you will only awake and arise! Yes, "believe, only believe" in the reality of God's compassion and tenderness towards the erring;—that no father ever loved his prodigal and desired his return more, than your Heavenly Father desires yours. The divine Shepherd leaves the ninety and nine, that He may search out the one, truant, wandering sheep; and He goes after it "*until* He finds it."

Mark farther, not only God's interest in Elijah, but *His considerate method of dealing with His servant.* He gives him *first* food for the body. He recruits his wasted, shattered, hunger-stricken frame, before He offers spiritual guidance or counsel. The angel stands by in silence, till the restorative refreshment had been partaken of; and *then*, but not till *then*, he *speaks* to him; gives him directions as to his journey, work, and duty. There is nothing more striking, did we carefully observe it, than God's wise and appropriate adaptation of His dealings to the peculiar state, circumstances, and necessities of His people. He knows the journey that is before each of them; He knows what storm, in leaving the harbour, the vessel will encounter. And as the best of commentators says on this passage, "He that appointeth what the voyage shall be, will victual the ship accordingly."* Reader, take no thought, no over-anxious, fretting, disquieting thought for the future. God will lead you by "*the* right way." If the journey be great, the strength needed will be vouchsafed,—"Thy shoes shall be iron and brass; and as thy day is, so shall thy strength be."

Conscious of Jehovah's kindly and beneficent care, and rejoicing in it, Elijah is himself again! He springs from his couch;—and as we behold him, with pilgrim staff in hand, strong in body, and brave in soul, once more speeding along the dreary wastes,—do we not seem to hear the solemn stillness of the desert air broken by the inspired melody of his fatherland?—"The angel of the Lord encampeth round about them that fear him and delivereth them. O taste and

* Matthew Henry.

see that the Lord is good, blessed is the man that trusteth in him." It was, observe, his at once partaking of the God-given food, which enabled him to set out on his journey. To us there is a spiritual lesson in this. Many sit at the foot of their juniper-trees, moping and in despondency: musing on their weakness, fretting themselves over their past sins,—the difficulties and trials of the spiritual journey,—and in this presumptuous despair, settle down in their old sleep of indifference, and perish miserably—the victims of their own unreasonable doubts. Their inward disquieting thought is, 'How can we possibly live out these desert privations: that simoom by day, these drenching dews by night? Where can we get food in these dreary leagues of arid sand, or drink amid these barren rocks and waterless channels?' The angel message to all such is, "Arise!" 'take the provided food; accept the offered gospel-terms, and trust God for all the rest. He who has provided food, will provide strength for the journey. Arise! *Do* the will of God, and ye shall know of the doctrine.' This is true Christian philosophy. Act up to God's directions—seek to fulfil His will, and in the very doing of that will, unbelieving torturing doubts shall take flight, and by the most convincing of all evidences—the inward, subjective, experimental,—you will be brought into captivity to the obedience of Christ. "Why liest thou on thy face?" said the Divine voice to Moses, when he crouched a sceptic at God's feet, pointing to the barrier mountains behind and the raging sea in front—"Speak to the children of Israel, that they go forward!"—'Up, do my bidding; and thou shalt see how I can make my way in the sea, and my path in the mighty waters.' Forward! said the rebuked hero, clasping the rod of faith which had been lying forgotten at his side, and rising in the might of Jehovah. Forward they *did* go; and what was their confession and anthem on the opposite shore?—"Thy right hand, O Lord, is become glorious in power; thy right hand, O Lord, hath dashed in pieces the enemy." "At Thy rebuke, O God of Jacob, both the chariot and horse are cast into a dead sleep." "O Lord God of hosts, who is a strong God like unto thee? Thou rulest the raging of the sea: when the waves thereof arise, thou stillest them."

On the Prophet journeys for a long hundred and eighty miles; forty suns rise and set on the desert sands, before he fixes on any resting-place. Various and conflicting motives, doubtless, had induced him to undertake this lengthened pilgrimage, and ultimately to select the spot where he now takes up his abode. While unquestionably guilty of a lamentable dereliction of duty in thus prolonging his flight; and while fear — unworthy fear and distrust, as we shall presently see—still clung to him and mingled with the better convictions of his newly-awakened soul,—yet he betrays also, in the very selection of his place of retreat, evidence of the recent revival of his faith in God, and of the depth and reality of his religious feelings. His predominating motive, we are inclined to believe, in directing his footsteps to Horeb, was to secure an opportunity of uninterrupted repose, meditation, and prayer; and thereby recruit alike his physical and spiritual strength. Where could he have discovered a more befitting temple?—where, (with the exception of the sacred city of solemnities—Mount Zion itself,)—could he find a nobler oracle of holy thought, than among the hallowed solitudes of Sinai?—those mysterious cliffs which, ages before the Exodus, the wandering shepherds—the Amalekite Arabs—had invested with awful sanctity as "The Mount of God," and, according to Josephus, forbade their flocks to trespass on its luxuriant pastures.* But subsequent ages and events had made these haunts more consecrated still. The vivid emotions which we in modern days experience in visiting the Holy Land, must have been shared by the Israelites of Elijah's time with reference to the Sinai desert. It was the Holy Land of that age. The Exodus and forty years' wandering formed the grandest

* See *Sinai and Palestine*, p. 46; *Dr Bonar's Desert of Sinai*, p. 394. —The following is the extract from Josephus:—"This is the highest of all the mountains thereabouts, and the best for pasturage, the herbage being there good: and it had not been before fed upon, because of the opinion men had, that *God dwelt there*, the shepherds not daring to ascend it." And again—"He (Moses) ascended up to Mount Sinai, which is the highest of all the mountains that are in that country, and is not only very difficult to be ascended by men on account of its vast altitude, but because of the sharpness of its precipices also; nay, indeed, it cannot be looked at without pain of the eyes, and, besides this, it was terrible and inaccessible on account of the rumour that passed about, that *God dwelt there*."—*Ant.*, b. iii., ch. 5, sect. 1. I add a note from Dr Bonar's appendix, which he gives in the form of a query, and which is interesting in connexion with our Prophet's special mission as the Destroyer of BAAL, the *fire-god*:—"Sinai seems to have been the mountain of Jehovah's true worship; and over against it rose Serbâl, the mountain of Baal's worship—long before Israel entered the wilderness. After the 'God of Glory' (the Shekinah) appeared to Abraham and led him out of Chaldea into Canaan, did He withdraw that glory to the desert, and take up His abode on Mount Sinai, (the hill of Jehovah,) and there gather round that Sanctuary a band of worshippers, of which Jethro was the representative? And did BÂL the *fire-god* (the imitator of the Shekinah) take up his abode on Serbâl and gather his worshippers around him there? Was thus the glory of the false worship set up right in view of the glory of the true?" —*Desert of Sinai*, p. 395.

epoch of their historical annals. The miraculous passage of the Red Sea had been sung and celebrated by inspired minstrels in their psalms, and by inspired seers in their prophetic rolls. Elim, Marah, Rephidim, and, above all, Sinai and Horeb, (Gebel-Mousa and Gebel-Attâka,) were names and scenes of imperishable interest. Imagine the Prophet's feelings, as he approached, in evening light, the majestic summits of "the mount of God," reddened with the fiery glow of the descending sun;—each peak a hoary rugged giant, compared with the old familiar mountains of northern Palestine—in themselves not devoid of grandeur—Ebal and Gerizim, Tabor and Hermon, Carmel and Lebanon. He wends his way, up the frowning steep, to the cave which to this day bears his name,—probably the same from which his great predecessor saw the "glory of God." He enters the cavern,—spreads his mantle on the rocky floor, with the determination, probably, to make it for some considerable time his place of abode. He may have uttered in spirit the plaintive prayer of Jeremiah, "Oh that I had in the wilderness a hiding-place of wayfaring men, that I might leave my people and go from them, for they be an assembly of treacherous men." And if such were his longing wish, it is now fulfilled: he has reached the sacred spot hallowed by the footsteps of Moses and the voice of God. He would be well content to say, "This is my rest; here will I dwell, for I have desired it." But his God will not leave him long undisturbed in his lonely grotto and in his wilful flight. The silent echoes of his retreat are awoke as with the voice of thunder. "*What doest thou here, Elijah?*"

XII.

The Drama of the Desert.

"And he came thither unto a cave, and lodged there: and, behold, the word of the Lord came to him, and he said unto him, What doest thou here, Elijah? And he said, I have been very jealous for the Lord God of hosts: for the children of Israel have forsaken thy covenant, thrown down thine altars, and slain thy prophets with the sword; and I, even I only, am left; and they seek my life, to take it away. And he said, Go forth, and stand upon the mount before the Lord. And, behold, the Lord passed by, and a great and strong wind rent the mountains, and brake in pieces the rocks before the Lord; but the Lord was not in the wind: and after the wind an earthquake; but the Lord was not in the earthquake: and after the earthquake a fire; but the Lord was not in the fire: and after the fire a still small voice. And it was so, when Elijah heard it, that he wrapped his face in his mantle, and went out, and stood in the entering in of the cave. And, behold, there came a voice unto him, and said, What doest thou here, Elijah?"—1 Kings xix. 9-13.

"Our God shall come, and shall not keep silence: a fire shall devour before him, and it shall be very tempestuous round about him. He shall call to the heavens from above, and to the earth, that he may judge his people. . . . Hear, O my people, and I will speak; O Israel, and I will testify against thee: I am God, even thy God."—Ps. l. 3, 4, 7.

THE DRAMA OF THE DESERT.

THE wanderer was alone, yet not alone. A voice he could neither mistake nor misinterpret had sounded in his ears the thrilling question—"What doest thou here, Elijah?" Every syllable was pregnant with meaning and rebuke. "What *doest* thou here?" Life (and none should know better than thee) is a great *doing;* not hermit inaction, inglorious repose, guilty idolatry. "What doest *thou*"—thou my vicegerent in these degenerate days,—thou whom I have honoured above thy fellows, and who hast had proof upon proof of my faithfulness? "What doest thou *here*"—here in this desolate spot—away from duty;—the Baal-altars rebuilding—my own altar in ruins;—the sword of persecution unsheathed, and the bleating flock left by thee (coward Shepherd!) to the ravening wolf? "What doest thou here, *Elijah?*" Thy very name rebukes thee! Where is God, thy 'strength?' Where are the prayers and vows of Carmel? Child of weakness, belying thy name and destiny, "*What—doest—thou—here?*"

That voice is responded to by an answer in which are still mournfully blended selfish mortification, wounded pride, sceptic faithlessness:—"I have been very jealous for the Lord God of hosts, because the children of Israel have forsaken thy covenant, thrown down thine altars, and slain thy prophets with the sword; and I, even I, only am left, and they seek my life to take it away." The question is repeated. But before this is done, God opens the volume of nature with all its grand and terrible, yet soothing influences. "The Lord is in his holy temple; let all the earth keep silence before him!" Let us take our stand with Elijah on the mount, and listen to the sublime utterances.

Let us endeavour to picture the *manifestation itself*—the historical scene here described.

Elijah is commissioned to leave the cave, and to stand in the mount before the Lord. "And behold," we read, "the Lord passed by." But the august Presence is preceded by a threefold manifestation,—three successive couriers or harbingers of the Divine Majesty,—storm, earthquake, fire:—three terrific voices crying in the wilderness, "Prepare ye the way of the Lord; make straight in the desert a highway for our God." First, "a great and strong wind rent the mountains, and brake in pieces the rocks before the Lord."* A tumultuous storm swept by; the

* "The scene of the address to Elijah is now localised in the secluded plain immediately below the highest point of Gebel-Mousa, marked by the broken chapel, and by the solitary cypress. There, or at Serbal, may equally be found 'the cave;' the only indication by which the sacred narrative identifies the spot. There, or at Serbal, equally may have passed before him the vision in which the wind rent the granite mountains, and broke in pieces the cliffs." The "word," observes the same writer, "rendered rocks, is 'Sela,' not 'Tzur.' It may be difficult to determine the relative meaning of the two words. But it is almost certain, that, of the *two*, '*Sela*,' like our word 'cliff,' is the grander and more abrupt feature." "The name '*Sela*,' is the same as that by which, in later times, the place now called Petra was designated."—*Sinai and Palestine*, pp. 47, 94.

'One or two chapels I passed at different halting places. Then came winged tempests of heaven are let loose from their chambers to wrestle with the old granite peaks;—they rush from cliff to cliff with a sound like the crash of armies in a shock of battle;—the splintered rocks lie scattered in the valleys beneath, driven to and fro as chaff in the summer thrashing-floor. Jehovah had arisen in the glory of His majesty to shake terribly the earth. "BUT," it is added, "the Lord was not in the wind." The Prophet, in trembling amazement, marvels what next was to follow. He may have expected, after this exhibition of Power, some audible expression of the Divine will; and that the "wind" was the trumpet-voice heralding its proclamation. But there was none! The hurricane has passed, the tempest is lulled, all is for a moment hushed in silence. It has left nothing but the memorials of its fury in the fragments which strew the scene of desolation. Again, however, a murmuring, muffled, hollow sound, reaches his ear. The sky is darkened, the earth is convulsed, the everlasting hills rock and tremble;

the fine hollow or basin more than half way up the hill, in the midst of which stands the old cypress, called Elijah's tree; hard by which there is a well or circular pond containing a little water. The chapel of that prophet is also shewn here. It is out of this mountain wady that the rugged top of Jebel-Moûsa rises like a cone out of the hollow of some vast crater. . . . We saw the 'great and terrible wilderness' around us. . . . No green spot, no tree, no flower, no rill, no lake, but dark-brown ridges, red peaks, like pyramids of solid fire. No rounded hillocks or soft mountain curves such as one sees even in the ruggedest of home-scenes—but monstrous and misshapen cliffs, rising tier above tier, and surmounted here and there by some spire-like summits, serrated for miles into rugged grandeur, and grooved from head to foot by the winter torrents that had swept down like bursting waterspouts, tearing their naked loins, and cutting into the very veins and sinews of the fiery rock—'a land of darkness, as darkness itself; and of the shadow of death without any order, and where the light is as darkness.'"—*Bonar's Desert of Sinai.*

fresh masses of stone come thundering down from the mountain summits, the leaves in the great volume of nature are again torn in tatters—tossed in the wild elemental war; "but the Lord is not in the earthquake." What next? Is there still to be no manifestation of Love and Mercy in conjunction with Power? The Prophet gazes, but the reeling of the earth, the last symbol of terror in this sublime panorama, is only to give place to a third. "After the earthquake, a fire." In that dim twilight hour, the sky was red with flame; a lurid glow converts every mountain summit into a ruby battlement; the valley at his feet blazes like a smelting furnace. Flash, it may be, succeeds flash, of brilliant Eastern lightning. This was the most terrible of all. Fire! It was the recognised emblem of Divine wrath. It was *fire* that was hurled down from heaven on the cities of the plain. It was *fire* that came forth from the Lord and consumed Nadab and Abihu, the two sons of Aaron. It was *fire* that burned on the top of that same Sinai when Jehovah proclaimed the decalogue. Elijah had recently seen his burnt-offering on Carmel, consumed by *fire*;—the symbol of that righteous vengeance, which must fall either on the sinner or on his vicarious sacrifice. There was nothing, therefore, in this last manifestation, to calm the fears of the lonely spectator. He must have bowed him down in crouching terror in the mountain cave. There was no lullaby to his soul in this new flaming harbinger. "The Lord was not in the fire." But this mighty parable of nature is yet incomplete. After the fire there was "*a still small voice;*"—a "still soft whisper," as the words may be rendered, like the tremulous cadence of sweet music falling on the entranced ear.

The Lord was THERE! Strange contrast to the hurricane and earthquake symbols which preceded it. It is a "voice"—a "*still* voice"—a "*small* voice." The chafed, riotous elements have rocked themselves to rest. All nature is hushed; the sky is clear; the soft evening shadows fall gently on the mountain-sides; and the Prophet's own perturbed spirit partakes of the repose. Nature's vast volume opens to a page on which is inscribed in gleaming letters—"*God is love!*" It is enough. The Prophet reads!—he adores!—he rejoices! Wrapping himself in his mantle, he comes forth and stands at the entrance of his cave. God has set him, as He set Moses, in the cleft of a rock, and made "all His glory to pass before him." He has proclaimed His name and ever-during memorial. "The Lord, the Lord God, *merciful* and *gracious.*" And Israel's illustrious seer, like Israel's sweet singer, can now give thanks unto the living Jehovah, for He is *good*—for His *mercy* endureth for ever!

Let us proceed, however, more especially, to consider the object of this manifestation and its designed lessons. We may warrantably regard it as a great acted parable, containing important truths, alike for the Prophet and for the Church in all ages.

We may look briefly, in the first instance, at the design of these parabolic utterances as regarded Elijah. His despondency, as we have previously noted, had manifestly arisen from a sinful and unworthy distrust of God's *power.* "I alone," said he, "am left." He had forgotten that even though his erroneous conclusions had been correct—though ten thousand knees had been bowing to Baal, and the merest wreck of true-hearted Israelites had been left; still there was ONE above, who could in a moment hurl every idol from its impious shrine, and quench every flame on the apostate altars. How, then, does Jehovah recall the Prophet's better convictions? He gives him an awful exhibition of His might and majesty. He makes dumb nature the preacher to revive the convictions of His servant in the great truth —that the "*Lord God omnipotent reigneth.*" He manifests Himself in the hurricane and the earthquake and the fire, so that the Tishbite could say with a deeper emphasis than the Psalmist, God hath spoken once, yea, *thrice* have I heard this, that "POWER belongeth unto God." These majestic symbols spake to him with awful eloquence. 'Poor craven-hearted Prophet! wilt thou distrust Me after this? Can I, who have the elements in my grasp,—who "thresh the mountains and beat the hills as chaff,"—I, who direct the volleyed lightning and give wings to the tempest,—can I not be trusted to protect *thy* life? Why afraid of the threats of a mortal, when thou hast the God of thy Fathers to stand by thee? "Who art thou, that thou shouldest be afraid of a man that shall die, and of the son of man that shall be made as grass; and forgettest the Lord thy Maker, that hath stretched forth the heavens, and laid the foundations of the earth, and hast feared continually every day because of the fury of the oppressor, as if he were ready to destroy? and where is the fury of the oppressor? . . . I am the Lord thy God, that divided the sea, whose waves roared; The Lord of hosts is his name. And I have put my words in thy mouth, and I have covered thee in the shadow of mine hand, that I may plant the heavens, and lay the foundations of the earth, and say unto Zion, Thou art my people!"'

But more than this. Although these tremendous natural phenomena preceded the Divine manifestation, it is expressly said, that the Lord himself was not in either wind or earthquake or fire. We must regard them, therefore, as conveying to the Prophet additional symbolic meaning. They were the reflected moods of his own mind;—his own impetuous turbulent self was mirrored in these agents and elements of nature. Earthquake and tempest and flame were the meet types of his past prophetic mission and character. He was denounced by his royal master as a "troubler in Israel;" and even in the eyes of the people he could not be regarded otherwise than as a minister of awe and terror,—an incarnation of righteous vengeance, passionate zeal, fiery courage,—at whose bidding both the natural and political horizon was black with cloud and portent and storm. And as he had begun, so doubtless perhaps might Elijah expect that with famine and FIRE and blood, he would complete his mission, and inaugurate the regeneration of Israel. God wished to shew him that all this stormy zeal—this flaming retribution—was not the wonted method of the Divine dealing;—that judgment was His strange work;—and that a mission begun thus in terror was to end in peace,—"a mission begun with John the Baptist's boldness was to terminate with John the Evangelist's love."* 'Enough,' He seems to say, 'Prophet of Fire. Thou hast awoke the people hitherto with the earthquake and tempest and flame;—thy battle hitherto has been that of the warrior, with confused noise and garments rolled

* Hambleton.

in blood. These august demonstrations may for the moment awe Jezebel's priests, and inspire the apostate nation with a salutary dread. But I wish with living power to speak to my covenant Israel. I wish to induce them to seek me in penitence and tears. This can only be effected by the ministry of love—the still small voice!' Elijah bowed in reverence! The gentle, silent symbol has opened to him a new volume. It is as a Being of *Love* that 'Jehovah liveth.' It invests His old motto with a new meaning. God has taught him that weak things can confound the things that are mighty. This vision and parable of Horeb might thus be translated into inspired words—"Not by might nor by power, but my Spirit, saith the Lord of hosts."

But leaving the primary object of the manifestation in its reference to Elijah, let us regard it in its practical bearings, as an Old Testament parable of God's method of dealing with individual believers in every age. First unfolding to them the terrors of the law,—convincing of sin;—then this heraldry of vengeance, followed by the gracious offer of gospel mercy,—the "still small voice" of Redeeming love. He takes first to Sinai; displays its thunders and lightnings and curses—manifests Himself as "the consuming fire," "that will by no means clear the guilty." Then as "God in Christ reconciling the world unto himself,"—desiring not the death of the sinner,—"waiting to be gracious."

Cannot many, in a spiritual sense, endorse from their own experience, the truth of this great Parable of nature? Do you remember the time when God laid you on a bed of sickness,—broke up, in a moment, your dream of earthly happiness,—brought you to the brink of the tomb,—and you felt that, all unmeet and unprepared to die, you were standing on the verge of eternity? As you lay tossing on that fevered couch,—the dim lamp of life burning to its socket—your mind filled with blank despair;—the past, with its ghostly visions of unrepented, unforgiven sin, rising up behind and before you in terrible memorial;—do you remember how conscience became to you a Horeb? God's Righteousness, and Justice, and Holiness, like the tempest and earthquake and fire, swept by you in terrible procession,—apparently heralding with trumpet voice, "vengeance and fiery indignation." But He spared you—in mercy spared you! And, as the ebbing pulses of life began to quicken, and the gleam of glad hope irradiated your silent chamber;—do you remember that gracious ray of peace,—that "still small voice" which whispered the glad, never-to-be-forgotten accents in your ear, "Awake, thou that sleepest, and arise from the dead, and Christ shall give thee life?" What wonders does that simple, sublime disclosure *of the love of God in Christ* effect, when once it breaks through the thick blinding darkness of the soul! How it sweeps every barrier down; and brings the maddened maniac—who snapped his fetters and chains like tow, and whom no other power could bind—to sit in lamb-like gentleness at the feet of his Divine Saviour! When did Elijah wrap his face in his mantle and come forth from the cave? Not when the hurricane was sweeping by, or the earthquake heaving, or the fire lighting up the wilderness with lurid grandeur. It was when he listened to "*the still small voice.*" So it is with all who have experienced the transforming power of gospel truth.

It is not the overawing *majesty*, but the *goodness* of God, that leads to repentance: not all the thunders of Sinai, not all the curses of Ebal, can melt and overpower and constrain like the believing sight of the *Saviour* of Calvary. Here is the gospel's great principle of gravitation,—"I, if I be lifted up from the earth, will draw all men unto me." As the sun of heaven with his silent heat can bend and deflect the iron which defies the power of hammer and anvil, so with the Sun of Righteousness: He can bend and subdue, when every other moral appliance fails,—when all other moral dynamics are powerless. Miracles, in themselves, will never convince. The most stupendous array of supernatural wonders will never melt the obdurate heart. Pentecostal marvels failed to do so; the resurrection of Lazarus and Lazarus's Lord failed to do so;—just as the terrific manifestations of fire and tempest and earthquake now failed to bring the moping Prophet from his cave. But "*the still small voice*" was omnipotent. Yes, we need not mourn, in this age of the Church, the absence of miraculous teaching and miraculous symbols; the heavens above us no longer break silence;—the earthquake and storm are no longer employed as evangelists to teach us as they taught Elijah. But *we* have still, what taught him better far, the sweet tones of this gospel voice,—"Christ the power of God and the wisdom of God unto salvation to every one that believeth."

And as it is the gospel's "still small voice" that whispers peace and hope to the individual believer, so is it this same silent agency, which is to form the mightiest lever in the world's regeneration. *Power* was the symbol of old imperial Rome. Her military emblem was the eagle—the bird of prey—with keen eye and strong talons. The empire of the Cæsars rose in vision to the Prophet of Babylon, as "a beast dreadful and terrible, and strong exceedingly; having great iron teeth which devoured and brake in pieces." But what has Rome, with her sister kingdom, Greece,—the two old-world representatives of *power*, alike physical and intellectual,—what have they done in solving the urgent problems of aching humanity? Nothing. Even in the higher domain of intellect, they only give, in one awful sense, the demonstration of knowledge being "power;" by shewing how mere intellectual greatness may be allied with moral weakness, mental capacity with spiritual degradation. Christianity introduced a new element of power, after tempest, earthquake, and fire had proved insufficient. "Cæsar and Alexander," said one of the sceptic great ones of modern ages, "conquered by arms,—Jesus Christ conquered by love." In the Roman catacombs, above which had thundered the tramp of these same victorious armies of martial Rome, there is carved, here and there, an image of the good Shepherd, carrying in His loving embrace the sheep that had wandered: underneath is the Latin inscription,—"*By this I conquer!*" The legions just referred to and their garlanded victors have left behind them no movement of enduring goodness;—nothing did *they*, to dry the tears, or soothe the sorrows, or tame and curb the passions of mankind. But the gospel of that good Shepherd "who gave His life for the sheep," has not uttered thus in vain its blessed words of peace and good-will to men. There is no speech nor language where that silent voice has not been heard; its line has gone through all the earth, and its words unto the end of the world;—purifying, soothing, comforting, elevating, regenerating, wherever its blessed principles have been diffused, and its healing influences have penetrated;—the true panacea for the evils of fevered, sin-stricken humanity;—the winged messenger of mercy, carrying the olive-branch of peace around the globe! That day shall come, blessed be God, to our earth:—the din of earthquake-war and whirlwind-passion is not to last for ever. The fitful moanings of the night-blast are the precursors of a brighter morning than has ever yet arisen upon the nations. And, what is dearer to us, as members of the *Church of Christ*, all her fierce contentions and fiery trials shall yet issue in rest and deliverance. Emblem after emblem of trouble and wrath and vengeance passed before the eye of the Prophet. At length came the whisperings of the voice of *peace!* He was thereby taught, that though manifold troubles were coming upon the Israelitish nation, there should be deliverance at last. So shall it also be with the Church in her militant state,—now rocked in storms, cradled in tempests, cast into a furnace of fire;—there is a day of tranquillity at hand. Her Lord is soon to let His voice of love be heard; then these elements of wrath shall be hushed for ever, and "the days of her mourning shall be ended."

While the scene in this passage of Elijah's life is full of lessons to the believer, are there no lessons of admonition and warning for the sinner? Yes, God is thereby telling each one, who may now be resisting Him, how manifold are the means He employs to bring to Himself:—the terrors of the law, the sweet and melting tones of the gospel; rousing providences, startling dispensations, sick-beds and death-beds. The King of terrors in tempest-form passes by, sweeping down the treasured memory of years, and leaving behind him a blighted and blackened wilderness. At other times, the Lord speaks by the gentle voice of prosperity;—by the blessings He pours into your cup,—by the tender voice of His own Word and Spirit,—calling upon you as weary and heavy-laden to come and find rest for your souls. What could He have done more for you than He has done? Look back on the past! Is not the picture presented, in this passage of the Prophet's life, the expressive symbol of the many ways Elijah's God has taken to arrest your souls and lead you to repentance? Can it be that all have failed? that judgments and warnings, love and mercy, have all been powerless to bring you to the Tishbite's place, with the mantle of humility around you, owning the combined greatness, and glory, and tenderness of a forbearing God? Solemn is the word in these text; ponder it and remember it,—"The Lord *passed by!*" God is "passing;" soon He will be "passed" altogether;—your means and privileges at an end, the day of grace fled, and fled for ever. It is an awful thought, that there is a time coming, when this wondrous appliance of power, and warning, and love, with some, will be irrecoverably *gone;* and they—self-destroyers and self-destroyed—left to brood over lost and forfeited opportunities, in the dark, gloomy Horeb-cave of irremediable despair! "What doest thou here?" is the question God puts to every careless sinner. "What doest thou here?"—still in thy sins, still unawakened, unconverted, unsanctified, unsaved. He hath "passed by" thee again and again;—awaking earnest thoughts of repentance; but where are they? Fugitive impressions; like the voice of the retiring thunder, growing fainter and fainter; or, like the wake of the vessel, leaving no trace behind it of its course. "Go forth and stand upon the mount before the Lord!" Go! remembering that "there is forgiveness with Him, that He may be feared." "With the Lord there is mercy and plenteous redemption!" Go! remembering that but for the bleeding, dying love of the great Surety, there could have been nothing for you, but the earthquake and tempest and fire,—the winged symbols of vengeance. "For ye are not come unto the mount that might be touched, and that burned with fire, nor unto blackness, and darkness, and tempest. . . . . But ye are come . . . to Jesus the mediator of the new covenant, and to the blood of sprinkling, that speaketh better things than that of Abel." Blessed be God for this secure refuge-cave;—this glorious "shelter,"—where we can flee from the sweep of the descending storm! Wrapping ourselves in the mantle of Redeeming righteousness, we can gaze on the symbols of blended power and mercy, of terror and love. Yes, safe in our trust on the Rock of Ages, we can go forth and 'stand on the mount'—exulting in the sublime assurance,—"A Man shall be as an hiding-place from the wind, and a covert from the tempest; as rivers of waters in a dry place, and as the shadow of a great rock in a weary land."

XIII.

The Seven Thousand.

"And, behold, there came a voice unto him, and said, What doest thou here, Elijah? And he said, I have been very jealous for the Lord God of hosts: because the children of Israel have forsaken thy covenant, thrown down thine altars, and slain thy prophets with the sword; and I, even I only, am left; and they seek my life, to take it away. And the Lord said unto him, Go, return on thy way to the wilderness of Damascus; and when thou comest, anoint Hazael to be king over Syria; and Jehu the son of Nimshi shalt thou anoint to be king over Israel; and Elisha the son of Shaphat, of Abel-meholah, shalt thou anoint to be prophet in thy room. And it shall come to pass, that him that escapeth the sword of Hazael shall Jehu slay; and him that escapeth from the sword of Jehu shall Elisha slay. Yet I have left me seven thousand in Israel, all the knees which have not bowed unto Baal, and every mouth which hath not kissed him."—1 KINGS xix. 13-18.

"AND THE ANGEL OF THE LORD APPEARED UNTO HIM IN A FLAME OF FIRE OUT OF THE MIDST OF A BUSH; AND HE LOOKED, AND, BEHOLD, THE BUSH BURNED WITH FIRE, AND THE BUSH WAS NOT CONSUMED."—EXODUS III. 2.

"FOR I, SAITH THE LORD, WILL BE UNTO HER A WALL OF FIRE ROUND ABOUT, AND WILL BE THE GLORY IN THE MIDST OF HER."—ZECH. II. 5.

THE SEVEN THOUSAND.

There is a striking analogy between God's proclamation to Moses in a former age, when He spake to him out of the cloud on the top of Sinai, and that made to Elijah now, in this sequel to the manifestation in Horeb. In the former, the revelation of the Divine attributes, as "merciful, gracious, long-suffering, abundant in goodness and in truth," was followed by the solemn averment of Jehovah's unsullied rectitude and holiness, as "the Punisher of Sin,"—"*and that will by no means clear the guilty.*" The similar revelation of "the still small voice," made to Elijah from the same stupendous Rocky Oracle, is succeeded by a like declaration; only, not enunciated, in his case, as a general truth or principle; but in the form of a commission, as "the Prophet of Fire," to prepare the two human instruments for the infliction of Divine vengeance on a guilty people and their reigning monarch. He was commanded to anoint one of these to chastise the nation by the sword; the other, to be the uprooter of Ahab and Jezebel's iniquitous throne, and the exterminator of their gross idolatries. "Anoint Hazael to be king over Syria, and Jehu the son of Nimshi shalt thou anoint to be king over Israel; and it shall come to pass, that him that escapeth the sword of Hazael shall Jehu slay." God is a God of *love*—the utterer of "the still small voice;" —but it is a love tempered by justice and unswerving hatred of iniquity. While "mercy and truth go continually before His face," "justice and judgment are the habitation of His throne."

We shall, however, in the present chapter, confine ourselves to the comforting assurance vouchsafed to the Prophet regarding *the present*, which accompanies the message of wrath; reserving the assurance regarding the *future*, for a separate chapter. His own sorrowful plaint respecting that present was, "I, even I only, am left." "Nay—not so!" says the living Jehovah, before whom he stands;—"*Yet I have left me seven thousand in Israel, all the knees which have not bowed unto Baal, and every mouth which hath not kissed him.*"* Erroneous as Elijah's conclusions were, let us, nevertheless, try to realise his emotions at this moment of his history, as he is still but half-awake from his dream—only partially as yet roused from his fit of hypochondria. He was haunted by that depressing feeling, which hundreds know so well, of utter loneliness and isolation in entertaining heart-convictions of truth;—misapprehended, misunderstood, vilified, with no kindly human voice to cheer him in his hopeless task. It was this, among other things, which made the pillow under his juniper tree, a few weeks before, moist with bitter tears,—that there was no eye to weep with him and no heart to comfort him;—"I, even I only, am left," a solitary pillar amid the crumbling ruins—a solitary bird, wailing in the desert with plaintive note, without one responsive echo!

There is a yearning, in every human heart, for sympathy. This is specially the case in the prosecution of a great

* Kissing the idol on the mouth and chin was usual in the worship of Baal.

cause or arduous work; and all the more so if it be a *holy* work. How Paul in the midst of his gigantic labours longed for it, and how he valued it when received! How he mourns the absence of Titus, and how, until he finds this young brother, "his spirit had no rest!" How he welcomes the sympathising convoy at *Appii-forum;*—how the gloom of his prison hours is cheered and lightened by the loving presence and loving words of Epaphroditus, Onesiphorus, and, above all, Timothy! Nay, see how a Greater than Paul yearned for human companionship in his unsolaced hour. See, in Gethsemane's Garden, with what earnest tones the Divine Redeemer charges the disciples—"Tarry ye here and *watch with me!*" If we read the annals of many a missionary in pagan lands, we shall be able to estimate somewhat of Elijah's heavy burden at this time. Again and again, in their instructive diaries, do these self-denying soldiers of the cross tell us how awful and oppressive—nay, (the word is not too strong,) how *agonising* often to their spirits is the thought of feeling and standing *alone* amid these millions of benighted heathen; no one to share the crushing load of anxiety, to cheer their faith and help their prayers—"I, *even I only, am left!*" In the case of our Prophet, God tells him his conclusions were false. Seven thousand earnest spirits were in Israel, linked with him in bonds of hallowed sympathy;—seven thousand who were in secret sighing and crying over the abominations of imported heathenism—ready, as he was, to die a martyr's death, rather than do homage at the shrine of the Sidonian God.

We may learn from this declaration of God to Elijah, in

reply to his complaint, *never to take too gloomy or desponding a view of the position and prospects of the Church.* However reduced in number and influence and piety the Church of God apparently may become;—however feeble the spark, it cannot be quenched—it cannot die. The true Israel often and again have been reduced to the lowest ebb; —the bush burning with fire ready to be consumed; but the living God was in the bush, and defied the destroying flames. Witness, in the days of Noah, when all "the remnant according to the election of grace," was contained in an ark of Gopher-wood;—eight souls, all that linked the antediluvian and patriarchal believers. Yet that ark (true symbol of the living Church within) rode triumphant through tempest and storm. Witness the Church in the apostolic days, when a handful of trembling hearts met for prayer in an upper chamber in Jerusalem;—their influence nothing;—their Master gone;—the world against them. Yet the stone "cut from the mountain," gathered strength as it bounded along, crushing in its course the venerated idolatries of centuries, and establishing itself into a kingdom that shall never be destroyed! Witness the Church of the middle ages,—hunted down, persecuted, "destitute, afflicted, tormented," driven to one small asylum amid munitions of rocks, in the Alpine Valleys of the Vaudois. Or in a later century, when the darkness was deeper still, and when one brave, outspoken man, previously alluded to as "the Elijah of his times,"—denounced with trumpet-voice the abounding corruptions, and awoke Europe from the slumber of death into new and glorious life! In these ages, as in our own, and in every age that is to come,—however sad the degeneracy, and apostate the faith,—there was, and there will ever be, a pious remnant, a blessed leaven that will preserve the mass from corruption and decay. Elijah, in his moody, moping melancholy, had no memory to recall Obadiah and the fifties he had been hiding in the caves of Israel; pious, lowly, humble ones, who were weeping in secret over the abominations of the land. Besides, he had been judging of the power and progress of true religion by a false standard. He had been taking his estimate from the jubilee of Carmel; just as many now do, from loud Shibboleths—flaming zeal—display of party. God forms *His*, from the lowly faith and love of His own hidden ones;—those seven thousand whose hearts are open and known only to Him who seeth in secret. Let us not, then, be among the number of those who, like Elijah, would take too gloomy a view of the times; who can see nothing but the exterminating sword of Hazael and Jehu;—the disastrous demolition of all churches, and the breaking up of all creeds; who, anticipating such lawless times, would leave in despair churches to decay and perish,—just as they would leave a wrecked vessel to go to pieces on the sands or rocks where it has drifted,—instead of using every effort to get it disentangled,—restore its shattered hull,—replace its shattered timbers, and set it once more afloat on the waters. "Uproot!—destroy!"—that is too often man's gloomy, destructive policy,—man's cure and panacea for evil;—"fling the reins on the courser's neck;—abandon the steam engine to its mad, unchecked career,—to carry terror and destruction in its course." 'Nay,' says God, 'mine is a nobler conservative philosophy:—"be watchful and *strengthen* the things that remain that are ready to die!"' Despite of all ominous and threatening signs of the times,—though infidelity with flaunting banners, and philosophy with sceptic pride, and profligacy with brazen brow, and crime with stained dagger, and Mammon with his hydra-head, holding all classes spell-bound with imperial sway;—though all these singly and combined should bode evil and disaster, — threaten to bring our altars into jeopardy, and cause many an Eli to be seated on the wayside trembling for the ark of God:—yet, fear not; that ark is in safe custody. There are ever, and there are now, faithful hands to guard it;—a holy leaven permeating the mass of society; —the true gold, undiscernible in the dross, but which will come to light in the time of refining;—true filings of steel, which, from the bed of dust, will leap to the attracting magnet. Even though witnessing in sackcloth, God will have His witnesses still. Oh, amid the sickening, harrowing tale of the world's corruptions and miseries, and the Church's lukewarmness and apostasy,—let us ever think of the loyal seven thousand who are keeping the fires of judgment in check, —arresting the angels in the outpouring of the prophetic vials. And even should darker days come, as come they shall,—when iniquity shall abound, and the love of many wax cold;—there will ever be a breakwater of "living stones," that will prevent an utter overflow of the destroying flood and subversion of the old landmarks. The Church of Christ, ransomed with His blood, cannot die. "God is in the midst of her, she shall not be moved, the Lord shall help her, and that right early." "I have left *Me*," says He;—*that* is the guarantee of the Church's indestructibility;—He will not suffer His own work to perish.

And to individual ministers of Christ there is a comforting and encouraging lesson, too, in all this,—in their relation to their individual flocks, as well as to the Church universal;—never to despond in their work. It may be growing, when they know it not. They may be mourning in secret that all they do is vain and ineffectual. They may go home from their pulpits with aching and saddened hearts; feeling that their words are powerless,—their success marred,—their usefulness impeded,—their congregations pulseless—lifeless—dead. Not so. There may be work, unseen and unknown to them, going on in many a heart. Souls arrested, stricken, comforted;—humble hidden ones wrestling for them and their work in secret;—characters moulded through their teaching;—noble resolves made and registered in the sanctuary under the words of eternal life. The sermon they thought least powerful,—(perhaps aimless and purposeless)—lo! some dying lip whispers with its latest breath—"These words were the first that went like an arrow to my heart, and taught me to think and to pray." They may have no Carmel heights, with their pomps and splendours. It matters not. Give them rather the lowly seven thousand scattered in the caves of Israel;—holy hearts—simple faith—obedient lives. "Who hath despised the day of small things?"

Arising from the lesson just drawn, and suggested by it,—we may farther learn to *beware of harsh judgments on our fellow-men and fellow-Christians.* There was unwarrantable self-sufficiency in Elijah—so boldly averring, "I, even I only, am left!" It was not for him, ("the man of like passions,") to make so sweeping and unqualified an assertion,—repudiating the faith of others, and feeling so confident of his own. The worst phase which self-righteousness can assume, is when we constitute ourselves religious censors; and on the ground of some supposed superior sanctity say, with supercilious air, "Stand back, for I am holier than thou." Elijah's feeling has developed itself in modern times in denominational exclusiveness;—sect unchurching sect. One saying—"I alone am left." I alone am "the Church," because of apostolic descent and sacramental efficacy. Another, "I only am left," because I am joined in a holy and scriptural alliance with the State, and Cæsar is my friend. Another, "I only am left," because I am independent of all State control, and have *no* friend in Cæsar. Another, "I only am left," for congregations around me are asleep, and mine only has undergone revival and awakening. Nay, nay; hush these censorious thoughts and hasty party-judgments. "Who art thou that judgest another?" Who art thou so ready to spy out the mote in thy brother's eye, and seest not the beam in thine own? We believe the judgment of God in this, as in other things, is in accordance with truth. *He* penetrates beneath all this narrow sectarianism. He sees His seven thousand clustering in the varied caves throughout Israel. He sees them in the cave Episcopalian, and the cave Presbyterian, and the cave Independent;—the High Church cave, and the Low Church cave. He sees some of these seven thousand in places visited by outward and visible signs of awakening. He sees some in the calm, unexcited throng of ordinary worshippers. He sees some under the fretted aisle of cathedrals. He sees others in the lowliest and least adorned of village sanctuaries. He sees some carrying the music of heaven in their souls, "amid dusky lane and wrangling mart." He sees others in cottage homes of lowly obscurity, or on beds of lingering pain and sickness. He sees one in the hoary-headed saint, waiting for his crown. He sees another in the little child lisping its evening prayer by its mother's knee! There has ever been, and ever shall be, "a hidden Church." "The kingdom of God cometh not with observation." There is often pure gold in the coarsest-looking ore;—there is often the rarest pebble in the most rugged rock;—there are often the loveliest flowers in the most tangled brake or remotest dell. We have the less ground for pronouncing harsh and severe judgments, when we think of the variety in mental temperament and constitutional character: this diversity prompting, in some cases, to loud expression on the subject of Christian experience; others, with undemonstrative reticence, keeping, like the lowly virgin mother of Nazareth, all these things locked up in their hearts. In a garden, we cannot refuse the epithet of "beauty and fragrance" to the violet, because it buries its head in its own lowly leaves; while the pretentious rose or lily at its side, is standing upright, and flinging a less delicate perfume on the passing winds. We cannot unchristianise a man, because he prays when others talk; and because, when he gives, he charges the left hand to keep the right in ignorance of its doings,—while others are tossing their ostentatious gift into the treasury. The dark murky clouds and weeping skies, muffle and obscure many a bright and beauteous star. So the dingy clouds and mists of our own censorious and false judgments lead us often to think dimly and darkly of many a true Christian. "When we come to heaven," says good Matthew Henry, in commenting on this passage, "as we shall miss a great many whom we thought to have met there; so we shall meet many whom we little thought to have met there. God's love often proves larger than man's charity, and more extensive." Doubtless, when Elijah, leaving Horeb, went forth on his return journey,—he did so with bitter reproach for his own self-sufficient ignoring of others as faithful as himself. God had assured him that he was not the solitary hero he imagined himself to be. He had brought him down from his pedestal of pride, and shewn him seven thousand pillars supporting the roof, of which he had thought he was the single column and monolith. The time was when he might have been offended by such plain speaking. He would have been so, perhaps, had the fact been told him as he slept on his pillow of self-sufficiency under the juniper tree. But he is now a humble, softened, altered man. The "still small voice" has taught him to hear and to bear anything. If his God only be glorified and Israel bettered, he cares not whether he be alone, or his faith be shared by thousands. Would that all of us could imbibe the meek spirit infused by the "still small voice" of gospel love;—"In lowliness of mind, let each esteem others better than themselves!"

Let us gather yet another lesson from this comforting assurance of God to Elijah;—it is the first time we have drawn it from the Prophet's past history,—*the influential power of a great example.* Elijah's feeling was, that he was alone; that he had toiled, and witnessed, and suffered in vain; that in vain he had uttered his high behests; borne publicly his testimony to the living Jehovah; lived his life of faith, and self-denial, and prayer. His saddening thought was, that he was now going to end a useless, fruitless, purposeless existence; that, for all he had done in the cause of Divine truth, he might still have been roaming a free-booter, or pasturing his flocks as a Shepherd in his native Gilead. 'Nay,' says God, to this mighty harvest-man,—'seven thousand souls have been reaped mainly by thy sickle.' His silent prayers had not ascended from his rocky oratory at Cherith in vain. The bold protest uttered by "the Prophet of Fire," before Ahab, denouncing the court idolatry, had kindled the smouldering embers of hope, and courage, and piety, in many a Hebrew household. His heroic example had put fortitude into many a faint heart. Ah! how many amid the thousands of Israel, could have repaired to his Horeb cave, to give the lie to his saying, "*I, even I only, am left!*"

Wherever there are brave, bold, honest, upright, God-loving hearts in this world, there is sure to emanate (there *must* emanate) a silent, it may be,—but yet a vast influence for good. "No man liveth to himself." What may not a word do!—a solemn advice!—a needed caution! That youth, coming for the first time into town, fresh from the hallowed precincts of home, and from the incense of the domestic sanctuary, to grapple with unknown temptations;—what may not a kindly word, a kindly deed, a kindly interest effect, in snatching him from the edge of the precipice, and confirming his moral and religious principles for life! And here too, lies one of the vast powers of the pulpit. There are words sown there (little seeds wafted to many a heart-plot,) which take root and grow for ever. Talk of the great Painters!

God's ministers are these;—mighty limners of the truth, decorating the halls and walls of the immortal spirit with frescoes for eternity. Ay, and this page in Elijah's history tells us that there is no such thing in the case of the Great and the Good as *failure!* Great heroic deeds may, for the time, be eclipsed, overborne; but, like the river of Egypt, lost in the sands, they will emerge, in due season, to roll on in an augmented volume to the ocean. *That* was apparently a grand failure at Carmel—that bold hero-deed. It ended in crushing disappointment. The brazen gates of Jezreel were ignominiously shut on the champion Prophet; an insulting message was hurled at his honoured head; he fled discomfited, panic-stricken, weary of life, to the bleak desert! —— Nay, not a failure: cheer thee, O Prophet of Fire! for seven thousand brave, and good, and true, are in these distant hills of Samaria, thanking God for thy bold heart and example! That was apparently a grand failure, as we see a prisoner in the Mammertine dungeon of the world's old capital,—his limbs cramped with the chain,—his body shivering in the winter's cold,—his lips sealed in silence! That was apparently a grand failure at the Colline gate of Rome, as we see this feeble, decrepit missionary, led along to the place of execution; and, with one stroke of the fatal axe, the head of the hapless victim rolling dishonoured in the dust! —— Nay, not a failure: cheer thee, O Paul of Tarsus! Thy glorious life has stirred the pulses of the world;—these footmarks on the sands of time, no wave of oblivion can ever obliterate;—the echoes of thy mighty voice shall circulate and reverberate to time's latest day!

Let us each strive to do our duty in our varied spheres,

nobly, usefully,—with an eye to God's glory and the good of others;—and then, though life should seem at times to be a failure,—our plans crossed, our purposes thwarted, the bright sunset of vermilion and gold all at once blurred and obscured in drizzling mist and rain;—we shall not, we cannot have lived to no purpose! Some of the seven thousand we have aided by our counsels, or prayers, or example, will gather round our grave, and let fall the unbidden tear. One of the great and the good of modern Elijahs,—an illustrious minister—who was wont to declare the truth with all Elijah's power; but who, with Elijah's temperament, as life's shadows were closing around him, was bewailing want of success,—glad to leave the scene where his work seemed discouraged—motives misapprehended—all a failure: would that he had seen the sequel; when the sceptic and the infidel of the town, who had trembled under his faithful words, came forth to bear his coffin on their shoulders to the tomb! "*I, even I only, am left.*" Hush, hush the thought. You may not have even seven, of the seven thousand. But, O man of God! that *one* converted sceptic, in humble attire, wiping the drops of labour from his brow, and the tear from his eye, as he bears thee to thy last long home! Oh, this—*this* forbids the word "failure" among thy dying utterances. The presence of that one mourner proves:—thou hast not lived, thou didst not die in vain!

XIV.

Return to Duty.

"And the Lord said unto him, Go, return on thy way to the wilderness of Damascus; and when thou comest, anoint Hazael to be king over Syria; and Jehu the son of Nimshi shalt thou anoint to be king over Israel; and Elisha the son of Shaphat, of Abel-meholah, shalt thou anoint to be prophet in thy room. And it shall come to pass, that him that escapeth the sword of Hazael shall Jehu slay; and him that escapeth from the sword of Jehu shall Elisha slay."—1 KINGS xix. 15–17.

"THEN FLEW ONE OF THE SERAPHIM UNTO ME, HAVING A LIVE COAL IN HIS HAND, WHICH HE HAD TAKEN WITH THE TONGS FROM OFF THE ALTAR: AND HE LAID IT UPON MY MOUTH, AND SAID, LO, THIS HATH TOUCHED THY LIPS, AND THINE INIQUITY IS TAKEN AWAY, AND THY SIN PURGED."—ISAIAH VI. 6, 7.

"IS NOT MY WORD LIKE AS A FIRE? SAITH THE LORD; AND LIKE A HAMMER THAT BREAKETH THE ROCK IN PIECES?"—JEREMIAH XXIII. 29.

"HAVE NOT I COMMANDED THEE? BE STRONG, AND OF A GOOD COURAGE; BE NOT AFRAID, NEITHER BE THOU DISMAYED: FOR THE LORD THY GOD IS WITH THEE WHITHERSOEVER THOU GOEST."—JOSHUA I. 9.

RETURN TO DUTY.

In the previous chapter we considered the comforting assurance regarding *the present*, which the Lord God of Elijah addressed to His servant before quitting the solitudes of Horeb. But there was a communication of mingled judgment and mercy given him also regarding *the future*. And, as an illustration of the minute, tender, sympathising interest God takes in the case of all His people, it may be well, in a single sentence, to mark how He therein meets and answers, one by one in succession, the complaints of the Prophet.*

The first subject of Elijah's grievance was, "The children of Israel have forsaken thy covenant;" the second, "They have thrown down thine altars and slain thy people with the sword;" the third, "I, even I only, am left."

'Go,' says Jehovah, in reply to the *first*, 'pour the consecrating oil on the head of Hazael. He is to be the rod of mine anger against apostate Israel. He will teach them, "by terrible things in righteousness," that it is not with impunity my covenant is forsaken.' And accordingly it was so. Some years after Elijah had been removed from the troubled scenes of earth to his glorious reward, the coasts and villages of the northern kingdom were ravaged and scourged by the Syrian

* These are well brought out by Dr Krummacher.

armies under this victorious captain;—the footprints of his desolating host, telling amid ruin and pillage and blood, that God is not a man that He should lie, nor the son of man that He should repent.

'Go!' says Jehovah, in reply to the *second* complaint, 'anoint Jehu the son of Nimshi;—he too is to be the minister of my vengeance against the royal house of Ahab and his unscrupulous queen.' And though this announced judgment was not accomplished in the days of Elijah, in due time the terrible doom was consummated by a work of extermination unparalleled in Hebrew history. Every relation, including the remotest kinsfolk of Ahab, was put to the sword, and Jezebel herself subjected to the most ignominious of deaths. A similar work of destruction was at the same time carried out regarding the Baal-worship. A vast temple, reared by Ahab in Samaria for idolatrous service, was crowded with votaries. At a preconcerted signal, eighty trusted soldiers rushed in on the crowd as they were engaged in offering sacrifice before the great stone statue of the Syrian idol. The smaller divinities were torn from their niches and pedestals; and, with indiscriminate slaughter, as described by Josephus, the doom uttered amid the solitudes of Sinai was fulfilled to the letter.

In answer to these two first complaints, we have Elijah's God coming forth as a God of judgment;—responding in the wind and the earthquake and the fire. But there is yet a third *comforting* assurance to be added, in answer to his concluding plaint. It is the God of "the still small voice" who speaks now. It is a word of *peace*. 'Go,' says Jehovah, 'anoint Elisha the son of Shaphat, of Abel-meholah, to be prophet in thy room. When thy voice is silent, I shall not want a faithful messenger, and the Church shall not want a faithful guide. Go, and say no longer, "I am left alone;" for this elect Israelite will be a sympathising friend to thee during the remainder of thy years, and shall take thy place at thy departure. "And it shall come to pass, that him that escapeth from the sword of Hazael shall Jehu slay; and him that escapeth from the sword of Jehu shall Elisha slay."' Thus did the Prophet of Fire prepare to leave his retreat with three swords gleaming before him,—Hazael's sword of war, Jehu's sword of justice, Elisha's sword of truth—the sword that wounds only to heal.* How this threefold assurance must have calmed his misgivings! He was seasonably reminded, of what should ever be a source of comfort to ourselves,—God's sovereignty alike in the Church and the world. By Him kings reign and princes decree justice;—He has manifold arrows in His quiver;—He can carry on His work, at one time, by a Hazael or a Jehu,—fierce, unrelenting, unsparing soldiers; at another, by Elisha, a man of love and peace—making the wrath of man to praise Him, and restraining the remainder of His wrath.

Elijah's memorable visit to Horeb was now over. The symbol vision was past. He found himself once more by the mouth of his cave alone. Nay, not alone! While standing there,—the noise of the whirlwind in his ear—the glow of the fire yet dazzling his eyes;—and, what was more, the blessed tones of the still small voice echoing through his heart of hearts;—a second time is the question addressed

* Matthew Henry.

to him, "What doest thou here, Elijah?" And after an answer similar to that previously made, but uttered in a far different spirit,—the Divine command was given: "And the Lord said unto him, *Go, return on thy way to the wilderness of Damascus;*" and it is further added, "*So he departed thence.*" Though, as regards the Prophet's *outer* life, the scene on Mount Carmel stands forth in pre-eminent grandeur and importance;—the manifestation on Mount Horeb, and more especially this its closing hour, was in many respects the most momentous crisis in his *inner* life. We may well, therefore, interrupt the thread of the narrative, and pause for a little on so solemn an incident in the Tishbite's history; making the direction addressed to him, afford subject-matter for a few practical thoughts of a more personal kind regarding ourselves. With these, we shall occupy the remainder of the chapter.

We believe that there are analogous Horeb experiences in the case of every Christian. Sacred spiritual epochs,—memorable turning-points,—associated with some peculiar revelation of God, either in His Word or providence; these resulting, as in the case of Elijah, if not in an entire alteration of thought and feeling, at least in a new impulse being imparted to the heavenly life. Such a solemn hour occurs with some at the crisis of an alarming illness, or during recovery from sore sickness; when "the still small voice" breaks the silence of the long night-watches and of the darkened chamber; and when life, given back from the gates of death, is devoutly consecrated to the great Restorer. Such a solemn season occurs, in the case of others, at a time of bereavement; when what we most fondly love has perished from our sight; and when, as "the still small voice" of heavenly comfort falls upon the ear,—the broken, bleeding tendrils of the heart, wrenched from creature-props, turn to the great unfailing Support and Refuge, and fix themselves there for ever! Such a solemn hour occurs, with others, at a sacramental season; when the God of the "still small voice" has "passed by;" and when, having partaken of the sacred symbols, and enjoyed near and blessed experience of the Saviour's presence and mercy, we have vowed a deeper love, and purposes of more devoted and earnest obedience. Reader, are any of these sacred and peculiar experiences now, or have they been recently, your own? and have you received, like Elijah, the summons to speed you back from your period of silence and seclusion, of awe and adoration, to the needful duties of life? Let us picture to ourselves some of the feelings with which the Prophet left his Horeb grotto, for "the wilderness of Damascus." We may find in them a reflection of what ours may possibly now be, in returning to engage once more in the calls and cares of a busy world.

As Elijah journeyed back through the desert, one of his feelings doubtless would be this—*Deep sorrow on account of his past faithlessness, and a salutary sense of his weakness for the time to come.* Every step of that backward journey must have recalled, with sorrow and shame, the remembrance of his unworthy flight and unworthy unbelief. Every weary league he retraversed;—every rock, and bush, and arid wady,—must have read to him a bitter rebuke and reproach; ay, and reminded him, that, "*strong*" as his name imported him to be, he was strong only in God. Perhaps, in his fit of sullen, morbid despondency, he had no time before, to ponder and realise the amount of his ingratitude and guilt. But now, after all he had seen and experienced in the mount, with what different feelings must he have bewailed the past:—that coward retreat from the gates of Israel;—that rash, passionate, prayer under the desert juniper tree;—the vain, proud, self-righteous apology, he had dared to utter in answer to God's remonstrance. How must all these have come home to him, as he hies him back, an altered man, to his God-appointed work. Could he ever forget the tremendous sermon on *sin*, preached in that great cathedral of nature;—Sinai the pulpit;—lightning and whirlwind and thunder the ambassadors of Heaven? Could he think of his heroic deeds and vows on Carmel, and the degenerate spirit he afterwards evinced,—and not hear the voice of impressive warning, "When thou thinkest thou standest, take heed lest thou fall?" Is this one of our feelings, in pursuing, after some recent solemn experience or 'manifestation,' our pilgrimage journey,—a deep, heartfelt, realising view of past guilt and unworthiness? Perhaps our besetting sins may not be of the same type as Elijah's;—peevishness, fretfulness, discontent, pride, unworthy distrust of God's ability and willingness to help. But be they what they may, do we set out anew, like him, feeling their vileness, deeply humbled, softened, saddened at the retrospect? Under the Divine teaching, have we seen sin, and our *own sin*, as that awful thing which, ere the still small voice of mercy could be heard, required that the tremendous heralds of wrath and vengeance should burst over the heads of a sinless Surety? And, farther, as we hear God's voice now saying, "Go, return on thy way to the wilderness;"—do we go, under a salutary consciousness of our own utter weakness and inability, in our own strength, "to pay the vows which our lips have uttered and our mouth hath spoken when we were in trouble?"—Do we go, uttering the fervent prayer, "Hold THOU me up, and I shall be safe?"

Another feeling Elijah had, in leaving his cave, must have been *a lively sense and apprehension of God's great mercy.* What, in the retrospect of the recent wondrous manifestation, would more especially linger in the Prophet's recollection? Not the wind, not the earthquake, not the fire; but "the still small voice." He would abundantly utter to himself the memory of God's great goodness. His heart would overflow with gratitude when he thought (despite of his coward flight) of Jehovah's varied ministry of kindness:—the bread and the cruse of water of the juniper tree;—the angel sent specially to spread a table for him in the wilderness; and, more than all, the Lord of angels,—the very Being he had offended and provoked,—meeting him in the cave of his despondency;—making heaven and earth,—the vastest agencies of nature,—to bring before him a magnificent series of sacramental signs,—ending the glorious display with *love;*—yes! *love* to *his guilty* soul;—hushing and calming his storm-tossed spirit, with that "*still small voice!*" Are *our* feelings, in this respect also, akin to those of Elijah? If God has accorded to us some signal providential interposition,—delivering our souls from death, our eyes from tears, and our feet from falling;—or if He has vouchsafed some special and peculiar manifestation of His grace;—spreading, it may be, for us also, as for his servant, some spiritual feast,—giving us manna from His own banqueting table—angels' food—the bread of life; and, by means of these sacramental symbols, in the still small voice, sealing and ratifying to us, all the blessings and benefits of the new covenant;—may we not well "return on our way" with our hearts pervaded and penetrated with a profound sense of His infinite mercy and loving-kindness; our lips attuned, like those of the Tishbite, as we picture him, once more, with girt loins and pilgrim staff speeding along the desert sands;—our lips attuned to the song, "What shall I render unto the Lord for all his benefits towards me?"

We may suppose another feeling entertained by Elijah in departing from his cave and returning through the wilderness, would be, *a fixed purpose and resolution of new and more devoted obedience.* Mourning an unworthy past,—penetrated by a lively sense of Jehovah's love,—he would go onward and forward, resolved more than ever on a life of grateful love and of active and unwavering service, until God saw meet to take him up in His chariot of fire. He would go, not only mourning his besetting sins, but seeking henceforth to watch against their occurrence. And it is worthy of note, that, from this time henceforward, we never again meet with the craven-hearted, petulant, impetuous Prophet. We may hear indeed no more, (with perhaps one exception,) of any great chivalrous doings;—heroic contests, or Carmel feats of super-human strength, like the race before the chariot to Jezreel;—but neither do we read any more of hesitancy, despondency, cowardice. If the torch of the Prophet of Fire has less of the brilliant blaze of former ecstatic exploits, it burns, at least, with a purer, steadier lustre. He may have less henceforward of the meteor, but he shines with more of the steady lustre of the true constellation. From this date he seems to enter on the calm, mellowed evening of life, following a troubled tempestuous day. Reader, if in some similar momentous crisis of your history, Elijah's God may be saying to you, as to him, "Go, return on thy way;"—is it in your case also with purposes of new and earnest obedience? Are you to leave your cave, whatever that may be, with the firm determination, in a strength greater than your own, that, whatsoever others do, as for you, you will serve the Lord? saying, Other lords, in time past, have had dominion over us, but "this God shall be our God for ever and ever?" And, while you go, like him, with the resolve to be holier, humbler, more meek, more gentle, more loving, more trusting;—go also, like him, feeling, that you have a great mission on hand;—a life of solemn work and duty;—preparation for eternity! God pointed out to Elijah special work to perform: "Go, anoint Hazael—Go, anoint Jehu;" and he *did* his Lord's bidding. He has work for each of us also, in our different spheres;—work for *Him;* work in our own hearts, work in our own families;—work in the Church, work in the world. "Go," says He; "return on thy way;" not to sleep under the juniper tree, but to active life;—to glorify me in your daily walk, and business, and station, and character. With this as our solemn purpose and resolution, may it be said of us, as of Elijah,—may God thus write down in His Book of Remembrance—"So he departed thence."

Bereaved! we have specially spoken of your experience, as being possibly similar to that of Elijah, in this eventful moment of his history. We may revert, therefore, yet once more, to God's monitory words addressed to him, as suggestive of thoughts more peculiarly applicable to your case and circumstances. "Go, return on thy way to the wilderness." Yes! "*the wilderness.*" This earth, to you, is a blighted world; "a land of drought, a desert not inhabited." As Elijah passed the old juniper tree, even the very angel's footsteps could not be traced: no fragment was left of his shining robes,—no echo of his voice. And as *you* return too, to the old familiar haunts; this voice and that voice are silent. Those who sat with you at your feasts in the wilderness, are gone: nothing is left but the black patch of smouldering ashes, where the banquet was once spread, and the mutual vow recorded. Gone! nay, *not* 'gone.' Many are like Elijah's angel,—only away to do higher behests of love and mercy in brighter worlds, and beckon you to follow after them! If you be left behind a little longer to tread the wilderness;—oh, let it be with you, as with the prophet;—let all God's dealings only quicken your footsteps to the true land of promise; meanwhile seeking to do your duty in your earthly sphere, with patience and faith, meekness and submission;—until God prepare your fiery chariot to descend and bear you up amid reunions that are to know no dissolution.

And if, perchance, some youthful eyes may fall on these pages,—let such suffer a word of exhortation. You are *unlike* Elijah, as he now stands before us at the mouth of his cave, girded for his journey; unlike this stern, rough man, who had fought for years the Lord's battles, amid famine and judgment;—and who was now drawing near to the close of his mission. The world is still all before you;—its Cheriths, and Carmels, and Zarephaths, and wilderness sojournings. And be thankful for this;—that you have yet time, and strength, and sphere, to serve God in your day and generation. Be thankful that you have yet, unforfeited opportunities;—that, with God's grace, you have the grand opportunity, which others have missed, of making that life and that mission a glorious one;—not by great Carmel-deeds of power and ostentation; but by faith, and love, and active lowly service. What would Elijah have given to live over again the past irrevocable days? What would he have given to stand again at Jezreel's gate, amid the rushing of the storm, when the tempter first came and assailed him, and led him captive? You *have* that future before you:—you have the unblotted pages of life's book yet to write. It depends much on your resolutions now, how they are to be written. To you, God does not say, as to Elijah,—"Go, *return*." It is, 'Go, *set out*;—the journey is all yet to be trodden.' Is it to be the faith and lowly submission of Cherith? the bold, devoted, heroic testimony of Carmel? or, is it to be the sullen, peevish discontent,—the unworthy inactivity of the wilderness of Beersheba? Is it to be a life for God and for heaven; or a life for earth and self? Many an old careworn, travel-worn Elijah envies you;—envies you this chance of a pure, godly, unselfish, elevated existence, which can be theirs no more! In entering the great world, you must expect to encounter its whirlwind, and earthquake, and fire. But let "the still small voice" be ever heard, amidst every hurricane of temptation. Go in the might of the Prophet's God. Let your name be "ELIJAH!" God's strength. "I write unto you, young men, because ye are *strong*, and the word of God abideth in you, and ye have overcome the wicked one." With pilgrim staff and girded loins, and "the still small voice" echoing in your ear, be it yours to say—"*We will go in the* STRENGTH *of the Lord God!*"

XV.

The Call of Elisha.

"So he departed thence, and found Elisha the son of Shaphat, who was plowing with twelve yoke of oxen before him, and he with the twelfth: and Elijah passed by him, and cast his mantle upon him. And he left the oxen, and ran after Elijah, and said, Let me, I pray thee, kiss my father and my mother, and then I will follow thee. And he said unto him, Go back again: for what have I done to thee? And he returned back from him, and took a yoke of oxen, and slew them, and boiled their flesh with the instruments of the oxen, and gave unto the people, and they did eat: then he arose, and went after Elijah, and ministered unto him."—1 KINGS xix. 19-21.

"ALSO I HEARD THE VOICE OF THE LORD, SAYING, WHOM SHALL I SEND, AND WHO WILL GO FOR US? THEN SAID I, HERE AM I, SEND ME."—ISAIAH VI. 8.

"RISE, HE CALLETH THEE."—MARK X. 49.

THE CALL OF ELISHA.

OF the three divine declarations, referred to in the commencement of the previous chapter, regarding "the throne and the altar of Israel," the last must have been especially cheering to the Prophet. After his recent experience of weakness and temptation, he may have sighed, as he never did before, for the friendship and sympathy of some kindred spirit. God had graciously provided a true "brother born for adversity." Accordingly, guided either by his own impulse and inclination, or by express authority, he inverts the order of the threefold direction, and speeds him first to find out the son of Shaphat. We have, in this new incident in his history, another of those rapid dramatic changes with which we are now familiar.

There is not a word said in the narrative about the long journey, by which, all alone, he retraced his steps to the north-east of Palestine. From gazing in thought on the awful solitudes of the Sinai desert,—the whirlwind and tempest and fire still blinding us with their terror, and the voice of God, more solemn than all, sounding in that magnificent sanctuary of nature,—we are transported, in a moment, to a quiet pastoral scene,—a peaceful home,—by the banks or on the plain of the Jordan. It is a picture of domestic sunshine;—twelve ploughs and teams of oxen are busy in early spring preparing the ground for the reception of the seed;—and the last of the twelve is guided by the hand probably of an only son,—doted on by fond parents, and he not slow in returning their love. It must have been, too, a joyous spring-time. With elastic step, must these eleven ploughmen, with their young master, have gone forth to the fields. For three years and a half had the oxen been "pining in empty stalls,"—the implements of husbandry unused, —and the sickles of harvest rusting in the desolate barns. But the sky had at last opened its windows. Man and beast, emancipated from their tedious thraldom, go forth to their appointed task. The furrows, once more moist with genial rain and dew, invite the seed. The ploughshare drives its way through the stubborn glebe; nature is about to spring from her grave, and rejoice in her new resurrection attire.

In the midst of this busy patriarchal scene, the toil-worn Prophet of Carmel and Horeb presents himself. We cannot point to the spot. It must, however, have been somewhere not far from the old familiar Cherith; or from the town of Pella, now hallowed to us through the remembrances of a later age.* The presence of the Prophet could not be other than a startling apparition. With no ordinary feelings must the son of Shaphat and his eleven husbandmen—when pursuing their quiet avocations—have seen all at once at their side, the stalwart figure of God's illustrious vicegerent;—one whose name had been for years a household word,—associated with mingled feelings of reverence and terror, awe and wonder! And the whole occur-

* Abel-meholah is placed by Robinson ten miles south of Scythopolis.

rence, or interview, if we may call it so, was equally strange, unique, dramatic. In silence,—without uttering a word,—Elijah takes off his well-known prophet's mantle—casts it on the shoulders of the young farmer—and then passes on. How soon and how faithfully has Jehovah's promise been ratified. Before the Seer reaches the skirts of the wilderness of Damascus, his own longings for human companionship are fulfilled. God has given him the first pledge of "the hidden church." He has discovered one family at least, of the reserved "thousands," still faithful to Him. A ray of new sunshine must at that moment have suffused itself over his soul. He must have felt as if an oppressive load were lifted off his spirit, and as if his own special mission of wind and earthquake and fire were now to be superseded by a gentler embassy. Here was the promised messenger of "the still small voice;"—the finisher of the work of which he had himself laid the rugged foundations. In the spirit of his great antitype, he would be willing to say, in joyful self-renunciation, "He must increase, and I must decrease."

Elisha, in his turn, sudden and startling as the whole transaction was, seems in a moment to have understood the symbol. He knew well, when he felt the garment touching his shoulders, that it formed the token alike of investiture in the sacred office, and of his adoption as son of the Tishbite.*

* "This ceremony has always been considered by Eastern people an indispensable part of the consecration to the sacred office. It is in this way that the Brahmins are still invested with the priestly character, a yellow mantle being thrown across their shoulders, which is buckled round the waist with a sacred ribbon; and it is in this way, too, that the Persian sooffees are appointed. The master, in the anticipation of death, selecting one of his favourite pupils, bequeathes his antiquated garment to the

There may have been, (there must have been,) a rush of conflicting emotions impelling him to cast the vestment aside, and reject summarily the proffered honour. 'What! I the successor of the great Elijah! I, who know nothing but of the sowing of perishable seed, to go forth scattering the imperishable!' But, under the human symbol, he saw the *divine* hand,—the indubitable commission of Heaven. "The still small voice" spoke too articulately to be mistaken or misinterpreted. To him, as to thousands since, that gracious promise may have come home as a balm-word of comfort—"He that goeth forth and weepeth, bearing precious seed, shall doubtless come again with rejoicing, bringing his sheaves with him."

Leaving his team of oxen, he speeds him after the great Prophet. Without one syllable of remonstrance regarding his acceptance of the divine call, he prefers the request—"Let me, I pray thee, kiss my father and my mother, and then I will follow thee." With similar brevity, without the

youth, who by that act is publicly recognised as his successor, and looked upon as inheriting along with the mantle, the virtues and powers of his venerable precursor. The Suffavean dynasty, who long occupied the throne of Persia, owed the origin of their family to the reputation which the founder of it enjoyed for sanctity. That person, who was universally regarded as a holy man, was succeeded by his grandson, Juncyd, who took up his mantle after the death of his grandsire, and a crowd of disciples flocked to him as the heir of the talents and qualifications of his deceased relative. It was evidently owing to the prevalence of the same Asiatic sentiments among the Israelites, that the succession to the prophetic office was determined by the descent of his master's cloak of camel's hair-cloth afterwards upon Elisha, and so well was the action understood, as conveying to the servant the spirit and authority of the master, that he was universally acknowledged as the successor of that eminent prophet, and the leading champion in his age of the cause of God."—See Dr Jamieson's "Eastern Manners," p. 313.

interchange of any words of courtesy—all silent as to the momentous future—Elijah simply says—"Go (or return) back again—for what have I done to thee?" 'Go!' as if he said—'But speedily return; for thou understandest well the token;—thou art from this hour the accredited messenger of God,—the consecrated seer of Israel.' Again, without venturing to reply, Elisha hastens to his home hard by, and communicates to his parents the startling tidings. In a brief hour, the destiny of a whole life is changed. In accordance with true patriarchal wont, the Prophet-elect assembles for the last time, around the domestic hearth, the faithful associates in his daily toils! A farewell meal must be partaken of by all. Father, mother, son, servants, seat themselves around the homely board; each heart, we can readily believe, filled with profound emotion.

In connexion with the feast, there occurs, in that dispensation of symbolism, another significant typical act. Elisha's agricultural labours are to be renounced for ever; he is to put his hand to a different plough, and never more to "look back." There must be some expressive outward token of that abandonment. The animals which he had driven before him in plough and harrow, are slain. The implements of husbandry are used as fuel to prepare their flesh for the entertainment. The very harness and tackling are thrown into the fire, to complete the symbol of entire and unqualified renunciation.

The feast is over. The long parting kiss is given to affectionate parents;—the father's blessing is received and returned;—and then, forth goes the ordained Prophet on his predestined mission. On overtaking his master, he immediately begins his lowly offices of ministration. We may picture in thought the two, journeying on in company to the cities of Samaria, encouraging one another in the Lord their God.

Among other practical lessons suggested by the calling of Elisha, let us note, *the variety of character among God's servants.* Never were there two individuals more opposite than these two lights of this age in Israel,—alike in training and in mental temperament. The one—as we have more fully delineated him in the opening chapter—was the rough child of the desert, without recorded parentage or lineage. His congenial and appropriate home the wilds of Cherith—the thunder-gloom of Carmel—the shade of the wilderness juniper—the awful cliffs of Sinai;—a direct messenger of wrath from heaven—THE PROPHET OF FIRE! The other, is trained and nurtured under the roof of a genial home,—mingling daily in the interchange of domestic affection—loving and beloved. No ambitious thought had he beyond his patrimonial acres;—tending his parents in their old age; ministering to their wants; and, when the time came, laying their dust in the sepulchre of his fathers. Even his physical appearance is in striking contrast with that of the other. In the future glimpses we have of his outer life, we look in vain for the stately mien and shaggy raven locks and rough hairy dress of the Bedouin. If we are most familiar with the one in rocky wilds, caves,—deserts,—mountain solitudes; we are so, with the other, among the homesteads of Israel, or leading a city-life, as a foster-father, among the schools of the prophets. If the one has been likened to the sun,—the other has the softened lustre of the moon, or of the quiet evening star. If the one be like his great future successor, "laying the axe to the root of the tree,"—making the thronging crowds tremble and cower under words of doom;—the other is surely a faint but lovely reflection of the Baptist's greater Lord, who would not "break the bruised reed nor quench the smoking flax;" loving ever to deal, in the case of sensitive consciences, with the utmost tenderness; as we see exemplified in his treatment of Naaman's scruples to bow with his master in the temple of Rimmon. Their very names stand in emphatic contrast. The one meaning either, as we have previously noted, "My God, the Lord," or else, perhaps, "The strength of God," or "The strong Lord;"—*strength*, the lion-symbol, being specially associated with the deeds of Elijah. The other, Eli-sha, "God is my Saviour," or, "God my salvation." If the Tishbite's motto was "Jehovah, the strong Lord, liveth,"—Elisha's might appropriately be that of a lowly saint of coming days, "My soul doth magnify the Lord, my spirit hath rejoiced in GOD MY SAVIOUR." The two, moreover, were raised up for different objects, and each possessed special qualifications for his appointed work. The one was a *destroyer;*—Baal, the reputed "lord of *force*" or "*power*," had, as we have seen, usurped the place and prerogative of Jehovah. Elijah's task was to overturn this false deity of force, and shew, by startling miracle and judgment, that "POWER *belongeth unto God.*" Elisha was *the healer;*—beneficence tracked his path. As his master's career was inaugurated with a miracle of drought and famine,—his, on the contrary, was inaugurated by the healing of the waters at Jericho, and the warding off the curse of barrenness! In a word, the one was the "Boanerges" of his time;—a "Son of Thunder!" the other was

Barnabas, "the Son of Consolation." The one stands before us "the man of like passions." The other, the man of like sensibilities.

And there are the same remarkable, the same beautiful diversities, to this hour, in the Church of Christ. As in external nature, a forest is not made up of the same trees,—or if the same in kind, each individual tree assumes its own peculiar shape; as every garden has its diversity of flower and shrub; as each field has its varied crop,—all different, yet all ministering to the common necessities of man; as each face has its varied features, with countless varieties of expression; and each body its varied organs—yet all necessary for the completeness of the frame;—so, we trace the same singular yet beautiful diversity in the moral and intellectual and spiritual character of God's servants. Moreover, He adapts them for their varied positions and posts of usefulness in His Church. To every man his work. Luther and Knox—the Elijahs of their times,—had *their* vocation in preparing the way for the Zuingles and Melancthons—the gentler messengers of peace;—blasting the rocks,—digging out the rough, unshapely, unhewn block,—to put it into the hands of these more refined sculptors to polish into shape and beauty. He has men whose province it is to carry the assault into the enemies' works by bold word and deed;—those distinguished for organisation;—ingenious in device for the outward lengthening of the cords and strengthening of the stakes of Zion. He has others, whose vocation is neither pulpit nor platform,—synod nor council,—ecclesiastical debate nor stern polemics;—but the quiet duties of the study or the closet;—men who are thinking while others are acting,—doing in their own way a secret work, without noise or ostentation;—who could not stand the shouts and clamour of Carmel,—thankful that there are Elijahs who can;—but who love rather to carry their influence amid the homes of Israel, and amid the schools of the prophets. Thank God for this unity in diversity, and diversity in unity. The division of labour, so needful in social and economic life, is illustrated with equal beauty in the diversity of gifts and operations in the Church of Christ: each, in his own way and sphere, labouring for one common end. In the building of the temple of old, the rough mountaineers of Lebanon were as much needed to hew down the cedar trees, as Hiram of Tyre's cunning workmen to prepare and cast the mouldings of brass, and carve the delicate interlacings of gold. Let us never depreciate one spiritual workman's avocation at the expense of another. Every "hammer, and axe, and tool of iron" is required to shape, and cast, and mould the varied parts; but all are tending to one ultimate object—the bringing forth of the "topstone with shouting," when the cry shall be made—"Grace, grace unto it!"

Although, however, we have spoken of the contrast in the mental temperaments of these two great Prophets, let us not therefore regard them as unkindred, uncongenial, antagonistic. We know how much the reverse was the case; how tender the sympathetic bond which united them. Opposite in character, they knew that they were embarked in one great and glorious work. As months rolled on, the golden link of friendship became stronger;—and when the last parting of all arrived, it is manifest how fondly the man of rough visage and iron will, clung to the loving heart from which he was about to be parted. See how these brethren love one another!

We may gather, as a second lesson, *the honour God puts on the ordinary secular occupations of life.* Elisha is found, —not engaged in temple worship in Jerusalem or Samaria, not even in meditation and prayer in the retirement of his father's dwelling, but at his plough,—driving before him his team of oxen. This is another of the reiterated lessons in Scripture as to the dignity and sacredness of labour, and the divine recognition of it. Moses was called to his high commission whilst in charge of the flocks of Jethro his father-in-law. Gideon, the great champion of his age, was called to be the instrument in overthrowing the gigantic power of Midian, while threshing wheat with his father's bullocks at the wine-press of Ophrah. The announcement of the Saviour's birth was made to the shepherds of Bethlehem while tending their flocks; and to the sages of Arabia while gazing on their eastern stars. Matthew, the apostle and evangelist, was summoned to attend his great Master while collecting the harbour dues at the port of Capernaum. Peter, and John, and Andrew, while busied with their boats and nets, were called to become fishers of men. Never let us imagine honourable employment in this work-day world to be incompatible with religious duty. God, in all these and other instances, sanctifies daily avocation and toil. Our worldly callings need not, and ought not, to interfere with the paramount claims of religion in the heart and life. The one rather should assist, stimulate, dignify, and elevate the other. Such secular pursuits indeed, are not to be confounded with an unreasonable and unseasonable entanglement with "the cares of this life,"—when religion is chased—hunted out of every chamber of the soul,—with the lash of engrossing worldliness;—when business or pleasure is suffered so to monopolise, that nothing but the merest crumbs and sweepings of existence can be spared for the claims of God and eternity. But if work and duty be faithfully and honestly intermingled;—diligence in worldly business, the faithful discharge of worldly claims, the engagement in active earthly pursuits and callings, ought to prove, and will prove, rather a stimulus to fervency in spirit, serving the Lord.

Once more—observe, in the case of Elisha and his parents, *the spirit of joyful self-sacrifice manifested at the call of duty.* Great, undoubtedly, as was the honour of becoming the consecrated prophet of God;—we cannot think of his acceptance of the high office, without, at the same time, having suggested the idea of self-renunciation. Judging from the brief narrative, he was no candidate for such honours. He had all which the world could give to make him happy. In his case the prayer of Agur had been fulfilled to the letter. He seemed to be in the enjoyment of an ample—a more than ample—competency. The heir of a small patrimonal inheritance in one of the rich plains of Gilead;—twelve pair of oxen and servants at his command;—a home, with the most hallowed of ties to bind him to his roof-tree,—the parents from whose lips he had been taught to fear and reverence that God to whom his public life was now to be consecrated. Then add to all this, not only did the severance and relinquishment of these dear family ties involve a struggle, but, in accepting the call of the great Prophet, he was placing himself in circumstances of formidable peril. He was abandoning a sphere of quiet, uninvaded seclusion, for the arena of public life;—exposing himself to the implacable resentment of Jezebel and her minions, whose fury had become more ungovernable than ever, since the recent discomfiture at Carmel. But there is not so much as one hesitating thought;—no converse with flesh and blood; —no tampering with expediency. The call was from God. There was no gainsaying it. In a moment, the most cherished objects, thoughts, hopes of life are surrendered; and he prepares to set out on his arduous calling. Nor does he even manifest, in this last hour spent under the home of his childhood and youth, the natural struggle which, in a heart like his, must have taken place. He keeps all sentimental feelings in abeyance. There is no moping sadness. He makes it even a joyous occasion. He hastily assembles parents, neighbours, friends, servants, around the social board, and bids an affectionate farewell. We have already noted the pledge of entire self-surrender, lest his heart might be tempted to yield to home influences in that trying hour. He not only kills the oxen; but ropes and tackle, plough and harrow, are cast into the flames. Like his true apostolic successors, he leaves *all* to consecrate himself to God. In a noble sense, he "denies himself, takes up his cross, and follows." But to him, as to all who have imbibed his spirit and copied his example, the great promise was fulfilled—"Verily I say unto you, There is no man that hath left house, or parents, or brethren, or wife, or children for the kingdom of God's sake, who shall not receive manifold more in this present time; and in the world to come, life everlasting."

Nor is it Elisha's conduct only that is worthy of note. That aged pair, who for years had fondly doted on a son all worthy of their affection, manifest an equally beautiful spirit of willing self-surrender. We have every reason to think of him as the prop and pride of their old age. Among the last thoughts that aged man and his wife entertained, was that of being severed from this light of their dwelling—the nourisher of their old age! With what fond interest would he daily be followed as he left the household. How would his footfall be joyfully welcomed, as he returned in the gray twilight to stall his oxen, and pen his flocks. Sad would be the day when either duty or death should render vacant his chair at the family hearth. That day has come. In a moment,—in the twinkling of an eye,—the parents are informed that the unexpected blow is impending;—that one plough less is hereafter to be seen in the plain;—that another voice has called him for a son; and that, henceforth, the quiet scenes of the Jordan valley are to be exchanged for the toil and anxiety of an exalted station. Do they remonstrate? Do they lay an arresting hand on him as he now stands before them, probably in the pride of full manhood, and plead, with tears, —their age—home claims—filial and parental love? No! Whatever may have been *felt*, not a tear is shed. It is the voice of God calling their loved one to a glorious, honoured work. If one misgiving come over them, as at that farewell feast they think of a happy past, and glance forward to the blank of the future;—their eyes rest on the hairy cloak of the man of God—mute but expressive symbol!

'Go, go, my son,' would be the words stammered forth from trembling lips, 'for the Lord hath called thee. "His work is honourable and glorious, and His righteousness endureth for ever!"'

What a lesson for us, this abnegation of self for God and duty. What *have we* surrendered of our worldly ease, our pleasures, our money, our children, our advantages, for Him and His cause? What have we done to disarm the power of besetting sins,—by cutting off, like Elisha, the occasion of them,—saying, 'Let oxen, implements, tackling, all go, and perish in the flames, if they rob our hearts of Christ, or Christ of our hearts?' Matthew locked the door of his toll-house behind him: he would never enter it again. The magicians of Ephesus burnt their magical books that they might never more incur the risk of being involved in their sorceries. And, if we be Christians indeed,—the disciples and followers of the Lord Jesus;—if a greater than Elijah has "passed by," and thrown the cloak of consecration around us;—as "priests unto God"—conscious of our high calling and destiny—be it ours, with some feeble measure of the apostle's lofty spirit of self-surrender, to say, "Yea, doubtless, I count all things but loss for the excellency of the knowledge of Christ Jesus my Lord."

XVI.

Naboth's Vineyard.

"And the word of the Lord came to Elijah the Tishbite saying, Arise, go down to meet Ahab king of Israel, which is in Samaria: behold, he is in the vineyard of Naboth, whither he is gone down to possess it. And thou shalt speak unto him, saying, Thus saith the Lord, Hast thou killed, and also taken possession? And thou shalt speak unto him, saying, Thus saith the Lord, In the place where dogs licked the blood of Naboth shall dogs lick thy blood, even thine. And Ahab said to Elijah, Hast thou found me, O mine enemy? And he answered, I have found thee: because thou hast sold thyself to work evil in the sight of the Lord."—1 KINGS xxi. 17-20.

"AND THEY COVET FIELDS, AND TAKE THEM BY VIOLENCE; AND HOUSES, AND TAKE THEM AWAY: SO THEY OPPRESS A MAN AND HIS HOUSE, EVEN A MAN AND HIS HERITAGE. THEREFORE THUS SAITH THE LORD, BEHOLD, AGAINST THIS FAMILY DO I DEVISE AN EVIL, FROM WHICH YE SHALL NOT REMOVE YOUR NECKS; NEITHER SHALL YE GO HAUGHTILY: FOR THIS TIME IS EVIL."—MICAH I. 2, 3.

NABOTH'S VINEYARD.

OUR narrative once more brings us in contact with Ahab, king of Israel, whom we now find in his palace of Samaria.* How changed since last we beheld him entering in state the gates of Jezreel,—the stalwart Prophet running before,—full of joyous hope! Now he lies on a bed in one of the royal chambers in helpless dejection,—moaning and tossing in feverish and restless misery. What catastrophe has overtaken that regal mourner?—why that settled gloom on these regal brows? Has the hand of death been in the palace halls?—has one of the princes of the blood royal been borne to the sepulchre of the kings of Israel—and left the aching void of bereavement in that smitten heart? Or, has it been some sudden overwhelming national disaster? Have the billows of war swept over his territories?—is the tramp of Benhadad's conquering armies heard at his gates, threatening to desolate his valleys, and carry the flower of his subjects captive to Damascus? No, no. His family circle is unbroken; and the trophies of recent victory adorn his walls. It is a far more insignificant cause which has led the weak and unworthy monarch to wrap himself in that coverlet, and to pout and fret like a petulant child. This lordly possessor of palaces

* A careful reader will gather that Ahab and his Queen were now residing at Samaria, twenty-five miles distant from Jezreel.

cannot obtain a little vineyard he has coveted;—and life is, forsooth, for the moment, embittered to him. Lamentable, but too truthful picture of human nature! Here is a King; —a man at the proud pinnacles of human ambition,—the owner of vast territories,—the possessor of one of the most princely of demesnes,—his ivory palace perched on the wooded slopes of Gilboa—looking across the wide fertile plain of Esdraelon. What our own Windsor is to Britain, or Versailles to France, so was this Jezreel, with its noble undulating grounds, to the kingdom of Israel. Even amid the miserable mud-huts of the modern Zerîn, the traveller can picture, from the unchanged features of the site, what the beauty of that summer park and palace must have been.* But on the outskirts of this regal domain, there happened to be one small patch of ground, the hereditary possession of a Jezreelite of the name of Naboth;† and on the occasion of one of the royal visits to this favourite hunting-seat, the eye of the king has lighted upon it. Its acquisition seems so de-

* "The village stands on an isolated rock, which may be said to be the most northern projection of Gilboa. There is no spot in the whole extent of the plain which offers so wide a view as this rock. From this point are seen Carmel, and the mountains of Nazareth—little Hermon and the hill of Bashan and Gilead—the heights of Gilboa and the lofty ridges of Shechem and Samaria. . . . Ahab certainly chose the best possible place for his royal residence."—*Van de Velde*, vol. ii., p. 370.—"An old square tower is in the centre, which in many respects much resembles one of our own Border strongholds, such as Hermitage Castle or Norham, only by no means so large or high. . . . To the east rise the mountains of Gilead, on either side of Jordan. From these hills the Prophet Elijah could see distinctly this palace of Ahab, and beyond it that Carmel to which he so often resorted."—*Dr Bonar's Land of Promise.*

† "The south-eastern fountain, Ain Zalûd, about a mile from the village, may very probably mark the site of the vineyard of Naboth."—*Ibid.*

sirable, that he resolves to have it at any cost, either by purchase or excambion. In the true spirit of an Israelite, however, Naboth rejects the royal proposal to alienate his patrimonial acres. Without palliating Ahab's puerile conduct, we may, at first sight indeed, deem that Naboth was an uncourteous, if not a disloyal subject, in thus thwarting the royal wishes;—that it would, at all events, have been no more than a becoming and graceful deference to the will of his sovereign, at once to surrender the desired possession. A little consideration, however, not only justifies Naboth's determined refusal, but greatly aggravates Ahab's guilt in urging the transaction. The soil of Israel belonged neither to Ahab nor Naboth, but to JEHOVAH. By the law of Moses, the owner of that vineyard at Jezreel was rigidly prohibited from parting with his paternal inheritance. Even in the case where debt necessitated a temporary transfer of property, that transfer was always coupled with the condition that the land could be redeemed at any time by the original and inalienable possessor; and, moreover, even without money redemption, it again reverted to him on the arrival of the year of jubilee.* When Naboth therefore rejected Ahab's offer, it was not on the ground of personal disinclination, far less in a fit of dogged obstinacy. There was nothing of churlish rudeness—no boorish discourtesy in his reply. With the calm self-possession of one who acted from high religious principle, he thus grounds his refusal, "The Lord forbid it me that I should give the inheritance of my fathers unto thee." We may not indeed altogether exclude the influence of personal considerations on Naboth's conduct.

* Lev. xxv. 13; Num. xxxvi. 7.

Like other Jews, he was doubtless deeply attached to the heritage of his ancestors. His vineyard would be a spot endeared by sacred associations. It had been the hallowed haunt of childhood;—the cradle of his earliest recollections. On these mountains of Gilead and Samaria, childhood's eye had gazed. Childhood's ear had drunk delight from the murmurs of the still existing fountain. Seated under the purple clusters of its trellised vines, he may have listened to instruction from reverenced lips. More than all,—the honoured dust of his sires doubtless reposed in some adjoining rocky cave; and holy memories would endear his "inheritance" beyond the compensation of all Ahab's gold.

But this, we repeat, was not his main motive in refusal; it was the resolve of a high-minded patriot Israelite, to fear his God, even though in doing so he should incur the displeasure of his king. That little ancestral plot of ground he felt to be his by a divine tenure. Infeft by Jehovah himself, and loyal to a Greater than Ahab, he had no alternative left him in dealing with the regal bribe. All honour to this noble-minded citizen, who resisted the talents and the royal smiles that would tamper with his conscience and his duty. We shall think of him as one of the seven thousand who loved, from his inmost soul, the God of his fathers, and refused to kiss the shrine of Baal. A pattern is he, to the many in every age, who would too often sacrifice principle and right on the altar of worldly policy; and, by base expediency, truckle to power and patronage. In these days, when we collect photographs of the great and good among our contemporaries, we may well find room for this bold sturdy peasant or vinedresser of Jezreel,—enrol him among the number of our moral heroes, and write under his name the motto—"*I must obey God rather than man.*"

But what is conscientious scruple? It is a myth and delusion to a mind blinded and demoralised like that of Ahab. He leaps in a passion into his chariot. As he drives back that long twenty-five miles to Samaria, it is with his countenance fallen. His wishes have been thwarted,—his royalty insulted,—his dignity compromised,—his will gainsayed,—his pride injured,—by a petty subordinate. The result is, he is *miserable;*—all his redundant possessions appear nothing, because he cannot call that patch of ground his own. Unworthy of a king,—unworthy of a man,—he flings himself on his bed, and sobs out to himself the tale of this most miserable disappointed ambition!

Is there no way by which these unroyal tears may be wiped away, and the coveted possession be yet obtained? If Ahab himself lack the moral courage to compass the wish by some foul and dastard deed, is there no one in the courtly circle who can gratify him, by means which imperious wills have often adopted before—cutting in two that conscientious scruple with the sword? One there was, able and willing for the task. Jezebel, who, as we already know, had inherited all the bold passions and oriental vices of her father, was the very heroine for the emergency. Quick as thought, she devises her accursed plot. By a series of easily planned perjuries, the royal equanimity will soon be restored; the royal park and pleasure-grounds soon have the desired appendage; and, what was better to her vindictive nature, Naboth shall learn at what cost he spurns the royal wish, and questions the royal prerogative. Getting into her possession the king's signet-ring, to give the appearance of a regal mandate to her proclamation, she causes letters to be written to the nobles and elders of Jezreel, to proclaim a fast; attainting Naboth at the same time of high treason—the charge to be supported by two suborned witnesses. Never was queen-craft more apparently triumphant and successful. Once get that recusant citizen accused of blasphemy, and, by a divine law, the property of the blasphemer and rebel reverts to the crown. Ahab, by an old statute, would become at once lawful lord of this petty vineyard. Two depraved men are induced without difficulty to perjure themselves, in order to compass the destruction of an innocent man. A fast is proclaimed. It is a hideous mockery in the name of religion. "A fast!" as if some dire disaster, in the shape of famine, pestilence, or war, impended over the city, or some dire sin needed expiation. The two "sons of Belial,"—the bribed witnesses who charged Naboth with the fictitious crime,—demand from the people summary vengeance on his head. He had "blasphemed God and the king"—the King as the visible representative of God. He had incurred the terrible penalties annexed to the boldest of transgressions, "Thou shalt not curse God, nor revile a prince among thy people."* O Justice! under thy sacred name how many crimes have been perpetrated;—how many traitors to sacred truth have dragged the innocent to destruction! It does give a terrible picture of the moral debasement at this period of Israel's history, that so many were to be found among nobles and elders—(the privileged classes,—the aristocracy of their day)—to aid and abet in so foul a deed. Not even one voice was raised in

* Exod. xxvii. 27.

protest against the enormous wickedness. No wonder, after weaving such a network of deceit as this, that Jezebel's name should have been handed down from generation to generation as the symbol and by-word of all that is execrable;—that it should be used in the last book of the inspired volume, by lips which cannot lie, as the emblem of wild fanaticism and licentiousness.*

The deed is done. The exasperated rabble have dragged Naboth out of the city, and "stoned him with stones;" and, as we learn subsequently, his innocent family were simultaneously involved in the cold-blooded massacre.† The king loses no time in forthwith claiming the wages of unrighteousness. He confiscates Naboth's goods; the coveted vineyard has lapsed into his hands. "And Ahab," we read, "rose up to go down (*i.e.*, from Samaria to Jezreel) to the vineyard of Naboth the Jezreelite to take possession of it." Yes, the plot had succeeded to a wish—a triumph of female sagacity. Not one noble or elder had divulged the terrible secret, which had given the semblance of legality to atrocious villainy. The bones of the murdered were heaped out of sight in some forgotten grave; and what was perhaps more than anything else to Ahab, Elijah was now, as he imagined, out of the way. He had heard nothing lately of his old troubler and tormentor.

* Rev. ii. 20, 21.

† "The blood of Naboth and the blood of his sons," (2 Kings ix. 26, compare Josh. vii. 24.) "From another expression in this verse 'yesternight,' we may perhaps conclude that, like a later trial on a similar charge, also supported by two false witnesses—the trial of our Lord—it was conducted at night. The same word, 'yesternight,' prompts the inference that Ahab's visit and encounter with Elijah happened on the very day following the murder."—*See note, Smith's Dictionary,* p. 529.

Perhaps some confused story had reached him of the wilderness flight;—that in a fit of misanthropic spleen, the Prophet had turned at once coward and hermit, and was spending the dregs of a fanatic life in the untrodden wilds of the Arabian desert. The king's fleet horses bear him along the highway to take formal possession of his dear-bought possession.* He enters the gates, and is already planning how this aceldama—this "field of blood"—can be turned to the greatest advantage. Ah, he hears it not! The dulled ear of conscience is closed; but the voice of Naboth's blood is crying from the ground, "O God, to whom vengeance belongeth, shew thyself."

Soon is the prayer heard. There was one close by, whose presence he little dreamt of;—one who had last conducted him in triumph, after a day of miracle and grace, to these same gates of Jezreel. Now he stands before him the messenger of wrath—"the Prophet of Fire"—an incarnate spirit of evil tidings. It is ELIJAH!—his own great, bold, brave self again: no longer daunted and panic-stricken by Jezebel, and ready, when his malison is delivered, to gird himself for flight. The prediction of Ahab's awful end might indeed well have struck fresh terror into his heart as he uttered it.

* "In the days of the kings of Israel it was the great highway from the south to the north of the country. The large stones with which that highway was laid still lie there, although for the most part broken up and thrown aside. It is not of Roman but of ancient Israelitish make; the large stones plainly indicate this, for the Roman causewaying of the roads in Palestine may be generally distinguished by their smaller quadrangular stones. . . . Ahab and . . . Elijah must often have passed along this road. And it must also have been trodden by the blessed feet of our Lord Jesus Christ in journeying from Galilee to Jerusalem, and from Jerusalem back to Galilee."—*Van de Velde,* vol. i., p. 370.

But he is another man since we recently met him in the Sinai desert. The frenzied queen may again vow vengeance as she pleases; he will not shrink from duty. The old visions of Horeb—the wind, and earthquake, and fire,—proclaim in his ears that "*Jehovah liveth.*" A career of unblushing impiety, on the part of Ahab, had now culminated in the most hideous of crimes, and the Herald of vengeance delivers unabashed his message. It is one of his former rapid, sudden, meteor-like appearances. Without warning or premonition, he confronts Ahab, like the ghostly shadow of the monarch's own guilty conscience; and, with a tongue of FIRE, flashes upon him the accusation—"Hast thou killed, and also taken possession?" We know not a grander subject for a great picture than this;—the hero-prophet standing erect before the ghastly, terror-stricken king; breaking through the barriers of court etiquette, and caring only for the glory of the God he served and the good of Israel, charging him with the murderer's guilt, and pronouncing upon him the murderer's awful doom.* The trembling monarch, awaking in a moment from his dream of iniquity to a sense of the presence which confronted him, shrieks aloud—"Hast thou found me, O mine enemy." "I *have* found thee," is the reply, "because

* The Jewish prophets were, in the best sense of the word, the guardians of public and social morality. Lamartine happily calls them "the sacred tribunes of the people," and represents the influence they exercised as corresponding with the modern power of the press. "Setting aside their divine commission," says the gifted living historian of the Jews, "the prophets were the great constitutional patriots of the Jewish state, the champions of virtue, liberty, justice, and the strict observance of the civil and religious law against the iniquities of the king and the people. They are always on the side of the oppressed. They boldly rebuke but never

thou hast sold thyself to work evil in the sight of the Lord." And then he proceeds to deliver the terrible sentence—The sword was to avenge the blood of the innocent. His family, root and branch, were to be extirpated;—the wild dogs of the city and the winged vultures of heaven should banquet on the flesh of his sons! The king cowered in despair. He rent his clothes, put sackcloth on his flesh, and in bitter misery bewailed, when it was too late, his aggravated sin. So heartfelt, however, was this agony of remorse, that the God he had insulted graciously respites his sentence. For three years, opportunity was given him, though in vain, for a fuller repentance and amendment, ere the weapon of deferred retribution descends. But the day of vengeance comes at last. At the end of that period, in going up to battle, to Ramoth-Gilead, he is mortally wounded. In a crimson pool, at the foot of the chariot, he lies in the last convulsions of ebbing life—"The chariot was washed in the fountain of Samaria, and the dogs licked his blood!"

Jezebel's end was more signal and appalling still. At that moment, which we have described, when Ahab entered to take possession of the vineyard of Naboth, two pages were seated at the back of his chariot, who overheard the stormy interview between him and the Prophet. The words Elijah

factiously insult their kings. They defend, but never flatter the passions of the people. In no instance does one of the acknowledged seers, like the turbulent demagogues of the Grecian or Roman republics, abuse his popular influence for his own personal aggrandisement or authority. . . . . Though false prophets might escape by dexterously flattering the powerful, the bold and honest discharge of the office demanded the highest zeal and intrepidity. Of all the prophets none united such distinguished qualifications or was so highly qualified as ELIJAH."—*Milman's History of the Jews, in loco.*

then uttered, sank deep into the heart and memory of one of these. It was Jehu the son of Nimshi. And when, from the position of an attendant he rose to the dignity of a conqueror, and entered with a triumphant army the streets of Jezreel;—though twenty long years had elapsed, he seems neither to have forgotten nor misunderstood his commission, as the scourge of God, and the avenger of innocent blood. When the Queen, savage and debased as ever, tried first by meretricious arts, and then by insult, to conquer or defy her invader, the blood of the incensed warrior rose in his veins; by his orders, she was thrown from her window outside the city wall—trampled under feet of the horses, and torn to pieces by the dogs.

"Go," said the merciless conqueror, "Go, see now this cursed woman, and bury her, for she is a king's daughter; and they went to bury her, but they found no more of her than the skull and the feet, and the palms of the hands. Wherefore they came again and told him, and he said, This is the word of the Lord, which he spake by his servant, Elijah the Tishbite, saying, In the portion of Jezreel shall dogs eat the flesh of Jezebel."

There are many voices addressed to us from Naboth's vineyard.

One of these is—*Beware of covetousness.* That vineyard has its counterpart in the case and conduct of many still. Covetousness may assume a thousand cameleon hues and phases, but these all resolve themselves into a sinful craving after something other than what we have. Covetousness of *means*—a grasping after more material wealth;

the race for riches. Covetousness of *place*—aspiring after other positions in life than those which Providence has assigned us;—not because they are *better*—but because they are *other* than our present God-appointed lot—invested with an *imaginary superiority*. And the singular and sad thing is, that such inordinate longings are most frequently manifested, as with Ahab, in the case of those who have least cause to indulge them. The covetous eye cast on the neighbour's vineyard is, (strange to say,) more the sin of the affluent than of the needy,—of the owner of the lordly mansion than of the humble cottage. The man with his clay floor, and thatched roof, and rude wooden rafters, though standing far more in need of increase to his comfort, is often (is generally) more contented and satisfied by far than he whose cup is full. The old story, which every schoolboy knows, is a faithful picture of human nature. It was Alexander, not defeated, but victorious—Alexander, not the lord of one kingdom, but the sovereign of the world, who wept unsatisfied tears. Ahab had everything that human ambition could desire. The cities of Israel his father had lost, had been all restored;—peace was within his walls, and prosperity within his palaces. His residences were unparalleled for beauty. His lordly park and demesne and gardens at Jezreel—stretching for miles on every side of the city—had every rare tree and plant and flower to adorn them. But what pride or pleasure has he now in all these? Plants bloom, and birds sing, and fountains sparkle, in vain. So long as that one patch of vineyard-ground belonging to Naboth is denied him, his whole pleasure is blighted. He cannot brook that insult of refusal. It has stung him to the quick, and sends him to pout and fret, in unroyal tears, on his couch in Samaria!

How many there are, surrounded with all possible affluence and comfort, who put a life-thorn in their side by some similar chase after a denied good, some similar fretting about a denied trifle. They have abundance; the horn of plenty has poured its contents into their lap. But a neighbour possesses something which they fancy *they* might have also. Like Haman, though their history has been a golden dream of prosperity;—advancement and honour such as the brightest visions of youth could never have pictured,—yet all this avails them nothing, so long as they see Mordecai the Jew sitting at the king's gate!

Seek to suppress these unworthy envious longings. "For which things' sake," says the apostle, (and among "these things" is *covetousness,*) "the wrath of God cometh on the children of disobedience." Covetousness, God makes a synonym for idolatry. He classes the covetous in the same category with the worshippers of stocks and stones. "Be content with such things as ye have." Paul was ever sound in philosophy as in religion;—his ethical, as well as his theological system, is one worthy of our profoundest study and imitation. Here is one of his maxims—"I have learned in whatever state I am therewith to be content. I know both how to be abased, and I know how to abound; every where, and in all things; I am instructed both to be full and to be hungry, both to abound and to suffer need." The secret of his contentment was, that he was possessor of those "true riches," which made him independent of all worldly honours and gains and distinctions. "I have coveted," says he, "no man's silver or gold or apparel." Why? because he had nobler treasures than the mines of the earth could yield or its looms fabricate. Having Christ for his portion, he could say—"I have ALL and abound." The vineyard which he coveted, was that which "God's own right hand had planted, and the Branch he had made strong for Himself!" Be assured that carping discontent will grow, if you feed it, till it comes to eat out the kernel of life's happiness;—a discontented manhood or womanhood culminating in that saddest of conditions, a peevish old age. In other sorrows, (the real trials of life,) the heart is upheld and solaced by sympathy, and by the nobler consolations of God's truth. But who or what could minister to a mind thus diseased? Who could pity the soul whining and murmuring in the midst of plenty? Who could throw away balm-words of comfort on those piercing themselves through with many sorrows, when these sorrows are chimeras—ghosts of their own discontented brain? As you value your peace, exorcise the foul fiend. Let Naboth alone in *his* vineyard, and enjoy *yours* just as it is. Impose not self-inflicted torture by longing for what you are better without. When shall we be taught in this grasping, avaricious, unsatisfied age, that a man's life, (his true being—his manhood—his glory,) consisteth not "in the abundance of the things which he possesseth!"

Another of the voices from Naboth's vineyard' is—*Keep out of the way of temptation.* If Ahab, knowing his own weakness and besetting sin, had put a restraint on his covetous eye, and not allowed it to stray on his neighbour's forbidden property, it would have saved a black page in his history, and the responsibilities of a heinous crime. Let us beware of tampering with evil. "If thy right eye offend thee, pluck it out, and cast it from thee." "Avoid it," says the wise man, speaking of this path of temptation, "pass not by it, turn from it, and pass away." If Achan had not cast his eye on the goodly Babylonish garment, the shekels of silver, and the wedge of gold, he would have saved Israel a bloody discomfiture and himself a fearful end. But he *saw* them; and the sight fed and fostered and stimulated the covetous master-passion,—the latent avarice of his greedy heart. It was David's wandering eye that led to the twin crime of adultery and murder. He, too, ventured to the place of temptation. He had become an idler when he should have been a worker. The old, heroic, chivalrous days were over, when he would have despised luxurious ease, and been away rather to share the hardships of his brave army then in the field. Instead of this, he was basking in inglorious unsolderlike fashion, after his noontide meal, on the roof of his palace. He was *out* of the way of duty, and *in* the way of temptation; and one fatal look, and one fatal thought, entailed a heritage of bitter sorrow on himself and on his children's children. Each has his own strong temptation,—the fragile part of his nature,—his besetting sin. That sin should be specially watched, muzzled, curbed;—that gate of temptation specially padlocked and sentinelled. One guilty dereliction of duty,—one unhappy abandonment of principle,—one inconsistent, thoughtless word or deed,—may be the progenitor of unnumbered evils. How many have bartered their peace of conscience for veriest trifles;—sold a richer inheritance than Esau's birthright for a mess of earthly pottage! And once the first fatal step is taken, it cannot be so easily undone. Once the blot on fair character is made, the stain is not so easily erased. Ahab's first and irretrievable blunder, was dated long anterior to the coveting of the vineyard. We have before noted that his thoughtless, unlawful, unprincipled union with a heathen princess, whose father's name and throne were blackened with infamy, was the commencement of his downward career,—the first instalment of that price, by which, we read, "he *sold* himself to work iniquity." He would never, in any circumstance, have been a great man; he had no native vigour or independence of character for that; but, under better fostering influences, he might have been moulded into a useful one. His facile, vacillating nature, might, by a better plastic power, have been brought to incline to the side of virtue. But Jezebel was his evil genius. He was a mere puppet in her hands. She took anything that was noble and generous from him,—instigating him only to execrable deeds. His better self surrendered to her base artifices, he became a depraved, effeminate weakling.

What we have already said, in a previous chapter, regarding the marriage union, is equally applicable to all business and social connexions. How many, in the formation of these, by looking merely to worldly advantages, make shipwreck of faith and of a good conscience! How many a young man has been lured, by the prospect of money-recompense, where his religious principles will be tampered with, or where he will be in danger of conniving at dishonest gains! The high sense of honour and integrity once lost or compromised, he becomes an easy prey to base arts,—underhand, dishonourable ways, and double dealings. No worldly gains or position can make up for the absence of true wealth of character and principle. All that Phœnician riches could secure or lavish, followed the Sidonian princess to her Hebrew home in Samaria. But what of this? Under that Tyrian purple there lurked a heart, which turned all she had into counterfeit and base alloy. Oh, rather far, the poorest, lowliest, most unostentatious lot, with character unsoiled, than gilded ceilings and array of servants, plate, and equipage, where the nobler element of moral riches is wanting. Rather the crust of bread and the crippled means, with unsullied principle and priceless virtue, than all that boundless wealth can procure without them.

Another voice from Naboth's vineyard is—*Be sure your sin will find you out.* Ahab and Jezebel, as we have seen, had managed to a wish their accursed plot. The wheels of crime had moved softly along without one rut or impediment in the way. The two murderers paced their blood-stained inheritance without fear of challenge or discovery. Naboth was in that silent land where no voice of protest can be heard against high-handed iniquity. But there was a God in heaven who maketh inquisition for blood, and who "remembered them." Their time for retribution *did* come at last, although years of gracious forbearance were suffered to intervene. As we behold the mutilated remains of that once proud, unscrupulous queen, lying in the common receptacle of offal and carrion outside the city of her iniquities, her blood sprinkling the walls;—or, in the case of the partner of her guilt, as we see the arrow from the Syrian bow piercing through "the jointed mail,"—or as he lies weltering in his blood—his eyes closing in agony—the wild dogs, by the pool of Samaria, lick the crimson drops from the wheels of his chariot and the plates of his armour;—have we not before us a solemn and awful comment on the words of Him who "judgeth righteous judgment:"—"These things hast thou done, and I kept silence; thou thoughtest that I was altogether such an one as thyself: but I will reprove thee, and set them in order before thine eyes. Now consider this, ye that forget God, lest I tear you in pieces, and there be none to deliver." * "He that, being often reproved, hardeneth his neck, shall suddenly be destroyed, and that without remedy." †

And are the principles of God's moral government different now? It is true, indeed, that the present economy deals not so exclusively as the old in temporal retribution. Sinners now have before them the surer and more terrible recompense and vengeance of a world to come. But not unfrequently here also, retribution still follows, and sooner or later overtakes, the defiant transgressor. They who "sow to the wind" are made to "reap the whirlwind;" the solemn assertion of a righteous God is not uttered in vain,—"I will punish the men that are settled on their lees, that say in their hearts, The Lord will not do good, neither will he do evil." Ay, and moreover, even should crime and wrongdoing be successfully hidden from the eye of man, *Conscience,* like another stern Elijah in the vineyard of Naboth, will confront the transgressor and utter a withering doom. How many such an Elijah stands a rebuker

* Ps. l. 21, 22. † Prov. xxix. 1.

within the gates of modern vineyards, purchased by the reward of iniquity! How many such an Elijah stands a ghostly sentinel by the door of that house whose stones have been hewn and polished and piled by illicit gain! How many an Elijah mounts on the back of the modern chariot, horsed and harnessed, pillowed and cushioned and liveried with the amassings of successful roguery! How many an Elijah stands in the midst of banquet-hall and drawing-room scowling down on some murderer of domestic peace and innocence, who has intruded into vineyards more sacred than Naboth's,—trampled virtue under foot, and left the broken, bleeding vine, to trail its shattered tendrils unpitied on the ground! And even should Conscience itself, in this world be defied and overborne; at all events in the world to come, sin *must* be discovered; retribution (long evaded here) will at last exact its uttermost farthing. The most awful picture of a state of eternal punishment, is that of sinners surrendered to the mastery of their own special transgression; these sins, like the fabled furies, following them, in unrelenting pursuit, from hall to hall and from cavern to cavern in the regions of unending woe;—and they, at last, hunted down, wearied, breathless, with the unavailing effort to escape the tormentors, crouching in wild despair, and exclaiming, like Ahab to Elijah, *"Hast thou found me, O mine enemy?"*

We may appropriately close this chapter with the impressive words and prayer of the Psalmist:—

"Surely thou wilt slay the wicked, O God: depart from me, therefore, ye bloody men. For they speak against thee wickedly, and thine enemies take thy name in vain. Do not

I hate them, O Lord, that hate thee? and am not I grieved with those that rise up against thee? I hate them with perfect hatred: I count them mine enemies. Search me, O God, and know my heart: try me, and know my thoughts: and see if there be any wicked way in me, and lead me in the way everlasting."

XVII.

Ahaziah and the God of Ekron.

"And Ahaziah fell down through a lattice in his upper chamber that was in Samaria, and was sick: and he sent messengers, and said unto them, Go, enquire of Baal-zebub the god of Ekron whether I shall recover of this disease. But the angel of the Lord said to Elijah the Tishbite, Arise, go up to meet the messengers of the king of Samaria, and say unto them, Is it not because there is not a God in Israel, that ye go to enquire of Baal-zebub the god of Ekron? Now therefore thus saith the Lord, Thou shalt not come down from that bed on which thou art gone up, but shalt surely die. And Elijah departed. And when the messengers turned back unto him, he said unto them, Why are ye now turned back? And they said unto him, There came a man up to meet us, and said unto us, Go, turn again unto the king that sent you, and say unto him, Thus saith the Lord, Is it not because there is not a God in Israel, that thou sendest to enquire of Baal-zebub the god of Ekron? therefore thou shalt not come down from that bed on which thou art gone up, but shalt surely die. And he said unto them, What manner of man was he which came up to meet you, and told you these words. And they answered him, He was an hairy man, and girt with a girdle of leather about his loins. And he said, It is Elijah the Tishbite."—2 KINGS i. 2-8.

"SHALL THE AXE BOAST ITSELF AGAINST HIM THAT HEWETH THEREWITH? OR SHALL THE SAW MAGNIFY ITSELF AGAINST HIM THAT SHAKETH IT? AS IF THE ROD SHOULD SHAKE ITSELF AGAINST THEM THAT LIFT IT UP, OR AS IF THE STAFF SHOULD LIFT UP ITSELF, AS IF IT WERE NO WOOD. THEREFORE SHALL THE LORD, THE LORD OF HOSTS, SEND AMONG HIS FAT ONES LEANNESS; AND UNDER HIS GLORY HE SHALL KINDLE A BURNING LIKE THE BURNING OF A FIRE. AND THE LIGHT OF ISRAEL SHALL BE FOR A FIRE, AND HIS HOLY ONE FOR A FLAME: AND IT SHALL BURN AND DEVOUR HIS THORNS AND HIS BRIERS IN ONE DAY."—ISAIAH X. 15-17.

AHAZIAH AND THE GOD OF EKRON.

THE events which are to occupy our attention in this chapter have a peculiar interest, connected as they are with the last exercise of Elijah's prophetic office. As he had begun, so he terminates his career,—the messenger of wrath—the rebuker of iniquity—"the Prophet of Fire." Three or four years have elapsed since last we followed his lightning-track, —traced his fiery footsteps in Naboth's vineyard, speaking God's word before kings, and not being moved. We are again to find him standing by a kingly couch;—bold as a lion; —discharging the last arrows in his quiver at the same presumptuous idolatries against which he had uttered a life-long testimony.

Ahaziah, (son and successor of Ahab,) had inherited the heathen vices and followed the idolatrous practices of his parents. Iniquity and irreligion are not always hereditary. But yet how often, by a righteous principle in the divine administration, are moral delinquency and impiety, with their bitter fruits, transmitted to children's children;—penalties of that great natural and divine law enforced and exemplified—"Whatsoever a man soweth, that shall he also reap." Troubled was the two years' reign of this unworthy king of Israel, and unhappy and inglorious his sudden and premature death. From the brief passing notice in the historical narrative, we are not warranted perhaps to stigmatise him as a coward. But we are led to surmise that dread of a violent death similar to his father's, had led him to shrink from the perils and calamities of war ;—suffering as he did, a daring revolt of long subject Moab to pass without an effort to repair the disaster. Exemption, however, from the dangers of battle could not purchase immunity from the smaller ills of life. He had now shewn him that God has other, and less glorious instruments of death than "the spears of the mighty," and that, after all, the post of duty (not that of coward self-preservation) is the real post of safety.

Let us pause for a moment, and read, from the case of Ahaziah, the impressive lesson, that all our care, forethought, and caution, cannot ward off accident, calamity, and inexorable death. He who escaped the Syrian's venturous aim, was laid low by an accidental fall from the flat roof of his palace in Samaria. He had probably been leaning against the screen or balustrade common on the tops of Eastern dwellings :—when, overbalancing himself, the slender rail or lattice-work had given way. He fell on the tessellated pavement below, stunned and mangled, and he was carried to a couch from which he was never to rise.

Age, character, rank, position, station can afford no exemption from such casualties, and from the last terminating event of all, the universal doom of dust. These royal robes encircled a body perishable as that of the meanest subject of his realm. The hand grasping that ivory sceptre, as well as the brawny arm of the strongest menial in his palace, must moulder to decay. "Trust not in princes, nor in the son of man, in whom there is no help. His breath goeth forth. He returneth to his earth. In that very day his thoughts perish." Poor and rich—the beggar and the prince—the slave and his master;—Dives with his purple and gold, and Lazarus with his crumbs and rags, are on a level here. The path of glory and royalty, of greatness and power, "leads but to the grave." The lattice on which the strong man leans—the iron balustrade of full health and unbroken energy—may in a moment give way. Sudden accident or fever may in a few hours write Ichabod on a giant's strength. The touch of the old slave in the conqueror's triumphal car is never more needful than when we are moving through life charioted in comforts—wreathed with garlands—regaled with music—"Remember thou art mortal!" None dare boast presumptuously of strong arm, and healthy cheek, and undimmed eye. It is by the mercy of God each one of us is preserved from the "terror that flieth by night, and the arrow that flieth by day, from the pestilence that walketh in darkness, and from the destruction that wasteth at noonday!" And when accident or evil does overtake, it is our comfort to know that it is by His permission. It is He who puts the arrow on the bowman's string. It is He who loosens the balustrade in its sockets. It is He who makes the lightning leap from the clouds on its mortal errand. It is He who commissions the coral builders to rear the fatal reef. It is He who guides the roll of that destroying billow, that has swept a loved one from the deck into a watery grave. It is He who says, (and who can gainsay?) "Thou shalt die, and not live." "As thy soul liveth, verily there may be but a step between thee and death." Saddest of all is it, when accident and "sudden death" overtake, without due preparation for the great change. Ah, yes, it is easy for us in health,—when the world goes well; when life's cup is brimming,—when the white sails are gleaming on its summer seas, and the music of its high holiday is resounding in our ears,—it is easy then to repress from thought the urgency of more solemn verities. But wait till the pillow of pain receives the aching, recumbent head;—wait till the curtains are drawn, and the room darkened, and that music is exchanged for the muffled bell, and the suppressed whisper, and noiseless footfall;—wait till the solemn apprehension for the first time steals over the spirit, that the sand-glass is running out, life's grains diminishing, and that awful hour which we have evaded, dreaded, tampered with, shrunk from, has come at last;—how solemn the mockery to try *then* to give to God the dregs and remnants of a worn existence and a withered love! How sad then to begin for the first time to utter the lamentation, "He weakened my strength in the way; He shortened my days. I said, O my God, take me not away in the midst of my days!" How much nobler, wiser, happier—to anticipate the necessities of that inevitable hour, that whether our summons shall come by the fall from the lattice, or the gradual sinking and wasting of strength,—whether by sudden accident, or by the gradual crumbling of the earthly framework,—we may be ready, in calm composure, to breathe the saying of the dying patriarch, "I have waited for thy salvation, O God."

Ahaziah was thus suddenly prostrated in the very midst of life—while manhood was yet in its glory. We are not indeed led to infer from the narrative, that there were at first any dangerous symptoms in his illness. It was sent and intended as a timeous warning—a seasonable remonstrance. Had he listened to the Divine voice,—or, like Manasseh in his affliction, had he "besought the Lord his God, and humbled himself greatly before the God of his fathers,"—or, like Hezekiah in his sore sickness, turned his face toward the wall, and prayed unto the Lord,—he might have been raised up to prove for years a blessing to his people, and a monument of saving mercy. We almost expect and hope, indeed, in reading the opening words of the story, to find a royal penitent, in the extremity of his mental anguish, recognising the chastisement of the God he had long despised,—sending messengers to summon the great Tishbite prophet to his sick-bed, that he might put forth on his behalf his "effectual, fervent prayers." Elijah's name and person and achievements must have been thoroughly familiar to him when he was yet a boy in the palace of Jezreel. He could not fail often and again to have seen, or, at all events, to have heard of that wild, rugged, stern Seer; nor, despite of his parents' hatred and scorn, could he be unimpressed with the story of his startling miracles and hero-deeds:—how he had restored a poor woman's son at Zarephath—brought him back, not from sickness, but from the chambers of death;—how, on the heights of that very Carmel on which he had gazed from his youth, he had brought down fire from heaven, and discomfited the Baal-priests;—and, last of all, he could not have forgotten how awfully verified had been the uttered judgments of this Herald of omnipotence regarding his own hapless father! Every time his eye fell on the now blighted and cursed vineyard of Naboth, would not the figure and mien of the Tishbite be before him;—his trumpet-voice sounding in his ears the solemn lesson, "Who hath hardened himself against God, and prospered?" Alas! how difficult it is, even in the midst of weightiest judgment, to overcome unbelief and prejudice! Nursed in the abominable idolatries of Jezebel, he clings to the last to the lie of heathenism. Messengers are summoned to his bed-side, with instructions to speed them to a well-known temple of Baal, to ascertain the issue of his trouble,—whether he should recover of his disease. This oracle was situated in Ekron, the most northerly of five cities of Philistia. The Sidonian god was here, under one of his manifold forms, worshipped as Baal-zebub—literally, "The God of Flies;" the supposed averter of the plague, common in the east, of swarming insects or gnats.* This temple at Ekron was the great rendezvous of heathen devotees. It was the Delphic oracle, or the Mecca of the Baal-worshippers. Thousands from the surrounding provinces and countries congregated at the shrine of the tutelary god, to get cured of diseases, otherwise supposed to be incurable. He was the Phœnician Æsculapius,—the god of medicine,—reputed to have power over demoniacs as well as bodily diseases. Hence the reference in the Pharisees' accusation regarding Christ, "He casteth out devils by Beelzebub."

In a literal sense, the parallel to Ahaziah's folly can in vain be sought now, in the changed aspects of the Church and the world. The heathen oracles are dumb. The prince of darkness, who seems in former ages to have wielded, by

* See Kiel, *in loco.*

means of these incantations, a mysterious power, has now changed his ground. But yet how many, in another form, have their Ekrons still?—in life as well as in death trusting to some miserable, false confidences; instead of reposing in simple faith on the Lord God of Elijah, and on the work finished and consummated on the cross of Calvary. Is it asked, What are these? There is the Ekron of *self-righteousness;*—the pride of what they themselves have done,—grounding their peace and confidence, alike for a living and a dying hour, on some miserable fragmentary virtues of their own—their charities and alms-deeds and moral lives;—the beggar proud of wearing some tinsel on his rags, the bankrupt proud of paying by farthings a debt which is accumulating by pounds and talents. There is the Ekron of proud *reason.* Men will not trust the simple word of the living God. The Bible doctrines, or, it may be, subordinate facts, do not square with their predilections and prepossessions,—their preconceived opinions and prejudices,—and they send their imperious intellectual messengers to this haughty oracle. Instead of coming to the divinely-authenticated page with the humble spirit of inquiry, "How readest thou?"—"What saith the Scripture?" their preliminary question is—'Science, what thinkest *thou?* Philosophy, what thinkest *thou?*' They come to the well of Sychar, not with the question, "Give me to drink;" but they must subject the water to chemical analysis; they must cast the Bible into their own earthly crucible, and subject it to their own earthly tests. Happy they who stoop down like the beggar at the running stream and quench their thirst; asking no vain questions; feeling nothing, and caring for nothing, but the precious adaptation of the water of life to their panting, needy souls. Happy they, who, spiritually enlightened, are not curious to know the process of cautery or cure, but who, gazing on the glorious uncurtained beauties of the moral world, before hidden from their view, can tell, in the utterance of a simple faith, "This one thing I know, that whereas once I was blind, now I see." Moreover, are there not many who make shipwreck of their peace and comfort by involving themselves needlessly in speculative questions,—profound transcendental doctrinal enigmas—with which they have no concern? As Ahaziah seems not to inquire *how* he was to recover, but *if* he was to recover, so how many there are who, like him, perplex themselves with the same question, in a spiritual sense; 'Am I ordained to be raised from the death of trespasses and sins? Am I among the number of the elect? Has God, by a predestined decree, placed me among the saved? Have I His seal on my forehead?' Vain dreamers! seeking to penetrate into the arcana of heaven—"the secret things which belong only to the Lord our God"—instead of giving themselves to the great practical work of applying the sovereign remedy of the gospel, already provided and already in their offer,—working out their own salvation with fear and trembling.

But to return to the narrative. The messengers of Ahaziah are now on their way—speeding along the plain of Esdraelon—charged to hasten with fleet foot to relieve the feverish anxieties of their lord. Laden, doubtless, with golden bribes and offerings, they expect to retrace their steps with a propitious response from the flattering oracle. But who is this, when the king's message demands such haste, that dares to thwart them in their mission, and to cross their path? What living oracle can this be, who seems to arrest in a moment that band of royal delegates, and send them back trembling and panic-stricken to the couch of their dying king? At that couch they stand :—and the monarch, with startled looks, seeing probably their trepidation, interrogates them as to the cause of this strange and speedy return. With the old smouldering passion kindling up in his languid eye, he demands, as if half guessing the dreaded truth, "Why are ye now turned back?" The reason was soon told: a wild, strange, unearthly being,—with hairy cloak,* and flowing beard, and leathern girdle, had stood in their way; and, with a voice of thunder, in the name of Jehovah, had exclaimed: "Go, turn again unto the king that sent you, and say unto him, Thus saith the Lord, Is it not because there is not a God in Israel, that thou sendest to inquire of Baal-zebub the god of Ekron? therefore thou shalt not come down from that bed on which thou art gone up, but shalt surely die."

We gather from the narrative, that these stranger Phœnician servants had either never personally seen 'the evil genius' of Ahab's house; or, at all events, they had not recognised the Prophet-messenger of the God of Israel, in that singular personage, who had met them on their way, like a lion from the dens of Carmel. But the king does not for a moment hesitate in recognising their description. He exclaims, "It is Elijah the Tishbite!" In

* Kiel throws out the remark, that the hairy garment of the Prophet was worn also "as a symbol of sorrow for the sins of the people, and the divine judgments thereby incurred."

his inmost soul, though he may try to conceal his guilty fears, we almost hear him echoing his father's words, "Hast thou found me, O mine enemy?" It is yet another of the Prophet's sudden appearances. He comes upon them like a flash of lightning; utters with thrilling brevity his solemn message, and then retires; for the description of the dramatic scene closes with the words, "And he departed." Bold, brave man! Here he was once more, "jealous for the Lord of hosts." Deeper affront could not have been offered to the Jehovah before whom he stood, than was perpetrated by the reigning monarch,—in ignoring the God of the Hebrew nation in the eyes of the heathen,—going down to Egypt for help. It was a base violation of the fundamental law of the theocracy, "Thou shalt have no other gods before me." "In Judah is God known; his name is great in Israel. In Salem also is his tabernacle, and his dwelling place in Zion." "Confounded be all they that worship graven images." As certainly as Saul's wild, heathenish, debasing mission to the cave of the enchantress at Endor sealed *his* doom, so does this impious insult of the son of Ahab seal his. It was doing guilty homage to an idol-god, in the face of almost unparalleled proofs of Jehovah's supremacy. Never, since the epoch of the exodus, had wonders and miracles been more profusely displayed than now, through the instrumentality of Elijah; and yet this apostate from the faith of his fathers, who had witnessed God's arm thus made bare, sends, in the very hour of righteous judgment and rebuke, the officers of his court to consult in his behalf with the miserable fly-god of Ekron, in Philistia. "Tell it not in Gath, publish it not in the streets of

Askalon, lest the daughters of the Philistines rejoice, lest the daughters of the uncircumcised triumph." "If we have forgotten the name of our God, or stretched out our hands to a strange god, shall not God search this out?"

There is yet one other incident worthy of note in this passage, ere we close the present chapter. It is the appearance of the august messenger—One mightier than Elijah—"Stronger" than "THE STRONG"—who sends him to meet the servants of the king of Samaria. He is called here "the Angel of the Lord," or rather, "*the* Angel, THE LORD;" "the Angel JEHOVAH." None other can he be than the Lord Jesus Christ Himself,—the great covenant Angel;—the same Divine Personage, who, anticipating as it were the period of His incarnation, had appeared to Abraham at Mamre, to Jacob at Peniel, and to Gideon at Ophrah. This idolatrous king of covenant Israel was sending to solicit the intercessions of heathen Baal—defiling his throne,—desecrating his country's altars;—like Nadab and Abihu, seeking to offer strange fire. The great future Intercessor of His Church arrests the messengers on their insulting errand; and shews, that if He be rejected as strong to save, He will manifest, in righteous severity, that He is strong to smite!

Terrible thought! to forfeit, by our own incorrigible sins, the intercessions of Him who alone can save us;—to have His rejected blood pleading, not *for* us, but *against* us—oh, whilst we see the life of Israel's monarch fast ebbing, as he lies on his royal couch at Samaria;—when we think, moreover, of his own daring impiety, as that which sealed his doom and hurried him to an early grave,—how solemnly do we seem to listen to the words of that insulted covenant Angel: "Their sorrows shall be multiplied that hasten after another god. Their drink-offerings of blood will I not offer, nor take up their names into my lips."

Yet, may we not, too, in this very sentence of death uttered by the angel Jehovah, derive a comforting reflection? Is it no solace to think that life and death are in the hands of that Angel-God; that what appears to us to be the most wayward and capricious of occurrences—the departure of a human being from this world—is directly under His sovereign control; that He gives the lease of life; and, when He sees meet, revokes the grant? He speaks indeed, in the case of Ahaziah, in righteous wrath; but, to each of His own people, as the divine Saviour—the Brother-man—He says, not in anger or judgment, but in love and faithfulness—"Thou shalt not come down from that bed on which thou art gone up, but shalt surely die." Death has no terrors when it comes thus as a message from death's great Conqueror. As He sent Elijah—the minister of flaming fire—with the tidings of doom to the chamber of the wicked; so does He send angels—glorious beings, who delight to do His pleasure—to the death-beds of His saints, to bear their disembodied spirits upward on wings of light and love to heavenly mansions. "Father, I will," (is His last and closing intercessory prayer in behalf of every member of the Church on earth,) "that they also, whom thou hast given me, be with me where I am; that they may behold my glory."

XVIII.

The Second Answer by Fire.

"Then the king sent unto him a captain of fifty with his fifty: and he went up to him; (and, behold, he sat on the top of an hill;) and he spake unto him, Thou man of God, the king hath said, Come down. And Elijah answered and said to the captain of fifty, If I be a man of God, then let fire come down from heaven, and consume thee and thy fifty. And there came down fire from heaven, and consumed him and his fifty. Again, also he sent unto him another captain of fifty with his fifty. And he answered and said unto him, O man of God, thus hath the king said, Come down quickly. And Elijah answered and said unto them, If I be a man of God, let fire come down from heaven, and consume thee and thy fifty. And the fire of God came down from heaven, and consumed him and his fifty. And he sent again a captain of the third fifty with his fifty. And the third captain of fifty went up, and came and fell on his knees before Elijah, and besought him, and said unto him, O man of God, I pray thee, let my life, and the life of these fifty thy servants, be precious in thy sight. And the angel of the Lord said unto Elijah, Go down with him; be not afraid of him. And he arose, and went down with him unto the king. And he said unto him, Thus saith the Lord, Forasmuch as thou hast sent messengers to inquire of Baal-zebub the god of Ekron, (is it not because there is no God in Israel to inquire of his word?) therefore thou shalt not come down off that bed on which thou art gone up, but shalt surely die. So he died, according to the word of the Lord which Elijah had spoken."—2 KINGS i. 9–18.

"FOR, BEHOLD, THE LORD WILL COME WITH FIRE, AND WITH HIS CHARIOTS LIKE A WHIRLWIND, TO RENDER HIS ANGER WITH FURY, AND HIS REBUKE WITH FLAMES OF FIRE."—ISAIAH LXVI. 15.

"AND I WILL GIVE POWER UNTO MY TWO WITNESSES, AND THEY SHALL PROPHESY A THOUSAND TWO HUNDRED AND THREESCORE DAYS, CLOTHED IN SACKCLOTH. AND IF ANY MAN WILL HURT THEM, FIRE PROCEEDETH OUT OF THEIR MOUTH, AND DEVOURETH THEIR ENEMIES: AND IF ANY MAN WILL HURT THEM, HE MUST IN THIS MANNER BE KILLED."—REV. XI. 3, 5.

THE SECOND ANSWER BY FIRE.

In last chapter, we considered the account given of the messengers who were sent by Ahaziah, from his sick-bed, to consult the oracle of Baal-zebub, the fly-god at the Philistine city of Ekron. While hastening on their journey, we found them suddenly arrested by none other than Elijah himself. We followed them as they returned to the chamber of their sovereign, bearing to him the Prophet's doom of death ;—the merited retribution for so impious a deference to an idol of the heathen, and so insulting a rejection of the God of Israel. We shall now pursue the narrative, and note how the message of these heralds of evil tidings was received by the prostrate king.

The unexpected intervention of Elijah was calculated to fill Ahaziah with dismay. He knew that the words and threatenings of the stern Prophet carried with them a terrible significance. That never-to-be-forgotten day on Carmel—the fire, the slaughter, the blood—must have engraven itself deep in his young memory. He might well have deemed it the height of madness to trifle with the sayings of one who could unlock the armoury of Heaven, and inflict summary vengeance on the adversaries of the God he served. Therefore, as a doomed man, we half expect, half hope, to see the tear of penitence trembling in his eye, and messengers forthwith despatched along the plain of Esdraelon, to endeavour to avert or modify the awful denunciation. But the blood of his mother Jezebel flows in this sick man's veins. The message of the Prophet rouses him only to wild and frenzied exasperation. He resolves that the Tishbite shall forfeit his liberty or his life for his bold presumption.

How sad when affliction, in whatever shape it comes to us, whether it be sickness, or bereavement, or worldly loss, is not accompanied with the humbling effects of resignation, penitence, submission! Outward trials, as we have remarked before, in speaking of Ahab, if they be not sanctified for softening the heart, must have the opposite result of leading to a deeper hardening and impenitency. So it was now with Ahaziah. We might have expected that his sickness would have proved a salutary monitor—a rousing messenger of rebuke and warning to his soul, humbling him in godly sorrow and tears, and leading him to cry for mercy. But instead of being like oil poured on the troubled waters —calming their fretfulness,—that sickness proved rather like oil thrown into the flames, feeding their fury. The dying man presents a picture of what, alas! is not unfrequently seen, though the saddest of all spectacles,—a scorner and spurner of the most solemn providential warnings at the very last gasp of life;—contending with his Maker—lifting his soul in proud defiance against God.

It is evident, from the troop of soldiers the king summons, that he deems the Tishbite no mean prey. An officer, with fifty men, is sent in hot haste to bring him dead or alive to the palace of Samaria. Elijah has meanwhile retired to "the top of an hill,"—"the top of the mount"—supposed with every probability to be Mount Carmel.* There he once more manifests in all its integrity, his old hero-spirit;—the truest of all bravery—that of unflinching faith and trust in his God. Seated on the summit, watching the armed band approaching, he would at once conjecture their hostile intent. Had he been the panic-stricken Prophet we so lately found wandering in the desert of Beersheba, he would have girded up his loins, and with the fleet foot which, on a previous occasion, nigh this same place, had outstripped the coursers of Ahab's chariot, he would have evaded the vengeance of his pursuers, either by distant flight, or by taking refuge in one of the many caves of Carmel with which he was familiar. But his old watchword and motto again rises to the ascendant. Nay, under the consciousness of the presence and nearness of the Covenant Angel—the Divine, mysterious Personage, whose voice had a few brief hours before addressed him—he could say, with a special emphasis, "The *Angel of the Lord* encampeth round about them that fear him, and delivereth them. O taste and see that the Lord is good: blessed is the man that trusteth in him." If one wavering unworthy thought might for a moment have obtruded itself, we may imagine him rebuking it in the words of the Psalmist King: "THE LORD is my rock and my fortress, and my deliverer; my God, my strength in whom I will trust; my buckler, and the horn of my salvation, and my high tower." Indeed, the lessons of

* "In this narrative, our version, as is too frequently the case, conceals the force of the original by an imperfect translation. 'A hill' should be 'the mount,' (הָהָר) the word always used for Carmel; and in connexion with Elijah, for Carmel only, with the exception of Sinai, which, of course, cannot be intended here."—*Art. Carmel*, "*Bib. Dict.*"

Horeb were now too indelibly written on his inmost soul to be forgotten. The time was when he might have been tempted to succumb before the storm, and in coward unbelief to utter the desponding plaint, "My heart and my flesh faileth." But since the Lord had "passed by," and spoken in "the still small voice," he had been taught that "Jehovah was the strength of his heart and his portion for ever." Though an host therefore *should* now encamp against him, his heart does not fear.

The officer or captain of the troop approaches within speaking distance, and exclaims, "O man of God, the king hath said, Come down!" "Man of God." This appellation may have been uttered in profane irony;—as if this godless captain of a godless king, would make stern proof of how bootless was the name, when fifty gleaming swords were ready to leap from their scabbards should resistance be attempted. But even had no such arrogant sarcasm been implied, it was crime and presumption enough to order thus summarily a prophet of Israel, who had done nought but deliver a message on his Master's authority, to surrender himself captive at the bidding of a recreant and apostate monarch. It was not so much contempt of Elijah, as insult to Him whose messenger and servant he was. Woe betide the earthly power that would dare dishonour an ambassador of the Most High!

Elijah, resolute and unmoved, majestically answered, "If I *be* a man of God, then let fire come down from heaven and consume thee and thy fifty." Grandly does the Tishbite appear at this moment;—not in anger, but with the calm dignity of conscious POWER, as the divinely-appointed minister of vengeance. He vindicates his mission and magnifies his office. He remembers that his own name signifies "God the Lord:" to rise up therefore against *him*, was to insult and desecrate the awful character he bore, as the representative and vicegerent of Heaven. That captain and his fifty, as the delegates of an earthly sovereign, had dared to defy and outbrave the warning of the King of kings,—"Touch not mine anointed, and do my prophets no harm." As THE PROPHET OF FIRE, Elijah gives the word. The lightning leaps from the cloud. At one flash, the captain and his fifty lie scattered on the green sward of Carmel—a mass of smouldering ashes—a silent, terrible testimony to the truth, "JEHOVAH LIVETH." "The Lord reigneth; let the people tremble." "A FIRE goeth before him and burneth up all his enemies round about; the heavens declare his righteousness, and all the people see his glory."

The king, meanwhile, has been waiting in the vain expectation of the return of his soldiers with the captured Prophet. He cannot brook delay. Another captain with fifty are commissioned to go forth on the same embassy; and bearing a still more urgent and imperious message. Unappalled by the spectacle of his smitten comrades, the leader of this second band delivers the summons, "O man of God, thus hath the king said, Come down *quickly*." But vain is the arrogant demand. Again the artillery of heaven opens,—the volleyed lightning speeds,—and the second fifty share the terrible fate of their predecessors. "The Lord also thundered in the heavens, and the Highest gave his voice; hailstones and coals of fire. Yea, he sent out his arrows, and scattered them; and he shot out lightnings, and discomfited them," (Ps. xviii. 13, 14.) Ahaziah could not fail, by this time, to be fully cognisant of these appalling judgments. He might possibly have ventured to put an atheist construction on the death of the first fifty;—that they had been the victims of unhappy and untoward accident;—that the lightnings—the capricious shafts from the quiver of nature—had, by sad mishap, fallen on the slopes of Carmel where his soldiers were. But now that the very same catastrophe had overtaken the second relay, there could surely be little debate that a Higher hand had put the bow on the string and made ready the arrows. Blinded indeed must that dying monarch be, if he still refuse to desist from his mad, impotent rage. If there be no reprieve from the merited doom pronounced on his own head, surely, at all events, ere the retributive sentence be executed, he will with his dying breath do homage to the Almighty Being he has insulted and provoked, and confess that the Jehovah of Elijah is the only true God. Alas! how much it takes to humble the proud heart. Apart from divine grace no outward trial can do it. Impending death itself, that hour when, we might suppose, all false confidences and illusions might well be shaken, finds the hardened and impenitent impervious as ever to conviction. Hence the miserable delusion of those who trust to the relentings and penitential feelings of their last hours. It is too often a vain unrealised dream. "As men live, so do men die!" The scorner in life, is a scorner at the last:—the blasphemer in life, is often a wilder blasphemer at the last. The unjust remain "unjust still," and the filthy remain "filthy still." Oh, it is the saddest picture of moral apostasy,—the saddest exponent of the enmity of the unregenerate heart;—when even the King of terrors brings *no* terror to the seared conscience and indurated soul;—the banner of proud defiance against God and His Christ waved, even when the awful gloom of mortal darkness is closing in all around!

The king's passion is still roused;—the fever of vengeance burns hot as ever; and the last miserable dregs of his life are spent in the renewed attempt to baffle Omnipotence, but only to squander afresh the blood of his innocent soldiers. A third troop of fifty are equipped and sent forth on the same luckless errand. Wise, however, at all events on this latter occasion, is their leader. On reaching Carmel, he sees from the awful memorials of rejected warning in the blackened skeletons around, how vain it would be, again contemptuously to summon Elijah to surrender; how vain rather, by assaulting the person of his ambassador, to rush with madness against the bosses of Jehovah's buckler. He falls down a suppliant at the Prophet's feet, begs his own life and that of his followers. He besought him, and said unto him—"O man of God, I pray thee let my life and the life of these fifty thy servants be precious in thy sight. Behold there came fire down out of heaven and burnt up the two captains of the former fifties with their fifties, therefore let my life now be precious in thy sight."

Be it ours to imitate the example of this soldier, and take timeous warning by the fearful fate of the despisers of divine vengeance. Every narrative of punishment in the olden time, is a parable;—the foreshadow of sadder eternal realities, written for our admonition on whom the ends of the world have come. The present incident is one of these

Old Testament prefigurations, of the certain doom that will overtake all who dare to fight against God. "Hand" here is "joined in hand;"—fifty by fifty league themselves against the Almighty; but their "swift destruction" reads to us the solemn moral, that "the wicked shall not escape unpunished." Yes, let all who make light of divine warnings and venture on high-handed resistance to God's word and will, gather around these heaps of smouldering ashes and splintered armour on the slopes of Carmel, and hear the silent voice of the silent dead proclaim the sterner verities of a world to come,—"Upon the wicked he shall rain fire and brimstone and an horrible tempest; this is the portion of *their* cup,"—"The chaff he shall burn with unquenchable fire!"

Ere we leave the scene of flaming retribution, let us connect it and contrast it, for a moment, with that other "answer by fire," which, ten years before, had descended on this same mountain. The two may not inaptly be taken as symbolic illustrations of the *law* and the *gospel*. The gospel lesson and picture is conveyed in the older narrative. The fire from heaven, invoked by Elijah, fell on the sacrifice as an atonement for the sins of the people. The thousands of Israel were gathered around, gazing in expectant silence, while the lone Prophet laid the bullock in pieces on the altar. As the fire at his intercession came down; not an Israelite was touched, not a hair of their head was singed;—the visible emblem of God's wrath consumed the vicarious sacrifice: then followed the rain clouds of blessing, and the multitudes dispersed with the praises of Jehovah on their lips, —"God is the Lord who hath kindled for us the flame.* . . .

* So the verse has been rendered.

Oh give thanks unto Jehovah; for he is good: for his mercy endureth for ever," (Ps. cxviii. 27, 29.)

In our present narrative, we behold the emblem of the *law*. That previous, ever-memorable day of sacrifice, seems to be guiltily forgotten and ignored alike by king and soldiers. The altar erected by Elijah is desecrated: the shrine of Baal-zebub at Ekron is madly preferred to it. And now, when above the same hallowed ground, the clouds of heaven again part;—the winged lightning—emblem of righteous vengeance—falls on the defiant sinners themselves. The rejected Deity manifests Himself under the awful revelation of "*a consuming fire.*"

Do we know the reality of this solemn alternative? "The Lord answereth by *fire!*" Fire—the wrath due to sin—*must* come down, either on the sinner or on the provided Sacrifice. Reject the Saviour and His great atonement, and however splendid or imposing may be our own moralities and boasted righteousness, "fire" must come forth from His presence and "mingle our blood with our sacrifices." Blessed are they who have been enabled to lay hold by faith on the glorious gospel declaration,—"Christ hath redeemed us from the curse of the law, being made a curse for us." We may devoutly say, in the words of the captain of the third fifty, as we address the true "Man of God"—the "Man of His right hand"—the God-man Mediator—"O man of God, I pray thee, let my life be precious in thy sight!" 'I have given thee,' may He not reply, 'the best proof which, (Omnipotent though I be) I *could* give, that your life is thus precious in my sight, in not sparing my own, that ye might have the gracious offer of a free salvation! The precious blood I shed, is the evidence and exponent of the preciousness of your souls to *Me!* "I came that ye might have life, and that ye might have it more abundantly."'

But to return. The supplication of the third captain is graciously heard. As it was with Elijah's Lord in Horeb, so is it with himself now; the voice of mercy follows the earthquake and the fire. The lives of the troop are spared. The Angel Jehovah of the preceding context, again addressing his servant, bids him fearlessly join himself to the armed band, accompany them back to the city, and confront in person the dying king. The Prophet accordingly descends from the summit of the hill, and, unaccoutred with human arms or panoply, joins the cavalcade. We may imagine them entering the gates of Samaria. There is an unusual stir in the royal city. A monarch, whose life is fast ebbing in the palace, would be theme enough of absorbing interest and excitement. But to this was added the strange tale, or rather the startling reality, of the holocaust on Carmel, and the terrible revival of Elijah's power. How the eager crowd would rush to the city-gates to catch a glimpse of the wonder-working Prophet—the captured hero,—loved and revered by many—dreaded by all! And, if such were the feelings of the general population, what must have been those of the king, when, in a few moments, the rough hair-clad man stands at the bedside of the monarch he has doomed! It was the hawk cowering in the presence of the eagle. We are again forcibly struck, indeed, with the calm dignity of Elijah's demeanour. There is no reference to the miraculous vengeance—the fire-smiting of the earlier part of the day,—no vaunting or parade of delegated omnipotence. As the minister of the Most High he simply utters his message, and then retires. He solemnly repeats, without comment, "the word of the Lord"—"Thus saith the Lord, Forasmuch as thou hast sent messengers to enquire of Baal-zebub the God of Ekron, (is it not because there is no God in Israel to enquire of his word?) therefore thou shalt not come down off that bed on which thou art gone up, but shalt surely die."* The delivery of this doom ends the remarkable interview. The king is silent. He is too much appalled in the presence of the man of God, or else his bodily strength is sinking too rapidly, to permit him to entertain the thought either of remonstrance or of vengeance. The pallor of death slowly gathers over his countenance;—for the solemn statement immediately follows, "So he died according to the word of the Lord which Elijah had spoken." It was the Tishbite's last meeting with the house of Ahab;—his last message of wrath,—his last protest against Baal. The hours of his own earthly existence were now nearly spent;—already the sentence was framing in the upper sanctuary, "Well done, good and faithful servant." It is pleasing to think of him in this his closing public act, true as ever to his great life-work and calling, as the unflinching Reformer of his day;—denouncing the degradations of the Baal worship, quenching the strange fires on the defiled altars of his country, and rekindling the sacred flames;—the same heroic spirit we found him when first presented to us on the sacred page; like Moses, not fearing the wrath of the king, but enduring, as seeing Him who is invisible. "Go down with him, be not afraid," said the Angel-Jehovah to

* It recalls the scene of a later age, Bishop Ken standing by the death-bed of Charles II., and rebuking him for his profligacies.

the Prophet. It is the same encouraging word Jesus speaks to us, in all time of our tribulation. He will Himself descend with us from our Carmels, to the battle of life;—from our hill-tops of prosperity to the valley of humiliation and trouble. He says to us, as He said to His church in Philadelphia, "I also will keep thee from" (yea, *in*) "the hour of temptation." "At my first answer," says Paul, "no man stood with me, but all men forsook me: . . . notwithstanding the LORD stood with me, and strengthened me; and I was delivered out of the mouth of the lion."

The reference to the incident which has occupied our attention in this chapter would not be complete, without taking in connexion with it that parallel passage in the Gospels, where two Apostles, in the blindness of a false zeal, sought to draw, from Elijah's conduct on this occasion, a vindication of their own unworthy desire of retaliation.* When our blessed Lord and His disciples were journeying together in this very district, on their way from Galilee to Jerusalem, —James and John were stung to the quick by the churlish inhospitality of some Samaritan villagers. These villagers had refused, to the Jewish strangers, the wonted courtesies accorded to travellers: and in their passionate misguided zeal, the two "sons of thunder," (as the Lord had well named them,) —perhaps a distant view of Carmel suggesting the precedent, asked permission of their Master, that, in imitation of the old Prophet, they might call down fire from heaven: "Lord, wilt thou that we command fire to come down from heaven, and consume them, even as Elias did?" The proposal was sharply

* Luke ix. 55.

rebuked and silenced. "Ye know not," said He, "what manner of spirit ye are of. For the Son of man is not come to destroy men's lives, but to save them." Jesus does not vindicate the conduct of the boorish, sectarian villagers; but He bids the imprecators of vengeance remember that they had grievously mistaken and misapprehended the character of the dispensation under which they lived. The days of Elijah were past. It was now no longer the economy of terror, judgment, visible retribution; but the gentle, peaceful era of the Gospel. The calling down of fire from heaven on the part of the Tishbite, was no more than the visible expression of the character of that severe, rigid dispensation, whose prophet and interpreter he was. It was different altogether under the dispensation of the Spirit—the newly inaugurated era of peace and love.

"The Son of man is not come to destroy men's lives, but to save them!" How this declaration rebukes the spirit of intolerance which has marked for centuries the career of persecuting churches, and more especially the apostate Church of Rome;—that Church which has sought to maintain its own supremacy, and to crush truth and freedom, by means of fire, prison, and the sword;—and this under the spurious name of "religious zeal." Whatever be the strength of our own convictions, we dare not, as the children of the new dispensation of light and love and charity, attempt to lord it over the consciences of others. Corrupt worship and practice are not to be uprooted and extirpated by violence and penal laws. The weapons of our warfare are not carnal. They who use the sword must perish by the sword. All acts of resentment, vindictiveness, revenge,—either on the part of Christians as individuals, or in their corporate capacity as a church,—are inimical to the spirit and character of Him, who was meek and lowly in heart, and whose dying utterances were words of forgiveness.

And if we may draw yet another lesson from this same passage, and one more specially applicable to the times in which we live,—it is, that the present tendency to inflame and foster "the war-spirit" is in every way opposed to the economy of the Gospel. Let us not be mistaken or misapprehended. All honour to the brave men who (noble examples of self-sacrifice) are willing to shed their blood and surrender their lives for their country's good;—the guardians of our homes, our liberties, and all that are dear to us! Moreover, as society at least now exists, we pronounce those to be the wildest dreamers, who, on spurious "peace-at-any-price" principles, would disband our armies;—convert our swords into ploughshares, and pave with cannon our iron highways.* But neither can we

* "Peace may be sought in two ways. One way is, as when Gideon sought it, when he built his altar in Ophrah, naming it, 'God send peace;' yet sought this peace that he loved, as he was ordered to seek it; and the peace was sent in God's way: 'The country was in quietness forty years in the days of Gideon.' And the other way of seeking peace is as Menahem sought it, when he gave the king of Assyria a thousand talents of silver that his hand might be with him. That is, you may either win your peace, or buy it;—win it by resistance to evil; buy it by compromise with evil. You may buy your peace with silenced consciences; you may buy it with broken vows, buy it with lying words, buy it with base connivances, buy it with the blood of the slain, and the cry of the captive, and the silence of lost souls—over hemispheres of the earth; while you sit smiling at your serene hearths, lisping comfortable prayers evening and morning, and so mutter continually to yourselves, 'Peace, peace, when there is no peace;' but only captivity and death, for you, as well as for those you leave unsaved; and yours darker than theirs."—*Ruskin's Lectures: "Two Paths."*

coincide with those who would draw from the stern conflicts and bloody exploits recorded in the pages of Old Testament story, argument and defence, if not encouragement, for the savage realities of modern war;—and for the reason already assigned, that the character of the dispensation is completely changed. As little dare we take the fierce campaigns of Joshua, Gideon, David, and others, with their cruel accompaniments, to justify the modern war-spirit,—as we can take the fact of Elijah's slaughter of the apostate priesthood, or Elijah's invoking the fire to descend on Ahaziah's soldiers, as a vindication of the minister or priest who now would gird himself for the work of a homicide;—or venture, with his own hands, to take bloody retaliation on the enemies of Him to whom vengeance belongeth. Elijah's age (symbolised in Horeb by the earthquake, the hurricane, and the fire) has passed away, and has been succeeded by that of "the still small voice." We maintain, therefore, that War,—meaning by that, either the wanton letting loose of the fierce passions of human nature, or the frantic lust of conquest and aggression,—is not more a blot on humanity, than a presumptuous violation and desecration of the spirit of the New Testament—that kingdom which "is righteousness and peace." May God, in His mercy, hasten the time, when the spirit of the new economy shall be more widely recognised and acknowledged;—when nations, as nations, shall listen to and obey the great law of the Gospel dispensation, enunciated by the lips of the Prince of Peace, its author and representative,—"This is my commandment, that ye *love* one another!"

XIX.

Farewell Visits to the Sons of the Prophets.

"And it came to pass, when the Lord would take up Elijah into heaven by a whirlwind, that Elijah went with Elisha from Gilgal. And Elijah said unto Elisha, Tarry here, I pray thee; for the Lord hath sent me to Bethel. And Elisha said unto him, As the Lord liveth, and as thy soul liveth, I will not leave thee. So they went down to Bethel. And the sons of the prophets that were at Bethel came forth to Elisha, and said unto him, Knowest thou that the Lord will take away thy master from thy head to-day? And he said, Yea, I know it; hold ye your peace. And Elijah said unto him, Elisha, tarry here, I pray thee; for the Lord hath sent me to Jericho. And he said, As the Lord liveth, and as thy soul liveth, I will not leave thee. So they came to Jericho. And the sons of the prophets that were at Jericho came to Elisha, and said unto him, Knowest thou that the Lord will take away thy master from thy head to-day? And he answered, Yea, I know it; hold ye your peace. And Elijah said unto him, Tarry, I pray thee, here; for the Lord hath sent me to Jordan. And he said, As the Lord liveth, and as thy soul liveth, I will not leave thee. And they two went on. And fifty men of the sons of the prophets went, and stood to view afar off: and they two stood by Jordan."—2 KINGS ii. 1-7.

"AS YE KNOW HOW WE EXHORTED AND COMFORTED, AND CHARGED EVERY ONE OF YOU, (AS A FATHER DOTH HIS CHILDREN.")—1 THESS. II. 11.

"AND THEY ALL WEPT SORE, AND FELL ON PAUL'S NECK, AND KISSED HIM; SORROWING MOST OF ALL FOR THE WORDS WHICH HE SPAKE, THAT THEY SHOULD SEE HIS FACE NO MORE. AND THEY ACCOMPANIED HIM UNTO THE SHIP."—ACTS XX. 37, 38.

FAREWELL VISITS TO THE SONS OF THE PROPHETS.

THE eventful time has at length arrived, when, from his changeful and chequered life-experience, the pilgrim seer is to be upborne in a fiery chariot to his heavenly rest and crown. And yet, notwithstanding the divine premonition he had evidently received of the honour in store for him, we never could guess from his bearing and demeanour that anything extraordinary was impending. Another day, and he would be soaring, in his magnificent flight, amid angels,—kindred spirits in the upper sanctuary,—ministers of flaming fire;—communing with the sainted fathers and patriarchs of his nation;—ay, gazing on the ineffable glories of God Himself. How such an anticipation would have overpowered most men, and made the repression of exultant feeling an impossibility! But it was different with this moral hero. He betrays no apparent emotion. We meet him on the way from Gilgal, walking side by side with Elisha—calm, unmoved, unagitated. He appears more like a father, making farewell visits to his scattered family, before undertaking some long pilgrimage. Even when he meets his friends in this his last journey, he makes no reference to the peerless honour awaiting him. He sounds no trumpet before him. He could easily have gathered all Israel to the heights of the Jordan valley, to witness the wondrous spectacle of his departure. But with the humility of true greatness he keeps the secret locked in his bosom: perhaps the one dominant thought in his great soul, with the vision of that fiery rapture before him, was—'What have I done, after all, to merit such an ovation as this?' "O thou noble Tishbite," says Krummacher, "how does thy august aspect cast us all into the shade! Thou desirest to be nothing that God may be everything, and tremblest lest thou shouldest be taken for more than a dark shadow to set off the divine glory. Concealing the secret of thy approaching triumph, thou fliest the eye of witnesses, and seekest a veil for thy glory, afraid lest any one should admire and praise, instead of the Sun, the little dew-drop that reflects his beams. And yet thou hadst not seen Him who spake, 'I am meek and lowly in heart;' 'I seek not mine own honour, but him that sent me.' We have seen Him—the Beloved of the Father;—and yet how clearly does His image shine in thee, compared with us! Yes, we penetrate thy motive—we understand thy wishes, and are covered with shame!"

As in the case of Naomi's remonstrance with Ruth in a former age, it is probable that Elijah, with the view of testing the fidelity and attachment of Elisha, thus addressed his trusted brother-prophet at Gilgal, "Tarry thee here, I pray thee; for the Lord hath sent me to Bethel." He repeats the same at Bethel; and yet again at Jericho. But Elisha's constancy was unshaken. He was no summer friend, forsaking the prop on which he had long leaned when it was about to be removed. No importunities would deter him from discharging the last offices of hallowed earthly attachment. Dissimilar as we have seen the two in many ways were, in feelings and character, Elisha had been taught too tenderly to love and revere that once rough, stern spirit, to whom he owed so much, to desert him in the closing scene. And he solemnly protests, "As the Lord liveth, and as thy soul liveth, I will not leave thee."*

We are introduced, in this concluding portion of Elijah's history, to some new localities—Gilgal, Bethel, and Jericho. In the previous passages of his life, with the exception of the one incident of his flight to the Sinai wilderness, our interest was concentrated in the northern kingdom around Samaria, Jezreel, and Carmel. In this closing chapter, it is transferred to the border cities of the two nations, the valley of the Jordan, and the giant mountain range on its eastern banks. Let us pause to say a word in passing, regarding Gilgal, the place from which the two prophets are represented as starting together in company, and whither Elijah had purposely gone to make the first of these his farewell visits. It is only recent explorers who have solved satisfactorily the topographical difficulties which surround this place of their departure. The old, immemorial *Gilgal*, which formed Joshua's first encamping ground after entering Canaan, was situated in the lower valley of the Jordan in front of Jericho. By a glance at any map of Palestine, it will at once be observed

* We cannot accept as satisfactory the motives imputed to Elijah by some commentators in making the above request to Elisha—viz., his old love of solitude, or his desire that his friend should not witness his translation, and be spared the pain of parting. The presence of Elisha, we shall presently find, was necessary in order to complete his own investiture with the sacred prophetical office by the hands of his departing father. And the fact of the former being an eye-witness, we have every reason to believe, was revealed to Elijah as an accompaniment in his translation.

that it would have been a strange circuitous route for Elijah to have taken in order to reach the ford of the Jordan, had he travelled, (as has been generally taken for granted,) from the Gilgal of Joshua north to Bethel, and thence from Bethel back to Jericho. Moreover, the peculiarity of the expression in ver. 2, "So they went *down* to Bethel," would be manifestly inappropriate with reference to the city of Israel's encampment. No one could be said to "*descend*" from it to "the holy city," seeing that the way from the Gilgal of the Jordan valley to Bethel, is a gradual ascent of twelve hundred feet. We must seek its locality, therefore, somewhere among the mountains towards the north. The remains of a city or village, Jiljilia, on a steep, flat-topped hill, in the borders of Ephraim, north-west of Bethel, from which Ebal and Gerizim and the distant Hermon are seen northwards, and the mountains of Gilead towards the east, seems conclusively to point to the real locality of Elijah's present sojourn.* Indeed, this "mountain-Gilgal" is incidentally mentioned long previously by Moses in connexion with the old Canaanitish kingdom: "Are they not on the other side Jordan, by the way where the sun goeth down, in the land of the Canaanites, which dwell in the champaign over against *Gilgal*, beside the plains of Moreh?" (Deut. xi. 30.)†

But leaving this point of mere geographical interest, let us proceed to note the object of Elijah's farewell visits to these three favoured cities.

There was an unwonted and unmistakable stir and excite-

* See Stanley's Sinai, note, p. 306; also Robinson and Van de Velde, *in loco.*

† See also the learned and conclusive note of Kiel, p. 399.

ment in Gilgal, Bethel, and Jericho that day. Companies of young men—called here "Sons of the Prophets"—are seen gathering in earnest and arrested groups;—and when the two reverend men of God are welcomed in their midst, they beckon Elisha aside, and the secret is with trembling lips whispered by the surrounding youth in his ears—"Knowest thou that the Lord will take away thy master from thy head to-day?" To this query, the reply was given with bated breath—"Yea, I know it indeed;—hush! be silent!"

This introduces us to a new and most interesting phase in Elijah's history. We have hitherto been contemplating him in his public aggressive character, as the bold reformer—the defender of the old faith—the unsparing "iconoclast"—the uncompromising antagonist of the Baal worshippers—God's ordained minister of fire and judgment against the workers of iniquity—the vindicator of the Divine righteousness—the avenger alike of Israel's defiled sceptre and polluted altars. Here we have him under a new representation;—no longer engaged on the outward bulwarks he had so nobly strengthened and defended, but occupied with an equally momentous work. Directed, doubtless, mainly by the Spirit of God, but inspired also by his own apprehension for the decay of true religion throughout the land in this period of degeneracy, he had spent his closing years in providing for the spiritual well-being of the generation to come by establishing three, if not more, "Schools;"—the Universities,—or, if we might be allowed the modern term, the "Divinity halls," or Missionary seminaries of the age. By instructing in these, the flower of the Hebrew youth, in the great principles of the theocracy and the religion of their ancestors, he ensured the existence of a seed to serve his God, when he should be gathered to his fathers in the Church above. We must regard these Colleges—these repositories of sacred truth and learning, specially as the institutes of Elijah. True, indeed, we read of similar "schools of the Prophets" in the age and under the venerable presidency of Samuel, in Gibeah and Ramah.* Interesting, however, as

* "The chief places where they appear in his (Samuel's) own lifetime is his own birthplace and residence, Ramah, Ramathaim-Zophim, 'the heights,' 'the double heights' of the watchmen. From this, or from some neighbouring heights, they might be seen descending in a long line or chain, which gave its name to their company, with 'psaltery, harp, tabret, pipe, and cymbals.' Or by the dwellings, the leafy huts as they were in later times, on the hill side—'Naioth in Ramah.' They were settled in a congregation, (such is the word in the original,) a church, as it were, within a church, and 'Samuel stood appointed over them.' Under the shadow of his house they dwelt as within a charmed circle. From them went forth an influence which awed and inspired even the wild and reckless soldiers of that lawless age. Song and music and dances were interwoven in some sacred union, difficult for us to conceive in these western or northern regions, yet not without illustrations even at the present day from the religious observances of Spain and of Arabia. But, unlike the dances of Seville and Cairo, the mystical songs and ecstasies of these prophetic schools were trained to ends much nobler than any mere ceremonial observance. Thither in that age of change and dissolution, Samuel gathered round him all that was generous and devout in the people of God. David, the shepherd-warrior and wandering outlaw; Saul, the wild and wayward king; Heman, the grandson of Samuel himself, chief singer afterwards in David's court, and known especially as the king's seer; Gad, the devoted companion of David in his exile; Nathan, his stern reprover in after-times, and the wise counsellor of David's wise son—all, however different their characters and stations, seem to have found a house within those sacred haunts—all caught the same divine inspiration—all were, for the time at least, drawn together by that invigorating and elevating atmosphere. Long before Plato had gathered his disciples round him in the olive grove, or Zeno in the Portico, these institutions had grown up under Samuel in Judea."—*Stanley, Lectures on Jewish Church*, pp. 395-397.

these earlier institutions were, they were temporary in their character, compared with those of the age of Elijah. They seem to have had no fixed external constitution or organisation;—to have partaken more of the character of voluntary associations or combinations of youth, whose object was very much the cultivation of sacred poetry and music, and which were discontinued and superseded in the reign of David, by the new era he inaugurated in the services of the sanctuary and in sacred song. Moreover, the people in the age of Samuel, mainly through their reverence and love for his exalted character, and their gratitude for deliverance by his prayers from Philistine oppression, were imbued with his pious spirit. Though the priesthood had degenerated, the heart of the nation was sound. Samuel's influence, were it nothing else, had secured their loyalty to the God he so faithfully served. In Elijah's age all was different. A withering blight had passed over the old theocratic devotion. The people were wofully demoralised. Seduced by court influence, and by their own corruptions, they had lapsed into abominable idolatries. So lamentable indeed was the general apostacy, that, as we have seen, he who was best conversant with the gangrened condition of the body politic, had uttered the desponding plaint, "I am left alone!" May it not have been one of the many sacred lessons Elijah was taught at Horeb,—or rather, may it not have been one of the practical results of the assurance given him there, that there were yet seven thousand leal-hearted in the land, his being led thus to adopt means permanently to secure some of this residuary "leaven," for the benefit of succeeding ages? What better method could he devise, for protecting and perpetuating the purity of truth and worship, than founding a number of godly Schools,—nurseries of devotion and sacred literature. What more hallowed or befitting occupation for the evening of his own life,—when silvered locks had now displaced the raven hair of former days, and the giant strength of Cherith and Carmel had to bow to the inexorable demands of advancing years,—than to be engaged in rearing up and indoctrinating a noble band of young Israelites in the principles of the old theocracy? He seems to have made the words and the prayer of the Psalmist his own: "O God, thou hast taught me from my youth: and hitherto have I declared thy wondrous works. Now, also, when I am old and gray-headed, O God, forsake me not, until I have shewed thy strength unto this generation, and thy power to every one that is to come."*

We can only form a dim conjecture and conception of these closing eight years of hallowed occupation in the southern cities of Israel. If the Tishbite's bodily frame was more fragile than in the chivalrous days of earlier manhood; his soul, at least, burned, as ever, with inextinguishable fire. We can think of him gathering these children of the corrupt faith around him,—expounding the great principles of the Levitical and Moral Law,—making them minutely conversant with the details of their sacred books—the design (so far as was then revealed) of the complicated typical and ceremonial dispensation:—alternating these several pursuits, as in the earlier schools, with the study of sacred poetry and music: above all, exhorting his hearers to holy boldness and steadfastness in the faith, in the midst of an infidel and apostate age; and to

* Ps. lxxi. 17, 18.

transmit the great doctrines of the faith unimpaired to posterity, that the people which should be created might praise the Lord.* We may only further add, that these schools, in the kingdom of Israel, so far compensated for the want of the Temple services and Levitical priesthood, instituted in the metropolis of the kingdom of Judah.† If it be a new light, therefore, it is surely an interesting one, to regard Elijah as the founder, in one sense, of Ecclesiastical Colleges; —the first head and principal of a Religious University;— gathering around him a band of ingenuous youth and imbuing them with the truth set forth in his own great life motto— "The Lord liveth before whom I stand!" Indeed, if he had done nothing else, he would ever have been honoured, in this connexion, as a benefactor of his people;—the *conservator*, as he had already proved himself the *defender* of the faith. What a joy to the aged man to see these altar fires kindled in the Temple of God before his own lamp was put out;—these stars lighting up the theocratic firmament, ere he vanished like the sun from their sight, to shine in a brighter hemisphere! How he would now feel rebuked for his old saying, "I only am left!" How unreasonable and unwarrantable would his gloomy anticipations now appear, when he beheld these "arrows in the hand of the mighty!" Happy would he be

* Lamartine, in visiting one of the remarkable grottoes in Mount Carmel remarks, "The only view from it is over the boundless sea, and the only noise that is heard comes from the breakers continually dashing against the ledges of the promontory. Tradition recounts that this was the School in which Elias taught the knowledge of the mysteries and of sacred poesy," vol. i., p. 189.

† We find, in a later period of Jewish history, reference made to these "sons of the prophets" living in chambers or cells attached to the Temple at Jerusalem.—*Jeremiah* xxxv. 4.

who had thus "his quiver full of them;" and who, in looking round on such "nourishers of his old age," could say, with a grateful heart, to the God he served,—"Behold I and the children whom thou hast given me."

We may cease to wonder, then, at these eager groups, gathered on that memorable day, around the city gates, at Gilgal, Bethel, and Jericho. The Spirit of God,—whose influence, we have reason to believe, was specially poured out on these Prophetical students,—had communicated to them the fact that their reverend head and father was about to be taken up to his glorious reward. Let us endeavour to realise the scene. Let us picture the youths assembled at one of the college-gates here mentioned:—say that of Bethel. 'Shall we ever see him again? Shall we get his farewell benediction and blessing?' Thus we may imagine them interchanging their hopes and fears; when, all at once, they descry in the distance the well-known figure, in company with Elisha. With hearts bursting with fond, yet mingled emotions, they go forth to meet him! They have gathered lovingly around the object of their veneration, outside the gates of the city, somewhere in the moorish track still scattered with the stones, out of which Jacob, ages before, made his rude pillow. With delicate reticence, they make no allusion to their Spiritual Father of the approaching event. *He* has said nothing of his severance from *them*;—and they, with becoming deference, do not broach the theme uppermost in all their minds. To Elisha alone they confide the eager question, 'Is it indeed the case? Is it true? Can it be?' "Yes, indeed, it is," is the reply, "I know it—be silent!"

As if he said, 'It is too tender a theme to be mooted. Let there be no parting scene;—give and receive the parting farewell, in mute expressive silence!'

Let us just listen, in passing, to the grand philosophy of death, contained in these simple words of the sons of the prophets,—(what a comfort to those mourning the loss of beloved relatives)—"Knowest thou that THE LORD will take" thy master—thy friend—thy husband—thy wife—thy child "away to-day." They are *taken;* but knowest thou not it is "the LORD." Oh rejoice, it is not until *He* calls they can be "*taken.*" "The Lord gave, and the Lord hath *taken.*" "HE turneth man to destruction, and saith, Return, ye children of men."

From Bethel, the two men of God start on another stage of this last journey. They pursue the old well-known valley —"the long defile"—leading from Ai to Jericho, "which, in other times, formed the route of invading armies into Palestine."* On reaching Jericho, the same touching scene, in an interview with the sons of the prophets residing there, is repeated. Last parting counsels and blessings may have been given by Elijah; but, if so, they are not detailed in the simple record. But surely, with reference to himself, it is a touching farewell memory, that his closing earthly thoughts and deeds are in connexion with those beloved sons in the faith, whom he had, for the last decade of his life, watched and tended with such paternal interest and solicitude. The old helmsman is about to resign his post; but his last thought is for those, who, after he is gone, are to steer the shattered vessel through the surging sea. We may with

* Stanley.

reverence put into *his* lips, the farewell words which a Mightier far employed in leaving *His* college of disciples—"Now I am no more in the world, but these are in the world, and I come to thee. Holy Father, keep through thine own name those whom thou hast given me!"

Elijah makes one last effort to test the attachment of Elisha. "Tarry I pray thee here, for the Lord hath sent me to Jordan." But he receives the same reply—"As the Lord liveth and as thy soul liveth, I will not leave thee:" and it is briefly added, "they two went on." They are seen descending the slopes from Jericho, and having crossed the hot undulating sands, they are now approaching by the shelving banks of the "arrowy river." But there is a last touching and significant incident presented in this picture of the old Prophet's collegiate life. As they are thus standing by the brink of the Jordan—high up on the terraces—the steep, abrupt ridge* behind,—there are ranged fifty of his old Students—fifty Sons of the prophets. If forbidden the gratification of giving him a personal convoy, they have come out to the most conspicuous of the heights around to follow their master with loving eye, which they could do for a long distance, in that clear Eastern atmosphere, till he be lost from their sight in the gorges on the farther side of the river; sorrowing, like the elders of Ephesus, when, on the shore at Miletus, they bid Paul farewell, that they should see his face no more. We may, surely, gather from this affecting scene, the tenderness of the tie which knit together the old Master and his young disciples; —the sternness of manner of his earlier years being now

* A later tradition assigned to these heights the locality of the Saviour's temptation.

mellowed and softened by age; or rather, by the grace that was ripening him for immortality. We see in it the realisation of his old vision at Horeb—his own character reflected in that sublime diorama of nature. The earthquake and whirlwind and fire were now past: the close of his life had its befitting symbol in the "still small voice." "Mark the perfect man and behold the upright, for the end of that man is peace."*

* From a notice in a subsequent chapter, the young men in these colleges seem, like the Jews in later periods of their history, to have been instructed in mechanics, husbandry, and other useful arts of life. The nearest modern reproduction of these old schools or training establishments at Bethel, Gilgal, and Jericho, is one visited by us two years ago—the Missionary Institution of St Crichona, in the Black Forest of Germany,—and which is becoming, every day, better known among the Churches of Christendom. An ancient church, situated on the summit of a romantic hill, has been fitted up and enlarged so as to form a commodious residence for professors and students. The College is presided over by a venerable man —its patriarchal founder—M. Spittler. Its object is to train young men for the Missionary life, and the "St Crichona Brethren" are now scattered throughout the Missionary world. One special feature in the Institution is the instruction imparted to these humble students in the useful arts of life —mechanics, husbandry, &c. Our visit, on the occasion referred to, vividly recalled the incident in the life of Elijah, on which we have now been dwelling, when the whole inmates of the College turned out on their "terraces" to welcome, by a hymn or sacred song, their reverend father and friend, when they caught sight of him approaching the valley.

XX.

The Chariot of Fire.

"And Elijah took his mantle, and wrapped it together, and smote the waters, and they were divided hither and thither, so that they two went over on dry ground. And it came to pass, when they were gone over, that Elijah said unto Elisha, Ask what I shall do for thee, before I be taken away from thee. And Elisha said, I pray thee, let a double portion of thy spirit be upon me. And he said, Thou hast asked a hard thing: nevertheless, if thou see me when I am taken from thee, it shall be so unto thee; but if not, it shall not be so. And it came to pass, as they still went on, and talked, that, behold, there appeared a chariot of fire, and horses of fire, and parted them both asunder; and Elijah went up by a whirlwind into heaven. And Elisha saw it, and he cried, My father, my father, the chariot of Israel, and the horsemen thereof. And he saw him no more: and he took hold of his own clothes, and rent them in two pieces. He took up also the mantle of Elijah that fell from him, and went back, and stood by the bank of Jordan; and he took the mantle of Elijah that fell from him, and smote the waters, and said, Where is the Lord God of Elijah? And when he also had smitten the waters, they parted hither and thither: and Elisha went over. And when the sons of the prophets, which were to view at Jericho, saw him, they said, The spirit of Elijah doth rest on Elisha. And they came to meet him, and bowed themselves to the ground before him. And they said unto him, Behold now, there be with thy servants fifty strong men; let them go, we pray thee, and seek thy master: lest peradventure the Spirit of the Lord hath taken him up, and cast him upon some mountain, or into some valley. And he said, Ye shall not send. And when they urged him till he was ashamed, he said, Send. They sent therefore fifty men; and they sought three days, but found him not. And when they came again to him, (for he tarried at Jericho,) he said unto them, Did I not say unto you, Go not?"—2 KINGS ii. 8–18.

"AND THEY HEARD A GREAT VOICE FROM HEAVEN SAYING UNTO THEM, COME UP HITHER. AND THEY ASCENDED UP TO HEAVEN IN A CLOUD; AND THEIR ENEMIES BEHELD THEM."—REV. XI. 12.

"AND I SAW AS IT WERE A SEA OF GLASS MINGLED WITH FIRE; AND THEM THAT HAD GOTTEN THE VICTORY OVER THE BEAST, AND OVER HIS IMAGE, AND OVER HIS MARK, AND OVER THE NUMBER OF HIS NAME, STAND ON THE SEA OF GLASS, HAVING THE HARPS OF GOD."—REV. XV. 2.

THE CHARIOT OF FIRE.

THE loving attachment of the "sons of the prophets" to the person of Elijah, is rewarded by the sight of the closing miracle of his life, the recollection of which could not fail ever afterwards to embolden and strengthen them in the midst of their labours and trials. He is to pass over Jordan. The old Gileadite, with that instinctive love of country and birthplace so common at life's close, seems desirous to get across the border-river, that the scene of his mysterious departure might be amid the secluded valleys and ravines of his Fatherland. There was a ford or ferry then, as now, across the Jordan. But as the public life of the Prophet began, so it would terminate, by an exhibition of divine power. The God he served would certify to him, by an outward visible sign, the truth of that promise, which others apprehend only by faith, "Lo I am with you alway, even unto the end of the world."

Elijah unties his well-known mantle or cape; wraps it tightly round and round (as the word means), in the form of a staff;—and, like Moses of old with his shepherd's rod, he violently * smites the waters of the river. These are divided hither and thither, and the two prophets cross through the dry channel. On reaching the opposite bank, they quietly

* So also it is denoted in the original.

resume their lofty converse. Elijah feels that his moments are numbered;—he must bid his best and truest earthly friend farewell: "What shall I do for thee before I be taken away from thee?" is the interrogatory with which he breaks silence. It was a startling, perplexing question. Elisha well knew how much the departing seer had in his power. But as we may well imagine, earthly ambition had no share in dictating his answer: the wealth, and honours, and prizes of the world had no fascination in the eyes of one, who had already given such noble proof of self-renunciation, and self-sacrifice. His thoughts are not on himself, but on the Church which is so soon to be orphaned: his one solitary wish and ambition is, that he might be enabled to follow the footsteps of his great predecessor, by glorifying God in his day and generation. What to him half so enviable or desirable, as to inherit a portion of that noble spirit;—to have his own soul enkindled with some sparks of that hallowed fire which is now to be borne from the altar of earth to that of heaven! "And Elisha said, I pray thee let a double portion of thy spirit be upon me." What meant he by this request? We never for a moment can entertain the supposition, which some have ventured to advance, that Elisha's humble nature could have prompted him to crave that he might be doubly endowed in comparison with Elijah, by the possession of superior gifts and graces. The expression he used was one well understood among the Hebrews. A double portion of goods always descended to the eldest son of an Israelite;—this bringing along with it the special birthright blessing. Elisha's request, therefore, was no more than this—that he would have the double portion of the first-born, and thus be served heir and successor to his illustrious Master.* Elijah, indeed, in reply, allows that he had asked "a hard thing;"—he refers the granting of it to the Divine decision; informing his companion that if he be permitted to see with his bodily eyes the miraculous ascension, he may accept this as a pledge and assurance, on God's part, that the farewell request is not denied.

The two holy men are now lost to the sight of the fifty spectators among the recesses of Gilead. "They still went on," we read, "and talked." What that talk was, we know not; although we almost wish we could lift the veil and listen to the interchange of thought at that solemn moment, when one of the two was standing on the threshold of eternity. It may have been about *Israel*;—the completion of the overthrow of idolatry—the continued revival of the olden faith, and the nurturing of a manly piety through the instrumentality of the schools of the prophets. It may have been about *themselves*:—Elijah may have been tendering some last faithful lessons to his successor, from his own failures and shortcomings:—by a mutual rehearsal of the divine dealings, they may have been "encouraging one another in the Lord their God." It may have been about the mysterious, unseen realities of that glorious *spirit-world*, on which the honoured Tishbite was about to enter. Be this as it may; a tem-

* "The phrase employed in Deut. xxi. 17, to denote the amount of a father's goods, which were the right and token of a first-born son, is literally 'a mouth of two,' a double mouthful. Thus the gift of the 'double portion' of Elijah's spirit was but the legitimate conclusion of the act of adoption, which began with the casting off the mantle at Abel-Meholah years before. This explanation is given by Grotius and others."—*See note, Smith's Bible Dictionary*, p. 535.

pest—a desert simoom—would seem to have swept over them. We are reminded of Ezekiel's vision—"And I looked, and behold a whirlwind came out of the north, a great cloud, and a fire unfolding itself—and a brightness was about it, and out of the midst thereof, as the colour of amber out of the midst of the fire."* The mountains in a moment glow with lurid light. The unearthly splendour has resolved itself above their heads,—or rather by their side, —into a Chariot of FIRE, and horses of FIRE. Seated in this flaming equipage,—the burning axles revolved by the fierce hurricane,—the Prophet is swept upwards to the clouds.† Who can follow that car of mysterious flame? Imagination feebly tries to realise the feelings of the rapt and wondering occupant. He who is now borne aloft—not as a Prophet, but as a Conqueror—must, in his upward journey, have undergone some marvellous transformation, alike in bodily and spiritual organism, the nature of which we can only dimly conjecture. He left earth, "the man of like passions," with the body of corruption and death: but mortality is now swallowed up of life, and the corruptible has put on incorruption. Nor can we attempt to comprehend the magnificence of that flight, as he passes, through suns, and stars, and worlds, into the presence of the Infinite. We can but faintly picture in thought, the bands of Angels—the Seraphim (the burning or fiery ones) welcoming their kindred spirit within the heavenly gates. We can think of another illus-

* Ezekiel i. 4.

† Ephraim Syrus thus paraphrases it: "Suddenly there came from the height a storm of fire, and in the midst of the flame the form of a chariot and horses, and parted them both asunder."

trious member of the covenant people welcomed by Abraham, and Isaac, and Jacob in the kingdom of God;—or, as he bends before the throne—uttering, as his first words, the old motto of earth, now the song and rejoicing of eternity—"JEHOVAH LIVETH BEFORE WHOM I STAND!" Prophet of FIRE, thou hast reached the source of thy brightness! "Then shall the righteous shine forth as the SUN in the kingdom of their Father."

Such may have been the scene in heaven—What was it on earth? The solitary companion of his pilgrimage stands awe-struck, trembling, confounded;—his eye scorched with the blaze of the dazzling retinue. He can only give vent through his tears to the unavailing lament—"My father, my father, the chariot of Israel and the horsemen thereof!" He speaks like a bereft fatherless child. It is another proof of the change which had taken place in the naturally rough, stern spirit of Elijah,—making him the object, not of dread or terror, but of affection and filial love. At a former period of his history he would more probably have been apostrophised as "Prophet of fire," "Herald of wrath;" but now, it is "*My father, my father.*" Moreover, in the loss to the Church on earth of that one man, Elisha saw a sadder calamity than if the hosts of Jehoram—fifty thousand strong—had been swept away. HE had been the true army of Israel,—its bulwark of defence—its phalanx of strength—its head and shield in the day of battle. The chariots and charioteers on which earthly kings depend for victory, had been concentrated, in the case of Israel, in him. His word had at one time closed the loop-holes of heaven; at another, it had unmasked its batteries, and brought the lightning from the clouds. Rending his own clothes in customary token of grief, Elisha catches up the mantle that had dropped from the ascending chariot. It was a precious memorial of departed worth;—the old well-known companion of many wanderings,—associated with the performance of many chivalrous deeds. More than this, it was the priceless badge of his own investiture with the prophetic office,—the guarantee that his parting request had really been granted, as well as a visible sign to others that the spirit of Elijah rested upon him.* The weeping, solitary prophet must not abandon himself to fruitless tears or disconsolate grief. With that cloak as a treasured keepsake, and a pledge of reunion in a better country where no chariot of fire could part them, he hastens back to work and duty.

Standing again by the Jordan, he folds up the mantle, and smites the water, saying, "Where is the Lord God of Elijah?"—(*lit.*, "Where is Jehovah, the God of Elijah, even He?") Elisha knew that he had received for his heritage not only Elijah's mantle and Elijah's spirit, but, what was better, the guidance and support of Elijah's GOD. His best earthly friend and protector was gone,—severed from him for all time; but he had an unchanging portion and refuge in his Heavenly Friend—the living JEHOVAH, the strength of his heart and his portion for ever. The smitten waters obeyed his summons. The sons of the prophets, who were still gazing from the Jericho terraces, had their faith still further confirmed by

* To this day, in the East, a reputed saint, when departing from life, indicates his successor by bequeathing to him his mantle, the symbol of his spiritual power; and although that mantle may be dirty, patched, tattered, or threadbare, it is deemed to be of higher price than the brockaded robes of kings, and the older it is, the more precious it becomes. Elisha well understood the sign."—*Kitto.*

this renewed miracle. It afforded them additional assurance that Elisha was divinely invested with the spirit and office of their beloved father. They came to meet him, and "bowed themselves to the ground, doing homage before him." With a natural incredulity, however, they could hardly be convinced that Elijah's translation had been real. He was wont often, in the same way, suddenly to disappear from the haunts of men, and as suddenly to shew himself when duty demanded. Might he not possibly still be found dead or alive amid these savage mountains? Might not that fierce whirlwind have only taken him up a little way in its wings, and dashed him down on some mountain or valley? He had disappeared nigh the same spot, where, in an earlier age, his great predecessor in work and spirit had withdrawn from mortal view; and then, if it had been true that God had taken the soul of His servant to Himself,—could they not rescue his remains, at least, from the oblivion and mystery which had rested for centuries around the obsequies and burial of the old Hebrew lawgiver? It was a labour of love at all events;—a befitting and gratifying homage to his memory, to send fifty bold mountaineers to search these cliffs and precipices. This they did for three days without success—"*He was not, for* GOD TOOK HIM."

Let us occupy the remainder of the chapter, in seeking to discover some reasons for the peculiar method of Elijah's departure in his equipage of flame;—carried soul and body to heaven without tasting the pangs of dissolution.

In the symbolic teaching of the Old Testament, the Chariot of fire could not have been without its significancy, as a befitting close to a life of flaming zeal. We cannot avoid comparing and contrasting it with a greater and yet kindred event in a later age. A mightier than Elijah ascended also to heaven from one of the mountains of Palestine. But His triumphal chariot,—appropriate to His divine character and person as Immanuel,—was *a cloud*,—the chariot of God—the invariable emblem of Deity—which bore HIM majestically from the gaze of the rapt disciples;—that same "cloud" on which, as Judge, He is to come again;—"Behold, He cometh *with clouds!*" But as Elijah was the flaming minister of vengeance in an apostate age,—the successive acts in whose life-drama were the fiery flashes of divine judgment,—what more appropriate, than that in a car of symbolic Fire—(the emblem of God's judicial righteousness and wrath against sin)—he should ascend to his crown! "Elijah," says Matthew Henry, "had burned with holy zeal for God and His honour, and now with a heavenly fire he was refined and translated."

Nor have we to go far to discover the special end and design which God had in view, in vouchsafing to him this strange anomalous exemption from the universal doom of mortality,—revoking in his case the sentence of dissolution. He wished, by a startling outward visible sign, to give evidence to these degenerate times of the existence and reality of another life. Three great beacon-lights of hope and comfort on the subject of the body's Resurrection and a separate state, were set up to illumine each of the three grand eras or dispensations of the Church. The patriarchal era had this "blessed hope" unfolded in the translation of ENOCH; the Mosaic era in the departure of ELIJAH; and the crowning and triumphant pledge of it was reserved for the Christian era, in the Resurrection of our LORD—"Christ the first fruits, afterwards they that are Christ's at his coming." Let us stand with Elisha in these awful solitudes of Gilead; and as we see the Prophet-hero, in a moment, wrapt in his chariot of flame, and soul and body together borne upwards to heaven,—let us regard the mysterious scene as a grand prophecy by symbol and vision of our own glorious future as believers in Jesus—"children of the resurrection." Let us accept it as the foreshadow and pledge of what will happen to all the saints, both those whose bodies shall, at that solemn hour, be slumbering in their graves, as well as those who shall be alive at Christ's second coming. "We shall not all sleep," says the apostle, "but we shall all be changed, in a moment." The world itself shall then be resolved into a fiery chariot;—"the elements shall melt with fervent heat, the earth also, and the works that are therein shall be burned up." But, far above this tremendous conflagration, shall be heard the song of the glorified, as they are upborne in the cloudy whirlwind to meet the Lord in the air,—"Nevertheless we, according to his promise, look for new heavens and a new earth, wherein dwelleth righteousness."

And is there not comfort and encouragement, too, for every desponding believer, in this final dealing of God with His servant,—ministering to him such an "abundant entrance" into a world of glory? Who was this transfigured conqueror? Was it not the same coward-prophet, who once sat moping under the wilderness juniper-tree—peevish—fretful—abandoning himself to unworthy despair? Yet out of weakness he had been made strong: he had risen "like a giant refreshed:" and for this "man of like passions," who had, once and again, too painfully manifested the infirmities of a fallen nature, there was decreed at last the most glorious of triumphs! In the prospect of the same hour of departure, there may be some reading these pages, who, by reason of present corruptions and infirmities, and the saddening memory of past unworthiness and sin, may, through fear of death, be all their life-time subject to bondage. Let not these recollections of past shortcoming and backsliding, and the consciousness of present infirmity, needlessly depress you. If, like Elijah, you have listened to the still small voice;—if you have resolved, like him, to rise from your posture of despondency, to grapple with duty, to face trial, and to make a renewed consecration of yourselves to God,—He will not deny to you the chariot of final triumph—and give you, in Jesus, victory over death.

Are we meet for the chariot of fire? Is our work done? Are we girded for the glorious dismissal? Can we say, as the New Testament Elijah could say, "I am now *ready!*" Could we meet the fiery whirlwind bravely, calmly, as the Prophet did? We can, if we have made his life-motto our own, "Jehovah liveth." Or rather, if we have heard the voice of Him who has taken the sting from death, and robbed the grave of its victory,—"Fear not, I am he that LIVETH, and was dead; and, behold, I am alive for evermore, and have the keys of the grave and of death!" Laying hold by an appropriating faith of these words,—the chariots of death become the chariots of salvation,—the gate of the grave and the gate of heaven become one. Elijah, by his symbolic act, tells us how the last enemy may be truly conquered. It was when, with his mantle, he smote the Jordan, that the chafed waters receded and opened for him a safe passage. We have a mantle, too, by which we can smite the Jordan of death. It is the mantle of Christ's finished work and righteousness. It divides the darksome waves, and enables us to sing with the Psalmist, "We went through the flood on foot, there did we rejoice in him." Even now, as we are journeying on towards Jordan,—some of us, it may be, near it,—Jesus asks each of His true servants, as Elijah did his of old, "What shall I do for thee?" "Whatsoever ye ask in my name, that will I give unto you." What shall our request be? Shall it not be that of Elisha,—that, as heirs of God, we may have the portion of His First-born;—that we be "heirs of God, and joint-heirs with Jesus Christ;"—that even now we may be enrolled as members of "the general assembly and Church of the First-born which are written in heaven!" God keep us all from any poorer request;—from bartering, like Esau, our heavenly birthright for any mere mess of earthly pottage.

Again, to pass to the other closing incident; as we see the mantle of Elijah falling on Elisha, let us ask ourselves, 'Has his mantle fallen on us?' What mantle? His true cloak was not that rough coverlet of sheepskin; that was the mere outer badge and symbol peculiar to his age and office. But the mantle in which we may all more or less be arrayed, is the mantle of his virtues;—the beautiful spirit of consecration to the God he served; active, self-denying, single-eyed, bold, unflinching, uncompromising. O Prophet of the Highest, *whose* work, in these degenerate days, could stand the fiery test and ordeal like thine?" "My father, my father, the chariot of Israel, and the horsemen thereof!"

One other thought. It was in a chariot of FIRE, Elijah was taken to heaven. Is it not in a similar chariot, in a figurative sense, He takes many of his people still? He brings them, as He did Elijah, to the brink of Jordan; keeps them for years hovering amid the rough, rugged glens and gorges of trial;—seats them in a flaming equipage;—reins in the fiery horses, until, *in the fire*, they are refined and purified as gold, and fitted for their radiant crowns! Many are making it their life-long effort to mount some worldly chariot—the chariot of riches, or the chariot of fame. God often appoints far other for His loved ones. It is *the chariot of* FIRE! He whispers in their ears as they enter it, "Through much tribulation ye shall enter into the kingdom!" Oh, how many can bless Him with their dying lips, for that *chariot;*—and can say, on the retrospect of years on years, it may be, of burning trial, 'But for that chariot of fire, and these horses of fire, we should never have reached the throne and the crown!' and whose eternal ascription, as they cast that crown at the feet of a Redeeming Saviour, is this, "WE ARE SAVED, YET SO AS BY FIRE!" If God from time to time may be taking some of us out amid Jordan valleys, to witness glorious departures, let us bless His name as we see the chariots ascending, that humbler saints far than Elijah are still left in the Church to strengthen the faith of the beholders;—to magnify the power of sovereign grace, and to cast down upon mourning survivors a priceless mantle of Christian faith and love and triumph.

Further, If any be like Elisha, mourning the loss of departed relatives, let these follow his example, by smiting the waters of death with the noble question, "Where is the LORD

God of Elijah?" Elijah has gone: but the Lord God he served still remains;—the creature has perished, but the Creator perishes not. The chariot of flame has borne my loved ones out of sight; I have to return to life-duties like the Prophet of Gilgal—all solitary and alone—the companionship I most prized and cherished, gone for ever! But where is Elijah's Lord God? He ever lives, He ever loves. Yes, I will go back to my stricken home,—from these ravines of sorrow, these waters of death,—exulting and saying, "The Lord liveth, and blessed be my Rock, and let the God of my salvation be exalted." "*They* shall perish; but Thou remainest." And when the Lord shall conduct me down to these same ravines, and dark Jordan-floods;—I will take courage, from seeing the dying grace manifested by them, to go boldly through the gloom: "Yea, though I walk through the valley of the shadow of death, I will fear no evil, for Thou art with me." I will sing as they sang, with trembling lip and faltering utterance, just as they were stepping into the car of victory—the horses of fire impatient for flight:—

> "Raise the eye, Christian, just as it closeth,
> Lift the heart, Christian, ere it reposeth;
> Thee from the love of Christ nothing shall sever;
> Mount when thy work is done,—praise Him for ever."*

---

* The above sentence was written at the time of the occurrence of two remarkable deaths in which the author was specially interested. He retains the reference, as a feeble tribute to the cherished memory, particularly of one of these,—a member of his flock—at once the greatest sufferer, and the most signal monument of Divine grace he has known in the course of his ministry. Gifted by nature in no ordinary degree, she was, nevertheless, permitted to wander during twelve years of apparently unsanctified suffering

amid the gloomy ravines of trial; "going through fire and through water," before being brought out into "the wealthy place." But after the long, weary week-day of unrest, the Sabbath of the soul came at last. "Chosen in the furnace of affliction," the work of the Refiner was, in His own good time, accomplished. He seemed, in a marvellous way, to transfigure her before He glorified her. "BUT IT SHALL COME TO PASS THAT AT EVENING-TIME IT SHALL BE LIGHT."

We may appropriately append to this chapter the following meditation of Bishop Hall:—

"Lord, what great favour was that which Thou shewedst to Thy Prophet Elijah: to send a fiery chariot for him to convey him up to heaven! I should have thought that the sight of so terrible a carriage should have fetched away his soul beforehand, and have left the body grovelling on the earth. But that good Spirit of Thine, which had fore-signified that fiery rapture, had, doubtless, fore-armed Thy servant with an answerable resolution to expect and undergo it. Either he knew that chariot, however fearful in the appearance, was only glorious, and not penal; or else he cheerfully resolved that such a momentary pain in the change would be followed with an eternity of happiness. O God, we are not worthy to know whereto Thou hast reserved us. Perhaps Thou hast appointed us to be in the number of those whom Thou shalt find alive at Thy second coming, and then the case will be ours, we shall pass through fire to our immortality; or, if Thou hast ordained us to a speedier despatch, perhaps Thou hast decreed that our way to Thee shall be through a fiery trial. O God, whatever course Thou, in Thy Holy wisdom, hast determined for the fetching up my soul from this vale of misery and tears, prepare me thoroughly for it; and do Thou work my heart to so lively a faith in Thee, that all the terrors of my death may be swallowed up in an assured expectation of my speedy glory; and that my last groans shall be immediately seconded with eternal hallelujahs, in the glorious choir of Thy saints and angels in heaven. Amen. Amen."—*Bishop Hall's "Breathings of the Devout Soul,"* p. 204.

XXI.

The Mount of Transfiguration.

"And it came to pass about an eight days after these sayings, he took Peter, and John, and James, and went up into a mountain to pray. And as he prayed, the fashion of his countenance was altered, and his raiment was white and glistering. And, behold, there talked with him two men, which were Moses and Elias: who appeared in glory, and spake of his decease which he should accomplish at Jerusalem. But Peter and they that were with him were heavy with sleep: and when they were awake, they saw his glory, and the two men that stood with him. And it came to pass, as they departed from him, Peter said unto Jesus, Master, it is good for us to be here: and let us make three tabernacles; one for thee, and one for Moses, and one for Elias: not knowing what he said. While he thus spake, there came a cloud and overshadowed them: and they feared as they entered into the cloud. And there came a voice out of the cloud, saying, This is my beloved Son; hear him. And when the voice was past, Jesus was found alone. And they kept it close, and told no man in those days any of those things which they had seen."—LUKE ix. 28-37.

"AND I SAW ANOTHER MIGHTY ANGEL COME DOWN FROM HEAVEN, CLOTHED WITH A CLOUD; AND A RAINBOW WAS UPON HIS HEAD, AND HIS FACE WAS AS IT WERE THE SUN, AND HIS FEET AS PILLARS OF FIRE."—REV. x. 1.

THE MOUNT OF TRANSFIGURATION.

In the former chapter we found the gates of glory closing on Elijah and his triumphal chariot of fire. He had entered that silent land, from whose bourne no traveller ever returns to this nether world. It was now a thousand years since he had taken his place among its redeemed multitudes; —a fixed star in the unchanging heavenly firmament. For many centuries, however, the whole Jewish nation had entertained a confident expectation of his reappearance somewhere on the old scene of his labours;—an expectation founded on the remarkable, though enigmatical words of Malachi,—all the more remarkable and memorable from being the last announcement of the last of their prophets—"Behold, I will send you Elijah, the prophet, before the coming of the great and dreadful day of the Lord." That utterance (partially and typically fulfilled perhaps in the ministry of the Baptist, but whose true and literal accomplishment may yet be future*) had as shadowy fulfilment also in the sublime scene we are now to consider.

In perfect keeping with the sudden dramatic changes of his older history, like some blazing meteor, the "Pro-

* The reader is referred to some interesting details on this subject in the Appendix, page 345.

phet of Fire" wanders back again to earth; or rather, as the satellite follows its parent sun, he appears in transfigured glory, by the side of the same "Living Jehovah," before whom it was his boast formerly to stand. But it was now JEHOVAH-JESUS—"God manifest in the flesh!" The mysterious humiliation of that adorable Being was about to terminate in a darker night of suffering. In the prospect of undergoing he agonies of the garden and the cross, His divine Father had decreed a preliminary hour of glory and triumph. On the height of one of the mountains of the covenant land, delegates from the redeemed Church in earth and heaven met to do Him homage;—sustaining His soul in the prospect of treading the wine-press of the wrath of Almighty God. Out of the glorious throng of ransomed worshippers in the upper sanctuary, from Abel downwards, two appeared as representatives of the Church triumphant. Whether they were specially chosen for this high behest by God Himself, or whether they volunteered their lofty services, we cannot tell. If the latter, we may imagine, how, as the adorable Father announced His purpose of delegating messengers to glorify the Son of His love; and as He asked the question, amid the hushed stillness of the glorified throng—"Whom shall I send, and who will go for us?"—*One* bright spirit, glowing amid the ranks of Seraphim, and still burning with the old unabated ardour of earth, is heard to respond, "Here am I, send me!" It was a magnificent spectacle, indeed, which last occupied our attention—the ascent of the Prophet-conqueror in his car of flame. But he himself tells the disciples, in the topic which engages their talk and thoughts on the Mount, that there is One theme infinitely more glorious than translation—viz., that mighty deed of dying love,—atoning suffering,—without which no horses of fire could ever have been yoked to the ascending chariot, nor any entering made within the gate into the heavenly city.

The contrast is striking and worthy of note, between the Old and New Testament delineations of the character of Elijah. In the one he is almost from first to last presented to us as the Minister of vengeance, the Herald of wrath—severe, vigorous, stern; while, if left to glean our estimate from the few incidental notices contained in the gospel, we meet him as the minister of kindness to the widow of Sarepta; —an example of the power of effectual fervent prayer,—"turning the hearts of the fathers to the children, and the disobedient to the wisdom of the just." "This remarkably illustrates," as a recent writer well observes, "the great differences which may exist between the popular and contemporary view of an eminent character, and the real settled judgment formed in the progress of time, when the excitement of his more brilliant but more evanescent deeds has passed away. Precious, indeed, are the scattered hints and faint touches which enable us thus to soften the harsh outlines or the discordant colouring of the earlier picture. In the present instance, they are peculiarly so. That wild figure, that stern voice, those deeds of blood which stand out in such startling relief from the pages of the old records of Elijah, are seen by us, all silvered over with the white and glistering light of the mountain of Transfiguration. Under that heavenly light, Ahab and Jezebel, Baal and Ashtaroth, are forgotten, as we listen to the Prophet talking to our Lord of that event which was to be the consummation of all that He had suffered and striven for."*

Let us then approach this pavilion of glory, and catch our last sight of the Prophet on earth, till we meet Him on a better Transfiguration mount, where we shall have the brightness of the earthly scene without any of its transience.

The traditional locality of the Transfiguration, which as early as the sixth century was assigned to Tabor, is now abandoned by all modern writers. That it was ever selected, seems to have arisen from the one fact, or rather misconception, that this mountain answered apparently better than any other single eminence in Palestine to the description of the evangelist Mark, "an high mountain apart." When, however, the passage in the gospel comes to be narrowly examined, the word "*apart*" is found really to refer, not to the position of the *mountain*, but to that of the *disciples*. Besides, the objections to Tabor are in other respects insuperable. It is shewn by the most learned of Biblical travellers, that a fortified town must, during this very period of our Lord's life and ministry, have occupied the summit of the hill, the ruins of which are still remaining.† More than this, the chronological order of the narrative gives to the old reputed site a strong improbability. Harmonising the evangelistic narrative, it will be found that the Redeemer had just been sojourning with His disciples in the region round Cesarea-Philippi, the extreme north of Palestine. It is far from probable, that during the intervening six days, He would take the

* Smith's Biblical Dictionary, art. "Elijah."

† Robinson, vol. ii., p. 359.

long journey of fifty miles to the foot of Mount Tabor, on the confines of Zebulon and Naphtali. It is much more likely that He would select one of the spurs or ridges of snow-covered HERMON as a meet high altar for this scene of "excellent glory." The expression in the original of St Luke is, "He went up into the mountain."* As he was at that time under the shadow of this great giant, the solitary Alp of Northern Palestine, no mountain could so well answer the distinctive epithet applied by the evangelist. "It is impossible," says Dr Stanley, "to look up from the plain to the towering peaks of Hermon, almost the only mountain which deserves the name in Palestine, and one of whose ancient titles was derived from this circumstance, and not be struck with its appropriateness to the scene. That magnificent height, mingling with all the views of the north, from Shechem upwards, though often alluded to as the northern barrier of the Holy Land, is connected with no historical event in the Old or New Testament. Yet this fact of its rising high above all the other hills of Palestine, and of its setting the last limit to the wanderings of Him who was sent only to the lost sheep of the house of Israel, falls in with the supposition which the words inevitably force upon us. High up on its sunny slopes there must be many a point where the disciples could be taken 'apart by themselves.' Even the transient comparison of the celestial splendour, with the snow where alone it could be seen in Palestine, should not perhaps be wholly overlooked." †

* Ἀνέβη εἰς τὸ ὄρος.

"Standing amid the ruins of Cesarea, we do not need to ask what that 'high mountain' is. The lofty ridge of Hermon rises over us, and prob-

Such, then, may have been the wondrous earthly frame to the dazzling heavenly picture. It is an old tradition of the Christian Church, that the Transfiguration took place on the anniversary of the death of Moses, the first day of the month Adar. If the *time* was thus possibly connected with one of the two illustrious saints, it was from a spot commanding a distant prospect of those very places where once he wandered about in sheepskins and goatskins, destitute, afflicted, tormented, that the old Tishbite seer now "saw his Lord's glory—the glory as of the only begotten of the Father, full of grace and truth."*

We shall endeavour in the present chapter to depict the circumstantials of the Transfiguration-scene itself;—leaving for the concluding one the more special objects it was

ably on one or other of those wooded peaks above us that wondrous event took place."—*Porter*, vol. ii., *in loco.*

"What other hill could it be than the southward slope of that goodly mountain Hermon, which is indeed the centre of all the Promised Land, from the entering in of Hamath unto the river of Egypt—the mount of fruitfulness, from which the springs of Jordan descended to the valleys of Israel. Along its mighty forest avenues, until the grass grew fair with the mountain lilies, His feet dashed in the dew of Hermon, He must have gone to pray His first recorded prayer about death: and from the steep of it, before He knelt, could see to the south all the dwelling-place of the people that had sat in darkness and seen the great light—the land of Zebulon and of Naphtali, Galilee of the nations;—could see even with His human sight the gleam of that lake by Capernaum and Chorazin, and many a place loved by Him and vainly ministered to, whose house was now left unto them desolate. And, chief of all, far in the utmost blue, the hills above Nazareth sloping down to His old home: hills on which the stones yet lay loose that had been taken up to cast at Him when he left them for ever."—*Ruskin on Mountain Beauty; Modern Painters,* vol. iv., p. 392.

* The following, from the graphic pages of a recent traveller, describing

designed to subserve, particularly in its connexion with the appearance of Elijah.

It was after a season of unremitting labour in the great work of His ministry, that the Redeemer ascended this "high mountain" for rest and prayer. We know that "the evening" was the season He usually selected for these "Sabbaths of His soul." Moreover, as the same evangelist informs us that the three disciples who accompanied Him were "heavy with sleep," and finishes his account of the transaction by stating that "*on the next day* they came down from the hill;" —are we not abundantly warranted in supposing that the Transfiguration took place during night? If this conclusion be correct, what an additional pictorial interest does it impart to the scene! The sun has already set, far to the west, over the great sea;—all nature is hushed to repose;—nothing is

a visit to Hermon and its vicinity, suggests another remarkable association and coincidence, viz., that Elijah must have been brought at this time into singular proximity with one of the great temples of the false deity whose worship it had been the main object of his life to overthrow;—the Prophet of Fire, probably within sight of one of the principal shrines of the "Fire God." "We went to the large temple, of which a great deal still remains *in situ*. It was placed with the angles to the cardinal points, in order that the south-west side should face the Baal temple raised on the highest point of Hermon." Of this latter temple the writer thus speaks:— "A massive wall once encircled the highest peak of the mountain, and a temple stood here. The ground is covered with the large hewn stones of the outer wall; a few of them were bevelled, and we saw some bold simple sculpturing on some of the others—the style reminding us of Dier-el-Ashayr. That a temple, dedicated to Baal, once existed here is to be gathered from the name of Baal-Hermon, applied in Judges iii. 3, and 1 Chron. v. 23. And St Jerome testifies to the fact. No one could stand on that summit and turn his eyes from east to west, from north to south, without feeling that no worshipper of the sun could have left so grand a spot unconsecrated to their God."—*Beaufort's Egyptian Sepulchres and Syrian Shrines*, vol. ii., p. 14.

heard but the rippling of the mountain streams;—nothing is seen but the pale silvery moonlight, falling on the everlasting snows of the mountain;—or, high above, myriad stars, like temple lamps lit in the outer court of some august sanctuary; —these, however, about to be quenched, for the time, by the seraphic radiance which is presently to stream forth from the Holiest of all.

We cannot resist pausing for a moment on the threshold of this consecrated shrine, in order to mark the grand prelude to the manifestation of the excellent glory—*Jesus* PRAYS. On that lonely hill top, or ridge, the Son of Man and Lord of all, pours out His soul, as a strong wrestler, in the ear of His Father in heaven. The moon and stars listen to their Maker's voice; and that voice, the voice of Prayer—pleadings for Himself,—intercessions for the world —the Church—for His disciples—for *us!* It is well worthy of note, though the remark be a trite one, that all the great events and crises of the Saviour's incarnation-life are hallowed by *prayer*. He prays at His baptism, and lo! the heavens are opened. He prays in the garden—"Father, if it be possible, let this cup pass;" and "being in an agony He prayed the more earnestly." At the cross He prays, "Father forgive:" "Father, into thy hands I commend my spirit." His very cry in the hour of His God-desertion—"My God, my God" —was an impassioned prayer! We have all in our diverse human experiences, though separated by an untravelled distance from those of the Divine Redeemer, our crises-hours—solemn emergencies—terrible moments of temptation—sore suffering—crushing disappointment—poignant bereavement. Shall we not learn, from the Prince of sufferers, our true preparation against the dark and cloudy day? If Almighty strength and Infinite purity needed to be thus girded for the struggle-hour, how can such weaklings as we are, dispense with the sacred privilege? Oh, that in all time of our *wealth*, when climbing the giddy heights of prosperity;—led out by Satan to "the exceeding high mountain;"—tempted to surrender or compromise principle in order to propitiate the world's maxims and fashions, and barter a good conscience for its perishable baubles,—obsequious to man, disloyal and unfaithful to God; or, in all time of our *tribulation*, when called to climb the mount of trial,—we would listen in thought for our protection and safety, our encouragement and example, to the voice of Him "who, when He was on earth, made supplication with strong crying and tears to Him that was able to save Him from death; and was heard in that He feared."

The three disciples selected from the apostolic company to be the representatives of the Church on earth, at their Lord's Transfiguration, are Peter and the two sons of thunder. Peter "the Rock,"—James, the first of the twelve who was to suffer death for his Master's sake—John, the favoured disciple, whose head afterwards leaned on the bosom of incarnate Love. Wearied with the fatigues of the day, these infirm watchers fall asleep. They continue locked in slumber till a strange unearthly light is felt playing on their eyelids. Is it a dream? a trance? They wake up; and lo! a spectacle of overpowering glory bursts upon them. The Lord they left praying, is now seen before them, arrayed in garments woven as with sunbeams;—His raiment emitting light, vying in whiteness with the virgin snow; or as St Mark, in his own graphic way of delineation adds, "So as no fuller on earth can white them." A bright fleecy cloud surrounds Him with a halo of glory; and on either side of the transfigured Saviour there is a glorified form. The apostles gaze in mute wonder. As their adorable Master is engaged in converse with these myterious visitants from another world the question must have passed from lip to lip—"Who are these arrayed in white robes and whence came they?" They do not require, however, to wait a reply. Either by revelation, or more probably from hearing their Lord addressing the two glorified ones by name, they know that they are in the presence of none other than MOSES and ELIAS. With what profound interest,—with what trembling transport,—would they gaze on the two Fathers of the Nation, whose names must have been embalmed in their holiest memories since the dawn of earliest childhood. "What!" we may imagine them exclaiming, as they fixed their eyes first on the older saint,—"Is this indeed the great Shepherd who led Israel like a flock; who did marvellous things in the sight of their fathers, in the land of Egypt, in the field of Zoan? Is this he whose rod smote the tongue of the Red Sea,—whose feet trod the steeps of Sinai,—who spake amidst its lightnings and thunders face to face with God? What! is this indeed the great Elijah—the old seer of Gilead—the faithful witness for Jehovah in Israel's most degenerate age—the mighty wrestler on Carmel—the homicide at the Kishon—the fiery minister of vengeance—the herald of righteousness,—whose earlier life of tempest and earthquake and fire merged at last into the still small voice of love,—he who was taken to heaven alive in a whirlwind, and who was prophesied of by Malachi as the precursor of the great and dreadful day of the Lord? The earthly character and mission of both, presented a lowly yet striking reflection of Him they had now come to honour. Their messages, had been received like His with scornful indifference. One had, in a noble spirit of self-sacrifice, surrendered his bright prospects as heir to the throne of Egypt; the other, with fearless devotion to truth, had confronted royal frowns, and offered a heroic protest against the nation's guilt, in the name of his dishonoured Master. No more befitting attendants surely could have been selected to do homage to Him, who "made Himself of no reputation;"—left His throne and crown for a manger and a cross;—"the faithful and true Witness," who came "not to do His own *will*, but the will of the Father who sent Him." The eyes of the earthly and the heavenly delegates are alike fixed on the great central figure of the group;—the toil-worn sorrow-stricken Man, who, a few hours before, had climbed the steep ascent with weary limb and burdened soul, but who is now radiant with superhuman glory, the true Apocalyptic Angel "standing in the sun." The face of one of these heavenly attendants, fifteen hundred years before, had been seen resplendent by the camp of assembled Israel, but it was a borrowed lustre. He had come forth from the presence-chamber of God on Sinai, and the ineffable brightness still lingered by reflection on his countenance. In the case of the Redeemer on the Transfiguration-mount, that glory was inherent. The rays of indwelling Deity, imprisoned in His body of humiliation, burst through the casement of flesh,—the lustre of eternity streamed through the veil of His humanity. "Moses," it has been observed, "only ***shewed*** the brightness of the Father's glory, He *was* that brightness." No wonder that Peter, in an ecstasy of impulsive joy, exclaims, "Lord, it is good for us to be here;" and that he even proposed the erection of three tabernacles, where their Lord and His glorified attendants might take up a permanent abode, and, enthroned on these majestic peaks of Hermon, reign over regenerated Israel.

But gaze we yet a little longer, and there is a new phase in this diorama of heavenly splendour. A cloud of yet more transcendent brightness descends on the head of the Saviour and His two celestial companions. It is nothing less than the *Shekinah*, or Divine glory, the symbol and emblem of a present Deity;—the same cloud which of old preceded in a pillar-form the march through the wilderness; which hovered over the ark in the tabernacle, and over the holy of holies in the Jerusalem temple. The three disciples seem, at this juncture, to have been shut out and excluded by the new cloudy canopy. They became greatly afraid; the appearance of the cloud struck them with awe. This feeling, moreover, increased as they felt themselves thus dissociated and dissevered from their Lord, whose presence a moment before, radiant though it was with almost intolerable brightness, had yet been to them the blessed pledge of security and safety. A voice issues from the cloud. A message comes to them from the midst of the excellent glory—"This is my beloved Son, in whom I am well pleased; hear ye him." It is the sublime attestation of God the Father. "He installs the Son as sovereign of the kingdom."* He consecrates Him as Prophet, Priest, and King for evermore.

* Olshausen.

If such be the utterance of the Eternal Father in this seraphic scene, let us return for a moment to Elias, and inquire what part he takes in the august conference. Are his lips sealed? Does he appear as a mere dumb witness, a passive spectator, mutely doing homage to his great Lord, and then silently winging his arrowy flight back among the ministering Seraphim? No, he *does* speak, and we listen with profound interest to the theme with which he breaks silence. He and Moses are the first messengers from the spirit-land who have visited our earth,—the first voyagers who have ever come back with tidings from the undiscovered shores! What then, we curiously inquire, is the theme which engrosses their thoughts;—what the subject of their heavenly converse;—what communications have they brought down with them from the realms of light, wherewith to gladden their Lord in His hour of glorification? When we last parted from Elijah it was when he was taken to heaven in his fiery chariot. Does he talk of this? or, now that the scenes of his old labours are faintly descried under the star-lit heavens, do these suggest to him the rehearsal of his own life-marvels, or those of his sainted companion? or does he commune of the nobler inheritance on which he had since entered—the thousand years—the millennium of bliss, since last he trod the earth?—does he speak of the last song in which he had joined with the celestial worshippers, or of the last embassy of love on which he had sped, or of his lofty association with the brotherhood of Seraphim,—ministers of flaming fire,—who keep the lamps of the heavenly temple continually burning? No, none of these. His topic of converse, and that of his illustrious compeer is the last we should have dreamt of as being selected for ecstatic triumph. It is DEATH!—"*Death,*" that awful anomaly in God's universe—"*Death,*" the theme of all others undwelt on in heaven, because there unknown. Death too,—*the King of Terrors,*—lording it over *the Prince of Life;*—for it was Death about to vanquish none other than the August Being who was now glorified under that canopy of dazzling splendour. Moreover, it was death in peculiar and abnormal form;—not the gentle dismissal of the soul to the unseen world,—not the tranquil sleep of His "beloved" which God gave to *one* of these saints, nor the holy beatific rapture he vouchsafed to the other,—but death specifically spoken about as occurring at "*Jerusalem;*"—a death mysteriously associated, at all events to the Omniscient Son of God, with a thorn-crown, and bitter anguish, and an accursed tree;—a fearful baptism of blood! Nor would it appear that the strange converse was limited to the glorified attendants;—the transfigured Saviour Himself joined in that wondrous talk. 'Speak not,' He seems to say, 'of my crown; speak to me rather of my cross; speak to me, even at this moment of my glorification, of that bitter humiliation which awaits me. It is by being "lifted up," not as now in glory, but lifted up in suffering and anguish, that I am to "draw all men unto me!"'

But the hour of triumph is at an end, the dazzling lustre has faded from the Redeemer's raiment, the celestial voices are hushed, the vision has passed away. Emerging from the cloud and returning to the three still terrified disciples, their Lord finds them, in the extremity of their fears, to have lost all consciousness. They are still "heavy with sleep." Alas! for weak, fragile human nature, even in seasons when it might well be expected to rise above its weakness. These disciples slept now in the hour of their Master's rapture, as they slept afterwards in the hour of His sorrow. Ah, men "of like passions!" If Elijah saw them then from his cloudy canopy, he would remember the juniper-tree, and be silent. "What doest thou here, Elijah?" What! my own disciples, "could ye not watch with me one hour?" Blessed for us who may be mourning over our dull, lethargic frames, losing by our slothfulness many bright transfiguration-experiences—the blessings of the mount:—happy for us that there is a day and a world coming, when the gentle rebuke of an injured Saviour shall never more be needed—"Why sleep ye?" For "there shall be no night there!"

But He is faithful that promised—"I will never leave thee, nor forsake thee." The hour of manifested glory has made no change in the sympathising tenderness of the Brother-man. He is still "that same Jesus"—He comes to the disciples, as He had done oft before, in their weakness and terror; touches them, and with gentle voice says, "Arise, be not afraid." They lifted up their eyes;—the cloud—the glory—the celestial visitants—the voice, were gone; "they saw no man—save Jesus only." The morning light was again tipping the eastern hills,—and they must hasten down the slopes of the mount, once more to encounter stern duty, temptation and trial.

XXII.

Lessons of the Mount, and Closing Thoughts.

"And, behold, there appeared unto them Moses and Elias talking with him. Then answered Peter, and said unto Jesus, Lord, it is good for us to be here: if thou wilt, let us make here three tabernacles; one for thee, and one for Moses, and one for Elias. While he yet spake, behold, a bright cloud overshadowed them: and behold a voice out of the cloud, which said, This is my beloved Son, in whom I am well pleased; hear ye him. And when the disciples heard it, they fell on their face, and were sore afraid. And Jesus came and touched them, and said, Arise, be not afraid. And when they had lifted up their eyes, they saw no man, save Jesus only. And as they came down from the mountain, Jesus charged them, saying, Tell the vision to no man, until the Son of man be risen again from the dead. And his disciples asked him, saying, Why then say the scribes that Elias must first come? And Jesus answered and said unto them, Elias truly shall first come, and restore all things."—MATT. xvii. 3–11.

"FOR YE ARE NOT COME UNTO THE MOUNT THAT MIGHT BE TOUCHED, AND THAT BURNED WITH FIRE, NOR UNTO BLACKNESS, AND DARKNESS, AND TEMPEST, AND THE SOUND OF A TRUMPET, AND THE VOICE OF WORDS; WHICH VOICE THEY THAT HEARD ENTREATED THAT THE WORD SHOULD NOT BE SPOKEN TO THEM ANY MORE. BUT YE ARE COME UNTO MOUNT SION, AND UNTO THE CITY OF THE LIVING GOD, THE HEAVENLY JERUSALEM, AND TO AN INNUMERABLE COMPANY OF ANGELS, TO THE GENERAL ASSEMBLY AND CHURCH OF THE FIRST-BORN, WHICH ARE WRITTEN IN HEAVEN, AND TO GOD THE JUDGE OF ALL, AND TO THE SPIRITS OF JUST MEN MADE PERFECT." —HEB. XII. 18, 19, 22, 23.

LESSONS OF THE MOUNT, AND CLOSING THOUGHTS.

HAVING in the previous chapter endeavoured to describe, as minutely as the details furnished by the three separate Evangelists enable us, the scene and significant incidents of the Transfiguration, we shall proceed, in these closing pages, to speak of the objects which this beautiful New Testament sequel to the life of Elijah seems mainly intended to serve.

These were various. We shall restrict ourselves to the one which, while in itself most prominent, has also a more special connexion with our Prophet—viz., the intimation thus given by visible symbol, that *the legal and prophetical dispensations were superseded by the gospel.**

Moses and Elias were the representatives of the two former. Moses, the great lawgiver, who had received the ten commandments, amid the thunders of Sinai, from the hands of God Himself; and Elias, as we now well know, the most distinguished in his own age, or perhaps in any age, among the Prophets of Israel. Both appear to do homage to *Jesus;* confessing their subserviency to Him, of whom both the law and the Prophets bore witness. They lay down, as it were, the seals of office,—the warrants for their temporary ministration,—at His feet;—Moses his

* See an admirable exposition of these various objects in one of Dean Horsley's sermons.

rod — Elias his prophetic-mantle, — acknowledging that neither they nor the dispensations of which they were the representatives, had any glory by reason of "the glory that excelleth." The law seemed to say, through *its* representative, 'O Lamb of God, all my bleating sacrifices pointed to Thee.' Prophecy seemed to say through *its* representative—'O Prophet of the Highest, all my picturings and prefigurations centred in Thee.' The shadow is transformed into the substance. 'In Thee,' says Moses as he gazes on his transfigured Lord, 'I see the end, and meaning, and reality of the Passover—the besprinkled lintels,—the smitten rock, the serpent of brass,—the blood-stained mercy-seat.' 'It was Thee,' says Elijah, 'I saw in the sacrifice on Carmel,—Thee, I heard in "the still small voice" of Horeb.' And when Peter, in the wonted ardour of his spirit, suggested the erection of three tabernacles—one to each of the glorified persons,—God gave a very significant intimation, that both the other ministers were to give place to "the minister of the sanctuary, and the true tabernacle which the Lord pitched, and not man." For "while he thus spake, there came a cloud and overshadowed them, and they feared as they entered the cloud; and there came a voice out of the cloud, saying, This is my beloved Son; hear ye him." "Hear ye Him." 'Ye have been accustomed to hear, and to regard with profound veneration, Moses and Elias and the other Prophets,—but a greater than these is here. This is the illustrious personage of whom your great lawgiver himself predicted, that "a Prophet would the Lord God raise up unto you of your brethren;"—this is He "of whom Moses in the law and the prophets did write, Jesus of Nazareth;"—

this is the true Elijah (" the strong Lord ") who shall " turn the hearts of the fathers to the children, and the heart of the children to their fathers." "This is my beloved Son; hear ye him." '* And then, when the glorious vision departed, Moses and Elias disappear, and leave "*Jesus only;*"—a beautiful emblem, designed to intimate that the former dispensations were now done away! Elias and Moses, two names which the disciples, in common with their countrymen, regarded almost with religious awe, were to give place to a greater. The work of the servants is done—merged in the glory of their Master; the rod of Moses is broken—the mantle of Elijah falls on the true Elisha—JESUS was to be hailed as " King of the Jews." By Him the moral law was obeyed—the prophecies accomplished—the types fulfilled. And now, in accordance with God's wonted dealings with His subordinate ministers, a solemn investiture takes place of the Great Antitypical-Priest, Lawgiver, and Prophet;—the glorious company of the apostles—the goodly fellowship of the Prophets—the noble army of martyrs—praise Him! Adoring Him as Redeemer, they proclaim through these, their two sainted representatives, " Behold the Lamb of God, which taketh away the sin of the world!"

The accompaniments of that scene of glory, too, were such as to vindicate the superiority of the gospel over any of the previous dispensations. The legal dispensation was ushered

* Stier well remarks—" He who fulfils the law and the prophets holds a select council with the personal representatives of the law and the prophets. Moses and Elias appeared together as closing the old covenant, (See Mal. iv. 4, 5;) and now, in the heavenly imperial council, before the throne of the excellent glory, they stand upon the threshold of the new covenant."

upon the world from the blazing summit of a mountain, amid a fearful canopy of cloud and darkness, thunderings, and lightnings, and tempest. The other, from the summit of a mountain, too; but now the thunders are hushed—the blackness has passed away; and in its stead a cloud of surpassing brightness overshadows. We behold Moses on the one—his language is, "I exceedingly fear and quake;" —Peter on the other, "Lord, it is good for me to be here." On the one, we listen to a voice which shakes the earth; and "they that heard entreated that the word should not be spoken to them any more;"—on the other, we hear a voice,—but it is the still small voice of love, pointing us to Christ, saying, "*Hear ye Him!*" Elias, on the same Horeb-mount, comes forth from his cave, muffling his face in his mantle, gazing with trembling awe on the winged symbols of vengeance that passed in succession before him. Now, with open face, he beholds, as in a glass, the glory of his transfigured Lord, and is "changed into the same image from glory to glory!"

As a further reason why Moses and Elias were employed on this occasion in preference to other ransomed saints, we may infer that they were sent to bear attestation to the great plan of the Redemption which is by Christ Jesus;— "that neither is there salvation in any other, for there is none other name under heaven given among men whereby we must be saved." Of those who had entered on the inheritance of the promises, if any there were, who could have attained heaven on the ground of their own good works and meritorious deeds, it would doubtless have been the two who are here with the Lord on the mount. We know well the history of the one,—how in his life of exalted purity, there is but one solitary recorded blemish—discovering him to be a "man of like passions." A similar intimacy with the other, would unfold a marvellous display of faith, humility, devotedness, heroic endurance, self-denial, and heavenly-mindedness. So that if any of the human race could have laid claim, so to speak, to the kingdom above, on the footing of personal merit, we should have pointed to these two illustrious representatives of the two earlier dispensations—these two heads of the sainted hierarchy. But we could not have been more powerfully or impressively told, that every Redeemed worshipper before the Throne, from the least to the greatest in the kingdom, owes his place there to another righteousness than his own. These mightiest of glorified mortals *talk of nothing but "the decease that was to be accomplished at Jerusalem!"* They appear in shining raiment;—but they proclaim that these robes owe all their brightness, these crowns all their lustre, to the Saviour of Calvary. We may regard them, therefore, not only as the representatives of bygone dispensations of type and figure on earth, but as the representatives of a higher dispensation of glory in heaven;—sent down from the ransomed multitude above, to tell to the world that not a robe is *there* from Abel's downwards, but what is washed in the blood of the Lamb;—that every jewel that sparkles in their crown they owe to His cross and passion. We may regard them as commissioned to tell of the intense interest with which that approaching "decease" was contemplated by the companies of the upper sanctuary. In this view of it, while the scene on the mount would greatly strengthen the faith of the disciples in the hour of trial, it would also tend, and was doubtless designed, to impart courage and consolation and support to the great Redeemer Himself, in the prospect of coming anguish. Oh! would He not be cheered and strengthened for His approaching conflict, when He descended the hill with the approving smile of His heavenly Father resting upon Him;—conscious that He carried with Him to the garden and the cross, the awakened interest and sympathies of a Redeemed multitude which no man can number, who waited in profound suspense for the moment of Victory, when He should cry, "It is finished," and bow His head and give up the ghost! Let us try to imagine the wondrous converse. "*They spake of His decease!*" They would strengthen His soul, by telling of the mighty results that decease was to accomplish;—the transcendent lustre it would pour around the throne of God,—magnifying every attribute of His nature—securing peace on earth, and glory in the highest. They would tell of the august lesson it would read to a wondering universe;—what an attestation to God's unbending holiness—His spotless truth—His hatred of sin, and yet His love to the sinner! They would tell of the countless multitudes who had died in the faith of this "decease," and were now rejoicing above in the prospect of its accomplishment;—of the myriads, in unborn ages, who were to reap its fruits, out of every nation, and kindred, and people, and tongue. Yes! we may conceive that the eye of the Transfigured Saviour (as of old from mount Pisgah did that of the lawgiver of Israel, who now stood by His side) would, from the top of this northern height, survey the land of covenant promise. Stretching far beyond the plains of Galilee. He would see, in majestic perspective, the nations of the earth confessing Him as Lord, and rejoicing in that very decease He was about to accomplish. Amid the stillness of that midnight scene, He would direct His own eyes, as He had done those of the Father of the Faithful ages before, to the starry firmament, and behold there an emblem of His unnumbered spiritual seed! Thus seeing of the travail of His soul, He would be satisfied. The thought that He should thus turn many to righteousness, who should shine as the stars for ever and ever, would mightily nerve Him for the hour and power of darkness. Oh! when, from this holy converse, the past, and present, and future, all seemed to combine in proclaiming the results which were suspended on His decease;—when He saw the tide of glory that would thereby roll in to the Throne of God;—when He thought of the mighty moral influence of His death, not on the family of earth only, but on unknown worlds—varied orders of intelligence throughout the universe;—in the dispensation of the fullness of time gathering together in one all things in Christ, both which are in heaven and in earth;—He would descend to the conflict rejoicing to think, that, though His own garments were to be rolled in blood, the garments of a myriad multitude should by that blood be made white;—contemplating such results as these, not only would He willingly enter the garden, and drink the cup, and endure the cross; but, as if longing for the hour of victory, He could exclaim, "I have a baptism to be baptized with, and how am I straitened until it be accomplished!"

In addition to this more special design of the Transfiguration, there are many other interesting and comforting truths which may warrantably be deduced from the consideration of the hallowed scene. Among these is the testimony borne to *the state of immediate bliss into which the souls of believers pass at the hour of death*;—that the moment the spirit leaves the walls of its crumbling earthly prison, it soars into the presence of God, and engages forthwith in active errands of love and duty. The appearance of Moses and Elias surely affords a conclusive refutation of the cold cheerless theory, which is not without its modern advocates, that, after death, the disembodied soul passes into an intermediate state of torpor and inactivity—a condition of lethargic slumber; that there is an arrest put on its spiritual activities, until the Resurrection morning welcomes it back from its sojourn in this dream-land, and reunites it to the raised and glorified body. If the case of Elias be deemed peculiar, he having been translated, soul and body together, without dying,—it is not so, at all events, regarding his brother delegate. The body of Moses was mysteriously entombed amid the solitudes of the Moab mountains, over against Baal-peor;—his limbs composed by angels;—his grave dug by God Himself, (for "God buried him,") though sedulously secreted from the eye of man. But we see the Hebrew Prophet on the Transfiguration-mount,—a visible, living, speaking, recognised representative of the family of the ransomed. He comes forth, along with a kindred spirit, from the brotherhood of the redeemed; and as if the theme, too, in which they had been just engaged with the adoring multitudes around the throne, were still thrilling on their tongues. His body slumbers amid the ravines of Pisgah;—it has long ago crumbled away in insensate dust; but the true MAN is a conscious, thinking, living being—a ministering angel before God—embarked in the ceaseless energies of holy service.

Behold, too, in visible symbol, the blessed bond of union which links together the Church on earth and the Church in heaven;—Moses and Elias, from the bright-robed company above,—the three disciples from the Church in the wilderness, have their eye centred on ONE peerless Object of adoration and love. The note which the two glorified ones last struck on their golden harps within the veil, is taken up on the earthly mount: "Worthy is the Lamb that was slain." It was for *Him*—in order that they might testify to His sufferings and their resultant glory—that these two immortal ones left their thrones and their bliss for that hour of earthly rapture; and it is in active embassies of love for "that same Jesus," that the redeemed are now delighting, and will delight to exercise the noblest energies of their natures through all eternity. Yes! as we leave the history of the great Prophet, whose life of marvel has so long occupied us, it is surely delightful and interesting to bear away the recollection that the last glimpse we get of him, as he is hidden from our sight by the enveloping Shekinah on the mountain summit, is *adoring the Redeemer of the world;*—casting all his mighty deeds, his zeal, his humility, his heroic endurance, his untiring self-consecration —*all* at the feet of the Lord who died for him! Ay, more, —we believe, were we to draw aside the mysterious curtain which hides the invisible, we should behold him still in his old attitude,—rejoicing in a living Saviour-God, before whom he stands. And as others among the company of the redeemed, who revered his hero-deeds on earth, might still love to rehearse them in his presence; we may imagine him, with the tongue of fire, now burning only with love, exclaiming in self-renouncing lowliness, 'Perish the memories of Cherith, Sarepta, Carmel, Jezreel, Jericho, the chariot-rapture,—" *God forbid that I should glory,* SAVE IN THE CROSS OF OUR LORD JESUS CHRIST!"'

Blessed thought—Christ the all in all of heaven! The saints may be lustrous, radiant points of light;—hallowed luminaries, emitting rays of sacred glory: "But the city had no NEED of the sun, neither of the moon, to shine in it; for the glory of God did lighten it, and the Lamb was the light thereof." We can think, indeed, of the Redeemed, bound to one another by the same mental and moral affinities and idiosyncrasies which affiliate them on earth;—bands of the white-robed multitude gathered around some favoured spiritual father,—embarked with him in congenial occupation, whether that be worship, or contemplation, or active service and ministry of love. We can think of Elijah, for example, —"Prophet of Fire," as ever,—gathering his band of Seraphim around him, enkindling them with his own unquenchable ardour,—yoking still his chariot with its fiery steeds, to speed him and them together in whirlwind embassies of flaming zeal, to comfort distant saints, or regenerate distant worlds; or we can suppose him collecting together contemplative spirits among the ranks of the ransomed, as he did of old the sons of the prophets, and pursuing in concert with them the deep studies of eternity. But all revolve around a more glorious centre. They—their persons, their deeds, their studies—have no glory by reason of the glory which excelleth.

In the great sidereal system, in the firmament above us, while dependent planets circle around their different suns, astronomers tell us these aggregate suns themselves own a mightier influence,—wheel in stupendous revolution around Alcyone, the supposed great common centre of the material universe. So, whatever may be the separate groupings among the Redeemed,—whatever their minor revolutions,—there is one peerless, sovereign Sun, around whom they all lovingly revolve;—one sublime song,—the music of these "heavenly spheres,"—which circulates to the remotest circumference of the celestial glory: "Unto HIM that loved us, and washed us from our sins in his own blood, and hath made us kings and priests unto God and his Father: to him be glory and dominion for ever and ever. Amen!" Thus the loftiest idea of a future heaven—the true "hill of God"—is that of an *eternal Transfiguration*,—the concentric circles of saints and adoring angels gazing with unquenchable rapture on the glorified Son of God, and exclaiming, "It is good for us to be here!"

If such were the lofty themes of converse which occupied the delegates from heaven on the heights of the Holy Mount, let us take a parting glance outside the cloud, when all is over, on the disciples—the representatives of the earthly Church. The heavenly messengers have come and gone;—the cloud, the radiance, the lofty converse, the august voice of paternal love,—all have vanished. The cold, chill, morning air, the drenching dews of early dawn, the fleecy clouds in the valley, the smoke in the distant hamlet—all denote that they are back to the dull world again—that soon they shall once more be involved in the rough contacts of daily life. What a contrast with the past night of seraphic bliss!

"Alone!"—ay, "yet not alone!" "When they lifted up their eyes, they saw no man, save *Jesus only.*" Bereft they are of their celestial companions; but they have *one* compensating solace for all they have lost. The stars and satellites and moons have waxed and waned and departed;—the taper-lights have been extinguished; but the great Sun still remains to illuminate their path, and perpetuate the bliss of that glorious Sabbatic hour and scene—"they saw no man, save Jesus only." JESUS ONLY;—it is enough—they ask no more. With His love and presence to cheer them, they pursue their path, ready for duty, for trial, for suffering;—animated by the sight of the crown, they descend more willing to bear the cross.

"*Jesus only*"—what a motto and watchword for *us!* Many of the most loving and beloved of human friends come only, like Moses and Elias, on angel visits,—illuminating the night of earth with a transient, yet blessed radiance,—ther leaving us, like the disciples, amid the chill, gray mists of solitude,—our path moist with dewy tears, as we hurry back once more to a cold, unsympathising world. But blessed be God, to His true disciples, as to the favoured three on Hermon, their *best* Friend is still left—"JESUS ONLY!" "Fear not," He said on another occasion to these same disciples, "I AM;* be not afraid." "I AM,"—then perish every desponding thought. "I AM,"—faithful among the faithless, changeless among the changeable! Oh, blessed antidote to all cares! blessed balm for all wounds! blessed compensa-

* εἰμί.

tion for all losses! blessed solace in all sorrows!—to descend from the mountain-heights of worldly bliss to the deepest valleys of humiliation and trial,—with JESUS ONLY!

"PROPHET OF FIRE," farewell! We shall long for thy return—if not in person,* at least in spirit—to rekindle the watch-fires on the walls of Zion! Let the last glimpse we have of thee on the inspired page direct every wavering eye to the source and secret of all thy greatness and power;—the *Transfigured* ONE, who alone can "baptize with the Holy Ghost and with FIRE!"

"HE WAS NOT THAT LIGHT, BUT WAS SENT TO BEAR WITNESS OF THAT LIGHT. THAT WAS THE TRUE LIGHT, WHICH LIGHTETH EVERY MAN THAT COMETH INTO THE WORLD."

* See Appendix.

APPENDIX.

A REMARKABLE expectation has ever been prevalent among the Jews as to Elijah's personal return as the Restorer of their nation. No attentive reader of the Gospels can fail to be struck with the singular way in which the conviction seems to have riveted itself in the Hebrew mind at the time of our Lord's coming. Not only had John the Baptist's miracles, his very dress, appearance, and ascetic habits, led to the conclusion that the Prophet of Gilead had become again incarnate—preaching his old doctrine of Repentance, and laying the axe at the root of the tree—"Art thou Elias?" but when a mightier than John had set all men musing in their hearts, the common people spoke out their strongly-felt presumptions, that the long dream of centuries was at last fulfilled, and Elias was risen again, baptizing "with the Holy Spirit and with *fire*." As it is well remarked by a discerning writer, "His appearance in glory on the Mount of Transfiguration does not seem to have startled the disciples. They were 'sore afraid,' but not apparently surprised. On the contrary, Peter immediately proposes to erect a tent for the prophet whose arrival they had been so long expecting. Even the cry of our Lord from the cross, [Eli, Eli,] containing as it did but a slight resemblance to the name of Elijah, immediately suggested him to the bystanders,—'He calleth for Elijah.' 'Let be, let us see if Elijah will come to save him.'"*

In the apocryphal book of Jesus the son of Sirach, we have the following address—"Thou, Elias, wast taken up in a whirlwind of fire, and a chariot of fiery horses; who wast ordained for reproof in its season, to pacify the wrath of the Lord's judgment before it broke forth into fury, and to turn the hearts of the fathers unto the sons, and to restore the tribes of Jacob. Blessed are they that see thee, and shall be honoured on account of thy friendship; there shall we possess the true life." It is added in a note by the same Bible expositor quoted above, with references to his authorities, "He is recorded [in the Talmud] as having often appeared to the wise and good rabbis—at prayer in the wilderness, or on their journeys—generally in the form of an Arabian merchant, (Eisenmanger, i. 11; ii. 402–7.) At the circumcision of a child a seat was always placed for him, that, as the zealous champion and messenger of the 'covenant' of circumcision, (1 Kings xix. 14; Mal. iii. 1,) he might watch over the due performance of the rite. During certain prayers the door of the house was set open, that Elijah might enter and announce the Messiah, (Eisenmanger, i. 685.) His coming will be three days before that of the Messiah, and on each of the three he will proclaim, in a voice which shall be heard all over the earth, peace, happiness, salvation, respectively, (Ib. 696.) So firm was the conviction of his speedy arrival, that when goods were found and no owner appeared to claim them, the common saying was, 'Put them up till Elijah comes,' (Light-

* See Smith's Biblical Dictionary, art. "Elijah."

foot, *Exercit.*, Matt. xvii. 10; John i. 21.) The same customs and expressions are even still in use among the stricter Jews of this and other countries, (see *Revue des Deux Mondes*, xxiv. 131, &c.)"

In a recent interesting and instructive volume, the writer, who was personally present in a house in Jerusalem at the annual celebration of the Passover, mentions, in a graphic description of the scene, "There were plates of lettuce and other herbs, and the bones of the roasted lamb, in dishes on the table; besides, the unleavened bread, and four cups of wine. Three of these, at certain parts of the ceremony, were passed round and partaken of by each individual, including the woman and baby; one cup of wine remained untouched, which was said to be for the prophet Elijah,—and we were told that, in most families, towards the end of the supper, the door of the room is opened, and all stand up, while the prophet is believed to enter and partake of the wine: among rich Jews this cup is frequently of gold, with jewels."* Nor has the veneration for the person and name of the Prophet been confined to the Hebrew nation. The Greek and Latin churches have delighted to honour him. The festival, or anniversary, of his ascension is still scrupulously observed by both, and a special service employed on the occasion. Monasteries and chapels, identified with his name, are found scattered through Oriental countries, from the solitary shrine amid the wild cliffs of Sinai, to the well-known monastery on Carmel, whose bare-footed friars own him as their patron saint, and the originator of their order. Even the Mohammedans hold his name in great repute. In their legends he is

* Beaufort's Syrian Shrines, vol. ii., p. 266.

represented as having drunk large draughts of the Fountain of Life, and so become immortal. "He is called Kheder, which signifies verdant, because from that time he enjoyed a flourishing and immortal life. According to them he lives in a place of retirement, in a delicious garden, where is the Tree of Life, and where the Fountain of Life runs; by the help whereof his immortality is preserved. Here he awaits the second coming of Jesus Christ, at which he is to appear once more in the world."* Dr Stanley mentions, in his reference to Sarepta,—the modern Sarafend,—that "close on the sea-shore stands one of those sepulchral chapels dedicated to 'El-Khudr,' or 'Mar Elias.' There is no tomb," he adds, "inside; only hangings before a recess. This variation from the usual type of Mussulman sepulchres was, as we were told by the peasants on the spot, because El-Khudr is not yet dead; he flies round and round the world, and those chapels are built wherever he has appeared. Every Thursday night and Friday morning there is a light so strong within the chapel that no one can go in."† In connexion with the name we have given this volume, we may add the following curious legend from a learned writer already quoted:—"The magi of Persia pretended that their master, Zoroaster, was one of the prophet Elijah's disciples. This fiction is founded on Elijah procuring FIRE from heaven, and his being carried away in a fiery chariot: the disciples of Zoroaster making the element of FIRE the principal object of their worship." A book seems to have existed, although no longer extant, called "The Revelation or Ascension of Elias," from which, Jerome tells us, is borrowed the passage of St Paul to the Corinthians,

* See Calmet, *in loco*.

† Sinai and Palestine, p. 274.

(1 Cor. ii. 9,) "Eye hath not seen, nor ear heard," &c., (*Hieron. Ep.* 101 *ad Pammach.*) Origen, in his citation of them, tells us that these words were nowhere found but in "the secret books of Elias," (*Hom. in Mat.*, xxvii. 9.)*

The expectation of the coming of Elias is still devoutly and strongly cherished by the Jewish people. Professor Hackett mentions, with reference to a spot visited in the course of his travels near the plain of Jezreel, that "within sight, on a neighbouring hill, was a pillar of stone which the Jews said was Elijah's seat, because he was accustomed to rest there as he journeyed through this region. He will come again a second time, they remarked to me, and will then change the pillar into gold."—(*Illustrations*, p. 154.) The same belief in the return of the Prophet is shared by all Christians of the literalist school, and among those many whose views are worthy of all consideration and deference. While it appears presumptuous to build with any degree of certainty on the few fragmentary and enigmatical allusions on this subject, we cannot think that the explicit words of the prophet Malachi,—the last notes of the Old Testament prophetic harp,†—can, in any advent that has yet taken place, have received their complete and final fulfilment. The words of our blessed Lord, moreover, to His disciples at the close of the Transfiguration, in answer to their question, "Why say the scribes that Elias must first come?" would seem to give the impress of a higher authority still for the expectation. Jesus on that

* Calmet.

† "Behold, I will send you Elijah the prophet before the coming of the great and dreadful day of the Lord: and he shall turn the heart of the fathers to the children, and the heart of the children to their fathers, lest I come and smite the earth with a curse."—MAL. iv. 5, 6.

occasion replied—"Elias truly shall first come, and shall restore all things. But I say unto you, that Elias is come already, and they knew him not; but have done unto him whatsoever they listed." This answer was purposely expressed enigmatically: but most trustworthy commentators, ancient and modern,* explain it as referring to a twofold Elias,—two distinct precursors of Christ; the one being the Baptist, the herald of his *first* coming; who, however, though he came in the spirit and power of the older prophet, distinctly declared, in answer to the question of the priests and Levites, "Art thou Elias?" "*I am not;*"—an answer he never would have ventured to give had he been the prophet referred to by Malachi. (Their question was evidently founded on Malachi's prediction;—and to aver that this unequivocal negative returned to it was a mere evasion on the part of John, would be a supposition surely unworthy of the bold outspoken honesty of his character;)—the other precursor of the second coming being none other than the Tishbite, who in a grand gospel sense will fulfil Isaiah's prediction by preparing the way of the Lord, and making straight in the desert a highway for our God. "Behold the day cometh," [the day of which the Prophet of Fire will be the forerunner,] "that shall *burn* as an oven; and all the proud, yea, and all that do wickedly, shall be stubble: and the day that cometh shall burn them up, saith the Lord of hosts, that it shall leave them neither root nor branch."† Nothing, indeed, can well be more explicit than the assertion of our Lord, (an

* Chrysostom, Bernardino, Maldonatus, Calmet, Stier, Alford, &c., &c. Indeed the ancient writers are almost unanimous.

† Malachi iv. 1.

assertion made, be it observed, *after* the Transfiguration, so that the predicted advent of His messenger could not have been fulfilled by His appearance on the mount,) "Elias, (the *real* Elias, as if He said,) *shall* truly come." 'The scribes have been right in their supposition. And though I say unto you "Elias is come already," it is only one in his spirit and power;—one who, despite all his fidelity, earnestness, and boldness, has failed to fulfil Malachi's predicted mission as "the Restorer of all Things."*

If the future restoration and conversion of Israel, (as it probably will, from the analogy of their early history,) be accompanied with miraculous agency, that glorious epoch may not impossibly be inaugurated by the personal appearance of the old Prophet, who would thus become the great instrument, under God, of "turning (nationally) the hearts of the children to their fathers;"—the morning-star of earth's grandest Reformation;—the harbinger of a brighter day than has ever yet risen upon the nations. Befitting would be the summons and apostrophe to regenerated Israel from the lips of the PROPHET OF FIRE—"*Arise, shine, for thy light is come, and the glory of the Lord is risen upon thee!*"

* "The double allusion is only the assertion that the Elias (in spirit and power) who foreran our Lord's first coming, was a partial fulfilment of the great prophecy, which announces the real Elias (the words of Malachi will hardly bear any other than a personal meaning) who is to forerun His greater and second coming."—*Alford, in loc.*

CPSIA information can be obtained
at www.ICGtesting.com
Printed in the USA
LVHW101023190422
716440LV00024B/342

9 783752 593280